Then Tajima made a de............................fe.
He announced to the cr..........................ill
enter the contest and ....nd
against the famous swor...........

The crowd stirred. '.....................ous
sword instructor defeat his own son, then go against the
fencer of Iori's caliber was an event that outweighed all other
considerations.

Jubei glared at his father. The tactic was so transparent that
Jubei could not bear the shame. "In the name of fairness," he
shouted, "it's only right that we also duel with real swords."

"It is only necessary that we compete," Tajima said firmly.
"There's no need to spill blood."

"No!" Jubei cried. "I'll accept your challenge only under
the same conditions that Iori fought."

The father stared at the son. The son stared back at the
father. "Please, Jubei," his sister begged, "don't you understand Father is trying to save you?"

Jubei brushed her aside. "Do you accept the conditions or
not?" he challenged.

"Prepare to fight," Tajima said, measuring out each word
like a dose of poison.

Shimabara

Shimabara

by
Douglass Bailey

BANTAM BOOKS
TORONTO • NEW YORK • LONDON • SYDNEY • AUCKLAND

SHIMABARA

A Bantam Book / September 1986

ISBN 0-553-25115-5

Published simultaneously in the United States and Canada

Bantam Books are published by Bantam Books, Inc. Its trademark,
consisting of the words "Bantam Books" and the portrayal of a rooster,
is Registered in U.S. Patent and Trademark Office and in other countries.
Marca Registrada. Bantam Books, Inc., 666 Fifth Avenue, New York,
New York 10103.

PRINTED IN THE UNITED STATES OF AMERICA

KR   0 9 8 7 6 5 4 3 2 1

For my mother and father

The author gratefully acknowledges the invaluable contributions of his wife Michiko, whose Japanese spirit animates these pages. And also, he wishes to thank his friend Morinaga Yasuhiro for his generous help in constructing the historical framework of this novel.

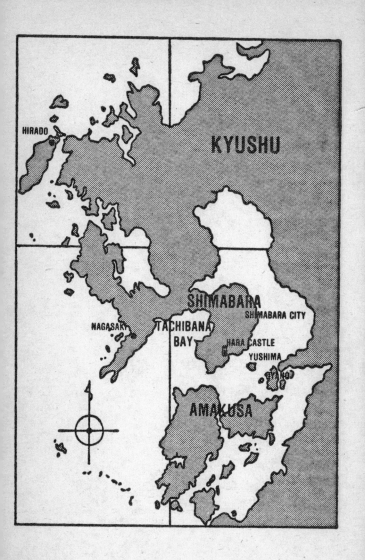

PROLOGUE

Osaka
Year of the Rabbit—1615
Hour of the Tiger

The spot had been chosen carefully. It was the place where the morning sun first broke on to Osaka Plain. Framed in an orange wash that spilled through a cleavage in the hills, the Shogun sat, his back rigid, his heart pounding inside his armor like a war drum. In the distance the great castle of the Toyotomi clan loomed over the plain. When the windows of the central donjon began to glow like cats' eyes, he knew that his agent inside the enemy fortress had accomplished his mission. The fires had been set.

Beyond the blaze of torches that illuminated the platform where the old warrior was sitting, a sea of samurai stood shoulder to shoulder in the predawn hush. Some with fierce eyes and clenched jaws. Some with vacant eyes and noisy stomachs. Some with eyes closed, their lips moving in silent prayer, their palms damp with the strong sweat of fear.

The Shogun flared his nostrils and filled his lungs with the morning air. Although the years had loosened his muscles and layered his midsection with rolls of fat, his heavy hooded eyes remained as bright as freshly minted coins. As he gazed down on the samurai in the front ranks, the Shogun thought he saw some old familiar faces, only to realize the faces belonged to the sons and grandsons of comrades long since dead—good men who had followed him when he'd been nothing more than a callow youth with a contagious vision. He'd dreamed of a land free of three hundred years of political turmoil and incessant civil wars, a united land with the strength to fend off the ravenous appetite of the Roman pope and his legions of scheming padres.

Unlike his Toyotomi rival, he had never allowed himself to be seduced by either the religion or the impressive scientific achievements of the round-eyed barbarians. Once Osaka Castle had fallen and the padres had nowhere else to turn for protection, then he would give the Christians his undivided attention.

Now only one more battle stood between him and the realization of his dream. At age seventy-three the last vestige of resistance to the Shogun's absolute military control of the Sunrise Land was about to collapse.

A ray of sun struck the golden tips of his war helmet, and a hundred thousand samurai stirred like leaves in a rush of wind as he rose to his feet. For several moments he stood still, letting his men absorb their shogun's presence.

"Samurai!" he boomed out, pleased to find that his voice still had brawn. "We stand in the shadow of Osaka Castle, the last impediment to peace. The gods have given us this moment to put an end to the war. The peace that has eluded this sacred land for three centuries is only one victory away." The Shogun stepped forward and pointed his folded war fan at the great walls of the castle. "Once before, when the Toyotomi threatened, I brought my armies to the very place where we stand now. But war was averted that time through negotiation and compromise. As a gesture of goodwill I gave my daughter's hand in marriage to the young Toyotomi lord . . . and he betrayed me. My son-in-law used the truce to buy foreign guns and reinforce his army with hired samurai." His hand shot out, and the war fan snapped open. "This time there will be no negotiations . . . no compromise . . . no truce. This time Osaka Castle will fall, and with it every last member of the Toyotomi clan! Be brave! Be strong! Be resolute! Tomorrow the sun will rise on a united Japan!" The Shogun raised the Tokugawa standard high in the air, and a guttural roar issued from the depths of his belly—a roar picked up by a hundred thousand voices. Again and again the shock waves reverberated off the hills and echoed over Osaka Plain.

Inside the vast complex of structures that comprised Osaka Castle, the fires raged out of control. Stonemasons, carpenters, artists, craftsmen, grooms, servants—every able-bodied man, woman, and child living on the castle grounds—joined the soldiers in a furious battle against the inferno. Fire gongs clanged over the roar of the flames. Beams buckled and collapsed. Buckets of water were passed from hand to hand. Great timbers crashed down in explosions of sparks. Paper screens on windows and doors turned brown from the heat, then burst into flame. Horses, wild-eyed with terror, broke down their stalls and bolted through the narrow streets, trampling the old and infirm where they fell.

Hideyori Toyotomi, lord of Osaka Castle, stood at a window of the central donjon, gazing down at the devastation below. The enormity of the disaster all around him had drained the arrogance from his youthful face, leaving him emotionally gutted. When his counselors spoke to him, he heard only words detached from meaning and merely stared back at them through glazed eyes.

So they looked to his wife for guidance, and Lady Sen dismissed them with a wave of her hand. They left with the knowledge that the situation was hopeless. The only decision of importance left for their lord was to choose the correct moment to end his life with dignity.

Lady Sen had taken it upon herself to order a room prepared for their seppuku. It saddened her to think that haste would tarnish the tragic beauty of this ancient suicide ritual, but there was precious little time left. Smoke was drifting up from the rooms below, the faint crackle of flames audible above the noise in the streets.

She glanced at the Zen monk Takuan, who had remained to act as formal witness at the seppuku. He nodded his head gravely, and Lady Sen approached her husband.

"It's time," she said softly.

Hideyori turned and saw that she had changed into her white death kimono. Comprehension unclouded his eyes. "I'll compose my death poem," he responded, still not grasping the urgency of the moment.

Lady Sen turned and silently appealed to Takuan to intercede.

"My lord," Takuan said in a respectful but stern voice, "there's no time."

Hideyori looked bewildered.

"Come," Lady Sen said, taking him by the hand like a little child.

She led him to a small antechamber where two tatami mats had been hastily arranged in the shape of a hammer. A covering of white silk had been spread over the mats. Hidden from view behind a white screen was a trusted servant holding two trays, each containing a razor-sharp dagger. At the apex of the mats a samurai from Hideyori's personal bodyguard was waiting to execute the final decapitating cut.

Hideyori hesitated at the door.

Noticing that Takuan and the nurse tending her infant daughter remained at a respectful distance behind them, Lady Sen used the opportunity to remind her husband of what he must do to honor the ritual. "Because of our precarious position, only the essence of the ritual can be preserved." Although he was looking directly at her, she could not be certain that he understood. It pained her to continue, but she went ahead anyway, trying to make her voice sound as calm as possible. "When you receive the dagger, wrap the blade in the silk cloth on the tray. There is no need to make any statement before you perform the lateral belly cut. If you feel it's necessary to make the vertical cut, your second will wait for you to lower your head before striking the final blow."

She saw that his eyes had become vacant again, and knew he was only a hair's breadth away from disgrace. Lady Sen guided him to the mat and asked him to open his kimono to the navel. He did it mechanically, as if undressing for the bath. Fearing that the purity of his final act might be spoiled by a sudden failure of nerve, she took Takuan aside and asked if he considered it proper to instruct the bodyguard to strike the killing blow the instant her husband's hand touched the hilt of the dagger.

"Isn't the gesture itself sufficient evidence of his honorable intentions?" she asked, knowing in her heart that it would be skirting the fringe of propriety.

A quick glance at Hideyori's face confirmed the wisdom of Lady Sen's plea. Takuan nodded his approval. "There's no shame in that," he reassured her.

"Then let it begin," she said, kneeling down beside Takuan.

The little monk gave the signal, and the bodyguard drew his sword. The servant brought the tray forward, bowed deeply, and offered the dagger to his lord.

Hideyori stared at the gleaming instrument for a long moment, then reached out as if to accept a proffered sweet.

Takuan flashed another signal at the bodyguard.

Lady Sen closed her eyes and heard the solid thud of steel slicing through flesh and bone. She opened her eyes to see her husband's headless trunk teeter, then topple to one side. A deep pang of grief threatened her control. Despite his enmity for her father, he had been kind to her. She thought of the nights he had invited her to lie with him, and silently thanked him for the child he had fathered.

Following the prescribed procedure the samurai picked up the head by the topknot and showed both profiles to Takuan. He bowed to the samurai, and the head was placed inside a wooden cask.

The heat from the fires was turning the tiny room into a bake oven. Lady Sen took her year-old daughter from the nurse and clutched the child to her breast one last time. When she looked up at Takuan, he could see that she was struggling valiantly to maintain her composure.

"As the daughter of the Shogun I learned to accept life as it came to me, without remorse or bitterness. It was in that spirit that I married my father's enemy. As a wife I did my duty and served my husband faithfully. Now I'm prepared to follow him into death." She took out a handkerchief and dabbed away the beads of perspiration that had collected on her daughter's face. "As a mother . . . I know it's my duty to take my daughter with me . . . to the Pure Land. But—" Her voice finally cracked. "But I'm not that strong." She held the child out to Takuan. "Take her, old friend. If you can save her, give her a new name and see to it that she is reared as a samurai. If you can't"—she swallowed hard—"please let her die swiftly."

Takuan bowed, then took the child from her mother and cradled her in his arms.

Lady Sen kneeled beside the body of her dead husband and opened the neck of her kimono. The samurai stepped back and raised his sword to the proper height for one of Lady Sen's rank. She ordered him to hold his cut until she lowered her head. With a steady hand she reached for the dagger, wrapped the blade in white silk, paused to take one final look at her daughter, then plunged the dagger into her throat. She let her head drop. The sword fell.

When Lady Sen's head was displayed for Takuan's identification, he did not prevent the bewildered child from reaching out to touch her mother's face. The world is full of ironies, he thought, and wondered if Lady Sen would have chosen him to witness her death if she'd known he was acting as a secret agent for her father. Would she have entrusted her daughter to his care if she'd known he was the one who set the fires that destroyed her husband's castle and drove him to his death?

Takuan picked up the dagger that had fallen to the mat and lifted the child's gown aside. She reached out and grasped his finger in her little hand. The simple gesture moved him, but he knew that he must not allow sentiment to thwart the Shogun's will. She looked up at him, her eyes brimming with tears and innocence. Her lower lip was quivering, but she made no sound. This child is Toyotomi, he reminded himself. But the longer he looked at her, the more he saw only a helpless baby—a little girl whose frightened face stirred the ashes of a long dormant memory.

What would the Shogun say if he knew that his most trusted agent, the cold-blooded instrument of his victory, succumbed to compassion which kept him from fulfilling his vow to eliminate the Toyotomi clan from the face of the earth?

Suddenly Takuan made a decision his instincts told him he would live to regret. "This will be a secret between us, little one," he whispered to the child. "A long time ago I had a daughter who was about your age when she died in my arms. I thought I'd forgotten her, but it seems I haven't. Her name was Akane, and now the name will be yours. If we can leave here alive, I'll find you a home and a family name worthy of your bloodline."

PART ONE

1

Edo
Year of the Horse—1630
Hour of the Dog

Word spread quickly through Edo Castle. The Shogun had returned from the hunt in a fouler mood than when he had left. The hawking excursion had been his wife's idea. She thought it might help lift the old man's sagging spirits. Now something had gone wrong. She called her first son in to explain what had happened.

"He lost his hawk," Iemitsu explained in response to her question.

"A bird?" Two thick swatches of painted eyebrows arched in disbelief. "You're telling me your father waited from dawn to dusk for some bird to return?"

Iemitsu fidgeted under her intense gaze. At eighteen the Shogun's designated heir had still not gained the confidence to speak to his mother as a man. Iemitsu struggled to find the right words to make her understand the importance of the hawk. "Father was fond of that bird. He said she was hardworking and steady, and when she failed, she didn't lose her confidence."

"And how did such a splendid bird get lost?" Her question was tinted with sarcasm.

"She was old," Iemitsu explained. "Father thinks she couldn't hear him when he tried to call her back. The circles kept widening, then she was gone."

She dismissed her son, thanking him for the information. Life had become increasingly difficult for her since the day, fifteen years ago, when the wars ended. Her husband had never been easy to please, and his disposition had not improved with age. She hoped a bath and some hot tea would calm him.

The Shogun let the silk kimono drop from his shoulders and stood naked in the soft candlelight. He stared straight ahead, unaware of the nimble hands that caught his robe before it touched the slatted floor of the bathing chamber.

The two women attendants each braced one of his elbows as he lowered himself onto the wooden stool next to the soaking tub. One of them ladled warm water over his body while the other began scrubbing his back with a tubular sponge. He leaned forward and inhaled the delicate scent of the sandalwood twigs smoldering in the brazier beneath the tub.

Without warning, embers of pain burst into flame, percolating misery from the pit of his stomach to his throat. The Shogun held his breath and counted to himself, One . . . two . . . three . . . This time the count reached twelve before the pain began to relent. Good, he thought, pleased that neither of the two women seemed to notice.

Their movements were fluid and unhurried, not a word spoken, not a motion wasted. When the rinsing was over, they helped their lord into the tub, and a cup of green tea was left close by.

The Shogun closed his eyes and listened to the night. Little by little the tension evaporated and the clamor of the day faded to a whisper. In his mind he saw the widening gyre of his lost hawk, and it made him sad. So many of the old ones were gone now . . . the ones who knew him as a man before they knew him as Shogun.

"Feeling sorry for yourself, my lord?"

The Shogun opened his eyes and squinted through the rising steam, searching for the source of the familiar voice. The room was empty. He realized his mind had tricked him into believing he had heard the voice of a dead man. "So this is the way senility begins," he mused aloud.

Then the shadows in the far corner of the room moved. At first he could see only eyes, then the silhouette of a man dressed in black moved into the light. The ninja drew back the dark wrap that covered his mouth and nose. "I wager you thought I was dead," he said with a smile.

"Takuan! Is that really you?"

"So it's true what they say, your eyesight is getting as bad as your hearing."

The Shogun chuckled. It had to be Takuan. No one but him would dare such impudence. Still, it was difficult to believe his old friend and most trusted agent had actually managed to set the fires at Osaka Castle and get out alive. "It's been fifteen years. I thought you were dead!"

Takuan sat down cross-legged next to the tub and removed the tight-fitting hood that covered his bald head. Time had been kind to him. The wrinkles at the corners of his tiny eyes had deepened, but his smile was still full of an anarchy of strong yellow teeth.

"You underestimate the resourcefulness of the ninja. Many of our agents are highly placed engineers. Whenever a castle is constructed, we see to it that secret passageways are built in, known only to us. I used one to get out of Osaka Castle."

"And Edo Castle . . . there are ninja passageways here too?"

"How do you think I got into your private bath undetected?"

The idea of his own castle honeycombed with passages he knew nothing about did not amuse the Shogun. He had always understood that dealing with the ninja was risky. For untold centuries two rival families of professional assassins and spies, the Iga and Koga ninja, had offered their clandestine services to the rich and powerful. Takuan, who was the leader of the Iga family, had aligned himself with the fortunes of the Tokugawa. The Koga viewed this break with tradition as further evidence of Iga treachery.

Despite his long and close relationship with Takuan, the Shogun knew little more than the average man about the shadow world inhabited by the ninja. He did know that to be a ninja, one had to be born a ninja. He also knew that they were capable of penetrating the most impregnable defenses, and once engaged in battle, these fierce fighters would never allow themselves to be taken alive. And he had heard that they possessed weapons beyond the imagination of the ordinary samurai warrior. But one thing was certain—the ninja kept all their dark secrets hidden from everyone except members of their own clan. They were a law unto themselves. Yet he had no regrets about his use of Takuan's services, who had served the Tokugawa long and well.

"So where have you been all these years?" the Shogun asked.

"Living in the shadows, where a ninja belongs. But now that you need me, I'm here."

"And what makes you think I need you now?"

"Because you are dying."

Takuan's pronouncement was delivered unemotionally, a statement of fact carrying no more drama than a "good morning"—or more importantly, the Shogun thought, "good night."

"Takuan, a long time ago, when I tasted my first defeat, I wanted to commit seppuku, but you told me it wasn't my time to die. You said a ninja can see death over a man's left shoulder. Do you see it there now?"

Takuan cocked his head to one side and asked, "Do you want me to lie?"

"Maybe so."

"I see nothing," he said with exaggerated innocence.

Activity stirred in the outer chamber at the sound of the Shogun's laughter. Takuan slipped back into the shadows a split second before a guard burst into the room.

"My lord . . ." he said, looking around, his hand on the hilt of his sword.

"Go away!" the Shogun commanded gruffly, and the samurai quickly backed out of the room. When the screen was drawn shut, he motioned Takuan to join him again.

"So old friend, you've come to say good-bye."

"No, I've come to find out how I can serve you after you're dead."

"What makes you think I'm going to die? Have you forgotten that the Emperor has issued a decree of deification?" There was a trace of mirth in the Shogun's eyes. "I'm a god."

"A dying god," Takuan chided him. "But, I suppose, a god nonetheless." He wiped away the beads of sweat that had collected on his bald head. "Who knows, maybe the real gods invented death to keep great men like you from taking themselves too seriously, *neh?*"

"It's not myself I take seriously, old friend—it's peace. As long as I remain alive, the peace is secure. Since I put an end to the Toyotomi, no one has dared oppose me . . . not even the Emperor. But it would be a grave mistake to imagine that there are no storms on the horizon."

Takuan knew exactly what he meant. For centuries after the Emperor lost military control of Japan and been reduced to a figurehead, the many daimyo who ruled over separate fiefs had vied for supremacy. The Sunrise Land had been in continuous turmoil until Lord Tokugawa emerged as the prominent military force. In spite of the Emperor's antipathy for the Tokugawa, his position was too weak to resist Lord Tokugawa's demand to be named Shogun—supreme military commander of the Japanese empire. It was clear that the nobles in the Emperor's court had never abandoned hope that one day real political authority would revert back to them. Although they no longer commanded large armies, they were constantly plotting with ambitious daimyo to undermine the power of the Shogun.

"It's true," Takuan agreed. "The nobles still dream of power. But do you really believe that their schemes can topple the Tokugawa?"

"They might be able to pose a serious threat if they managed to rally the Christian daimyo around the Emperor and forge an alliance with the Portuguese." The Shogun gripped Takuan's arm. "The foreign devils taught me a very important lesson about warfare. Firepower is the key to victory. Whoever controls guns, controls the destiny of Japan."

"It takes gold to buy guns," Takuan responded. "From what I hear, your tax levies have all but drained the treasuries of disloyal daimyo. Where will they get the gold to buy weapons? From the Jesuits?"

"Surely not the Jesuits, nor their Franciscan rivals," the Shogun scoffed. "They came here to plunder gold, not to spend it. No. They plan to harvest Japan through intrigue and religious conversion, just as they did in the New World. So far I've been able to keep them off balance by alternately favoring the Jesuits, the Franciscans, the Dutch, and the English. But it's a juggling performance that takes considerable skill, skill I'm not convinced my heir possesses. That's why, if the Tokugawa shogunate is to survive for generations to come, my son Iemitsu must have the help of someone like you."

Takuan bowed slightly. "I'll serve your son just as I've served you," he promised.

"Good. See to it that the Emperor confers the title of Shogun on him when I die. The nobles will do everything in their power to resist the appointment, but they must not be allowed to interrupt the succession."

"I'm entering my sixth decade," Takuan reminded him. "If anything happens to me, I see no leader among the Iga ninja to take my place, and the Koga cannot be trusted. They sell their services like whores."

"Then look for a successor outside the ranks of the ninja," he commanded.

"Do you have someone in mind?" Takuan asked.

"There is one man I've been observing over the years. On the surface he seems to have all the qualities we're looking for. He's a solitary man, an expert listener who always takes in more than he reveals. He's mastered the art of wearing his face like a mask. As for his prowess with the sword, his style has become the standard by which all others are judged. . . ."

The Shogun paused, as if inviting him to guess, but Takuan refused to commit himself until he heard more.

The Shogun decided to prod him with a few more hints. "He's a clever man, some say too clever for his own good. You see, his rise to power was a little too rapid to suit certain members of my council. They suspect he has ambitions beyond his present position as my sword instructor. But most of all they fear his reach may *not* exceed his grasp."

"Lord Tajima," Takuan said, nodding his head pensively.

"So you know him," the Shogun replied, eager to hear Takuan's opinion.

Takuan considered telling the Shogun the secret he had kept hidden from him all these years, but decided it would serve no useful purpose. "We met once, not long after he inherited the Tajima School of Fencing from his wife's father."

"And?"

"And the rumors of his ambition are well founded." Then he added, "But I can't think of a better choice for the job."

"Good." The Shogun wiped perspiration off his face. "Observe him. Test him. And when you're certain he's the one to follow in your path, go to him—" The words caught in his throat as the pain welled up in his belly like molten lava. This time he made no attempt to dissemble.

"Here." Takuan handed him a packet that he took from his medicine pouch. "Put a little in your tea—it will ease the pain."

The Shogun drank, and the fire subsided. "Will we meet again?" he asked Takuan.

Takuan shook his head and retreated into the shadows.

On an impulse the Shogun called out the first part of a secret recognition signal used exclusively by the ninja. "All men are thieves. . . ." He listened, wondering how Takuan would react to an outsider uncovering one of their impenetrable secrets.

From far away he heard Takuan laugh, and then came the response: "And it will rain tomorrow."

The Shogun grinned. Now they were even. He had his revenge for the clandestine passageways.

The light from the lantern Takuan had left hanging in the passageway cast a small circle on the wall. As he lifted it off the peg, the lantern's halo fanned out over the slick granite.

The circle widens, he mused, thinking back to that night long ago when he brought the Shogun's granddaughter to Lord Tajima's quarters. "Take the child. Rear her as your own," he remembered telling Tajima.

"Whose child is this?" Tajima had asked.

"Her name is Akane," he had responded. "I can tell you nothing more than that."

Takuan recalled the absence of expression on Tajima's face as he sat drumming his fingers on his knee. "Why should I do this for you?" Tajima had asked shrewdly.

"No reason . . . unless you value my gratitude."

After a moment of deliberation, Tajima agreed to accept Akane as his daughter on the condition that Takuan use his influence to have him named Sword Instructor to the Shogun.

It was a bold gambit, one so brazen that Takuan suspected Tajima had somehow guessed the identity of the child. But the bargain had been struck. Since that time Tajima had never given him cause to regret his decision.

Now, years later, Takuan found himself questioning what he'd done. By intervening to save the child, a stone had been tossed into the waters of fate—and after all these years, the circles were still spreading.

On a hillside just beyond the gray walls of Edo Castle, Lord Tajima was standing in his west garden pondering the meaning of the unexpected gift the Shogun had sent him earlier that day. It was a magnificent granite boulder shaped like a cresting ocean wave. The great rock towered over the young fruit trees and flowering shrubs planted there. Lord Tajima could not help being struck by the perfect harmony it imposed on his garden. The trees and shrubs that lay in its wind shadow were no longer tormented by the force of the prevailing ocean breeze.

Except for his slightly stooped shoulders, which was an unconscious compensation for his unusual height, Tajima looked much younger than his thirty-six years. His rugged face might have been handsome if it hadn't been for the early damage done to the bridge of his nose when he was just learning how use the wooden kendo sword. He wore his hair in the traditional samurai style, oiled and plastered to the side of his head. One long tuft of hair was folded double at the crown, tied and pulled forward over his shaved forelock. He was backing away from the rock when a gust of wind caught the double strand of hair and knocked it askew. As he reached up to recenter it, Tajima suddenly grasped the significance of the Shogun's gift. The key to the mystery had been in the poem the Shogun had sent along with the rock. Tajima reached inside his kimono, took out the poem, and read it again.

Beyond the shelter of the solitary rock,
A wind-stripped branch.
Inside the wind's shadow frail blossoms cling.

The Shogun was using the image of the frail blossoms to express his concern for the frailty of the peace he had so carefully constructed. He was worried that without rock-solid support, his newly established shogunate might be blasted away by hostile winds. The gift of the rock suggested that the Shogun was looking to the Tajima family to provide the shelter the Tokugawa clan needed to grow and flourish.

A deluge of satisfaction washed over him. After fifteen years of dedicated service—fifteen years of cultivating powerful friends and allies, while at the same time managing to steer clear of all the petty intrigues that dominated life inside Edo Castle—he had finally been rewarded with the Shogun's confidence.

Tajima folded his wiry arms across his chest and silently wondered what all this meant for him and his family. But he knew there was nothing he could do except wait for the Shogun to take the next step. Not far away, Akane sat facing the doorway to the west garden, watching her father contemplate the Shogun's strange gift. It was dusk, and the wind had picked up, as it always did at twilight.

Akane shivered.

"Are you cold, child?" Lady Tajima asked as she ran the comb down the length of her adopted daughter's hair.

"No," she replied. "It's the dusk. For some reason it always makes me feel uneasy." She gazed into the distance, where the ghostly spectre of Fujiyama seemed to float above the horizon.

"It's a fragile time . . . an uncertain moment between a beginning and an end," Lady Tajima said, making another long pull through Akane's lush, dark hair.

She could not have loved Akane more if the girl had been her own daughter. At seventeen Akane had developed into a lissome beauty whose oval face made a perfect setting for her almond-shaped eyes and elegantly arched cheekbones. Lady Tajima, who was short and pudgy, with a round face as plain as a bowl of boiled rice, kept dreading the moment when Akane would begin to wonder about the extraordinary physical differences between them, and begin to raise delicate questions even *she* could not answer. Her husband had simply turned the child over to her without a word of explanation. Although love had never completely dissolved her curiosity, she was content to let Akane believe that she was her true daughter.

For Akane this was a very special night. Lord Iemitsu, the Shogun's designated heir, had arranged a party to celebrate her brother Jubei's return after five years of study with the warrior monks of Hiei, and his elevation, at the age of nineteen, to the rank of *shinan*—just one step below the rank of swordmaster. Initially every student in her father's kendo school had been invited, everyone except her. Although it disappointed Akane, it had not surprised her. She was accustomed to being shunned by the male students in her class. They viewed her as an unwelcome interloper in a domain exclusively reserved for men. Despite denials to the contrary, she was certain that Jubei had used his influence with Iemitsu to get her name added to the guest list.

It had been more than five years since her father had

dramatically altered her life by ordering her to separate from
the other girls her age and study the art of fencing with the
sons of high-ranking samurai enrolled in his kendo school.
Stunned by the news, she pressed him to explain the purpose
of this unprecedented move. He told her that one day he
planned to assign her to guard the Shogun's daughters. "The
women's quarters are a great source of invaluable information
. . . information that I can use to promote the fortunes of this
family."

So, day after day she sparred with the wooden swords,
absorbing blows without flinching. Night after night she lowered her battered body into a hot bath, and summoned all
her strength to face the next day. No one, except her mother,
seemed aware of her misery.

But the night before Jubei had to leave for Hiei, Akane
returned to her room to find a jar of whale-oil balm on the
tatami next to her bedding. Beside the jar was a sprig of
blossoms taken from the plum tree in the garden outside
Jubei's room. It was a simple act of kindness she had never
forgotten.

"Fuji-san is lovely, *neh*?" Akane said to her mother as she
watched the silhouette of the great volcano fade, then vanish
like a piece of magic.

Lady Tajima grunted through the comb she held clenched
between her teeth.

"*Hahaue*," she said to her mother, who was buzzing around
her like a fly, pulling on this, tugging at that. "Do you think
Jubei's changed much?"

Lady Tajima took the comb out of her mouth and laid it on
the cosmetics tray. "He's grown so much I hardly recognized
him. I wish he'd shave his forelock, though," she complained.
"It's unseemly for a young man his age to wear his hair tied
back like a little boy."

Akane liked the idea that her brother wore his hair the way
it pleased him, but she decided not to mention it to her
mother for fear of stirring up a hornet's nest. "No, I mean he
might have changed . . . inside."

"Age changes everyone in certain ways. What are you
afraid of, child?"

Akane wasn't sure, so she didn't answer. She had always
felt especially close to Jubei when they were growing up. He
had been her guardian, her protector. She recalled the day

he brought her to kendo class for her first lesson. At first the boys reacted with stunned silence. Then one of the older students began to grumble out loud. Jubei said nothing, but when the time came to pair off for sparring drills, Jubei selected the grumbler as his partner. Within seconds after the sparring began, she heard a terrible groan and saw the grumbler collapse in a heap. Jubei had crushed one of his ribs and broken his arm in two places. After that episode the animosity toward her retreated into the shadows.

When Jubei went off to Hiei, his absence left a void in her—an emptiness that even the uncompromising rigor of kendo could never seem to fill. And now that he had returned, she was afraid that time had eroded their special affection for each other.

Lady Tajima accepted Akane's silence and began applying her daughter's makeup. First she dusted her face with rice powder, then lengthened her eyes with long dark brush strokes. Next she painted her lips in the shape of a perfect bow. When her hair had been lightly oiled and arranged so that two strands formed loops that draped over her shoulders, she stepped back to survey every detail of her work.

"Well," Lady Tajima sighed. "I've never seen you look more beautiful."

Akane beamed. When it came to compliments, her mother was as frugal as a miser. She took a long look at herself in the Portuguese looking glass. All the tiny flaws that always troubled her had somehow vanished under her mother's masterful hand.

Then Lady Tajima insisted that she practice the pigeon-toed shuffle required to navigate in a formal kimono. Considering how little time Akane had to practice the feminine graces, she thought her daughter's walk created a passable illusion of floating.

"Didn't you forget something?" Lady Tajima called after her as Akane started down the path to the front gate.

"Oh, my gift for Jubei!" Her mind had been on the party.

Lady Tajima handed her the dwarf plum tree Akane had grown from a cutting off the tree outside Jubei's room. It had taken her five years to shape it into an exact replica of the mother tree.

Akane gripped her mother's hand. "Thank you for making me feel beautiful tonight."

"Go now," Lady Tajima said gruffly, her heart nearly bursting with pride.

The inn Lord Iemitsu had chosen for the celebration was located near Nihonbashi—the famous bridge that marked the beginning of the Tokaido road, linking Edo with the old capital of Kyoto. By the time Akane's palanquin arrived, the festivities were well under way.

She paid the porters and followed the noise through the central garden to a large room with a riot of shadows playing on the paper panes of the shoji screen. Akane recognized Lord Iemitsu's voice rising above the clamor. She put the plum-tree gift beside the door, slipped out of her sandals, and went inside.

Everyone was caught up in the rock-paper-scissors drinking game. On the leader's signal, pairs of contestants made simultaneous hand gestures indicating one of three choices—a clenched fist for rock, an open hand for paper, two fingers for scissors. Rock breaks scissors, scissors cut paper, and paper covers rock.

"One . . . two . . . three!" Iemitsu shouted.

Hands flew, then winners gloated and losers drank. It was evident from the high color of the revelers' faces that the game had been going on for some time.

As guest of honor, Jubei was next to Iemitsu on a raised dais at the far end of the room. He was wearing a silk kimono of deep indigo, which served to intensify the brilliance of his dark eyes. The contrast between the two young men was striking: Jubei was nearly a head taller than Iemitsu and much more solidly constructed. It was as if a bolder hand had carved Jubei out of rougher stone. Compared with Iemitsu's delicate features and studied grace, even Jubei's smallest gesture seemed overpoweringly masculine.

Akane caught Jubei's eye and waved. For a moment he just stared at her, then his eyes widened with delight and the warmth of his smile made her blush with pleasure.

"Akane?" Iemitsu peered at her through bleary eyes. "Can this lovely creature be *our* Akane?" he teased. "Come up here," he commanded, gesturing to a spot next to him. "It wouldn't be proper for such an elegant lady to sit among the rabble."

Laughter broke out and applause followed Akane to the

dais. She kneeled by Iemitsu's side, promptly took up the porcelain *tokkuri*, and filled his cup with sake.

Iemitsu surprised her by returning the courtesy. Although she hated the taste of sake, it would be an unthinkable breach of etiquette for her to refuse to drink. "*Kanpai*," Akane said, raising her cup.

Then the congratulatory speeches began. One after another the students of the Tajima style of kendo rose to pay tribute to their new fencing instructor. They praised his swordsmanship, his qualities of leadership, and his courage. The accolades went on and on, each more lavish than the one before.

Akane held her breath, silently praying that Iemitsu would not call on her. Her relief was enormous when Iemitsu wobbled to his feet to make the final speech.

There was a hint of deviltry in his eyes as he stood with his hand braced on Jubei's shoulder. "What could a poor orator like myself add to the eloquence already expressed here this evening? Instead I'll concentrate my efforts on correcting one of Jubei's most glaring deficiencies." Iemitsu waited for the murmurs to die down before continuing. "You've all been praising our new *shinan* for his mastery over the sword, and I suppose it may be justified . . . in a limited sense."

"Limited!" someone in the crowd shouted. "Who handles the sword better than he does!"

"Wait!" Iemitsu retorted. "It's not Jubei's expertise with the two swords he wears in his obi that's in question. It's the one he carries between his legs that I'm talking about."

Iemitsu's bawdy joke was greeted with a burst of cheers, while Akane stared at her hands, wondering where this was leading.

"Unfortunately Jubei's dedication to the two killing swords has left him little time to develop the skill required to handle his third sword—the pleasure sword." Iemitsu waited for the laughter to die down. "A dreadful situation I've taken steps to correct this very evening."

He clapped his hands and the shoji screen slid open. Standing in the doorway, flanked by two attendants, was the most famous courtesan in Edo, a woman known to everyone by her professional name only—Haruna. Her presence stunned the room into silence.

Akane had never seen anyone so magnificent. Her cobalt hair was swept back and gathered at the nape of her neck,

mysteriously held there by two tassled *kanzashi* no longer
than a pair of chopsticks. She was wearing an opulent robe of
five-colored silk over her sky-blue kimono.

The hem of her robe swirled around her feet like foam in
an eddy as she made her way to the dais, her bow to Jubei as
graceful as a seabird suspended on the wind. She raised her
head, her eyes sparkling with secret knowledge, yet her
smile made her seem sky and vulnerable, conveying a sense
of childlike innocence.

Jubei smiled back and motioned her to his side, the room
exploding with spontaneous applause.

Compared with Haruna, Akane felt awkward and ridiculous—
like a little girl dressed up in women's clothes. Every move,
every gesture she made, seemed clumsy in the face of this
courtesan's perfectly honed femininity and grace. Akane stole
a look at Jubei, who was focused on Haruna.

At the first opportunity Akane excused herself and slipped
away into the cool night.

Leaving Jubei to soak in his tub, the innkeeper's chubby
daughter loaded her arms with fresh towels and scurried
down the hall to the room where Haruna was bathing. She
was consumed by an urge to see what mysteries were hidden
underneath the courtesan's fancy clothes.

As she entered the room, Haruna was emerging from the
tub. The steamy room, the dim light, and her own poor
eyesight conspired to make a truly thorough examination
impossible. So she announced her presence with a polite
cough, and moved a few steps closer.

Haruna looked up and saw a pair of myopic eyes squinting
at her through the steam. It gave her a start, then she
realized it was the innkeeper's half-wit daughter. The girl's
shameless gawking would have been offensive had it not been
so comical. Instead of scolding her, Haruna decided to surprise her with a sight few women outside the Floating World
had ever seen.

"As long as you're here," Haruna said guilelessly, "would
you be kind enough to wipe off my back?"

She waited while the girl wet a small towel and wrung it
out. When she got very close, Haruna turned her back toward
the light and listened for the gasp of amazement she was
sure would come. And it came, just as she'd anticipated.

The girl stood gaping at the intricate designs that started at the small of Haruna's back, ran up her spine, and fanned out across her right shoulder blade—leaves and flowers intertwined with fire-breathing dragons and fierce samurai warriors in a riot of colors more elaborate than a Chinese tapestry.

"Go on, you can touch it," Haruna said. "The pictures were etched into my skin by a master. They can never be removed."

Tentatively the girl passed her fingertips over her back. She asked Haruna if it were her imagination, or had the colors actually brightened by her touch?

"It's true," Haruna told her. "The colors respond to stimulation. I'm told they become most vibrant at the height of sexual stimulation."

The girl jerked away her hand.

Haruna laughed, and dismissed her with a wave of her hand. "Tell Lord Tajima's son that I'll be honored to receive him when he's through with his bath."

"*Hai.*" She stopped at the door. "Haruna-san, may I ask you a question?"

"Just one," Haruna said as she slipped into her white sleeping kimono.

"Why did you have your skin decorated?"

"Tell me, will you ever forget what you've seen here tonight?"

"No . . . never."

"And neither will any man who ever sees me."

The innkeeper's daughter left, feeling as if she had just learned something of great importance, but not quite sure what it was.

Haruna finished preparing herself, then slipped into the sleeping chamber. She was pleased to discover that her two young attendants had prepared the room well. The three large candles had been placed at different levels so that the eye would be drawn to the flower arrangement situated on a stand at the far end of the room. Water had been heated for tea, and all the utensils had been laid out perfectly. The temperature of the room was neither too warm nor too cool.

Yet something was wrong.

Haruna closed her eyes and formed an image of the young man she was entertaining. Although he was tall, he possessed none of the awkwardness of most men his size. All the fuss about his swordsmanship had made him uncomfortable, but he managed to suffer through it in good spirits. While the others drank themselves into a stupor, Jubei drank only enough to loosen his laugh. Over the course of the evening he had spoken sparingly, preferring to listen and watch. On the surface he appeared at ease, but she sensed a tension about him—like a drawn bowstring, or a cat poised to spring. Suddenly she knew what was bothering her. The air had been too heavily scented for someone with his keen senses.

She went to the brazier and removed two of the four sandalwood chips smoldering on the charcoal. Then she slid the door open a crack to let the night air dilute the fragrance.

A few moments later Haruna heard Jubei coming down the hall. She took her place across from the door and bowed deeply as he entered the room. "Please be welcome here," she greeted him in a lovely, musical voice.

Jubei kneeled down across from her and drank in her beauty. Without makeup her pale skin had a rosy glow, like fresh snow at dawn. Artists painted women like this, he thought, and poets wrote verses about them. But until now Jubei never really believed they existed. He was spellbound.

While she was preparing the tea, Haruna chatted about the party, punctuating her observations with amusing impersonations of some of the guests. Jubei began to relax. The sound of her voice was as soothing as the purring of a cat. By the end of the second cup of tea, he was laughing and telling her stories about his life among the monks of Hiei.

When it came her turn to relate a tale, there was a moment's pause as she looked deep into his eyes. "You must be tired," she said softly, and glanced at the futon.

Jubei's stomach muscles tightened. "I won't try to pretend that I'm experienced in pillowing," he said candidly.

Haruna smiled. "Good, then I won't pretend that I'm not." She went to the futon and drew back the comforter. "First lie here and let me take some of the tension out of your body."

At her bidding, Jubei took off his sleeping kimono and stretched out facedown on the futon. Haruna leaned over his tight, athletic body and began kneading the muscles around his neck and shoulders. As she worked her way down his back, she spoke to him about the art of pillowing.

"There's only one secret worth remembering. All the rest— the delightful variations of pillowing—will grow and bloom in its own time. You must learn to empty your mind to make room for your senses. Savor the moment . . . the scent of hair and breath, the feel of skin on skin, the motion of muscle against muscle, the taste of moist salt on your lips, the sensuous sounds of breathing." She drew her nails down the length of his back. Jubei shivered. "Never force yourself to act unnaturally. There will be times when your need is urgent. Take your woman with the passion a hungry man reserves for food. At other times you'll want to go slowly, tasting her delights like an emperor at a banquet. There are as many ways to love as there are moods to feel." She patted Jubei's shoulder. He rolled over and looked up into her dark eyes. "And nothing you feel is wrong."

Jubei undid her obi, then opened her kimono and let it fall from her shoulders to her hips.

Haruna remained still, inviting him to explore her body with her eyes, his hands, his lips.

Instead he reached out and drew her down beside him. Bending over her, he said, "You are a wise and beautiful woman."

"No, Jubei. I'm only a woman who has leaned how to satisfy a man's needs. One day, if you're lucky, you'll discover there's more . . . much, much more."

"Perhaps you're right," he said, pressing closer to her. "But for this moment you're everything I need."

It was not yet dawn when Jubei woke up. The sake had left his throat parched and his mouth tasting sour. It took him a moment to realize he was not in his own room, and a moment more to recall he was in a room at the inn.

He sat up and looked around. The woman was gone, but the delicate scent of her musk lingered in the room. The aroma rekindled disjointed recollections of her supple body moving against his, the warmth of her breath on his lips, chest, stomach, and thighs; the intertwined limbs and the soft moans of pleasure.

Had she known this was his first time? What does it matter? he thought as he dressed to leave. "The mystery is over," he said softly to himself.

Despite the aftereffects of the sake, Jubei felt expansive. Instead of going home, he took a path that led to a hill overlooking Edo. When he reached the summit, he tucked his kimono between his legs and sat down to watch the city wake up.

Night-soil collectors, with their pots of human waste balanced on each shoulder, shuffled along waist deep in the heavy mist that lay in the streets of Edo. Farm women, bent double under the weight of produce, streamed in from the countryside. Along the waterfront most of the fishing boats were gone. Soon the lucky ones would return with fish for the morning meal.

The sun lifted off the rim of the ocean and gathered strength. The mist thinned and the city began to stir. Charcoal braziers were lighted, and the pungent scent of miso flavored the air. Street merchants began to hawk their wares. Doors slid open and closed. Women gathered at neighborhood wells to collect water, exchange bits of news, and complain about their husbands.

On the high ground above the city, a stone's throw from where Jubei sat, loomed the massive walls of Edo Castle. Why the Shogun, with all of Japan at his feet, had chosen this miserable piece of barren marshland as the site for his castle, was the subject of considerable head shaking and shoulder shrugging among the samurai who found it necessary to move here. Those who viewed the great Shogun with kindness, thought the decision quixotic. The others thought it insane.

Hundreds of thousands of stonemasons, carpenters, craftsmen, and common laborers had been pressed into service. Crude houses and makeshift shelters had sprung up all around the castle grounds. Moats were dug and land filled. Granite was hewn, lumber milled, and workers died and more came to replace them as the walls rose higher and higher. Merchants came and built, the price of the land went up, and Edo prospered and grew into the most muscular, vibrant city in the Sunrise Land.

Most of it had happened in the nineteen years since Jubei had been born. He had grown with the city, and in his own way had also prospered, for today was the day of his elevation to the rank of *shinan*, a teacher of the Tajima sword style—the style selected over all others to be taught to the Shogun's samurai. It was the proudest moment of his life.

Jubei listened. It was not a sound he heard, but rather the absence of sound that alerted him. He felt his stomach muscles tighten and the skin on the back of his neck tingle as if touched by a feather. Jubei suppressed a shiver. Someone or something was watching him.

Without turning, he probed the stillness, fixing the source at a point a few paces behind his right shoulder. Casually he leaned forward and scooped up a handful of loose gravel with his left hand. He took a deep breath, then pitched forward in a somersault, releasing an ear-splitting *kiai* as he landed on his feet.

"Hold!" Takuan shouted.

It was too late. The monk caught the blast of gravel full in the face. He dropped his staff and buried his face in his hands.

Jubei rushed to aid the little old man moaning and writhing on the ground. As he drew near, the monk raised one hand in a piteous gesture of defense.

"Don't kill me, please, I beg you," he wailed. "I'm only a poor servant of Lord Buddha. I possess nothing of value."

"You have nothing to fear from me, *obo-san*," Jubei said gently. He reached out and took the monk's hand in his.

"Oh, thank you, young sir. Thank you." He drew Jubei's hand to his lips as if to kiss it, then suddenly sank his teeth into the fleshy part of Jubei's thumb and hung on like a pit bull.

Jubei shrieked. Searing pain shot up his arm, followed by numbness that returned to searing pain at the slightest movement.

When Takuan let go, Jubei slumped to the ground and massaged the spot on his thumb marked by teeth prints. There was no feeling from his neck to his fingertips, his useless arm hanging from his shoulder like a fish on a meat hook.

Neither man spoke. Takuan was busy groping through his bag. He found a bamboo tube containing water, and seemed oblivious to Jubei's existence as he washed the dirt out of his eyes, then dabbed at his eyes with the hem of his robe.

"You crippled me," Jubei said in a voice that came out smaller than he wanted it to.

"You blinded me," Takuan said flatly.

Jubei looked at the monk and hoped it was true.

Takuan rinsed his face again, then turned toward Jubei. His eyes were red and swollen, but there was still sight in them. "You can stop feeling sorry for yourself. The numbness you feel is only temporary."

Jubei was not convinced, and began to vigorously shake his arm.

"Why did you attack me?" Takuan asked.

"Why did you sneak up behind me?"

He shrugged and smiled. "I don't know. I suppose I wanted to see if I could do it."

"That's absurd!"

"Of course it is." Takuan threw his head back and laughed until tears rolled down his cheeks.

Now Jubei was certain he was dealing with a madman.

"You see," Takuan went on, "I used to be a glorious sneak, maybe even famous. But it's bad manners to boast. When you get to be as old as I am, you start to wonder if you can still do the things you were good at when you were young. Let's say I just got the urge to practice."

Jubei stared at him in disbelief. "What if I had killed you?"

"Then I would be dead, *neh*?" With that Takuan sprang to his feet and ordered Jubei to turn around.

Jubei was not prepared to turn his back on this lunatic. He merely eyed the old man warily.

"What's the matter? Do you think I'm going to bite you?"

Jubei laughed despite himself, and turned around. He felt the monk slip his hands inside the neck of his kimono and probe around with his fingers. When he found the spot he was looking for, he pressed hard with his thumb. Jubei felt a slight tingling in his fingertips. The old man pressed again, and a stab of pain shot down the length of his arm. Jubei pulled away while Takuan squatted down and waited for Jubei to realize that sensation was returning to his arm.

The clang of the swordmaker's hammer rang out above the hustle and bustle of the throngs that filled the main street. Jubei directed the monk's attention to a banner that bore the simple inscription KOTETSU OF ECHIZEN. Lesser craftsmen would have added the word *swordmaker* to the sign, but Kotetsu's swords were so famous, nothing more needed to be said.

Takuan glanced at the shop, then wrinkled his nose and tested the air like a lost dog. "Ah, *udon*," he sighed. The way he said it sounded more like an invocation than the name of a noodle. He glanced at Jubei to see if the suggestion of food had produced the desired effect.

Although Jubei was hungry too, he had no intention of spending any more time in the company of this eccentric. He had allowed himself to be persuaded to show the monk the way to Kotetsu's shop, and now he was anxious to get rid of him as quickly as possible.

"If you'll excuse me," Jubei said politely, "I'm expected at the castle to assist my father with kendo instruction."

"Your father is the sword instructor at Edo Castle?"

"*Hai.*" Jubei nodded, pleased that the revelation had made an impression on the monk.

"Could it be that *you* are the son of the renowned sword instructor Lord Tajima?"

Jubei lowered his eyes modestly. "He's my father."

With that Takuan dropped to his knees in the middle of the street and executed a protracted bow.

"Please," Jubei muttered, embarrassed by the monk's inappropriate obeisance. "This is not necessary, not necessary at all." People were stopping to stare, and it was all Jubei could do to keep from bolting. Finally he squatted down and whispered urgently, "Get up. You're making a fool of yourself!"

Takuan lifted his face to Jubei. "Excuse me, I was overcome. Why don't you buy us some *udon*?"

By now nothing the monk did or said could astound Jubei. If the price of putting an end to this ludicrous spectacle was a bowl of noodles, so be it.

Takuan ate like a man possessed, ramming huge loads of noodles in his mouth, then packing in the dangling ends with his chopsticks. He finished his second bowl, drained two cups of tea in rapid succession, and burped with enormous satisfaction.

"Praise be to Buddha," he said, wiping the noodle drippings off his chin with a hot steaming cloth. "This is truly an auspicious day." He didn't seem to notice that Jubei was not sharing his enthusiasm. "Of course, it started off badly enough, but misfortune is necessary to preserve the balance of nature, *neh*? How else could we recognize luck when it came our way?"

In a conspiratorial tone Takuan then told Jubei the story he had fabricated to explain his purpose for coming to Edo. He revealed that a certain unnamed daimyo was living under the

threat of assassination. Those closest to him could be trusted
the least. The plot, he feared, involved members of his own
family. For this reason the daimyo had commissioned him to
conduct a secret search for an expert swordsman to act as his
personal bodyguard. Since Edo was full of masterless *ronin*
with formidable reputations as swordsmen, his plan was to
organize a contest, open to all samurai. The last man standing
would be declared the winner and awarded the prize of a
coveted Kotetsu sword. If it turned out that he was also a
man of character, he was empowered to offer him a high
position in the daimyo's service.

As plausible as his story sounded, it was difficult for Jubei
to imagine that someone like the monk would be charged
with such an important assignment. "If your mission is so
secret, why are you telling me?" he asked.

"Because I need your help."

Jubei nearly choked on his tea.

"Or, more precisely, I need your father's help. You see,
permission to conduct a contest of this sort would raise a lot
of questions from the authorities . . . questions that I'd prefer
not to answer, *neh*? However, if Lord Tajima were to sponsor
the contest, I could remain in the shadows . . . and think of
the talent your father's name would attract."

Jubei shook his head slowly. "With all due respect, *obo-
san*, I think you're crazy."

"Well, perhaps your father is a better judge of sanity than
you are. Anyway, I don't have time to argue with you. We've
got to pick up the sword from Master Kotetsu."

Before Jubei could protest, the monk dragged him across
the street into Kotetsu's shop.

The tiny one-room workshop was saturated with intense
heat from the swordmaker's forge. Next to the forge was a
trough of water, and through the shimmering waves of heat
Jubei could see the swordmaker's tools hanging from hooks
on the wall. Kotetsu was kneeling on a plank raised a few
inches above the earthen floor. In his right hand he gripped a
long pair of tongs which held the blade of the sword he was
forging, his concentration absolute. The *hajimaki* tied around
his head was soaked, and sweat poured into his eyes. His lips
formed secret prayers of his craft as the sinew of his body
glistened in the reflected light of the glowing bed of coals.

Jubei watched in silence as Kotetsu grappled with the

mystery of steel. It was an awesome battle between raw iron and Kotetsu's will, a holy war where every slam of the hammer, every thrust into water, every turn of the grinding wheel took on religious significance. Kotetsu was more than a craftsman, more than an artist—he was a shaman, an alchemist who breathed life into steel.

Although fire and water and iron and skill determined the quality of the blade, in the end it was the swordmaker's spirit that animated the sword and shaped its distinctive personality. There were lucky swords, bloodthirsty swords, swords that drove their owners to madness—all kinds of swords with famous names and enduring legends.

Not a word was spoken as Kotetsu worked. Jubei did not know much about the art of tempering steel, but he instinctively sensed that Kotetsu was involved in a split-second gamble between water and hot steel.

As they watched the swordmaker, a burly *ronin* with a pockmarked face and a filthy kimono that smelled of neglect swaggered into the shop. He was one of many masterless samurai who had crowded into the cities after the wars had ended. Since their swords were no longer in great demand, these "wavemen" wandered from place to place in search of a daimyo who might be willing to take them on as a retainer. The situation had become so desperate that some *ronin* had actually renounced their samurai birthright to become farmers. A few had even swallowed their pride and descended into the lower two classes of artisans and merchants. But most preferred to starve or steal rather than give up the privilege of wearing the two swords.

The *ronin* brushed past Jubei and went straight for Kotetsu. His lead-weighted kimono hem swung dangerously near the open forge. "Hey, Kotetsu," he shouted rudely. "I've come for my sword."

Whether Kotetsu even heard him was a matter of speculation. Not a muscle moved, and his narrow eyes remained focused on the shaft of bloodred steel at the end of his tongs.

"Are you deaf or just stupid?" he growled. "I left my sword here to be polished. Finished or not, I want it now!"

Kotetsu rammed the blade into the water trough near the *ronin's* foot. A dense cloud of steam rose up, choking the *ronin* and forcing him to step back. When the air cleared, the

ronin charged at Kotetsu and delivered a murderous kick that
sent the old man sprawling against the wall.

Outraged at the assault, Jubei started for the *ronin*, but the
monk's hand gripped his arm like a vise. "Wait," he whispered.

Jubei obeyed, but he was seething as the *ronin* rummaged
through the shop until he found the sword he was looking for.
It was longer than usual and the hilt was dressed in white.
Jubei realized that this *ronin* was a member of the White Hilt
Mob, a notorious gang of thugs who had been terrorizing the
citizens of Edo for years. Even the *doshin* who policed the
streets of Edo avoided confrontations with the White Hilt
Mob.

The *ronin* drew his sword from the scabbard and inspected
the gleaming blade that instantly collected vapor on its blue-
hued surface. He grunted his approval, slid the sword into
his obi, and started for the door.

As he brushed past Takuan, Jubei heard a solid thud and
the snap of bone, then saw the *ronin* crumple to the floor.
But he never saw the blow that dropped him.

Moving calmly, Takuan took a small purse from the *ronin's*
obi and counted out some coins. "Please forgive the interruption," he said to Kotetsu, pressing the coins into his hand and
helping him to his feet. "I will come for the sword at a more
propitious time." Takuan bowed deeply. Kotetsu politely removed the *hajimaki* from his head and returned the bow.

Together Takuan and Jubei dragged the unconscious *ronin*
outside and left him lying in the street.

"Let's go," the little monk said to Jubei. "I'm anxious to
see your father."

Akane lay still, watching leaf shadows dance on the rice-
paper door that faced the east garden, waiting for her dream
spirit to settle down after its disturbing night journey. Her
lingering sadness and shame had not been dispelled by the
morning light. The same dream had come again, and this
time it truly unnerved her.

The dream had taken her to a place of unearthly beauty—a
golden lake with water as smooth as Portuguese glass. It was
neither dusk nor dawn, yet the mist that collected on the
surface of the lake was colored with an eerie glow. In the
distance she saw the figure of a boatman, poling his craft
toward the shore where she was standing. Despite the chill in

the air, he was wearing only a loincloth. As he drew near, she recognized the boatman as her brother Jubei.

He motioned her to him, and Akane lifted her kimono and waded out a few steps into the warm water. Jubei gazed down at her, as if seeing her for the first time. His eyes were deep pools of quiet pleasure. The way he looked at her made her feel beautiful.

He reached out, and she felt herself being drawn into the boat. The tension was frightening and delicious, and she did not resist when he lifted the kimono off her shoulders and let it fall away. The only sound was the soothing slap of ripples against the boat.

Jubei leaned closer, and her bare breasts brushed against his chest, bringing a shiver. He gathered her closer and held her so tight that she could feel their hearts beat in unison. "Though you are my brother," she whispered near his lips, "you are my one true and only love."

His kiss flooded her with a warmth that penetrated to the marrow of her soul. Locked in his arms she felt herself drifting back until his full weight was on her. Then she loosened her thighs and took him inside her body.

Their lovemaking was long and luxurious. When it was over, she looked up and gasped. Her father was standing over them with a sword in his hand. Jubei's blood-drenched hands covered his face. Gently Akane unraveled his fingers. Where his eyes had been, there were now only empty sockets. She opened her mouth to scream, but no sound came. Then she awoke.

Lord Tajima refolded the note Jubei had brought him and tucked it away inside his kimono. To satisfy his curiosity, he cracked open the shoji screen and peeked out. Takuan was coming across the dojo, poling his way along with a large walking staff. His oversized head glistened in the sunlight like burnished bronze.

So this is what he looks like, Tajima mused. The legendary shadow-warrior who people said could leap backward over a ten-foot wall, transform himself into a whole menagerie of animals, stay submerged in water for days, be in three or four places at the same time, track footprints over solid rock, appear and disappear at will, and read the heart of a woman—

this spy, this sorcerer, this ninja of a thousand fantastic tales, had a comical face composed of ungainly features.

It was the first time Tajima had seen him in the light. The night Takuan brought Akane to him, he had been dressed in ninja garb. The meeting had been a brief one. Takuan asked him to rear Akane as his own child, and he agreed. Not another word had passed between them since that night.

Tajima greeted the monk formally, bowing deeply from the waist. "Takuan, I'm honored that one of your stature would deign to honor this humble school with a visit."

Takuan returned the bow. "*Iai*," he said with a wave of his hand. "I'm only a doddering old fart living out his years. It's the Tajima School of Fencing that's achieved stature."

Takuan's crudely put compliment was accepted with another bow, this one perfunctory enough to signal his willingness to dispense with the formalities and get down to business.

"As you may recall," Takuan said, "I have a weakness for speaking directly."

Tajima nodded, also recalling his penchant for withholding all but the most essential information. All that he had been told about Akane was that she was the daughter of an important samurai family, and no more.

"This time I've come to ask you to perform a special service for the Shogun."

"The Shogun commands my unbounded loyalty," Tajima responded. "Whatever he asks of me will be done."

"Good." Takuan inched closer. "Understand then, nothing I'm about to tell you can leave this room."

Tajima excused himself and went outside. His kendo students were gathering at the dojo exercise ground for the morning sword instruction. Some were standing around chatting and working on their equipment. Others were doing stretching exercises. No one was near enough to overhear anything. Just to be safe, Tajima ordered Jubei to begin the workout. He waited until everyone had paired off and the dojo was noisy with the clatter of wooden practice swords, then took a quick turn around the building and went back inside.

"Your reputation as a cautious man is well deserved," Takuan said. "It's one of the many qualities you'll need to perform your mission successfully."

"Perhaps it would be useful to name some of the other

qualities in case one of my many deficiencies would disqualify me for the task you have in mind."

"That's precisely what I intend to do. I'm going to ask you some questions, and your answers will determine whether or not we'll pursue the matter further or let it drop. Think carefully and speak your mind without fear of censure. All I want is the ungarnished truth." Takuan paused a moment, then said, "I know your opinion of the Shogun. What do you think of his first son, Iemitsu?"

"As his sword instructor I've seen a side of him that others may not." Tajima paused to assemble his words carefully. "Lord Iemitsu inherited his father's stubborn nature . . . and little else. He's a bright young man, but he tends to use his intelligence and position to bully. He can be willful and shows evidence of recklessness. And . . ." Tajima hesitated.

"Go on," Takuan commanded.

"And he shows an unnatural attraction for young boys."

"Is that a flaw?"

"It's an observation."

"Not a very flattering portrait," Takuan remarked. "Tell me, which son is best qualified to succeed the Shogun, Iemitsu or the second son, Tadanaga?"

"Tadanaga," Tajima answered firmly.

"And what will you do when Iemitsu becomes the next Shogun?"

"I will defend him with my life."

"In spite of your . . . reservations?"

"I have no reservations when it comes to supporting the Tokugawa. I've seen enough bloodshed and chaos. I'm convinced that the only way to keep Japan from sliding back to civil war is through the establishment of a hereditary shogunate. Serving one mediocre Shogun is insignificant compared with the prospect of continued stability and order. The fact that Lord Iemitsu may be a weak link is all the more reason for peace-loving men to rally around him. It is our role to keep the Tokugawa chain from being stretched to the breaking point by power-hungry opportunists."

"Are you prepared to lie to achieve this end?"

"I am."

"To murder?"

"I am."

"To sacrifice your own family if it becomes necessary?"

Tajima thought for a long time before he answered. "If that is the price of peace, I would pay it."

Satisfied with his responses, Takuan told Tajima about his meeting with the Shogun. "For many years the Iga ninja have served the Tokugawa from the shadows. My brothers and I have done all the dark deeds that no honorable leader could ever do overtly—murder, arson, theft, character assassination— all the things that are absolutely indispensible if a leader is to govern effectively without squandering the trust and respect of his subjects. Look at me closely, Lord Tajima, and you'll see the Shogun's other face—the ugly, twisted face that must never be worn in public . . . the ruthless face of power." Takuan paused to let the impact of his words sink in. "Are you willing to put on this face?"

Tajima realized he was being offered access to power greater than he had ever dreamed possible. The price was steep, but irresistible. "How can I refuse?" he said solemnly. Then he tapped the bridge of his ruined nose with a finger, and a wry smile creased his lips. "Especially since I already have such a good start on the proper features."

Takuan nodded. "So you do. From this moment forward you and your family will do whatever is required to maintain the Tokugawa grip on the shogunate. Your official title will remain Sword Instructor, but now you'll sit on the governing counsel and assume responsibility for maintaining law and order in the capital. Your real function, however, will be to gather information and conduct clandestine operations. You'll take your secret orders directly from the Shogun." Takuan cocked his head to one side and smiled. "Welcome to the shadow world, Lord Tajima."

"There are so many questions—"

Takuan cut him off with a wave of his hand. "All in good time. First tell me about your son. I hear he's good with the sword."

Tajima weighed his son's strengths and weaknesses in his mind. "Jubei's an enigma. He has exceptional speed and agility, but he uses these gifts to cover flaws in his technique. The problem is, he's arrogant. None of the other students are capable of pushing him . . . except, perhaps, Akane."

"A girl!"

Tajima smiled wryly. "A very unusual girl."

"She must be, if she can hold her own against an opponent with the gift of *haragei*."

"*Haragei?*" Tajima asked. "Who has the gift of inner vision?"

Takuan nodded. "This morning I tried to take your son by surprise. His back was turned, but he saw me coming with his third eye. He measured my distance, and reacted with utter confidence. I'm telling you, his awareness is not tied to the five senses."

Tajima pondered Takuan's insight. "I knew he had uncanny instincts, but I never imagined it was *haragei*." He stroked his chin thoughtfully. "The edges are still rough, but I can tell you this—there are moments when I think I've never seen anyone better."

Coming from a swordsman of Tajima's renown, the statement made a profound impression on Takuan. However, he had seen too many students of the sword show signs of brilliance on the practice grounds, only to fall to pieces when they faced cold steel. "What would you say if I told you I want to test your son in a real duel?" he asked.

"I would tell you he's not ready." Tajima studied Takuan's face for some kind of reaction. Takuan's eyes were like ice-glazed puddles, reflecting more than they revealed. "It's the flaws," Tajima explained. "If only he was a little more consistent."

"Why not let me see for myself," Takuan said, getting to his feet. "Perhaps these flaws can be corrected before they become *fatal* flaws."

Tajima led Takuan across the dojo to the shaded observation platform. About twenty or thirty sons of high-ranking retainers had formed a ring around two combatants who were circling each other cautiously, holding their wooden practice swords high above their shoulders like woodcutters in mid chop. As Takuan mounted the platform, he noticed that one of the combatants was a girl.

"Is that Akane?" he asked.

Tajima nodded. "I'm training her in the Tajima style. I plan to assign her to guard the Shogun's daughters when they are inside the women's quarters."

"A unique idea." Takuan moved a few paces to one side, to get a better look at the contest. "I'm surprised your male students are willing to give her a match. I would have thought they'd consider it demeaning."

"I'm afraid most of them do." Tajima smiled slyly. "But not for the reasons you may think. Watch."

Her opponent was several years older than Akane, but not much taller. It was clear from the expression on his face that he was not taking his opponent lightly. He feigned a rush and Akane stood her ground.

"She has steady nerves," Takuan commented.

The second rush was real. He faked low, whirled around, and came in high with a Smacking Parry that almost succeeded in dislodging the sword from her hands. Akane dropped to one knee at the last second, just as the concluding cut whistled perilously close to her head. Then, with a bold counter, she caught him totally off balance. There was a solid thud as Akane's sword found his midsection, and a spontaneous roar of approval went up from the spectators.

"That was a reckless counter move," Takuan said to Tajima. "She was lucky she didn't get her head taken off."

"When you've seen her do things like that enough times, you stop thinking of it as luck."

Tajima clapped his hands, and the students scrambled to take their places in front of the platform. Jubei was the last to kneel. His eyes were riveted on Takuan. It was evident from the look of dismay on his face that he had not expected his father to waste much time on the monk, let alone invite him up on the platform.

"Your son thinks I'm just a crazy monk," Takuan whispered. "Let's not disabuse him."

Since Tajima could think of nothing credible to say about Takuan's presence on the platform, he simply left the monk unexplained and commenced the lesson. "We'll begin the morning session with a demonstration of a basic strategy," he announced to his students. Then he called Jubei and Akane to the front of the class.

Akane's light steps and cheerful face made a stark contrast to Jubei's slow saunter and detached expression. "He walks like a man who thinks he's dangerous," Takuan commented out of the corner of his mouth.

"I told you he could be arrogant," Tajima answered.

Jubei and Akane took positions facing each other, and waited for their instructions. Tajima ordered them to demonstrate the Fire and Stones cut and the Red Leaves counter.

"Why is he trying to embarrass me? He asked Akane his sister. "He knows those are my two weakest moves."

Tajima called out the starting signal.

Raising his sword waist high, Jubei struck out, using the power in his hands and legs to break through Akane's parry. Deftly Akane rolled her shoulders and managed to beat down the point of his sword. Only Jubei's quickness saved him from her counter cut.

Jubei recovered and struck again. Akane deflected the blow easily and answered with another skillful stroke. Parry, thrust, parry, thrust, again and again, faster and faster, until Jubei got in a stunning blow that knocked Akane's sword out of her hand and sent it tumbling across the mat.

"Did you detect the slight hitch in Jubei's downstroke?"

Takuan nodded. "And the faulty weight distribution."

"You have a keen eye," Tajima said.

"I wish it were so, but the truth is, the flaw was flagrant."

The monk closed his eyes, seeming to go inside himself. Except for the steady breeze that rippled the banners, the dojo was silent. The students sat back on their heels and waited for further instructions.

Takuan asked Tajima to start them again. He watched intently. Again. The result was always the same. Jubei barely escaped disaster and won on overwhelming strength.

Suddenly Takuan sprang to his feet and called Tajima aside. He raised both hands over his right shoulder, assuming the strike position. "Tell me, Lord Tajima," he said, "what does the Fire and Stones cut have in common with the Red Leaves counter?"

Tajima thought for a moment. "They're both basic cuts," he answered. "Cuts that a student of Jubei's ability should have mastered easily."

"True, but what else?" Takuan's voice was charged with excitement.

Tajima searched his mind. "I'm sorry . . ." He shrugged, unable to fathom what the monk was driving at.

"It's so simple that I almost missed it." The old monk's eyes sparkled with childlike delight. "Watch," he said as his hands traced the two cuts in the air. "Both moves originate from the right-side attitude!"

"And?"

"And your son is left-handed."

"Left-handed?" Tajima had almost forgotten how difficult it had been to break him of the shameful habit of favoring his left hand. He recalled the constant chiding of Jubei's mother as time and again she shifted the chopsticks from his left hand to the correct hand. In the end she won, but now it appeared that the problem had merely been buried only to reemerge in a corruption of his skill. If it had been anyone but Jubei . . .

"I should have noticed," Tajima said abjectly. "It's inexcusable that I missed this defect."

"Defect?" Takuan chuckled merrily. "I call it a breakthrough. You've done your son a great service. Think of it—you forced him to use an unnatural posture, and look at what he's accomplished! Imagine what he'll be able to do when we put the sword in his left hand."

"A left-handed fencer?" Tajima scoffed. "It's outrageous!"

"Of course it's outrageous. That's why it has to be done. Picture yourself in combat with an opponent with Jubei's skill. You draw your sword with your right hand, he draws with his left. Immediately you're thrown into utter confusion. How do you fashion your attack? Everything's backward, like looking into a mirror. Who has the advantage?"

"The edge clearly belongs to the left-hander," Tajima admitted.

"Turn him over to me for a month. If he needs to be pushed, I'll push him. This much I promise you—when I'm finished with him, he'll be ready for his first real duel."

Tajima was skeptical. "A month is a short time. Can it be done?"

"Your son's no ordinary samurai, and I'm no ordinary teacher. I tell you it can be done."

"Forgive me if I sound selfish," he told Takuan, "but Jubei is my only son. Now that I'm operating in the shadows, I'll need him and his skills more than ever. What if he's killed?"

"You have to trust me. This is not a whim. If I am successful, your son will only become that much more useful to you. Besides, how can we discover the true depth of his talent until we put it to the ultimate test? I suggest you place him in my charge and leave the outcome to the gods."

After his earlier pledges of unqualified commitment, Tajima could hardly refuse. But he did reserve the right to reconsider the duel at the end of the training period.

* * *

That night Jubei vanished without a word. In keeping with Takuan's policy of never telling anything to anybody who didn't need to know, Akane was not told where her brother had gone or what he was doing. All her father would say was that Jubei was safe and would return home in about a month. She went through her daily routine mechanically, counting the days until Jubei returned.

As for Jubei, his month with Takuan become the most grueling experience of his life. The little monk drove him like an animal, making relentless demands on his body and mind for more, always more—more speed, more agility, more concentration, more practice, more of everything except rest. Jubei suffered thirst and hunger and pain and all manner of torment at the hands of his teacher.

When he wasn't practicing kendo, the monk gave him impossible tasks to complete, riddles to solve, intellectual knots to unravel. When Jubei finished them, he was given more. Whatever he did was not enough. Not a word of praise, not a hint of approval, ever passed his teacher's lips. Accomplishments were greeted with stony silence. Flaws were exposed, dissected, and criticized with savage intensity. If ninety-nine out of a hundred thrusts found the mark, the monk only saw the miss. Imperfection was treated with scorn and ridicule.

Beneath the layers of anger and resentment, Jubei realized that something good was happening to him. The ordeal was taking him to the boundaries of his own limitations.

Though Takuan withheld praise, Jubei's progress with the sword surpassed his expectations. He made the conversion to his left hand quickly, and by the end of the second week Jubei was fighting with equal facility from either side.

But honing his natural talent to a fine edge had been the easy part of the training. The hard part was breaking down Jubei's arrogance without destroying his pride. Like most gifted people, the temptation to cross the line from self-assurance to self-satisfaction kept Jubei from developing the character he needed to become a true master of the sword. Whenever Takuan detected signs of cockiness, he would goad Jubei into making a mistake and leave him with a welt to help him remember his error. The black-and-blue marks all over Jubei's body were testimonies to both men's persistence. By the end of the month it was clear that Jubei had become a little more circumspect about crossing the line into arrogance.

However, another flaw emerged during the course of the training, and Takuan had not been able to correct it. At unpredictable moments Jubei would lose control and snap into a cold rage, leaving himself vulnerable to counterattack. It worried Takuan, but not enough to keep Jubei out of Lord Tajima's fencing contest.

2

Edo
Year of the Horse—1630
Hour of the Snake

The site that had been chosen for the contest was a clearing in a stand of cryptomeria on the outskirts of Edo. Lots were drawn shortly after dawn, and by late morning only three contestants remained. One was the vulgar White Hilt *ronin* who had abused the swordmaker Kotetsu. Despite his crude manners, this *ronin* turned out to be an excellent fencer, dispatching several accomplished opponents with comparative ease. Although Tajima had decreed that only wooden practice swords could be used until the final bout, the White Hilt *ronin* had still managed to kill two of his three opponents and seriously maim the other one.

The second contestant wrapped himself in mystery, choosing to identify himself only by his surname, Iori. In manner and appearance he was the polar opposite of the burly *ronin*. His lithe body and refined features appeared to be more suited to the fine arts than the martial arts. Yet whatever he lacked in brawn was more than made up in grace. His movements were so fluid that his opponents tended to misjudge his speed, which turned out to be a grave mistake.

The last swordsman to emerge from the pack was Jubei. Of all the morning's duels, his had been the most thrilling. In every bout he seemed to blunder into some impossible situation, only to rally and pull it out at the last second.

"What's wrong with you?" Takuan complained after a close call in one of the early matches.

Jubei smiled. "A clever hawk hides his talons," he said, and walked away to join his sister.

After that Takuan worked his way through the crowd, making every bet he could on Jubei. And Jubei continued to make the fleecing easy by never putting out any more effort than he needed to win.

Since an odd number of opponents had ended up in the semi-final round, straws were drawn to determine which one of them would miss a turn. The White Hilt *ronin* drew first and pulled a short straw. He was in. Jubei drew next and got the long one. He was out. Iori bowed to Tajima and went off to prepare himself.

Someone passed a flask of sake to the *ronin*, who had been making a conspicuous display of guzzling rice wine before each of his bouts. He contemptuously jerked the flask to his mouth and put on a great show of swallowing hard.

Akane was sitting close enough to see through the sham. "Watch him," she said to Jubei. "He's not really drinking."

"I know. He's not as stupid as he looks," Jubei said dryly. "This time he realizes he's in for a real test."

Throughout the morning Akane had tried to keep her spirits up, but now she felt incapable of bravado. She had been dying piecemeal with every duel her brother fought. His narrow escapes had shaken her confidence in him. It seemed that his month's training had been worse than useless. All along she had been secretly praying that Jubei would lose in one of the early rounds, while wooden swords were still being used, but he always managed to disappoint her. Now, with a real sword in hand, he would have to face the winner of the next bout, and she was afraid either of the two could beat Jubei. From the grim expression she saw on her father's face, she knew she wasn't the only one concerned.

Akane dampened a cloth, wiped the sweat off her brother's forehead, and tried to put the impending duel out of her mind. "Karma is karma," she said to comfort herself. But it didn't help.

After each of the two combatants finished tying back the sleeves of their kimonos, they approached Tajima and bowed. He was about to give the signal to start the bout when Iori asked for permission to speak. Tajima gave his consent.

Iori pointed at his opponent. "This thing who calls himself a samurai," he said in a loud voice, "is an insult to the spirit of kendo." A murmur rushed through the crowd. The *ronin* flushed with rage. "I refuse to honor this ape by playing kendo with him."

"Coward!" the *ronin* snarled.

Iori ignored him and continued to address himself to Lord Tajima. "Instead, I ask your permission to dispense with wooden swords and fight this duel with *katana*."

"It's your right as a samurai to issue a challenge to another samurai," Tajima answered. "If the challenge is accepted, I won't interfere."

"I accept!" the *ronin* growled, yanking his sword out of its scabbard.

A roar went up from the crowd, and money began to change hands at a feverish pace.

"Before I hack you to pieces," the *ronin* shouted at Iori, "have the good manners to identify yourself properly."

It annoyed Iori that the *ronin* had chosen to exercise his prerogative as a samurai and demand that he reveal his full name. "My family name is Miyamoto," Iori responded reluctantly.

"He's Musashi's son!" someone in the crowd yelled. The *ronin* blanched at the information.

There was not a person there who had not heard of Iori's lengendary father. Musashi, born forty years ago in the small town of Miyamoto, had become the most famous swordsman in Japan. Before retiring into seclusion at twenty-nine, Musashi had won more than sixty duels. The unique sword style he had developed made him invincible. It was rumored that Musashi had actually fought his last few duels with a wooden sword carved out of an oar—and won!

His reputation was so enormous that Iori had found it difficult to move out of his father's shadow. Intent on forging an identity of his own, at sixteen he had taken to the road in search of recognition as a swordsman. For the past four years he had been traveling from one fencing contest to another, hoping to catch the eye of someone in a position to recommend his services to the Shogun. Iori thought that winning a competition sponsored by the Shogun's own fencing master could provide him with the credentials he needed to accomplish his goal. It troubled him that he might have to kill Lord Tajima's son to do it, but for the moment his mind was focused on the problem at hand.

Without waiting for the signal to start, the White Hilt *ronin* charged Iori, who held his ground. At the last instant Iori ducked under the vicious slash aimed at his head, and the *ronin* almost stumbled and fell. Iori let him recover before he casually drew his own sword.

The *ronin* bowed his neck and came at Iori slowly this time. Iori let him close to within striking distance, leaving his midsection exposed. The *ronin* unleashed a swipe at his belly, and his sword found nothing but air. Once again Iori waited until he regained his balance. Then to the astonishment of the crowd, he turned his back on the *ronin* and walked away.

The *ronin* dashed after him. Suddenly Iori stopped, whirled around, and slashed at the *ronin*'s trunk. The *ronin*'s mouth dropped open, his eyes bulged, and the upper part of his body toppled off his hips like a jug dropping off a table. Iori didn't look at the corpse as he calmly cleaned the edge of the sword with a piece of rice paper and replaced it in his scabbard.

Tajima looked at his son, whose face revealed nothing but admiration for the victor. He wondered how long it would take before Jubei began to connect his appreciation for Iori's skill with the realization that he was next. Akane, who had already made that connection, dug her fingers into Jubei's forearm and held him like a vise.

Then Tajima made a decision calculated to save his son's life. "By chance," he announced to the crowd, "Iori has been forced to undergo one more contest than his final opponent. The strain of each battle takes its toll. In the name of fairness I will enter the contest and duel my son. The winner will stand against Iori for the Kotetsu sword."

Iori glanced at Jubei, then back to Jubei's father. He nodded his approval and sat down, resting his back against the trunk of a large tree to wait out the results.

Once again the crowd stirred. There was some grumbling, but in general the opportunity to see the famous sword instructor defeat his own son, then go up against a fencer of Iori's caliber, was an event that outweighed all other considerations.

Jubei glared at his father. The tactic was so transparent that Jubei couldn't bear the shame. "In the name of fairness," he shouted, "it's only right that we also duel with real swords."

"It is only necessary that we compete," Tajima said firmly. "There's no need to spill blood."

"No!" Jubei cried out. "I'll accept your challenge only under the same conditions that Iori fought."

The father stared at the son. The son stared back at the father.

"Please, Jubei," Akane begged, "don't you understand—father is trying to save you."

Jubei brushed her aside. "Do you accept the conditions or not?"

"Prepare to fight." Tajima measured out each word like a dose of poison.

Turning away, Tajima tried to compose himself, but his anger interfered with the mental picture he wanted to form of Jubei in combat. It would be necessary to wound him. He knew Jubei's flaws and how to exploit them, but wondered if he had the skill and precision to attack them surgically enough to incapacitate him without killing him. In his mind's eye he pictured Jubei carelessly lowering his right shoulder after parrying the Red Leaves cut. He saw only one of Jubei's knees flex properly when he attempted the Ox Neck maneuver. Calm came to him like a good falcon, swiftly and quietly.

Jubei was wearing the short *happi* jacket and kendo pants. He wondered why his father had refused to change his clothing, choosing instead to fight in the more cumbersome kimono. Jubei knew it couldn't be either arrogance or oversight. It had to be tactical. But what possible advantage could there be in limiting his own mobility? Then an answer came to him: his father was planning to conserve motion, using the extra length of the kimono to disguise the position of his feet, making it more difficult to gauge his intentions.

The two combatants stood about ten paces apart. The lanky, slightly stoop-shouldered father was going about his preparations as if he were dressing for an afternoon stroll. The aura of calm about Tajima contrasted sharply with the excitement running through the crowd of spectators. From the moment he had taken up the challenge, he had not so much as glanced at his son.

The somewhat shorter, but more powerfully built Jubei was watching his father intently. There was no trace of anger in his eyes. It had dissipated quickly after the initial confrontation was over. Now he was wearing the slightly quizzical expression of someone who had asked a troubling question and was waiting patiently for an answer. Having lost rage as an ally, Jubei was searching his mind for a reason to go through with the duel. When it dawned on him that the man he had challenged to mortal combat was his own father, he suddenly realized that the resentment he felt at having been handed over to a stranger for a month of humiliation and torment was hardly sufficient justification for patricide. Yet he could not deny that something deeper was eating away at him, something elusive that kept on stoking the furnace of his resolve. But what? It had to be more than stubborn pride. In some perverse way Jubei thought it might have something to do with earning his father's respect.

But the answer Jubei was searching for lay hidden one layer deeper. It was not respect he was after—it was love. From the time he was a little boy, he had practiced endless hours with the sword just to please his father, had suffered a long, lonely separation from his family at his father orders, all of which might have been bearable if his father had shown him the smallest sign of affection. But there had been nothing, and the love he once felt for his father had withered and died from neglect.

Jubei gripped the scabbard and pressed his thumb against the hilt of his sword. Things had gone too far for either of them to back down now, and it was too dangerous for him to let regret—or any other emotion, for that matter—tamper with his will to win. Drawing on the hard lessons he had learned over the past month, Jubei emptied his mind and allowed instinct to take over.

As Tajima tied back the sleeves of his kimono, he scanned the treetops and took mental note of the position of the sun. When he finished his preparations he checked the ground to see where the sun hit with the greatest intensity. Then he turned and positioned himself so the sun would be directly in Jubei's line of sight.

Takuan, who was enjoying himself immensely, agreed to

preside over the match. He clapped his hands over his head and shouted, "*Hajime!*"

Tajima stood still and let Jubei circle him. Jubei held his sword with both hands high over his right shoulder, in the striking position. Tajima centered his sword in the parry position, gripping it with a floating feeling—neither tight nor loose.

Jubei narrowed his eyes and lowered both shoulders so that energy flowed into his legs from his abdomen to the tips of his toes. He focused his eyes on his father's stomach to keep from being deceived by irrelevant movement, and as he slowly circled, sensed a split second of indecision and dashed at his father, ramming his sword directly at his face. Tajima just managed to dodge the cut by deflecting the point and riding it down to the left. Jubei rolled and came up to his feet, this time with his sword poised over his left shoulder.

Jubei had assumed the left attitude, and just as Takuan had predicted, Tajima experienced a moment of utter disorientation. Jubei rushed again, and with Tajima off balance, his cut slashed through the front of Tajima's kimono. Their swords locked, then their eyes locked.

Tajima saw something he'd never seen in any man's eyes. It was as if Jubei was seeing everything and nothing. If ice could burn, it would look like that. His son was gone, and in his place was a stranger—a demonic instrument of death. For an instant Tajima understood the meaning of terror.

Then instinct took over, obliterating all thoughts except survival. Tajima was not even aware that the front of his kimono was soaked with his own blood. A kind of euphoria enveloped him. Life's complexities had come down to one perfect banality—kill or be killed.

Tajima pressed on relentlessly with slash after slash in masterful combinations, but amazingly, Jubei countered each with uncanny precision. As fatigue set in, the advantage seemed to favor Jubei's youth over Tajima's experience.

Panting more heavily than he needed to, Tajima began backing up, luring Jubei. Then he stopped, set himself, and dropped his guard dangerously low, inviting an assault from the upper attitude. Jubei darted in, cutting down straight from his shoulder. Simultaneously Tajima jerked his hands up, catching Jubei flush in the face with his sword guard. The sword dropped out of Jubei's hands and he crumpled into a heap at Tajima's feet. Akane scrambled on top of her brother, shielding him with her body.

For a moment Tajima stared down at his daughter, her face full of misery. "Declare Iori the winner," he said to Takuan, sheathing his sword.

As Tajima loomed over them, Akane rolled Jubei onto his back and gasped. It was a scene out of her dream. Jubei's right eye socket was a pool of blood. She took a soft piece of paper out of her kimono and pressed it against his face. Jubei had not moved, but his breathing was deep and steady.

Tajima reached inside his kimono, took out a small purse, and threw it on the ground next to her. "If he lives," he said to Akane, "take him to town and find him a place to stay. Stay there with him as long as you need to, but don't try to bring him home. He is no longer my son."

"No! Please," Akane wailed, clutching at her father's feet.

Tajima jerked away and walked down the hill.

The crowd was beginning to drift away when Takuan placed his hand on Akane's shoulder. "Gather some wood and build a small fire," he said. "I'll do what has to be done."

While she was gone, Takuan removed Jubei's crushed eye and rinsed the cavity out with sake. Then he opened his medicine pouch and took out a packet containing a fine yellow powder. This he poured into Jubei's eye socket, and watched until the bleeding slowed to a trickle and stopped.

Nearby, Akane blew the smoldering tinder into flames, then added some dry pine needles and a few pinecones.

"Give me your *kaiken*," Takuan ordered as Jubei began to stir.

Akane handed him her short dagger, and he plunged the blade into the flames. When the steel turned red, he told Akane to kneel on Jubei's arms and pin his head between her knees. When she got into position, Takuan closed Jubei's eye and sprinkled a pinch of gunpowder on his eyelid, then laid the glowing dagger across his empty eye socket. The gunpowder crackled. Jubei lurched and gasped. The pungent stench of seared flesh made Akane gag, but she managed to hang on until Jubei went limp.

Takuan checked to make sure the wound was completely cauterized. Satisfied, he applied some salve to the burned area and bandaged Jubei's face.

Akane sat with Jubei's head cradled in her lap. She stroked her brother's ruined face and sobbed uncontrollably.

"Don't weep, child," Takuan said to her. "Few men who choose the path of the sword live to know the joys of old age. Your brother will live a long life now, a life full of children, grandchildren, and peace." He rose to his feet and slowly shook his head. "But what I wouldn't have given to see this boy reach his full potential."

3

Lisbon, Portugal
Year of Our Lord—1630

The wind came in hard off the ocean, cool and heavy with rain. The leaves on the catalpas rolled over, silver side up to the darkening sky. Cassocks flattened out against the backs of the seminarians standing at the grave, and their sweat turned to ice water. Off in the distance there was a deep rumble in the bowels of the storm. The Father Vicar glanced at the sky and picked up the pace.

One seminarian stood a few paces away from the others, his intense violet eyes fixed on the casket of his former teacher. Like the others, he wore a plain black cassock, but the similarities ended there. Although Jan Kriek's mother was Portuguese, he had inherited the ash-blond hair and chiseled features of his Dutch father. For this reason he had always been treated as an outsider by his brother seminarians. It mattered little to them that he was half Portuguese. The other half was Dutch—the mortal enemies of the Holy Church. Whenever they spoke Jan Kriek's name, it was spoken slowly and through clenched teeth, as if it were a profanity. Even though most of the young men attending the seminary were stockier and more powerfully muscled than the slender

Kriek, very few risked openly expressing their contempt. There was something unsettling about Kriek, something that cultivated wariness.

Jan Kriek was concentrating hard now, trying to intercept meaning from the cascade of words that gushed out of the Father Vicar's mouth like fast water over loose rock. But all he could hear was metallic Latin sounds, uttered without sense or feeling.

Fighting back his anger, Kriek reminded himself over and over again that the repose of Father Sebastio's departed soul was not in the hands of this mechanical priest. It was in the hands of God. Still, he couldn't find it in his heart to forgive the Father Vicar for the way he was brutalizing this good priest's funeral.

It had been Father Sebastio who had made life at the seminary bearable for him. The departed priest had been drawn to Jan Kriek because he had been an outsider too. Like the young seminarian, he'd had a foot in two worlds. Portuguese by birth, Father Sebastio had spent most of his adult life as a missionary in the Japans, and it had changed him profoundly. The other Jesuit fathers had treated him correctly, but without affection. They found his obsession with the Japans tiresome.

Jan Kriek did not. Father Sebastio stirred his imagination with stories of silk-robed samurai, proud and dangerous, with ice-blue swords that cut through iron like ripe melons. He'd conjured gruesome images of severed heads of countless soldiers impaled on stakes and lining the road from Osaka to Kyoto, and lovely images of windswept pine with roots like tentacles, clinging to seaside rocks; of a sacred volcano so serene and majestic that the sight of it caused men to weep; and doll-like ladies with powdered faces and scarlet lips and hair the color of a crow's wing. Exotic pictures, rich and textured, took root in Jan Kriek's imagination and began to feel like memories.

Fat drops of rain pocked the pile of earth next to the grave. The wind quickened, and Kriek thought of the hours they had spent together poring over the Japanese syllabary, working on a language that little by little become more than isolated words, more than brush strokes on paper. For Kriek, learning to speak Japanese had become a new way of seeing.

As the priest droned on, Kriek reached inside his cassock

and took out a folded piece of rice paper. He looked at the
elegant brush strokes and saw his teacher's practiced hand at
work.

The final words were spoken, as the rain came hard. The
casket was lowered into the ground and the cemetery emptied. Only Kriek remained behind to read Father Sebastio's
death poem:

> A falling leaf disturbs the quiet pond
> The pond is still
> Another leaf falls

He dropped the rain-ruined poem into the grave and
commended his teacher's soul to the mercy of the Lord.

The Father Vicar tossed another piece of wood in the
fireplace. The fire and a change of clothes had not helped
much. The chill had gone too deep. He poured himself a
heavy dose of brandy and let the fumes clear his sinuses
before he took a swallow. The alcohol warmed the walls of his
stomach, and a glaze of perspiration formed on his forehead.
This, he knew, was not the effects of the brandy—it was the
beginning of a fever.

"Damn that Sebastio!" the Father Vicar grumbled to himself. He wiped his forehead, then sneezed into his linen
handkerchief. "God forgive me," he said, looking up at the
crucifix over the fireplace. But in his heart he knew that the
Society of Jesus was far better off now that the old curmud-
geon was out of the fray. He was certain it had been Sebastio's
incessant letters to the Father General complaining about
Jesuit interference in Japanese politics that had led to his
recall from the Japans. He wondered how many times the
Father General had been assailed with the same tripe *he* had
been subjected to ad nauseam. "Minister to the flock and
leave politics alone," Sebastio had said again and again. "If
we don't, the gates of heaven will be drenched in the blood of
martyrs."

The Father Vicar drained his glass. Where would the Church
be today without the blood of martyrs? he thought. Had not
Christ himself defied the earthly powers and shed his precious blood as an example for all true Christians to follow?
Let the Franciscans cringe at the feet of the Emperor. Let

the Dominicans content themselves with droppings from the Shogun's table. Jesuits were the soldiers of Christ, the whip that drove money changers out of temples, the vanguard in the battle with Satan's legions. Thank God the pusillanimous ravings of hopeless idealists like Father Sebastio had fallen on deaf ears.

The door of the study burst open. The Father Vicar turned abruptly and saw that the indiscretion had been committed by his own secretary. "Have you forgotten how to knock?" he snapped.

The young priest fumbled with his cross and stammered, "It's the Father General."

"What are you saying?" the Father Vicar demanded.

The secretary pulled the door shut and approached. "Excuse me, Father." He swallowed hard. "The Father General just arrived with a guest. He asks you to receive him."

The color drained from the Father Vicar's face. "Yes, of course," he muttered, then caught himself. "No, wait. Give me a few minutes to . . . just make some kind of excuse."

As the secretary hurried out of the study, a shiver coursed through the Father Vicar's body. An unannounced visit from the Director of the Society of Jesus! Blessed Mother of God, what could it mean? He quickly poured himself another brandy, then thought better of it and poured the drink back into the decanter, spilling most of it down the sides. He drew a deep breath, wiped his clammy palms on his cassock, and put on what he hoped was a convincing smile.

The Father General entered. "My brother," he said, extending his hand.

The Father Vicar dropped to one knee and kissed his superior's ring. "I am honored by your visit, your excellency."

"I'd almost forgotten how foul Lisbon weather can be this time of year," the older priest said, moving to warm himself by the fire.

"Yes, the rain was quite unexpected."

"Like my visit." He chuckled amiably.

"I assure you, in terms of surprise there can be no comparison." They exchanged smiles. "May I offer your excellency some brandy?"

"I'd be a fool to refuse," the Father General replied. "You know, Portuguese brandy is hoarded like gold at the Vatican. Naturally our Italian brothers insist that their brandy is superior, an opinion that says more about their patriotism than their taste."

The conversation meandered along pleasant paths that afforded the Father Vicar no insight into the real purpose of the visit. "My secretary mentioned something about another guest," the Father Vicar eventually remarked, carelessly nudging the conversation toward some kind of resolution.

"Ah, yes," the older priest said, as if he'd just remembered. "A most interesting woman. I think you'll agree when you meet her."

The Father Vicar thought he saw a trace of deviltry in his eyes. He had heard tales about priests in the Vatican—but God forbid, not the Father General! he thought.

"I took the liberty of asking your secretary to find us some accommodations for the night," he continued. "I'm afraid she's been through a rather arduous trip."

"I'm looking forward to meeting the lady." Then letting his displeasure show, the Father Vicar added, "Unlike your excellency, it is a rare privilege for those of us who lead the cloistered life to enjoy the company of a woman."

As soon as he said it, he knew he had gone too far. The Father General stopped in mid sip and glared at him over the rim of his brandy glass, stranding his lascivious remark in silence and letting it hang there like a cocked fist.

The moment was salvaged by the secretary, who returned bearing a silver tray with small cakes on it. "The lady is in the anteroom," he announced, setting the tray between them.

"Shall we ask her to join us?" the Father Vicar asked deferentially.

"Just one moment." There was a hard edge to his voice, which hadn't been there before. "Since you are wondering why I have come to your seminary, I'll put an end to your . . . speculation, and come to the point. There is a priest here who can be of service to me. His name is Father Sebastio. Have him summoned immediately."

"I'm sorry, your excellency. Father Sebastio was only recently summoned to our Lord."

"You're telling me he is *dead*?"

The Father Vicar nodded. He had expected shock; what he saw was anguish. "He was laid to rest this very afternoon."

The Father General went to the fireplace and gazed into

the flames as if trying to divine meaning there. "Show the lady in," he said, still looking at the fire.

Nothing had prepared the Father Vicar for what he saw when his secretary returned. Through the door came a young woman with almond-shaped eyes and a wealth of onyx hair with strands that looped over each shoulder, rose at the nape of her neck, then plummeted like a waterfall to the small of her back. She was wearing a tubular silk gown unlike anything he had ever seen. The colors embroidered in the silk were brighter than a freshly painted fresco. The long sleeves of her gown fluttered as she shuffled toward him, giving the impression of an exotic bird about to take flight. She stopped a discreet distance in front of him and inclined her head in a bow.

"Allow me to introduce Lady Arima," the Father General said, savoring the moment of his host's stupification. "However," he added, "she prefers to use her Christian name, Maria."

"You are Japanese?" he muttered lamely.

The Father General answered for her. "Maria's father is Lord Arima, a daimyo and a faithful Christian who rules over a fief located on the southern island of Japan known as Kyushu. Not long ago Lord Arima's territory included the port city of Nagasaki, which as you know is the only port where our Black Ship is permitted to conduct trade with the Japans. I've just learned the sad news that the Shogun, using some dubious pretext, has taken control of the port from Lord Arima and placed Nagasaki under the authority of the *bakufu*—the government officials appointed by the Shogun to execute his policies."

The Father General rotated the stem of his glass in his long, thin fingers and watched the candlelight play against the crystal before continuing. "I suspect the Shogun's decision had something to do with Lord Arima's Christianity, but it probably had a great deal more to do with diverting Nagasaki's trade revenues into his own treasury." He drained his glass in one swallow. "But be that as it may, Lord Arima has defied the Shogun's order prohibiting all unauthorized travel abroad, and sent his daughter here with a message for Father Sebastio."

"I see," the Father Vicar said, leading Maria to a chair near the fire. When she sat, he noticed her feet did not reach the floor. "But why take the risk of sending her to Portugal when it would have been so much safer to pass the message on through the captain?"

The Father General shrugged his shoulders. "I was hoping Father Sebastio could answer that question. All I know is that she was ordered to deliver her message to him and no one else."

"It seems we have a problem."

The Father General reached out and took Maria's hand in his. "Maria," he said slowly, "Father Sebastio is dead." He studied her face for some sort of reaction and saw none. "Do you understand?"

"*Hai, wakarimasu*," she said. "I understand."

"Good." He sat down opposite her. "And do you understand that this changes everything?"

Maria smiled painfully. "Please?" she said, not understanding.

"Sebastio is dead." Maria nodded. "Give . . . message"—he pointed at his chest—"to me."

Maria lowered her eyes, and the Father General slumped back in his chair and began massaging his temples with his fingertips.

"Your excellency," the Father Vicar said, breaking the silence. "Father Sebastio taught one of our seminarians to speak Japanese. If you think it would be useful, I'll have him brought here."

"I suspect language may be the least of our problems, but perhaps a translator would be helpful," the older priest said wearily.

"Shall I send for him?"

"Tomorrow will be soon enough. Have the lady taken to a room. I'll see your seminarian in the morning."

Father Sebastio's room was dank and musty. After thirteen months at sea Maria had gradually grown accustomed to the rancid body odor of foreigners. But here, in this room, the air was old and heavy and smelled of sickness. She forced the window open, breathed deeply, and tried to think of other things.

The secretary came in with a pitcher of lukewarm water and a large porcelain bowl and put them on top of the lacquer trunk that held her belongings. Except for the wooden pallet where Father Sebastio had slept, and a crucifix mounted on the wall, the room was empty. The secretary apologized for the poverty of the accommodations and asked if there was anything further he could do.

Maria looked at him quizzically.

"Good night," he said finally.

"Good night, Padre," she answered.

As soon as he left, Maria kneeled on the floor and looked up at the crucifix. The emaciated body of Jesus, weak from loss of blood, had fallen forward, his hands and feet straining against the spikes. He was close to death but still had enough strength to turn his head away, averting his eyes so that no one could see the shame of his agony.

Maria closed her eyes to pray. As always, the picture of God that formed in her mind wore Father Sebastio's face. She thought of the time she had mentioned this to him. It had upset him terribly, and he'd tried to convince her to discard the habit.

"It's not easy to pray to a spirit," she argued, and he explained that that was the reason God put on human flesh and came into the world as Jesus. "But I like your face better," she persisted. "Even if it does look like a pile of broken rocks."

Maria remembered the warmth of his laughter, and her mind drifted back to the last time she had seen him, nearly five years ago, when she was only twelve years old. He had made the long trip from Nagasaki to Hara Castle on foot.

She looked up and saw him standing quietly at her door, watching her sew. Without remembering to bow, she ran to him and threw her arms around his waist. No matter how hard Father Sebastio tried to love all God's children equally, she knew she was special to him.

"What's wrong, child?" he asked, feeling her shudder.

She looked up at him, her eyes brimming with tears. "I've heard that my father is in great danger."

"What kind of danger?" he asked.

"A messenger arrived from Edo this morning with a summons from the Shogun, ordering father to attend a

ceremony in Edo three days from today. Father says he can't make it to Edo in less than four days."

Father Sebastio had little difficulty figuring out what was happening. Ignoring the Shogun's summons was unthinkable, and arriving late for the ceremony would constitute an unpardonable insult, providing the Shogun with just the excuse he needed to get rid of one more Christian daimyo. Without Lord Arima's protection, the persecution of Christians would extend to Shimabara—the last safe haven for Japanese Christians.

Father Sebastio's somber expression confirmed her worst fears. "Is the Shogun going to make Father seppuku?" she asked in a small voice.

"Only God knows the future. We have to put our trust in Him, and pray for your father's safety." He lifted her chin with his finger. "Shall we pray together?" She shook her head sadly. "You don't want to pray for your father?" The question was tinged with gentle reproof.

"It won't make any difference."

Father Sebastio raised his eyebrows. "Why do you say that, child?"

"You taught me that God knows everything," she explained. "And I believe this is true." Father Sebastio nodded his approval. "If God has decided to take my father from me, who am I to ask Him to change his mind? I'm only a girl . . . He is God."

He smiled. "Ah, little daughter, if you were only a boy, what a fine Jesuit you would have made." He hugged her to his chest. "I'm afraid I can't refute your logic, but I can tell you something I truly believe. Logic may be the greatest barrier to true understanding. The supreme act of faith is the act that makes no sense at all. It is the stuff miracles are made of. You can accept miracles or reject them, but you can't explain them, can you?" She shook her head. "Well, nobody can . . . and that's the point. Christ forced everyone who witnessed His miracles to either deny what they saw or admit there may be a truth beyond logic. So when we pray, God wants us to come to Him with our hearts, not our minds."

She took him by the hand and led him to the shrine, where she lit a candle below the image of Mary. When they finished praying, Father Sebastio took a small pack-

age out of his cassock and gave it to her. Inside was a small golden cross of Moorish design.

She held it in her palm, enthralled by the elaborate workmanship. "It's beautiful," she said in a hushed voice.

"It belonged to my mother."

"What was your mother's name?"

"Maria."

"May I take her name when I'm baptized?"

"That would make me very happy," he said.

"Padre, if anything happens to my father, I want to become a nun. That way we can be together."

The moment had come. Father Sebastio knew it would be difficult to tell her, but he hadn't counted on this much anguish. "My child—" His voice choked, and he turned away to clear his throat. "I've come to say good-bye."

"Good-bye?"

"The Father General has ordered me to return to Portugal. The Black Ship will pick me up at dawn."

She clenched the cross tightly in her hand, her head bowed. When she looked up, her cheeks were streaked with tears. "You must go?"

"I'm afraid the Father General thinks I'm getting too old to be useful here. He's ordered me back to Lisbon to train younger padres to take my place."

"Then take my father with you," she pleaded. "I can write and tell you when it's safe to return."

"I doubt that he—" Suddenly he clapped his hands together. "The Black Ship! That's the answer—the Black Ship!"

When the Black Ship came to Hara Castle to pick Father Sebastio up for the trip back to Portugal, he convinced the captain to take her father aboard and deliver him to Edo a day ahead of time. Although she had come to understand it was an action that only delayed the blow that would one day fell her father, it was an act of kindness she would never forget.

Maria said the "Our Father" and asked God to help her decide what to do now that Father Sebastio was dead. Should she disobey the orders of her father and give his letter to the

Father General, or honor her samurai oath and remain silent?
Perhaps the morning would bring the answer, she thought.

Maria removed the obi that bound her waist, and stepped
out of her kimono. The room was fresher now. Outside, the
rain had stopped, but a stiff wind, thick with moisture, still
came in off the ocean. Despite the chill, the breeze felt good
against her skin. She took her time washing, shivering as
trails of goose bumps formed in the wake of the washcloth.
Closing her eyes, she tried to imagine she was home.

In the courtyard below her window Jan Kriek was returning
from vespers. Out of habit he glanced up at Father Sebastio's
room, and the breath stopped in his throat.

There, framed against the backlight of a single candle, was
the silhouette of a woman—a seemingly young woman with a
beautifully sculpted body. For an instant he thought his eyes
were playing tricks on him. He could think of no rational
explanation for her presence there.

Kriek looked away, then looked back again.

She was still there, passing her hands over her narrow
shoulders then down her slender arms while her head swayed
in rhythm with each graceful movement. Held in thrall by
the perfection of this silent, sensuous dance, he knew he
should turn away, but could not. It was as if a figment of his
most erotic fantasies had materialized before his eyes.

He saw her lift one arm to the nape of her neck and
remove a long thin stave, sending a cascade of loose hair
tumbling down the length of her back. He stood transfixed as
she ran a comb through her hair. With each long stroke, her
lightly weighted breasts seemed to rise and fall like calm sea
swells. Then she leaned over to blow out the candle, and he
watched her vanish in the dark.

Tormented by a turbulent mixture of guilt and desire, Jan
Kriek rushed out of the courtyard like a thief.

The Father General took his morning coffee alone in the
Father Vicar's study. A night of uneven sleep had rumpled
his disposition. Reading over the reports from the Father
Visitor, the highest Jesuit authority in Japan, did nothing to
soothe him. The dispatches indicated that things had gone
from bad to worse in the fifteen years since the fall of Osaka
Castle. In retrospect the Society's decision to secretly support the Toyotomi claim to the shogunate had been a disas-

ter. But at the time the prospect of trying to reach some accommodation with the mercurial Tokugawa Shogun seemed remote. Now it had become virtually impossible.

Ever since the collapse of the Toyotomi, the Shogun's grip had been tightening around Christian throats. First the practice of Christianity was banned in Edo, then high-ranking samurai were forced to renounce their Christian faith or lose their family name—a punishment tantamount to social execution. Next, all priests who hadn't been expelled for supporting the Toyotomi were confined to Nagasaki. And now Nagasaki was in the hands of the Shogun.

According to the Father Visitor, one renegade Jesuit—the fiery Father Alcala—was lurching around the Japans like a loose cannon, fomenting rebellions among Christian farmers and forging secret alliances, all without the sanction of the Church. Furthermore, he had apparently undergone some kind of mystical vision, the details of which remained unclear. The Father Visitor, however, had made it very clear in his report that he had serious doubts about Father Alcala's sanity. He promised to order him back to Lisbon the moment he was able to locate him.

A soft knock on the door invaded the Father General's funk. Its timidity annoyed him, so he ignored it. The second knock was louder.

"Come in," he called out in a gruff voice.

The Father Vicar stuck his head in the door. "The seminarian I mentioned—the translator—is awaiting your pleasure."

"Send him in."

As Kriek crossed the room and made his obeisance, the Father General studied him. The first thing he noticed were his Saxon features—the light hair and violet eyes.

"You are not Portuguese, my son?" he said.

"My mother is Portuguese. My father was a Dutch pilot and a Catholic. Because of this, and his marriage to my mother, he lost his license to sail on Dutch ships. So he came here and offered his services to the Portuguese."

"As a pilot?"

"Yes," he said with undisguised pride. "On the Black Ship."

"*Hmm.* You'll forgive me if I tell you I find the notion of a Dutchman piloting a Jesuit trading ship somewhat . . . shall we say, unusual."

"Experienced pilots are extremely rare, as I'm sure your

excellency knows. This particular pilot had a wife in Lisbon and a son in a Jesuit seminary, factors that tend to ensure loyalty."

"So, you are here as a hostage to your father's career."

"My tenure as a hostage ended two years ago, when I learned that my father had died. Now I am here because I choose to be."

The Father General had learned to trust his instincts, but this time his instincts were not sending him clear signals. There was an uneasy tension about the handsome young seminarian, like an unsprung coil. Yet it could not be described as nervousness—restlessness, he thought, fit better. He had one quality the Father General liked—the ability to say no more or less than he meant to say. A rare gift in one so young.

"Do you know why you've been summoned?" he asked.

"I only know that my ability to translate Japanese might be of some service to you."

The Father General motioned him to take a seat. "Wait here." He left Kriek alone with his thoughts.

Since he had no information on which to base an intelligent guess, Kriek cleared his mind and gazed out the window at the garden. The door latch clicked and Kriek turned. The moment he caught sight of Maria entering the room, he knew she was the woman he'd seen bathing at Father Sebastio's window. His face flushed.

"Good morning," Maria said, smiling.

"*Ohayo gozaimasu*," he answered, hoping to cover his embarrassment by shifting to Japanese.

Maria tilted her head in a slight bow. "It's comforting to hear my language spoken again," she said, reverting to her native tongue.

"I regret that my knowledge of your rich language is woefully deficient," he replied, using the self-deprecatory form he had been taught was proper to begin a conversation.

The Father General cleared his throat, indicating his impatience to get the interrogation under way. He began by asking questions about her father's situation.

She told him that although her father still remained master of Hara Castle, his every move was monitored by the Tokugawa. "As a woman, I enjoyed the freedom of the insignificant," she concluded. "That is how I managed to leave undetected."

"And your connection with Father Sebastio?" the Father General asked through Kriek.

She told him that Father Sebastio had baptized her and her father, and heard their confessions. "He was a close friend of the Arima family."

"I see. That's why he suggested that you report to Father Sebastio." His choice of the word *suggested* was deliberate. He watched her attentively. As she framed her answer, she looked directly at the Father General.

Kriek translated: "The lady says it was not a suggestion, it was a command."

"Yes, of course," he said. "Tell her it was an unfortunate choice of words."

The Father General shifted the conversation to the current status of Christians in Arima prefecture.

"The persecution is spreading from the samurai class to the lower classes," she explained. "In the past the farmers had been left alone. Now even they are being forced to renounce their Christianity or lose their land. It appears to be only a matter of time."

"For what?" the Father General asked.

"*Konzetsu.*"

He looked to Kriek for the translation.

"Eradication," Kriek said.

There was a long pause before he asked the next question: "Am I correct in assuming that you are bearing important information that may be helpful in preventing this . . . *konzetsu?*"

Maria told him that she was not qualified to assess the importance of the information.

"Then, my child, you must allow me to evaluate it."

She lowered her eyes. "I was ordered to give it only to Father Sebastio," she said softly.

The Father General slammed his fist on the table. "Father Sebastio is dead!" he shouted. "If you remain silent and thousands of innocent Christians are martyred, their blood will be on your hands. Do you understand?"

"I understand," she answered, and for the first time he saw a trace of uncertainty tamper with her exquisite serenity.

"And still you refuse to speak?"

Maria said nothing. Behind her beautifully composed features a profound struggle had begun. Maria was samurai to the core of her being. For her, a command was an obligation, and obligation was a trust. There was no shame greater than the betrayal of a trust. Yet Father Sebastio's death had altered things. She could choose to carry out the letter of her father's command, and abort the mission to retain her honor. Or she could use her own judgment, respond to the change in circumstances, and hope that giving the message to the Father Vicar would accomplish her father's purposes. It was an option that involved making a guess as to her father's true intentions. It was a risk she was loath to take.

The Father General reached out and took her hand. "Any Japanese who leaves the country without permission from Edo is forbidden to return home. You know that . . . your father knew it when he sent you here. Do you think he made his decision frivolously? Would he have made such a terrible sacrifice without good reason? I think not. I think it was an act of Christian courage that should serve as an example to you. Unless you find the courage to serve your father with intelligence rather than blind obedience, his sacrifice will have been in vain."

He listened to Kriek translate his plea. Although he could not understand a single word, he heard his own passion conveyed in the translation, and it pleased him.

"Go to the chapel and pray for guidance," he said to Maria. "When God has given you your answer, return here. . . . I'll be waiting."

The rosette window in the apse of the chapel took the full force of the setting sun, drenching Maria's face in a dazzling array of pastel light. She was kneeling, as she had been for hours—her eyes closed, her hands clasped at her waist. Kriek marveled at her stamina. He sat and waited while she prayed. Judging from his own discomfort, she should be in misery, yet she showed no signs of distress.

Before long the seminarians would be coming in for vespers. Deciding it was time to put an end to her ordeal, Kriek laid his hand on her shoulder. She opened her eyes. "It's time to go," he said softly.

"Yes," she said.

On the way back, Kriek asked her, "What do you intend to do?"

"I don't know."

He walked on, Maria following a few steps behind. He slowed his pace to allow her to catch up, but still she lagged behind. Then he tried taking smaller steps. Maria gained a little, then fell back again. Now his steps were so short and slow he had trouble maintaining his balance. Finally he stopped and waited for her.

Suddenly it occurred to him that the kimono was not the only reason she was having such trouble keeping up. The woman had been on her knees for an inordinate amount of time. Her legs must be cramped and aching.

"Shall we sit down a moment?" he asked, gesturing toward an oak bench situated among a small grouping of olive trees.

"Are you not feeling well?" she said, with a look of deep concern.

"No, I'm fine. Why do you ask?"

"Excuse me . . . it's just that you seemed to have difficulty walking."

"Not at all. I thought you—" Then he understood. "You were trying to stay a few paces behind me, weren't you?"

"Of course," she said, more than a little bewildered by the question.

"You see," he explained, "here in Europe women are expected to walk alongside men. As a matter of fact, in our culture ladies of your rank are revered by men. It's considered an honor to serve them."

"Really? And how do European ladies serve men?"

"They don't serve men," he said. "They adorn them."

"Like jewelry?"

"Very much so."

"Forgive me, but it seems a terrible waste to reduce a capable woman to a trinket."

According to Father Sebastio, samurai women served their men with the same intense devotion that the samurai man served his liege lord. A wife was no more a slave to her husband than he was to his master. "Everyone is looking for someone to follow," Father Sebastio had explained. "The Japanese have merely refined the process by taking speculation out of the search."

"I'm sorry, but do I call you 'Padre'?" Maria asked.

"No, I'm not yet ordained. Please call me Jan."

"Jan-san," she said, adding the honorific *san*. "Strange, your name isn't so difficult to pronounce."

"It's Dutch."

"It sounds Chinese."

They talked, and time passed. She asked him the Portuguese names for things. As he asked her about things Father Sebastio had taught him, the shadows lengthened and the sky lost its pale color.

"Jan-san," she said, laying her hand on his arm, "why didn't God speak to me?"

"I think he's already spoken to you. You just haven't heard Him."

"I don't understand."

"You're a Christian. God speaks to Christians through the example of His son. The decision you have to make isn't that complex. It's a matter of simple decency and compassion. I believe God expects a Christian to be able to see the moral difference between a commitment to deliver a message to a dead man and an obligation to do something that might save the lives of innocent people. God expects you to see and make the correct choice without demanding His personal intervention."

She listened without comment, and drew her kimono tighter to her neck. "There's a chill in the air, Jan-san. Perhaps this is only a false spring."

They met again at dinner. Maria had heard it was true, and now she'd seen it with her own eyes: in a silver platter in the center of the table, the severed leg of some kind of animal. The noxious stench exuding from the fuming hunk of semi-charred flesh took her breath away. When the Father General himself took up a knife and proceeded with the dismemberment, she was barely able to stifle a gasp. Handling dead animals was a loathsome task relegated to *Eta*—the dregs of society. Yet here was the Director of the Society of Jesus cutting away at an animal's leg with undisguised relish.

He forked a large piece onto a plate, drenched the meat in its own fluids, and handed the plate to her. "Here, my child, try some of our famous Portuguese lamb."

"Lamb?" she asked weakly.

"Baby sheep," Kriek translated.

Maria blanched, and bolted from the room. Kriek followed her outside, where he steadied her as she took great gulps of fresh air. With superb effort she managed to hold down her gorge. At Maria's insistence, Kriek left her alone and rejoined the Father General and the Father Vicar.

"I trust she's recovering," the Father General said to Kriek between mouthfuls, "because I intend to get to the bottom of this mystery as soon as we've finished this excellent repast."

"Her color is coming back. She asked me to convey her apologies and say that she expects to join us after dinner."

"A pity she's not feeling well." He forked a piece of meat into his mouth. "The lamb is exquisite."

"I suspect it was the lamb that upset her."

Kriek started to explain that the Japanese diet did not include meat, but something told him the Father General was well aware of that fact, so he said nothing.

"The Japanese are strange people," the Father General said. "If one were to take Francis Xavier's journal as a guide, there are no people on earth more ripe for conversion than the Japanese. Yet compared with the Spanish experience in *Nueva Espana*, our progress has been slow—painfully slow."

"I've always favored a more aggressive posture," the Father Vicar said with uncharacteristic passion. "Unfortunately my opinion wasn't shared by certain missionaries who seemed to favor appeasement over principle."

This thinly veiled criticism of Father Sebastio did not sit well with Kriek. He viewed it as nothing more than a transparent attempt to curry favor with the Father General, the very man who had recalled Father Sebastio because of his alleged pro-Japanese sentiments.

Kriek couldn't help feeling a tingle of pleasure at the Father Vicar's disappointment when he was asked to leave the room after the brandy had been drunk. Once he was gone, the badinage ended and the Father General sent Kriek out to fetch Maria.

"My child," he began, "I want you to understand that I'm not insensitive to the dilemma you're facing. If you'll indulge me by answering a few questions, perhaps a solution can be found without compromising either your pledge to your father or your duty to your church."

"I'll assist you in any way I am able," she responded through Kriek.

"What would have happened to you if you had been caught leaving Japan without permission from the *bakufu*?"

"I'd have been taken into custody and ordered to reveal the purpose of my mission."

"It's rare for the *bakufu* to fail in an interrogation. Which brings me to my point. Your father, Lord Arima, has a reputation as a cautious man. Considering the risk, I find it difficult to believe that the information we are seeking is contained in your mind."

Maria did not reply.

"So I took the liberty of searching your belongings while you were in the chapel. Needless to say, I found nothing. I was prepared to concede that my instincts might have been unreliable in this instance, until I remembered a small detail that seemed insignificant to me at the time. The kimono you're wearing today is different from the one you wore last night. Yet the obi around your waist is the same, and if I may be so bold, it is of a color that a lady of your impeccable taste would surely consider inappropriate . . . especially since several of the other ones I discovered in your trunk were clearly a better match."

"You have a very critical eye," she said.

"Would you mind removing your obi?"

"Here?" she asked.

"I'm afraid so." He leaned forward and said in a voice barely above a whisper, "If I am wrong, I owe you my deepest apologies. However, if I am right, and the information we seek *is* in your obi, you can honestly tell your father that you did not surrender the information willingly, it was taken from you . . . which is exactly what will happen if you don't comply with my request."

Flushing, Maria reached behind her, untied the knot, and let her obi fall to the floor. She held her kimono closed with her hand.

The Father General picked up the obi and felt it from end to end. Finding nothing, he took a knife out of the Father Vicar's desk and slit the stitching. Inside he found a diaphanous lining covered with inked characters.

"Do you know the contents of this message?" he asked Maria.

She shook her head. "I only know that I was to deliver this obi to Father Sebastio."

The Father General handed the paper to Kriek and asked him to translate.

"*From Lord Arima to Father Alfredo Sebastio, S.J.*

"*It is late winter and the snow is deep, the cold severe. The warmth that your companionship brought to my home is sorely missed.*

"*I have sent my daughter across the great sea with a message of the greatest importance. I have compiled a census of all the Christians in Shimabara perfecture. The count has been completed as accurately as possible. Please refer to your syllabary should you encounter any difficulty understanding the information.*

"*Spare yourself as the weather changes.*

> "*Sixth year of Kanei, 1629*
> *Second month. Twenty-fifth day.*"

Kriek studied the rest of the message in silence. "What follows," he told the Father General, "is a list of villages and the number of Christians living there."

"Is that everything he wrote?"

Kriek nodded.

The Father General wrinkled his brow and began gnawing on his lower lip. "So it seems we are back at the starting point."

After a pause he handed Maria her obi and said, "I had hoped this moment could be avoided, but now I must insist that you deliver your father's *true* message to me."

"There is no other message," she answered, calmly retying her ruined obi.

"Come, come, my child. You are asking me to believe that your father smuggled you out of the country and sent you halfway around the world to deliver a census report." His voice turned to acid as he added, "I'm not an utter fool!"

"I'm sorry you find my father's message disappointing, but that's the message I was ordered to deliver."

"Then your father is the fool!"

Kriek hesitated, hoping the Father General would reconsider his words.

"Translate exactly what I said," he demanded.

Maria's eyes widened. "I will not hear my father ridiculed."

"And I will not be played for a fool!"

Maria bowed her head. "With your permission I'll retire to my room."

"Go!" he shouted, and turned his back on her. As she was leaving, he called out, "Wait." He pointed his finger at her and asked, "Do you understand the consequences of excommunication?" Maria nodded. "Do you believe in Hell?" She nodded again. "Then swear on the holy cross of Our Lord that you are speaking the truth . . . and remember that your immortal soul hangs in the balance."

Maria grasped the cross she wore around her neck, then let it go. "A samurai does not swear oaths," she said stubbornly. "It's an insult to our integrity."

"Very well. I'll deal with you in the morning."

From her window Maria could see the rose-colored dawn gather in the eastern sky. There was a year of ocean between here and her home, a distance so vast and incomprehensible that it could only be measured in terms of loneliness. Once, her world had been small and comfortable, a place where births and deaths were large, where things were noticed and cared for. But on the ocean she had learned the meaning of insignificance. She saw her existence reduced to the size of a flyspeck, neither enlarging nor diminishing the world. The sight of the rising sun hurt her, so she closed her eyes.

She heard footsteps on the stairway, followed by a soft knock on her door. She recognized the voice whispering her name.

"Jan-san?" she called out.

"Yes," Kriek responded. "Please let me in. I have to talk to you."

Maria adjusted her sleeping kimono and opened the door. Kriek hurried in, carrying a leather-bound manuscript under one arm. In his other hand he held a candle that was little more than a stub. The dark circles under his eyes gave him the look of a half-mad zealot.

"It's here, in this letter," he began, as if she had been following his train of thought throughout the night. "The message was nothing more than a ruse, a piece of clever misdirection."

"I told the truth," she protested.

"Yes, of course you did. That was how your father protected you, and the real message." Kriek saw that in his excitement he had lost her. "Look." He spread the letter out on the table. "Your father tells Father Sebastio to use the syllabary if he can't understand the language. Ridiculous. There's not a word in his letter that a man of Father Sebastio's fluency would have the slightest difficulty with, and surely no one knew that better than your father."

"Yes, that is strange."

"No stranger than this census." He tapped his finger on the list of villages. "Here is the village of Fukae. How many people would you guess live there?"

"It's small—perhaps no more than a few hundred."

"Exactly. Now look at the number of Christians in that village."

"Nine hundred and twenty-one." Maria shook her head. "That's clearly an error."

"Now look at the castle city of Shimabara. According to Father Sebastio's records there are over thirteen thousand people there, yet the census lists the number of Christians at seventy-four!"

"Impossible."

"The whole document is riddled with impossible mistakes."

"But why?"

"That's the same question I asked myself all night. Finally the answer came to me. The numbers are all part of a code." He opened the syllabary and laid the letter beside it. "Look." He pointed to the first number in her father's census report—79. "Now look at the sound that's numbered seventy-nine in the syllabary."

"It's *ka*," she said, still puzzled.

"Now, what's the next number in the report?"

She glanced at the letter. "Forty-six."

Kriek turned to the syllabary and found sound numbered 46. "You see, it's *bu*, and the next one is eighty-five—*ki*." Kriek showed her the decoded message. "The first word is made up of the three sounds *ka, bu, ki*."

She sounded the word. "Kabuki . . . It's a popular form of theater."

"Yes, I know." He held out a piece of paper for her inspection. "When I finished cross-referencing all the numbers, I found this message."

KABUKI ACTOR UNMASKED
ALCALA VANISHED
SITUATION DESPERATE
MUST HAVE GUNS

"What does it mean?" Kriek asked her.

" 'Kabuki actor unmasked'," she mused. "My father must be refering to Okubo Nagayasu, a former Kabuki actor who was supervisor of the Tokugawa gold mines until he was imprisoned for pilfering a large amount of the Shogun's gold. So far he's refused to reveal where it's hidden. Apparently the Shogun believes that he planned to use the gold to finance a Christian uprising."

"Is it true?"

"There are always rumors of rebellion, but I have no way of knowing if this story is true."

"What about Alcala?"

"Every Japanese Christian has heard of Father Alcala and his famous prophecy."

"What did he predict?"

"He said a godchild of incredible beauty would appear to save God's people. When he comes, the clouds of heaven will burn and the land will rumble. Flowers will bloom out of season and white flags will flutter on fields and mountains. Then Christian power will swallow heresy."

"He saw this in a vision?"

"Yes. Some people think he's mad, but most Christians believe him."

"He vanished?"

"No one has seen or heard from him for some time. As for the guns, I've heard rumors that there is a vast stockpile of matchlocks hidden somewhere in Shimabara. Whether they're real or imaginary, I don't know."

Kriek quickly gathered up his things. "The Father General may have a better idea about what all this means. In any case he'll want to see it right away."

"Are you sure he won't be disappointed again?" she asked with pointed irony.

Kriek shrugged. "There's a chance that only Father Sebastio could have made sense out of those phrases. But we'll know soon enough."

As he started out the door, Maria caught his arm. "Thank

you, Jan-san," she said softly. "You were very clever to break the code."

Kriek smiled broadly. "I know."

Maria barely had time to hide her laughter behind her hand. "In all my life I've never heard anyone receive a compliment quite like that."

"And I have never heard a laugh as lovely as that."

She acknowledged his compliment with a bow of her head.

Standing in the amber candlelight, her hair spilling over her shoulders like liquid night, her beauty moved him in a way that felt something like fear. When she raised her eyes, he was still gazing at her. She smiled, and he hurried off to waken the Father General.

There could be little doubt from the Father General's reaction that the information Kriek decoded was significant. For a long time he paced the floor of the study, lost in concentration. Several times he seemed on the verge of voicing his thoughts; then he went back to pacing.

Finally he stopped and stared hard at Kriek, much like a magistrate about to pass sentence. "You are to prepare to leave for Japan on the next Black Ship." The order slammed into Kriek's brain with physical force. "You say your father was a pilot—did he teach you anything about ships?"

"I sailed with him a few times when I was a boy."

"Do you think you could pass yourself off as a seaman?"

"A very green seaman, perhaps."

The Father General tapped his finger against his lips. "You will report to Captain Nunes. He will instruct you in the duties of a deckhand, refamiliarize you with the language of the sea, and provide you with forged documents representing you as a seaman apprentice with experience aboard a Dutch trading ship."

The Father General clasped his hands behind his back and resumed his pacing. "Word has reached me that the Shogun has forbidden any more missionaries to enter Japan. Those who are there are harassed and their movements scrupulously watched. All Portuguese are suspect, even the sailors on the Black Ship. Only the Dutch are permitted anything resembling the freedom we once enjoyed.

"For that reason, you will disembark at Macao and sign on as a crewman on the first Dutch vessel bound for Japan."

Once again the Father General fell silent. After a few moments he drew a chair close to Kriek and sat down. "My son, the situation is far more perilous than I had suspected. Events seem to have taken an ominous turn. Perhaps the damage is irreparable, perhaps not. Of this I'm sure—the Father Visitor is the highest Jesuit authority in Japan. It is he who must react to the shifting winds of fortune there, and he who must bear the burden of responsibility for the deterioration that has taken place. There is a Jesuit there, a Father Alcala, who I hear is behaving uncontrollably."

Kriek noticed that his face had taken on a kind of weariness usually associated with aging.

"The Father Visitor was my teacher and my friend," the priest said, more to himself than Kriek. "Such a good mind. Now his reports are disorganized, almost useless. The little details that told me so much are gone. What's happened to him?"

"People grow older," Kriek said. "They get tired."

"Perhaps so, but whatever the cause I'm no longer willing to . . ." He couldn't seem to find the right words, so left the thought dangling. "You will deliver a letter to the Father Visitor instructing him to provide you with any assistance and information you need to carry out your mission."

Kriek waited for the Father General to continue, but when he remained silent on the definition of his mission, Kriek asked for clarification.

"The details will be spelled out in my letter to the Father Visitor. For now, the less you know the better." He drew closer to Kriek and lowered his voice. "But let me assure you, there is a great deal at stake here. It would not be an overstatement to say that the very survival of Christianity in Japan may hang in the balance."

"Your excellency, may I ask why you chose me, a seminarian with only book knowledge of Japan, for a mission of such consequence?"

"A fair question. Aside from being reasonably fluent in the language, you have impressed me in other ways that are too obvious to mention. So let me focus on your greatest asset. You are half Portuguese, but the light hair . . . the eyes are Dutch. If you're caught sneaking into the mainland, which is probable, the blame will fall on the heads of the Dutch. It will be they, not our Jesuit brothers, who will feel the Shogun's wrath. Does that answer your question?"

"It does, but I hope you won't be greatly disappointed if I tell you I don't intend to get caught."

The twinkle in Kriek's eye brought a smile to the Father General's lips, who raised his hand in a blessing. But before the priest could speak, Kriek said, "Excuse me, your excellency. What will happen to Maria?"

"The Black Ship leaves next year. Both you and Maria will be on it. Every reasonable attempt will be made to smuggle her into Nagasaki. In the meantime I'd suggest you use the opportunity to enhance your understanding of the Japanese language and customs. Maria should be an invaluable asset to you."

Kriek nodded, and dropped to one knee. The Father General made the sign of the cross over him and said, "Go with God, my son. Trust Him and all things are possible."

4

Kyoto
Year of the Horse—1630
Hour of the Monkey

A short time after Maria arrived in Lisbon, a meeting that was to have a profound effect not only on her life, but the lives every Christian in Japan, took place in the old capital of Kyoto. The meeting was called by Prince Sanjo, the son of the Emperor's favorite consort. On the surface Sanjo affected many of the feminine mannerisms so fashionable among the other nobles at the Imperial Court, but in fact he had never reconciled himself to a life of poetry, painting, flower gardening, and tea. He was obsessed by a single idea—restoration of the political power the nobility had lost centuries earlier, when the nobles allowed themselves to become too effete to wage war, forcing the Emperor to appoint a military commander from the samurai class to lead his armies into battle.

The title conferred on the supreme commander was *shogun*, and by tradition a shogun's authority never extended beyond the battlefield. However, in the thirteenth century a politically ambitious shogun from the Minamoto clan shattered that tradition. After successfully concluding a war, the Minamoto shogun refused to relinquish his command. Instead he established his own government in Kamakura.

Except for a few brief periods, from that time forward the samurai ruled Japan. Although bestowing the coveted title *shogun* still remained one of the Emperor's prerogatives, in actual fact his choices were limited. The samurai who wielded the most political power was also the one who controlled the treasury. The Emperor, the "Son of Heaven," had become an emasculated god, just as the nobles became political eunochs.

Sanjo was determined to rectify that state of affairs, but to accomplish this goal he needed three things: gold to finance a war against the Shogun, armies to fight the war, and guns to win the war. As much as he despised the Christians, he knew that without them all was lost. Sanjo needed Lord Arima to forge a military alliance with other Christian daimyos, and he needed Father Alcala's charismatic leadership and access to Portuguese armament. As for the gold, if everything worked according to plan, he would be able to provide more than enough to challenge the might of the Shogun.

"Our first task is to find a way to break the back of the Tokugawa shogunate," he told his two guests.

It was the first time Father Alcala had met the prince, and his impressions were not favorable. Prince Sanjo appeared to be the perfect expression of the extravagant foppery that had become the fashion among the nobles. He spoke in a high-pitched voice, and affected feminine mannerisms to the extent of coloring his lips, powdering his face, and painting dark swatches representing eyebrows high on his forehead. He had even adopted the custom of blackening his teeth like a married woman. In his hands the prince held a long-stemmed peony, which he sniffed from time to time during the conversation. The Jesuit listened to his statement, and chose not to respond.

Lord Arima was uneasy about being included in this meeting, but it was he who raised the practical question of how this "back-breaking" was to be accomplished. "I don't mean to belabor the obvious," he said, "but the combined armies of all the Christian daimyos are not strong enough to topple the Tokugawa, even with the aid of the Portuguese guns."

"Quite so." Sanjo extended his cup to his wife, and she replenished it with green tea. "It would be far better to let the Tokugawa topple themselves, *neh*?"

Arima took a quick sip of tea. And it would be far better if horses could fly, he thought. But since he was Prince Sanjo's guest, he curbed his tongue.

Father Alcala felt no such constraint. "Nonsense!" he said bluntly. "I see no indication that the Tokugawa are bent on self-destruction."

"Ah, Padre." Sanjo flashed his black smile. "Forgive me, but I was told that your God honored you with a vision that promised the defeat of the heathen Tokugawa."

"At the hands of Christians," he countered. "Not by their own hand."

"Surely you're not saying that you'd turn your back on a little help from your enemy?"

"What makes you think the Tokugawa would cooperate in their own downfall?"

"We all carry within us the seeds of our own destruction—petty vices that make humans such interesting creatures. For some of us it's vanity, for others lust for money or power, or some other peccadillo. But there's always one critical weakness in everyone's character that can be exploited by those who learn to look carefully. All you have to do is listen to what a man says that he hates most in other people. That's invariably the very flaw he fears most in himself. Once it's found, it can be nurtured until it grows ripe for the harvest."

After all Alcala's years in Japan, the Japanese penchant for meandering around in metaphors when a simple declarative statement would do the job still set his teeth on edge. "You're telling us you've uncovered the Shogun's fatal flaw?"

"I'm not interested in the present shogun. It's the future shogun, Lord Iemitsu, who interests me. However, there are many—including the Shogun's wife—who'd prefer to see her second son, Tadanaga, inherit the title. Already strong factions are forming around both of them. The Shogun is under increasing pressure to pass over Iemitsu and name Tadanaga the next shogun. The seeds of suspicion are sprouting in Edo Castle, and a little judicious gardening could produce just the kind of fruit we're looking for."

"So you're hoping that a rift develops between the two brothers that can be turned to our advantage."

"My dear Padre, nothing so lukewarm as that. I intend to see to it that they go for each other's throats."

Arima began to feel uneasy. Up until now all the talk against the Tokugawa had been just that—talk. But no longer. Sanjo was preparing to act. Arima felt like a fish who had been nibbling at the bait and suddenly found himself tasting the hook. He resisted the impulse to run. Instead he sat quietly as Alcala tried to draw Sanjo out. After several questions were deftly deflected, it became clear to Arima that Sanjo had revealed as much as he intended to reveal, and they would learn no more about his plans that night. So at the first opportunity Arima made his excuses, and Sanjo saw him to the door.

"Trust me," Sanjo said to him. "You have nothing to fear. My work will be done in the shadows. It may be a long time before we'll be ready to go to war. Meanwhile act the part of the Shogun's loyal retainer. If you're forced to renounce your religion, do it. When the day comes that power is restored to the Emperor, you and every other Christian in Japan will be free to worship your God without fear of persecution."

Arima found his words reassuring. He left carrying the hook in his mouth, but was not yet landed.

It wasn't Arima who worried Sanjo. He could be controlled. Alcala was another matter. There was something unstable about the priest. He was a genuine zealot—a true believer. Some way had to be found to keep him from going off half-cocked on his holy mission to Christianize Japan. What was his flaw? Sanjo watched him from the doorway. Alcala was staring at his wife. There was a strange intensity in his eyes that he hadn't seen before. His wife felt it too.

Princess Yugiri kept her eyes downcast, stubbornly refusing to let her husband take any pleasure in her discomfort. She despised Sanjo, just as he despised all women, a fact that was driven home with diabolic force five years ago on their wedding night. She had come to him that night fresh from the bath, dressed in her finest kimono. She was sixteen; he was almost thirty. When she arrived at his chambers, she found a young boy there. Sanjo ordered her to stay and watch while the boy serviced his twisted sexual appetite. She soon came to understand that her husband derived some kind of erotic enjoyment from her humiliation and misery. From that moment on Princess Yugiri resolved to deny him the response he expected from her. She continued serving him dutifully, if not sexually, in the face of unspeakable degradation.

Sanjo pretended not to notice Alcala's fascination with his wife. He picked up the conversation, asking him how much support the Portuguese were prepared to lend to the struggle.

It was a question Alcala was loath to answer, because he had never been able to extract a clear commitment from his superiors. In the beginning the Church had put all its energy into converting Japanese to the Faith, focusing on high-ranking daimyos like Arima. Initially this plan to take Japan by conversion had met with extraordinary success. Impressed by the superior science of the West, Japanese flocked to the Church in droves. Later on, when the Shogun learned of Pope Clement's edict dividing Japan between Spain and Portugal, the padres' troubles began. All hope of converting the Shogun vanished, and the rush to Christianity slowed down to a trickle. The emphasis then shifted from conversion to intrigue. Plots were hatched, and uncovered. Secret alliances formed, and fell apart. Then the outright persecution began. One after another the Christian daimyos who were unwilling to risk Tokugawa displeasure began to renounce their faith. By the time the Church Fathers realized that the model for the Spanish conquest of the New World was not going to be replicated in Japan, the Church was in retreat and no one seemed to know how to turn things around.

"When God is ready for Japan to join the family of Christian nations, certain unmistakable signs will be revealed," Alcala said confidently. "No Portuguese who calls himself a true Christian would dare ignore the will of God. We shall have the support we need."

"And the guns?" Sanjo asked. "Will we have the guns we need?"

"I've been able to smuggle a few thousand muskets into Shimabara. There's a vast stockpile in Manila, but until I get the gold you promised, that's where they'll stay."

"As you know, Padre, the one man who knows where the gold is hidden is imprisoned in Edo. He's under heavy guard, so freeing him might take months—even years. But I assure you, it will be done."

"You'll forgive me, but I find one thing troubling," Alcala replied. "You need Lord Arima to raise a Christian army. You need me to equip the army with Portuguese guns. Tell me, Prince Sanjo, why do we need you?"

"You need me because you need the legitimacy I can bring to your holy war. There is only one eternal authority in Japan—the Emperor. If you fight in the name of the Emperor, enemies of the Tokugawa will rally to your cause and you can win. But if you choose to fight in the name of your foreign god, you'll lose. It's as simple as that."

Although Alcala was a zealot, he also knew the truth when he heard it. The first order of business was to pry the fingers of the Tokugawa off the Church's throat. If that involved temporarily turning power over to the nobles, so be it. God would settle the issue in His own time, he thought. Still, his reservations about dealing with a man like Sanjo dictated caution.

"God works in mysterious ways," he said philosophically, shrugging his shoulders. "Who knows what the future holds?"

Sanjo studied Alcala, probing for the critical weakness that could be used to subvert his independence and force him to submit. It was difficult for him to read character in a Western face. All their features were as exaggerated as their speech. Alcala was no exception. A great hooked nose dominated his gaunt angular face, making his weak chin appear weaker. There was no luster to his brittle hair, which sprouted from his head like rain-starved weeds in an untended garden. However, it was Alcala's eyes that commanded Sanjo's interest. They were truly unusual, even for a Westerner. Close set and small, his restless round eyes were constantly darting from point to point, like a hungry vulture standing guard over his meal.

Gradually an idea began to take shape in Sanjo's mind. Something he had overheard earlier might be just the thing he could use to gain the leverage he needed. But it would have to be handled carefully.

He turned to his wife and ordered her to bring some sake. After she had left the room, Sanjo turned the conversation to the subject of Alcala's religious vision. "Did I hear you mention to Lord Arima that you had recently returned from a solitary retreat to seek further guidance from your god?"

"That's true," Alcala replied. "I spent forty days in fasting and prayer."

"And may I ask if your efforts were rewarded with success?"

"God spoke to me in a dream. He told me that it was my sacred duty to father the child destined to save Japan from heresy."

"How extraordinary!" the prince exclaimed, pretending he hadn't known. Word of this remarkable vision had quickly circulated in the Christian community, and it had been passed along to him. "Think of it, not only has your god chosen to reveal his prophecies through you, he's selected you to be the instrument of his will!"

"No one is more astonished than I," Alcala said humbly.

"Tell me, Padre," Sanjo inquired, "have you found a mother for this godchild?"

"I haven't begun my search. Why do you ask?"

"Well, it seems to me that the sooner the godchild is conceived, the closer we'll be to our moment of triumph, neh?"

"This is something that can't be done in haste," Alcala chided.

"Of course not. It's just that . . ." Sanjo paused and shook his head. "No, it would be presumptuous of me to offer advice."

"Please, feel free to speak your mind," Alcala insisted, his curiosity piqued.

"Actually, I know a woman of noble birth who might be the perfect mother for your child."

"Who is this woman?"

"Princess Yugiri."

"Your wife!" Alcala was stupefied. "This must not be treated as a joke."

"Forgive me, Padre, but I thought you found her attractive."

"That has nothing to do with it," Alcala stammered. "Men don't give their wives to other men. That's adultery!"

Sanjo shifted closer to him. "I assure you, my wife is still a virgin."

"You're telling me your marriage has never been consummated?"

"Unfortunately not." Sanjo lowered his voice to a whisper,

his eyes carefully watching the priest. "You see, I suffer from
an embarrassing condition. . . ." Alcala nodded his head sym-
pathetically. "It's a cruel fate for a woman to be deprived of
bearing a child. Although she'll feel it's her duty to protest,
you'd be doing a great service for her, and fulfilling your
obligation to your god at the same time."

Alcala closed his eyes and prayed silently. After a few
minutes he looked up at Sanjo. "God has accepted this woman,"
he said solemnly.

5

Edo
Year of the Ram—1631
Hour of the Monkey

The Shogun was dead.

In the furnace room of the public bathhouse where he
worked, Jubei was lying back against a stack of cordwood,
listening to the rain and the muffled tolling of the temple
bells. Outside, the streets were almost deserted. Most of the
people of Edo had gathered at the castle walls to pay their last
respects to the Shogun's earthly remains.

Jubei felt around for the sake jar he kept by his side. His
hand brushed against it, and tipped it over. Nothing spilled
out. He picked it up and held it upside down over his open
mouth. There were only a few drops left. He closed his good
eye.

The high wooden getas on Akane's feet made sucking sounds
as she struggled through the sloppy streets on her way to see
Jubei. He was working in a rough section of the city—a place
for hard drinkers and used-up prostitutes. The few who were
out in the rain kept their wide straw hats pulled low over
their faces and paid no attention to her.

The latch on the gate to the alleyway that led to the back of the bathhouse had broken and the wind was slamming it open and closed, forcing Akane to time her entrance carefully. The overhanging eaves provided scant protection from the slanting rain. She was soaked to the skin. At least the furnace room would be warm and dry, she thought.

She found Jubei asleep. His breathing was heavy and sour and smelled of cheap alcohol. Akane put the *bento* containing rice, fish, and yellow pickles by his side. Then she stripped off her straw rain cape and warmed herself by the furnace.

Akane kept her back to Jubei. No matter how often she came, no matter how many times she saw her brother yellow-eyed drunk—his kimono torn and dirty, his scraggly hair half tied—it always hurt. Although she continued to pay rent on a small room for him in a better section of Edo, the owner told her that Jubei never slept there anymore. Iori, who had accepted the offer to replace Jubei as the new *shinan* at her father's school, inquired around for her and learned that Jubei often spent the night under a bridge where beggers and whores went to escape the elements. Even though she had long since given up trying to persuade him to change, there were times when the tears came suddenly and could not be stopped. At other times it was all she could do to keep from killing him.

There was a clamor behind her. Akane turned to see the owner of the bathhouse burst into the furnace room. He was a bad-tempered little man with comical legs that looked like they had been molded over a barrel. When he spotted Jubei, he grabbed a bamboo staff, rushed at him, and smacked him on the soles of his bare feet.

Jubei let out a howl and jumped in the air. The owner kept after him, lashing out viciously with the staff. In his condition Jubei was not as quick as he needed to be to fend off all the blows.

"You lazy"—*swat*—"good for nothing"—*whoom*—"piece of monkey dung"—*whack*. "Put some wood in that furnace before my customers freeze to death!" *Swat*. "Are you trying to ruin me?"

Jubei stumbled over some loose wood and slipped down to his knees. Taking advantage of the opportunity to get in a good solid blow, the owner charged at Jubei with the staff raised high over his head. In a pitiful gesture Jubei lifted up one arm to protect his face. The owner picked his spot and struck. In one deft move Akane sliced off the shaft just above the hands, causing the man to lose his balance and tumble on top of her brother. Before he could regain his footing, Akane had him by the topknot, the point of her *kaiken* poised under his chin. The owner froze, his eyes bulging with terror.

"My brother is samurai," she hissed through her teeth. "You dare to curse and beat him like a common dog?"

Under the law, the slightest breach of etiquette and the most insignificant hint of disrespect was sufficient justification for a samurai to summarily execute an offender of any other class, and the owner of the Kuma-no-yu bathhouse knew the law. "Please," he pleaded. "I'm sorry. I forgot he was samurai . . . truly . . . truly . . . the string on my spleen broke. I didn't know what I was doing."

Akane let him whine and apologize until the heat of the moment passed. Although she was seething inside, Akane had to concede that it would not be hard for anyone to forget Jubei was samurai. Still, the shame she felt for her brother forced her to prolong the little man's suffering. "In the future show proper respect for samurai," she commanded, "and perhaps this insult can be overlooked."

When she released him, he groveled at Jubei's feet, running through a whole litany of apologies. Jubei reached out and touched his shoulder. The owner cringed. "Please get up," he said, and the owner was surprised to hear kindness in his voice.

Cautiously he lifted his face off the floor and slowly got to his feet. Jubei bowed his head. "I'm sorry for my indolence. You've been fair to me, and I've neglected my duties. Please accept *my* apology."

"No!" Akane snapped at her brother. "Have you lost all sense of pride? A samurai does not apologize to a merchant."

"Samurai?" Jubei said with a wry smile. "How many samurai do you know who have to stoke furnaces to eat?"

"You mean drink, don't you?" As soon as the words were out of her mouth, she regretted having spoken them.

Jubei went over to the woodpile, collected an armful of firewood, and fed the furnace. The owner slipped out of the room, casting sidelong glances at both of them as he went. When the fire took hold, Jubei sat down with his *bento* and began to eat.

Neither one spoke.

Making conversation with Jubei was not easy. It was as if his past ceased to exist the day he lost his eye. He would listen to a little castle gossip she had picked up in the women's quarters, and he seemed mildly interested in her progress with the sword. Not once in the year since the duel had Jubei asked, or had Akane volunteered, any information about their father. She suspected that he knew his father had been made a member of the Shogun's council. But in Jubei's shameful condition, she could never be sure of what he knew, or what he had once known and forgotten.

After he finished the last of his rice and pickles, Akane took a note out of the fold in her kimono.

"Do you remember the monk who sponsored the competition for the Kotetsu sword?" She tried to make her question seem casual, not knowing how Jubei would react to her first reference to the incident that cost him his eye. Akane held out the note. "He asked me to give this to you."

Jubei stared at her for a long moment, then took the note. There was not much light in the room. He walked over to the furnace, opened the fire door, and read: "Meet me in the dueling grove tomorrow at dawn."

Jubei crumpled the note and tossed it into the flames. Flickering light played over him as he watched it curl and vanish in a yellow burst.

Akane gathered up the empty food containers and put them back inside the *bento*. She had no idea why the monk had wanted to contact Jubei or what the note said. All she knew was that someone from his past had reached out to him, and Jubei had turned away. Although she no longer tried to convince him to change, she continued praying for some kind of breakthrough—anything that might shake him out of this debilitating ennui. For no good reason the monk's note brought hope, and now she was feeling the effects of the crash.

As Akane passed Jubei on her way out, she stopped, put her arms around his waist, and laid her cheek against his back.

"Jubei," she said tenderly, "when my hair was cut straight across my forehead, you taught me how to walk on bamboo stilts. When I fell down, you put me on your back and ran so fast the wind dried my tears. Each time I look at you, I try to see you as you were then, and each time it gets harder . . .

harder to see past the filth and degeneration to find the brother I worshiped like a god.

"The day you lost your eye and lay bleeding on the ground, I thought I was suffering the greatest pain I would ever feel. But I was wrong. Day after day, watching you destroy yourself with alcohol and self-pity, hurts more. And the worst part is . . . tomorrow I'll come back with more soup and rice, and the next day, and the next."

The rain beat down firm and even on the roof tiles. It ran off into full water barrels and splashed into puddles and filled the night with sound.

Jubei listened to the sliding door open and close. He slammed his fist into the furnace wall, and the pain felt good.

All the way to the dueling grove Jubei kept asking himself the same question: Why am I going? He hadn't intended to go. There was nothing to say to his former teacher. Seeing him again would only dredge up painful memories of a past that was gone forever. But despite a particularly heavy dose of sake the night before, Jubei had awakened before dawn. Unable to go back to sleep, he'd gotten up and gone for a walk. After a few abortive attempts to change direction, he gave in and headed for the grove.

Jubei spotted the little monk across the clearing. He was hunched over, cleaning his toenails with a sliver of bamboo.

"I'm here," Jubei announced.

"I know," Takuan said without looking up from his work. "I smelled you coming." He finished off one more toe before raising his head. "Your sister told me you're working in the bathhouse."

"That's right."

"Well, you certainly make a dismal advertisement for your establishment."

"Did you ask me to come here because your tongue was losing its edge?" Jubei shot back.

"Partly," he said. "And partly because it's time you stopped wallowing in self-pity and did something useful."

"I agree," Jubei said. "The trouble is, there's not a lot of demand for crippled swordsmen."

Takuan narrowed his eyes and studied Jubei. "You know, I came here thinking there might be something left to salvage, but I believe you're right. You really are a hopeless cripple."

"I dedicated my life to the sword—"

"Dedicated!" Takuan snatched up his robes and flashed his bare bottom at Jubei. "That's what I think of your dedication!" Jubei, who thought nothing the crazy monk did would surprise him, was flabbergasted. "Let me tell you something, young man. You don't know the first thing about dedication. You're a skimmer—nothing more than a flat rock skipping over the surface of life. You were never a swordsman. A swordsman dives, deep. You were only an athlete who wielded a sword. There's a big difference—a difference you haven't even sniffed."

"What about the month I spent with you?"

"A month," Takuan scoffed. "We barely scratched the surface."

"What about the pain and the abuse I took? Doesn't that count for anything?"

"At first you took it because you were told to, not because you wanted to. Later on you took it because you were mad . . . mad at me and mad at your father. That doesn't prove you're a swordsman. It just proves you're stubborn and spiteful."

"Maybe so," Jubei admitted. "But whatever chance I ever had to become a real swordsman ended when I lost my eye."

Takuan pointed at the two swords Jubei wore in his obi. "I see you haven't quit carrying them with you."

"It's my right. I'm still samurai."

"Let's see what kind of samurai you are." Takuan backed off a few paces. "Draw your sword." Jubei did as he was told. Takuan bent over and picked up a handful of stones. "Block these with your sword."

Jubei set himself. The first stone came right at his face. Jubei flicked his sword, missed, and the stone hit him flush in the mouth. He wiped the blood off his lip with the back of his sleeve. "Again," he called out. This time the stone struck him in the neck. Jubei shrugged it off. "Again!" Time after time Jubei misjudged the speed and distance of the stones. When Takuan finally ran out of stones, Jubei was bloody and bruised, and he hadn't blocked a single one.

"Sit down," Takuan said in a voice that was almost gentle.

"One more time!" he shouted, adjusting the black patch that covered his ruined eye.

"That's enough," Takuan said, handing his bamboo water

tube to Jubei. "It's water," he added sardonically. "I know it's been a long time, but maybe you still remember what it's used for."

Ignoring the monk's sarcasm, Jubei twisted the top off the tube and put it to his lips. As he started to take his first swallow, a strange sensation—an ill-defined, but certain inner perception of ominous presence sent a shiver down his spine. Jubei knew that someone, far enough away not to pose an immediate threat was watching from the hillside behind him. He was just about to wheel around, when he noticed the monk staring directly at the spot where he sensed the presence.

"Who's there?" Jubei whispered.

Instead of answering, Takuan called out in the direction of the hillside. "Did you find out what you want to know?"

Jubei's father stepped out from behind the cover of a large boulder and started down the hill, toward them.

"What's he doing here?" Jubei snapped.

"Why don't you ask him?"

"I have nothing to say to my father."

Jubei began to walk away, but Takuan grabbed his wrist. "Then why don't you practice listening?"

It was hardly a suggestion. The increased pressure on the nerve at the base of Jubei's thumb transformed Takuan's suggestion into a command.

Lord Tajima stopped a few paces away, and Takuan released his grip. Jubei made no attempt to leave. He stood his ground and returned his father's wilting gaze. If he's come here to satisfy his curiosity, Jubei thought, let him get his fill. Let him see the filth and smell the stench of utter failure. Let him look at the fruit of his loins, his only son and heir, his hope for the future of the Tajima clan. And let him drown in despair!

Tajima broke the silence. "Jubei, the duel is over."

"No, I don't think it will ever be over."

Jubei's response did not shock or surprise Tajima. Deep down he sensed the truth of what his son had just said, but at that moment it didn't matter. He'd come to ask for his son's obedience, not his affection. Based on what he had just seen transpire, he was inclined to agree with Takuan that his son's reclamation might be possible. If so, Jubei could become very useful to him. Tajima decided to test the waters.

"Do you want to learn how to stop those stones?" he asked.

The question caught Jubei totally off guard. His first instinct was to ridicule the notion. But he knew now that his father had been watching him try to block the stones and surely realized how desperately he wanted to regain his skills. So why deny the obvious?

"It takes more than desire," Jubei said, tapping one finger on his eye patch. "It takes two good eyes."

"Suppose I told you it may be possible to regain, and perhaps even surpass, your old skills."

Jubei forced a laugh. "I'd say you've never tried to block a stone with one eye closed."

Takuan, who had been listening quietly, suddenly ran to the place where he had been standing a few moments earlier. He reached inside the monk's bag he wore slung over his shoulder, took out a saffron-colored cloth, and tied it over his eyes. Then he raised his walking staff chest high and shouted out to Jubei. "Pick up one of those stones and throw it at my head as hard as you can!"

"This is madness!" Jubei shouted back at him.

"Don't defy me, you arrogant young cur!" Takuan goaded him. "Believe me, there are still a few things in this fleeting world that even you don't understand."

"Can you bring him to his senses?" Jubei appealed to his father.

Tajima picked up a flat stone and held it out to his son. "Why don't you do as he says?" he suggested.

It was his tone of voice that surprised Jubei. He had been used to commands from his father, not requests. For that reason alone Jubei took the stone, but he quickly made up his mind to alter the rules a bit. Instead of aiming at his head, Jubei planned to fire the stone at his chest. It would raise a painful welt, but at least it wouldn't split his skull.

"Are you ready?" Jubei called out.

Takuan grunted and set his feet.

Jubei reared back and fired the stone with all his strength. Takuan flicked his wrists, there was a sharp crack of wood, and the stone caromed off into the trees.

Jubei did not utter a sound. He just stared in amazement as Takuan took off the blindfold and rejoined them. "Would you like me to teach you that little trick?" he asked Jubei.

"More than anything!"

"You'll have to learn to see again, in a way you never

dreamed possible. It will take time and *real* dedication, but you have the power to do it. The only question is, do you want it enough to go after it with every fiber of your being?"

"I would give anything to feel whole again."

"Don't give me your final answer until you've heard what your father has to say."

It had been Takuan who introduced Tajima to the idea of recruiting Jubei to work with them as a secret agent. He argued that the widely heralded rift between him and his son provided the perfect cover for using Jubei against the enemies of the Tokugawa. After the incident at the dueling grove, few would ever suspect Jubei of working for the father who had crippled him then disowned him publicly.

At first Tajima resisted the notion, arguing that the wound had diminished his son's martial skills. Takuan countered by promising to teach Jubei how to compensate for his impaired vision by refining his other senses. He insisted that Jubei could be taught to "see with his entire body." Knowing Takuan, Tajima knew it was no idle boast. Yet his doubts persisted. He believed there was something unstable about his son, perhaps nothing more than a youthful rebellious streak which would atrophy with age and responsibility, but perhaps it was more enduring. However, despite his reservations, and despite the tension that had grown up between them, Tajima could not disregard the simple fact that they both shared the same blood. A son might rebel against his own father, but betrayal was unimaginable. More than anything, it was the security of a blood bond that persuaded Tajima to attempt a reconciliation with his son.

In broad strokes Tajima sketched out his secret involvement with the Tokugawa. He did it without preface, asking Jubei for nothing more than his attention. The revelations implied an implicit trust which was not lost on Jubei.

"It's an awesome responsibility," Tajima concluded, "not meant for the weak or squeamish. If you choose to stand with me, you must be prepared to abandon traditional concepts of honor. The stakes are too high to be handicapped by ordinary scruples, because if we fail, the enemies of peace will surely plunge this land into a new age of chaos and bloodshed." Tajima paused to let the impact of his dire prediction take hold of Jubei's imagination. "Now that the Shogun is dead, the wolves are coming out of their lairs with their hungry eyes fixed on Lord Iemitsu's throat. I want you to help me keep them at bay."

Jubei shared his father's commitment to peace, and had no trouble transferring his allegiance from the late Shogun to his heir, Iemitsu. What *did* disturb him was his father's insistence on renouncing the ethical principles of Bushido—the code of conduct defining samurai honor. "You always taught me that death is preferable to dishonor," Jubei said, voicing his reservations. "Have your values changed?"

The question touched a raw nerve. Tajima was not clear in his own mind how much of a role naked ambition had played in his decision to act as the dark fist of the Tokugawa.

"Yes, my values have changed!" he retorted quickly. "I know now that the ethics of Bushido is a luxury reserved for the individual, not those who bear responsibility for the lives and welfare of a whole nation of people. It would be an act of supreme selfishness for me to fight for peace with one hand tied behind me, and risk losing the battle to satisfy some petty notion of personal honor. I'm asking you to rise above common standards of morality and join me in a selfless struggle to save this nation from the ravages of war."

His response sounded reasonable to Jubei, but something about the speech lacked the resonance of true conviction. "How would I be expected to serve?" he asked.

"For now you'll continue leading your life exactly as you have since the day of the duel," he said. "The dissipation, the sloppiness, the self-pity, the spite, the drunken binges—"

"Why did you come to me?" Jubei asked, for to him, his final decision turned on the answer to that question.

"You are my son," Tajima replied simply. "I need you."

Jubei bowed to his father. "Then I accept."

They both stood there, each one testing the weight of the moment, wondering where the future would take them.

Takuan broke the silence. "Try to get as much rest as you can during the day," he told Jubei, "because the night belongs to me." There was an impish gleam in his eye. "You see, I've decided to bend a few rules and introduce you to the art of *ninjitsu*."

Jubei stared at the little monk in disbelief. "You are ninja?"

Takuan grinned. "A very famous ninja."

"Who are you?"

"My real name is Takuan."

"Takuan . . ." Jubei mouthed the name. It was the same name he had used as a child whenever he played "ninja" with his friends. How different Takuan had looked in his imagination! Little by little the pieces began to fall together. There was still a great deal left to figure out, but at that moment it didn't matter at all.

In the ensuing months after the reconciliation, Tajima passed along several assignments to Jubei. One particularly troublesome daimyo lost all his grain supplies in a mysterious fire, and had to turn to the Tokugawa for help. Lord Iemitsu, acting on Tajima's advice, generously resupplied the daimyo from his own stores of rice, thereby placing a potential enemy securely in his debt. In another incident, the *doshin* called in to investigate a robbery at the home of a wealthy Christian merchant accidentally uncovered hidden ledgers proving that he'd been falsifying his accounts to avoid paying taxes to the Tokugawa. The merchant protested his innocence, claiming that the ledgers were forgeries probably planted there by a competitor, but he was executed and all his property confiscated. After the success of these incidents, Tajima had to admit the arrangement with Jubei was working out well, very well indeed.

However, his relations with the Emperor's envoy left something to be desired. On the surface Prince Sanjo appeared to be a model of cooperation, offering only token resistance to a speedy confirmation of Iemitsu's claim to the shogunate. But Tajima could feel something wrong in the marrow of his bones. The longer the Emperor could hold out against formally naming Iemitsu shogun, the longer the seeds of discontent would germinate—and the closer the country moved toward civil war. Every delaying tactic, every excuse had been ancitipated. Moves and counter moves had been worked out well in advance, to thwart the nobles' attempts at procrastination.

Then why was Prince Sanjo going out of his way to be reasonable, Tajima asked himself, when all he needed was a stalemate to create the kind of political vacuum that served to cast doubt on the legitimacy of the Tokugawa shogunate?

Legitimacy. The most powerful weapon in the nobles' arsenal. On the Tokugawa side was military might. Yet using raw power to force the Emperor to bestow legitimacy on the

Tokugawa rule was unthinkable. No one, not even the most powerful shoguns, had dared risk the consequences of bludgeoning the Son of Heaven into submission. It would be an outrage no Japanese of any rank could tolerate. The process of maneuvering the Emperor into an untenable position was a matter of supreme delicacy.

Sanjo knew this. Yet day in and day out he sat in council squandering one opportunity after another to obstruct the aims of the acting Shogun. His performance was pathetic. Sometimes he appeared befuddled, other times he seemed bored and impatient to have done with the whole thing. It was like watching a toothless bitch in a dogfight.

Some of the council members were beginning to laugh at Sanjo behind his back, confusing his Kyoto foppery with incompetence—but not Tajima. He knew Sanjo was no fool. Beneath all that powder and paint he saw a cunning schemer with the instincts of a weasel. He warned the council not to underestimate Sanjo's capacity for guile, but it didn't surprise him when his admonitions were greeted with impolite silence. The record would show that the council had been warned, and that he had been the one who warned them.

Worst of all, Lord Iemitsu had turned a deaf ear to the possibility of deception. Now that he was acting Shogun, all that remained was securing the Emperor's formal sanction. In his haste to secure his title, Iemitsu was throwing caution to the wind. He seemed prepared to accept Sanjo's bumbling incompetence at face value. Shrugging off Tajima's suspicions, Iemitsu dismissed the nobles as nothing more than a nuisance. He was convinced that the meager stipend sustaining the Imperial Court would keep the nobles too impoverished to mount a serious threat against his appointment. "As long as the Tokugawa hold the purse strings," he argued, "the schemes of the nobles will remain as empty as their treasury."

It sounded plausible, except for one thing: Where was the fortune in gold that the former Shogun's Commissioner of Mines had siphoned off? Obubo's ties to the Christians were a matter of record. The Portuguese who had taught him his mining skills had been based in Kyoto, and Tajima suspected there might be collusion among the nobles in Kyoto, the Jesuits, and the thief Okubo.

Systematic torture and even the execution of his entire

family had not loosened Okubo's tongue. They were no closer
to recovering the gold or tracing its dispersal than on the day
he was captured. If only he could be made to talk, Tajima felt
certain he'd have the evidence he needed to expose a sinister
Christian-noble plot to destroy the Tokugawa shogunate.

The sound of rain falling on the terra cotta roof soothed his
mind. Tajima opened the sliding door that faced the west
garden and watched the downpour. The city below was dark
except for the lights that burned in the pleasure houses of
Yoshiwara.

The Yoshiwara district of Edo was located in the middle of
a dismal mosquito-infested swamp. It had been established
there to keep prostitutes off the streets. In fair weather the
brothels did a brisk business, despite their unfortunate location. But now that the rains had come, only the wealthier
patrons could afford the exorbitant fares boatmen charged to
transport them across the swamp.

Courtesans of the first rank, with their clientele of rich
merchants and well-off samurai, were the least affected by
the foul weather. In better times even the lowest-ranking
courtesan could refuse to pillow with a customer she found
distasteful. But while the rains were choking off business, it
was not wise for any of them to be overly choosy. The mood
of the *okami*, who controlled every detail of their lives, had
turned as ugly as the weather. Only the new boy from Kyoto
was spared the pressure.

Although he had not yet reached the age of fourteen,
Konosuke had acquired social graces that outshined all the
other courtesans at Yoshiwara. After all, his skills had been
honed in the ancient capital, and there were rumors that he
had actually been the catamite of a very important noble in
the Imperial Court.

Being a young man of impeccable discretion, Konosuke
had neither confirmed nor denied the rumors. But it was
certain that Konosuke was expensive; just how expensive, no
one knew except the *okami*. Yoshiwara gossip had it that he
had been brought in to attend to the needs of one very rich
and powerful client. Although the comings and goings of any
patron were held in the utmost confidence, the identity of
this particular visitor was scrupulously guarded, even from
the other courtesans. The mystery only served to elevate

Konosuke's already considerable prestige and fan the fires of jealousy among the women courtesans.

Holding a mirror in each hand, Konosuke turned to examine himself from every angle. He adjusted the back of his kimono so that a little more of the powdered skin at the nape of the neck was exposed. Then he cocked his head to one side and inspected the fine line running from his earlobes to the corners of his mouth, the line separating the intense white below from the lighter application on his face. It was nicely done. The total effect was satisfying. As he repositioned the mirrors, an image appeared in the glass over his shoulder. The mirror fell out of his hand.

"I see you haven't forgotten me," Sanjo said to Konosuke. The cruel mocking voice, high pitched and nasal, brought back the terror and pain the boy had experienced at Sanjo's hands during the years of service as his catamite.

Konosuke fell to his knees and touched his head to the mat. "Please be welcome, Prince Sanjo." Although he tried to hide his fear, the sound of his voice gave him away, as it always had.

Prince Sanjo chuckled. "Surely after such a long separation you might have affected a more . . . shall we say convincing greeting." Konosuke started to respond, but Sanjo cut him off with a wave of his fan. "But never mind." Then he added, "For one who aspires to a career in the theater, your talent for deception is woefully underdeveloped."

"I'm sorry that my greeting displeased you, my lord. I'm afraid your unexpected arrival caught me . . . unprepared."

"As it was intended," Sanjo replied, assuming a cross-legged position opposite Konosuke.

Remembering that Prince Sanjo rarely drank sake, Konsuke set about preparing the tea, improvising idle chatter to disguise his discomfort.

"And do you miss Kyoto?" Sanjo asked.

"Edo and Kyoto are different worlds," the boy replied, sidestepping the question.

"Alas," the prince lisped. "Our present rulers are far more impressed with physical power than refinements of the spirit. But what can one expect from samurai?" He pronounced the word with unbridled contempt. "You can rest assured that when the rival clans begin carving themselves up again, the nation will turn back to our beloved Emperor, just as it always has."

"I was under the impression that all the rival factions had been subdued and the country is secure under Tokugawa rule."

"Oh, my, I had no idea you'd become such an astute political observer," Sanjo said sarcastically. "You must have found an excellent tutor here in Edo."

Konosuke noted Sanjo's sly smile and the mocking intonation of his voice. Did he know? the boy wondered, and said, "I only repeat common gossip, my lord."

"Really? I would hardly characterize pillow talk with the Tokugawa heir as 'common gossip.'"

Konosuke saw there was no further need to dissemble. Sanjo knew Lord Iemitsu had become his lover. "You are well informed, my lord."

"Would it surprise you to learn that I arranged the liaison?"

"Is that why you sold me to Yoshiwara?"

"Indeed. Did you think I'd tired of you?"

"And Lord Iemitsu, does he know about this arrangement?"

"Of course. And thanks to your considerable skills, I've earned the gratitude of our future Shogun."

"I understand."

"Do you?" He lifted Konosuke's chin with one finger. "I think not. Surely you've known me long enough to realize that currying favor with the Tokugawa is hardly something I'd find palatable."

"Forgive me, I didn't mean to imply a lack of subtlety."

Sanjo let his hand drop onto Konosuke's thigh. He felt the boy's muscles tighten against his touch, and it stimulated him more than he cared to admit.

"There is a family of Kabuki actors preparing to establish a theater here in Edo," Sanjo said. "Unfortunately the family is not blessed with a son who's skillful enough to play the women's parts. I hear they're looking for a promising boy to adopt. Have you any suggestions?"

Konosuke's eyes blazed with excitement. "My lord, you know that is my one dream in life."

"Is it a dream worth risking your life for?"

"Yes," Konosuke answered without hesitation.

"Then listen carefully." He leaned close to the boy. "Cooperate with me and I'll see to it that you realize your dream.

But know this—your role is critical. The slightest failure of nerve, the tiniest mistake, could jeopardize the whole plan and cost you your life. Do you understand?"

Konosuke nodded.

"If I tell you anything more, there can be no turning back. Shall I continue?"

This time Konosuke took his time answering, but in the end the bait was too succulent to refuse. He bowed his head. "As always, I am your servant."

"Before the week is over I'll make arrangements for you to leave Yoshiwara and begin your training as a Kabuki actor. You will vanish without a trace, leaving Lord Iemitsu broken-hearted and bewildered. When his grief has had sufficient time to flower into agony, you will contact him and suggest a secret rendezvous. If he comes, your role is over."

Konosuke's hand went to his throat. "You're going to—"

Sanjo laughed his metallic laugh.

"Please tell me," Konosuke begged.

"And would my answer affect your resolve?"

Konosuke gazed at Sanjo's narrowed eyes, and his blood ran cold. "As you said, my lord, it's too late to turn back."

"I'll tell you this much. If the plan is successful, no harm will come to your lover. If not . . ." He closed his eyes and spread out his palms. "Do we curse the wind for plucking a blossom when its season is over?"

6

Lisbon
Year of Our Lord—1631

In the spring preparations were under way for the Black Ship's return voyage to Japan. At the Father General's request, Maria had stayed on at the seminary, tutoring Jan

Kriek in Japanese. She had been given small but comfortable quarters in a cottage that belonged to an elderly grounds-keeper. She spent her free time wandering through the seminary gardens, drinking in a delicious mixture of exotic sights and sounds.

Kriek often accompanied her on her walks, answering questions, explaining things that confused her. He spoke in Japanese, and though his pronunciation was faulty, his syntax tortured, and his phrasing too musical, the sound of her own language eased her loneliness. Yet language alone could not explain the comfort she experienced while with him. For a foreigner, Kriek had an unusual sense of Japanese inner rhythms. Unlike other Europeans, who seemed compelled to fill up every silence with chatter, Kriek knew how to remain quiet. He seemed acutely attuned to nuances in the weather, aware that days, like people, have their moods.

They usually saw each other in the early morning, before matins, and in the evening after vespers. While he was taking classes, Maria occupied herself by writing in her journal and sewing. Although the time they spent together in the evenings was generally devoted to Japanese lessons, they sometimes took long walks outside the seminary to places Kriek thought might please her.

One evening, a few days before the Black Ship was due to sail for Japan, he brought her to a small village where the wisteria was in full bloom. The night was warm, but there was still a tinge of spring in the air. Maria remembered a poem she had read in the *Tale of Gengi*, a note sent by a court lady to her lover. She recited the lines for Kriek.

*"Come join me in regrets for the passing of spring
And wisteria now aglow in the evening light."*

To her astonishment Kriek responded by quoting the lover's sorrowful reply.

*"I grope my way through the gathering shades of evening
With no great hope of coming upon wisteria."*

"Jan-san," she said, her eyes sparkling with delight. "Where did you learn that?"

"Lady Murasaki's book was one of the works Father Sebastio left me. It's beautiful. I've read it many times."

"It is beautiful, but I'm surprised a man would find pleasure in a woman's tales of love."

Kriek saw that she was teasing him, and he tried very hard to keep from blushing. At times like this he was certain his attraction to her was ridiculously obvious. Although it disturbed him deeply, his confessor made light of his distress. "You will face temptation of this sort all your life," he'd been told. "With God's grace you'll find a way to overcome your natural desires." By immersing himself in books, and focusing his mind on the final examinations prior to his ordination, Kriek had succeeded in crowding her out of his mind—until moments like this, when the full radiance of her presence disintegrated his defenses.

Unable to think of a way to extricate himself, Kriek continued the conversation, trying to adopt a more scholarly tone. "Lady Murasaki's book is intriguing, especially to someone who practically grew up in a seminary. I know very little about women, and even less about love."

"So you've never been in love," she said playfully.

"Have you?"

"Oh, yes." She hid her smile behind her hand, her mahogany eyes sparkling over her fingertips. "Many times."

"I see," he said, and knew immediately that his disappointment was transparent.

"Why, Jan-san," she teased, "I think you disapprove."

"No, it's just that . . ."

Maria let him dangle for a minute, then came to his rescue. "All my romances were very poignant, very sad, and . . . very innocent. I have a box full of love notes that were never sent. Maybe someday I'll use them to write love stories even sadder than Lady Murasaki's."

"Why do they always have to be sad?" he asked. "All the stories I read are about broken hearts and unrequited love. Can't you write about lovers who get married and live happily ever after?"

"I could, but no one would believe them. In my country love and marriage are separate things. Love is a beautiful sentiment that's expressed in poetry and song. It's a cherished daydream locked away inside a woman's heart, like a precious heirloom that can never be corrupted by the ravages of reality. On the other hand, for Japanese, marriage is a political and economic event—a union between families, not individuals. It's the glue that holds our society together. It has nothing to do with love."

"You're saying that sharing your bed with a man and bearing his children has nothing to do with love?"

"Jan-san, you've learned to speak the Japanese language, but you still have much to learn about the Japanese mind. Our way may not be perfect, but I can't imagine what would become of a society where inexperienced young people were free to choose their husbands and wives based on an emotion as volatile as love."

"Surrendering your own happiness for the good of society is a very noble gesture," he replied, "but I wonder if the benefits are really worth the sacrifice. It seems to me that God never would have given us the gift of love if He meant for us to throw it away for security."

"If you truly believe that, Jan-san, why have you decided to throw away this precious gift to become a celibate priest?"

Kriek thought for a moment. "Love takes many forms," he said, knowing he had not really answered the question for Maria, or himself.

A few days after this conversation took place, the Father Vicar called Kriek into his study. For a long time he stared at the young seminarian, pressing the tips of his fingers together, his lips pursed. Kriek tried to keep the theatrical pause from annoying him, but he knew his enmity for the Father Vicar was difficult to hide.

"I'm afraid I have bad news for you, my son," he began. "It seems that the Black Ship will be setting sail for the Japans earlier than had been anticipated. You must make preparations to embark on tomorrow's tide."

"As you wish, Father," he responded, barely able to contain his excitement.

"This, of course, means it won't be possible to arrange your ordination before you leave. However, I have written a letter to the bishop of Macao, asking him to accept your final vows when the Black Ship arrives there. I hope it's not too great a disappointment for you."

"I am a servant of Christ," Kriek said. "I accept the delay as an expression of His divine will."

The Father Vicar nodded gravely, and motioned for Kriek

to sit down. "The Father General left a sealed envelope containing your instructions. They are to be opened by the Father Visitor when you reach Nagasaki. Since you'll be sailing out of Macao on a Dutch ship, I suggest that you sew the envelope inside your jerkin. Needless to say, it would be a disaster for you and the Holy Church if it were to fall into Dutch hands."

"I will take the utmost precautions to keep that from happening," he assured the Father Vicar.

"When you reach the Dutch trading center on the island of Hirado, you are to contact a Japanese woman named Oman. She is a Christian who works at the Inn of Eternal Blossoms. She will help you reach the mainland. Once in Nagasaki you are to report directly to the Father Visitor. He will provide you with the assistance you need to carry out the Father General's directives. Is that clear?"

After Kriek repeated his instructions, he was handed an envelope fixed with the Father General's seal. "Guard it with your life," the Father Vicar commanded.

Kriek kneeled to receive the Father Vicar's blessing, then started out the door when the priest called out to him. "One last piece of advice, my son." Kriek thought he detected a malevolent cast to the priest's thin-lipped smile. "Our God is a jealous God. There is no secret of the heart hidden from His eyes, and terrible calamity awaits those who provoke his wrath. Think on this as you voyage to Macao, Jan Kriek."

Kriek thought on it often during the six months' voyage, but by the time the Black Ship approached Macao, it had become impossible for him to avoid the awful truth any longer. He had tried to find some innocuous word for the powerful emotions Maria stirred in him. Words like *affection*, *attraction*, and *fondness* were as satisfying as watered grog, compared with the intoxicating effect of Maria's nearness. She filled up his senses and dominated his every thought. After all attempts to define her out of his heart had failed, Kriek stared the truth dead in the eye and finally conceded that he was desperately in love with her.

He reacted to the realization by fighting it with all his might. The prescription was hard work and prayer. When the bilges needed cleaning, it was Kriek who volunteered to go below and remain there for hours in the malodorous darkness, picking and scraping until his fingers bled. No job was too arduous or dirty for him to accept. His crewmates regarded him with bemused suspicion. The captain just smiled and watched the young seminarian transform himself from a pale-skinned scholar into a nut-brown, rock-hard seaman. No one, not even Maria, had the slightest notion of the internal struggle ripping him apart.

Each night, almost as a test of his will, he went to Maria's cabin to continue his studies. For Kriek it was a time of sheer joy and agony. While he fought to appear normal, the closeness drove him mad with passion. Sometimes she would brush against him, or he would catch the scent of her hair, and it was all he could do to keep from taking her in his arms. Maria sensed the tension, but when she asked him what was bothering him, it only seemed to drive him away from her, so she stopped prying.

The night before the Black Ship was due to arrive in Macao, Kriek came to Maria's cabin at the usual time, prepared to take one last Japanese lesson. She was more than a little surprised, even disappointed, that he was treating this night like all the rest. Since it would be their final evening together, she had expected some indication that the time they'd spent together at the seminary and aboard ship held special meaning for him. Surely he understood how important he had become to her—how her spirits soared when he was with her, and how empty she felt when his duties kept him away. This much he had to know, even if she could never let him see the true depths of her longing for him. As the night wore on, Maria began to lose her patience.

"No, no!" she reprimanded him sharply. "The character for the word *jisei*—restraint—ends with a strong downstroke, followed by a taut lift on the upstroke—like this . . ." She took his hand and guided the brush movement down, then up. "You have to cut off the stroke before it has a chance to get started. You should feel *jisei* when you finish the stroke." Kriek grinned. "What?" she asked. "Did I say something funny?"

Kriek chuckled to himself. "It's just funny that this particular character is giving me trouble."

"Don't be so hard on yourself. *Jisei* isn't easy to do properly."

"No," he said softly, looking directly into her eyes. "It isn't easy at all."

Something about the way he looked at her made her feel uneasy. She took the writing brush out of his hand and put it away with the ink stone. "The lessons are over," she said in her best teacher's voice.

"I know."

Maria rummaged through her belongings and brought out a package wrapped in a thin blue cloth. "Here," she said, holding out the package to him. "An ordination gift."

Kriek peeled back the folds and took out a white silk chasuble with a scarlet cross running from the neck to the hem of the poncholike vestment. In the center of the cross Maria had embroidered the image of a crane nesting in a crown of thorns. The mother crane was opening a wound in her breast so her hungry chicks could feed on drops of her own blood.

"It's exquisite," he said, deeply moved by the scene and the incalculable effort it must have taken to execute such a magnificent work.

"Now you know how I spent my time while you were in your classes. I planned to give it to you at your ordination, but when it was postponed, I had more time to work on it."

"Yes," he said. "The postponement gave me more time too."

His comment puzzled her. "More time for what?" she asked.

Kriek realized he had come to the crossroads. If he didn't speak his heart now, he knew he would regret it the rest of his life. There was a good chance he would never see Maria again. And even if he did, the next time they met he would be a celibate priest.

"I didn't know it at the time, but delaying my ordination allowed me to put off a commitment I wasn't ready to make." Maria listened, her face cast in the golden glow of a swaying lantern. "Do you remember the night you asked me why I was becoming a priest if I valued love so highly?" Maria nodded. "It was a question I asked myself over and over again that night, and I couldn't find an answer. I realized that the days we'd spent together had changed me. I didn't understand what had happened to me, but I did know what it meant to feel alive, truly alive. Little by little I came to accept the truth. Being a priest was becoming less important than being with you. I could never take my final vows as long as there was a chance of making a new life with you."

Maria blinked, and her hand raised to her throat. "Jan-san," she murmured in a voice barely above a whisper. "I didn't know."

"And now you do," he said simply.

She turned away to collect her composure. How was she supposed to respond? she wondered. If she admitted that she shared the same feelings tormenting him, where would it lead? She wanted nothing more than to bare her soul and pour out her heart to him, but it would be an act of unconscionable cruelty to fan the fires of his passion when there was no hope of consummation—no hope at all. They belonged to separate worlds, and even love could never bridge the gulf between them.

"Is it enough that I know?" she asked, turning back to him.

"Maria, tomorrow I'll leave the ship and we may never see each other again. If there's a chance for us, say so. I won't take my final vows in Macao. I'll go to Japan and complete my mission. After that I'll go to Hirado and live as a Dutch trader. You can join—"

"Stop!" Maria cut him off. "This is pure fantasy! It's utter madness!" She took his callused hand between hers, and her dark eyes softened. "Jan-san, I'm a samurai—the daughter of a daimyo. What you're suggesting is unthinkable. I belong to my family, and you belong to the Church. Nothing either of us feels can change that."

"Maria, I'm asking you to follow the path of your heart."

Maria shook her head. "Please try to understand."

"If you can look at me and tell me you won't hurt, you won't feel an emptiness inside you when I'm gone, then I'll understand."

Maria summoned up all her resolve and looked him straight in the eye. "You're my friend, and I'll miss you as a friend . . . that's all," she lied.

Kriek tucked her gift under his arm and went to the door. His hand rested on the latch for a moment, then he stepped out into the night.

The door closed.

A tear started down her cheek.

* * *

The gangplank was lowered, and Kriek hoisted his seabag to his shoulder. There was a lot of pushing and shoving as the lucky seamen with the first leave jostled for position at the rail. Some of the old hands who had been to Macao many times before were shouting out the names of whores they had known into the heavy morning mist. A few women answered back in broken Portuguese, provoking near riot on board.

Kriek stood alone, waiting for the mob at the gangplank to be piped ashore. It had been a difficult night. The agitation that had kept him tossing and turning on his bunk had settled into a poisonous funk, a seething anger as raw as an open wound. The creaking of the ship, the soaking mist, the rowdy clamor of the sailors with the elbowing and boisterous laughter—especially the laughter—grated on his nerves.

The pipe sounded. Despite his resolve, Kriek turned for one last glance at Maria's cabin. She was standing in the doorway, looking down at him. Kriek's stomach tightened as if he had taken a blow. He saw her lift her hand, and he turned away before the final wave was offered.

Maria watched him go, feeling more alone than she had ever felt in her life. All night she'd tried to think of a way to let him know how much she cared for him, how much she wished the world they lived in were a different kind of place. Yet a wish, no matter how beautiful, remains a wish. If the world were round, as Jan-san said it was, it would be round tomorrow and the next day and the next. And there would always be a year of ocean between her home and his—wishes couldn't change that. So in the end Maria decided to say nothing. Instead she depicted a new world in her imagination, one in which wishes govern events and lovers never part.

Along the waterfront the stench was overpowering, the streets littered with refuse. Near the fishmongers' shops buckets of entrails were dumped in alleyways and left to molder in the sun. Large-eyed monkeys were picking through a pile of decaying fruits and vegetables. A cripple pleaded for alms, while a brown-skinned whore with sagging breasts grabbed Kriek's arm and tried to entice him with a smile stained red by the juice of betel nuts. The humid air was heavy with the odor of human waste.

Kriek kept moving inland until he came to a place where the main street forked into two branches on either side of a palm tree. An old woman was sleeping beneath the tree, her head resting on a bamboo cage. Through the veil of long white hair that spilled over the sides of the cage, he could see a tiny monkey peeking out at him. Next to her a younger woman was squatting in the dirt, cooking something white and gooey over a small fire.

"Jesuit mission?" he said to a the young woman, hoping one of the words might be understood.

The woman just stared at him.

"Padre." He made the sign of a cross, then folded his hands in prayer.

"Chreestean?" the woman asked, pointing at him.

Kriek nodded vigorously.

She gestured toward the left fork.

Soon afterward Kriek found what he was looking for. Compared with the dilapidated hovels around it, the mission looked almost grand. In keeping with the Portuguese tradition, there was only one door in the front, flanked by two round towers. The entire facade had been freshly whitewashed.

Through the door he could hear the sound of a hand bell being rung to signal the consecration of the host. Kriek decided to wait outside until the morning mass was finished.

After the worshipers filed out, Kriek went up to the priest, identified himself, and asked for an audience with the bishop. The meeting was arranged quickly, and Kriek was ushered into the bishop's study and greeted warmly by an avuncular-looking cleric with sad rheumy eyes.

The first hour or so was spent slaking the bishop's thirst for news of Lisbon. Finally, almost regretfully, he got around to asking the purpose of Kriek's visit.

"I was ordered to deliver this letter to you," Kriek said, handing him an envelope sealed with the Father General's stamp.

The bishop took the letter and held it in his hands as reverently as if it were a relic of the True Cross. Kriek couldn't tell whether his hands were trembling from emotion or from a slight palsy.

"Is something wrong?" Kriek asked as the moment lengthened.

"Forgive me, my son. My health is failing and I was beginning to fear that I'd never see Lisbon again. Until now all my letters to the Father General had gone unanswered."

He slit the wax seal with his thumbnail. "I had almost given up hope."

Although Kriek knew the general thrust of the letter, he silently prayed that the Father General had also remembered to respond to the old bishop's requests.

When he looked up from the letter, the light had drained from his eyes. "So you're to be ordained," the bishop said pleasantly enough, but his voice betrayed his deep disappointment.

"I'm afraid that's a decision you'll have to make after you've heard my confession," he replied somberly.

The bishop regarded him quizzically. Kriek's gaze was steady, but troubled. It was an expression he had seen on the faces of so many of the postulants who presented themselves for ordination. It's a woman, he said to himself, and his heart went out to the young man with the sad, violet eyes. "Well," the bishop said, "shall we see to it then?"

In the half light of the confessional Kriek spoke of his love for Maria. "Last night I promised to give up the priesthood if she would agree to marry me. I am here now only because she refused me. There's nothing I can say in my defense. I'm ashamed of my weakness, but I cannot renounce my love for this woman." Kriek bowed his head and waited for the bishop's response.

"My son, you are not the first man to come to the priesthood after losing the woman you love, and I daresay you won't be the last. Remember, Our Lord doesn't demand perfection from his servants, only obedience."

"But I tried to obey, and I failed," Kriek said abjectly.

"Perhaps this was God's way of reminding you that you are a man, not a god," the bishop said quietly. "Even the apostle Peter, a man who had walked with Christ, denied Our Lord . . . not once, but three times. And yet Christ took him back when he returned. Is your indiscretion greater than Peter's?"

"I can't be sure that I won't stumble again, your grace. That's what frightens me."

"And you should be frightened. The priestly vows are not to be taken lightly. But God grants us special grace to help with our special burdens. Try to accept this woman as a measure of God's grace. Think of her as a gift to carry in your heart, and perhaps the purity of your love will keep you safe from further temptation."

This was a turn of mind that caught Kriek completely off guard. He had come to the confessional expecting castigation; instead he found compassion. What the bishop had told him was true. Maria was a gift from God. She would be with him always, owning a part of him that no other woman could ever have. The rest belonged to God.

"*Ego te absolvo*," said the bishop. "Go in peace. The Lord hath put away all thy sins."

7

Edo
Year of the Monkey—1632
Hour of the Boar

Tajima looked up from his writing desk. The rain had stopped. The trees and shrubs glistened in the muted moonlight, and the air smelled of pine and washed earth. The opening into the garden was more than a passageway, it was a picture frame. Each tree, each bush, each rock had been carefully chosen and placed to form a natural composition of serene harmony. Stepping into the garden was like merging with a work of art that spoke to all the five senses in the language of the seasons.

The path to the teahouse wound through the garden, and the flat stepping-stones were perfectly matched to his strides. As he reached out to touch a moist leaf, he noticed an unusual shape to the wind shadow at the far end of the garden. A few steps farther and Tajima could make out the figure of someone—no, two people standing close together. They appeared to be in deep conversation, speaking in hushed tones.

It was Akane who first realized they were not alone. She

pressed her finger against Iori's lips and listened. Tajima rounded the bend and feigned surprise at seeing them there.

Iori managed to stammer out a greeting.

"Please be welcome," Tajima said, adding, "although I must apologize for my daughter's bad manners . . . she neglected to tell me you were coming." He couldn't show it, but Tajima was secretly pleased that Iori had finally worked up enough courage to act on his clumsily concealed attraction to Akane. It had been evident from the first day Iori agreed to take Jubei's place as chief sword instructor of Tajima's school.

"Please, sir," Iori answered, "the blame is mine. You see, Akane had no idea—"

"Oh?" he said, turning to Akane for verification.

"It's true, Father. Iori came to speak with you."

"With me?" He looked at Iori. "At this late hour?"

Akane answered for him. "There is a matter he wanted to discuss with you. I brought him into the garden to try to persuade him to come back at a more . . . acceptable time."

Akane seemed unusually agitated. Tajima wondered if Iori was bypassing the services of an intermediary and preparing to ask him directly for his daughter's hand in marriage. If so, it was a breach of etiquette that could not be easily overlooked.

"Does the matter concern you?" he asked Akane.

Akane shook her head and glared at Iori, who seemed to be struggling with some internal dilemma.

"Well?" Tajima's voice was stern.

"It concerns Jubei," Iori said.

"Go on," he ordered Iori. Tajima's features seemed carved out of granite.

"There was another raid on the Tokaido road last night. One of the bandits was captured and brought to me for interrogation. We pressed him for the name of his leader. . . ." Iori lowered his eyes. "He named Jubei."

Iori waited for some response. When none came, he continued. "Earlier this evening I sent a note to Jubei asking him to meet with me. I wanted to give him a chance to answer the accusation."

"And?"

"I was told he destroyed my note without reading it."

"The man you captured—do you believe him?"

"All the other information he gave us was checked thoroughly, and in every case it proved accurate."

"I asked if *you* believe him."

Iori met Tajima's hard gaze. "I do."

"Then why are you here?"

"I thought you'd want to know."

"Is that all?"

"And to ask you how to proceed."

"Arrest him and turn him over to the *doshin*."

"Father, please," Akane pleaded. "Jubei is still your son. At least give him a chance to defend himself."

Tajima looked past her and spoke directly to Iori. "You know your duty. Do it." Then he turned to Akane. "And you are forbidden to interfere in any way. Is that understood?"

"*Hai*," she said, refusing to bow in submission. "I understand that you are as guilty as Jubei."

Tajima slapped Akane across the face. "You understand nothing!" he snarled.

The following morning Jubei plodded down the street with his sandals in one hand, an empty sake jar in the other. Crowds of revelers, undeterred by the mosquitoes and oppressive heat, had taken to the streets in celebration of the *bon* festival—the day the souls of the dead came back to mingle with family and friends. It was also a day for settling old debts.

Outside the *zakaya* where Jubei did his social drinking, a group of men had gathered around an old woman who was dancing to the rhythms of a huge drum booming away in the heart of the city. Jubei stopped to watch.

"*Odoru aho ni miru aho, onaji aho nara odoranya son son*," they sang: Those who dance are fools, and those who watch are fools. If you are a fool anyway, you may as well dance.

"*Aii!*" the proprietor shouted when he spotted Jubei. "My business is saved. Jubei has finally come to pay off his account!" A cheer went up from the crowd.

Jubei dangled a small pouch of coins high over his head. "It's all here, you old thief," he shouted back. "But first, in honor of your father's spirit—a man whose only fault was his inability to teach his son to serve an honest drink—I demand a song."

"I'll give you your song and dedicate it to your mother's spirit—an honest woman who couldn't teach her son to tell the truth," he said with a grin.

The crowd laughed, and the proprietor leaped up on a sake barrel and began singing a familiar *ondo* song. The old woman caught Jubei's hand and drew him into the dance. Soon others joined in. Round and round they went, swaying to the music.

A short distance away Iori and a half dozen of his students watched the merriment. When the proprietor's song finished, the crowd broke up. Jubei and some of the others went inside. The rest drifted away.

"Wait here," Iori ordered his men. He crossed the street and entered the *zakaya* alone.

Jubei was sitting cross-legged on the mat at the far end of the room. A serving girl was pouring sake into his cup while he picked at a wooden tray filled with a variety of seafood. Iori noticed that his long sword was lying on the tatami by his right side, his short sword tucked in his obi. The year since the duel had changed him, Iori thought. His face was leaner and stubbled with a week's growth of beard. His body seemed to have filled out considerably. Whether it was fat or muscle was hard to tell in the dim light. Had it not been for the distinctive black patch on his right eye, Iori might not have recognized him.

Cautiously Iori approached him from the blind side. Without turning his head to look, Jubei reached out his arm and gestured toward the space next to him. "Sit down, Iori," he said through a mouthful of dried quid. "It's been a long time."

"Yes, it has." Iori wondered if Jubei knew how baffled he was. He sat down and laid his sword across his lap.

Jubei handed him a cup and poured the sake. "*Kanpai*," he said, lifting his cup.

"*Kanpai*."

They drank the liquid slowly. Jubei poured another. This time etiquette did not require Iori to drink.

"Who do you think would have won?" Jubei asked flatly.

Iori had to chuckle at the way Jubei cut through fat, muscle, and bone, and went right for the heart. "I can't say. I had the experience and technique. You had speed and the intensity of a badger." Iori shrugged. "I've often wondered."

Jubei nodded thoughtfully. "So have I, so have I."

"I was told you'd given up the way of the sword."

Jubei tapped his finger on his eye patch. "You can't carry water in a leaky bucket."

"I have also heard there is a remedy for everything except death."

Jubei shifted his weight to his right hip. "Shall we continue to trade adages or do you want to state your business?"

"I've been ordered to take you prisoner."

Jubei's shoulders tensed, and Iori dropped his hand to the hilt of his sword. A swarm of flies circled the bowl of rice Jubei was holding in his left hand. "So, your prisoner talked," he said.

Iori nodded.

Jubei picked up his chopsticks. Several flies had settled on the heaped rice.

"Do you intend to resist?" Iori asked.

Jubei brushed the flies away and watched them resettle on his rice. "Surely you're not worried about resistance from a cripple?"

"I don't want to kill you," Iori said.

Then Jubei did a remarkable thing. He reached out and snatched a fly with his chopsticks, then another and another. It was the most amazing feat of dexterity Iori had ever witnessed.

Jubei wiped his chopsticks on his kimono and smiled at Iori. "Do you mind if I finish this rice? I hear prison food is awful."

Iori did not respond, and merely stood by as Jubei finished, picked up his sword, and handed it to him. Then Iori said, "I'll take it, but I have a feeling you never planned on using it."

"Really. Why do you say that?"

"If you had, I think I'd be dead now."

Alone in the tiny windowless cell, the fetid air and unrelenting darkness seemed to grow heavy with each breath he took. Off in the distance Jubei could hear the *bon* festival drum pounding in synchrony with his heart. Something strange was happening to him. His breathing was becoming labored, his skin cold and clammy. If this was fear, it was unlike any he had ever experienced before, except in nightmares. Jubei slumped to the floor. He gripped his knees and counted seconds, hoping the monotonous act of counting would take his mind off the suffocating darkness.

After what seemed like an eternity, the cell door opened. "Jubei?" the voice behind the candle said. "What's wrong with you? You look terrible." The voice belonged to Takuan.

"It must have been the darkness, *sensei*," Jubei said softly to his teacher.

"Well, well," Takuan chuckled, "so the fearless warrior finally caught a whiff of his own vulnerability. The next thing you'll be telling me is that you squat down and move your bowels like the rest of us mortals."

Jubei raised up on one elbow. "Takuan," he said, "do you understand what I'm telling you?"

"If I told you I did, you wouldn't believe me anyway, so go ahead and explain it to me."

"There was something about being closed up in darkness that unnerved me. At one point I think I would have done anything . . . anything to get out of here. And this is what you have to understand. . . ." Jubei took a deep breath. "I can't tell you it won't happen again."

"You know what's wrong?" Jubei shook his head. "This is a different kind of cell than the one you're used to. The one you're comfortable with has little peepholes in it that create the illusion that you're not locked up."

"I don't understand what you're talking about," Jubei complained.

"Of course you don't!" Takuan threw his hands up in disgust. "Understand, understand, understand—what have you got when you 'understand'? Secondhand information, the cheapest form of knowledge. You know a lot more than you think you know, but you won't trust your knowledge until somebody makes a word out of it, defines it for you, and puts it in a sentence."

Jubei had heard it all before, and he still didn't know what Takuan was driving at.

"But," Takuan sighed, "since you insist on turning ignorance into an art form, I'll do my best to lead you out of the darkness." He sat down on the hard-packed dirt and drew his feet under him. "The prison cell you're used to is your own body. I've heard it argued that your spirit was put inside your body as a punishment for some misdeed in a previous life. I don't know, and the truth is I really don't care why we end up there. But like any prisoner who's been locked up in one place for a long, long time, we start to get comfortable—so comfortable that if somebody came up and threw the cell door open, we'd be terrified to go out. It's too scary, because all we know about the world outside is what we see through the tiny peepholes we use for eyes. So most of us cringe inside our little cells until death comes along and drags us kicking and screaming into the light."

"You're saying that death is like being let out of prison."

"No, it *is* being let out of prison," Takuan corrected him. "Someday you may learn how to get out before you die."

"What's the secret?"

"The secret is, the door's not locked. Once you find that out, all you need is the courage to let go and walk out the door."

"Can you get back in?"

"The door is never locked until your sentence is up."

"Forgive me, *sensei*, but if it's as easy as you say it is, why don't people do it all the time?"

"Did I say it was easy?" Takuan shook his head. "In our tangled lives the most obvious things are always the hardest to see."

Jubei got to his feet and stretched. He didn't care what Takuan said, he was not looking forward to spending any more time in the cell. "How long am I going to be in here?" he asked, casually scratching an imaginary flea bite.

"You'll be moved to another cell tonight."

"One with air, I hope."

"Stop worrying about your physical comfort, and put your mind on the job at hand."

"It would help if I knew why I'm here."

"How much did your father tell you?"

"Only that there was a small gold shipment coming down the Tokaido from the mines in Izu. The raid was to take place in broad daylight near the Nihonbashi Bridge. One of my men would be taken prisoner and during the interrogation he'd reveal my name. When they came for me, I was to give up without a fight. That's as much as I know."

"Good," Takuan said. "Your father is a cautious man." He bent forward and lowered his voice to a whisper. "Not long after the former Shogun had made himself lord of the eight provinces of the Kwanto, he invited a group of Kyoto Kabuki actors to perform at Edo Castle. Among the entertainers was a clever scoundrel named Okubo. Hearing that the Shogun was desperate for money, Okubo concocted a bold plan. He told the Shogun that the most efficient way to generate capital for the wars was to go straight to the source. 'Extract the precious metal directly from mines,' he said. The Shogun asked him who had the expertise needed to survey the land and operate the mines. Okubo said if he was appointed commissioner of mines, he'd arrange everything. Having nothing to lose, the Shogun granted his request.

"The experts turned out to be foreigners, but when the gold started flowing in, no one raised an eyebrow . . . least of all the Shogun, who was busy with his campaigns.

"After the fall of Osaka Castle the Shogun had more time to pay attention to the mines. An investigation turned up evidence of massive embezzlement. In addition it was discovered that Okubo was a Christian. He was arrested and imprisoned, but despite the most drastic measures, he has remained silent. The whereabouts of the missing gold is still a mystery."

"How much was taken?" Jubei asked.

"Enough to cause us serious problems if it falls into the wrong hands. But the more significant question is, Why? Here's a man who rose from the ranks of an outcast to an important government position. It was more than any actor could ever dream of, yet he went ahead and risked everything. For what?"

"Greed?" Jubei suggested.

"There's no indication that he spent any of it on himself."

"Then why?"

"That's the question we want you to answer. After I go, you'll be put in a cell with Okubo. Befriend him and win his confidence"—Takuan pressed a small medicine packet into Jubei's hand—"then save his life."

"Is he sick?"

"Not yet. But soon we'll start feeding him a slow-acting poison. When he's hanging by a thread, give him this antidote. I suspect he'll be grateful."

"Do you really think he's going to be grateful enough to tell me what you want to know?" Jubei asked skeptically.

"Of course not. That's why we're going to let you both

escape. With a lot of luck and a little trust, he may lead you to the answers."

From down the hallway came the sound of footsteps. Takuan looped his prayer beads over his hands and began chanting a sutra. The guards waited impatiently for the monk to finish praying. For their benefit, and Jubei's amusement, Takuan launched a passionate tirade against the evils of crime, then limped off shaking his head and muttering about the sad state of today's youth.

8

Hirado
Year of the Monkey—1632
Hour of the Horse

The whores on the streets of Hirado were like none Jan Kriek had seen anywhere in the world. They were clean. The fine white powder on their faces and necks had been applied judiciously, not caked on in layers to cover dirt and defects like the whores of Europe and Macao. Their lips were painted the color of spring apples and looked delicious when they were moist. Most sat in open windows behind wooden grilles, waiting for sailors to approach them. Not one stared or called out as he and his chief mate passed by. Women walking on the street kept their eyes downcast, their wooden sandals slapping out a rapid beat as they hurried along, intent on getting wherever they were going.

"So you thought old Troxie was spinnin' out stretchers when he told you about these Jappo women, did you?" When Troxie laughed, his breath smelled of stale beer, dried herring, and tooth decay. "Just wait till you get yer hands on one of them toy women. They got skin so soft it'll make you weep!"

Troxie snatched off his stocking cap, swept it under his arm, and aimed an elaborate bow at a girl in one of the windows. "The name's Johann Troxell," he bellowed. "Chief mate on the foulest garbage scow in the Dutch fleet, at your service." His performance was greeted with a look of curiosity mingled with disbelief. "Stay right where you are," he told her. "Soon as I get this gut full of good Dutch cookin' I'll be back for you." Troxie slapped his belly and roared with laughter. Below his bulbous nose a heavy mustache jiggled up and down, dislodging tiny pieces of leftovers from his morning meal.

He grabbed Kriek by the arm and dragged him off toward Piet Brock's Grog Haus. "I swear I been doin' nothin' but dreamin' of Ou Brock's stew since we left Macao. Big chunks of meat swimmin' in a sea of honest-to-God Dutch grease!"

The pungent smell of simmering meat saturated the air outside Piet Brock's. Inside, a couple of sailors were hunched over bowls stuffing food in with both hands. At one table another sailor was lying face down in his own dish. A fat baldheaded man stood over him cursing as he dumped a pail of water on his head. "Pigs!" he shrieked. "I tell you to go easy on the meat, but nobody listens. This is a grog house, not a ship's head, you bunch of saltwater vermin!"

"Kill the bastard!" Troxie pointed at the fat man. "Ou Brock's poisonin' the crew."

"Troxie? Johann Troxell?" Brock screwed his face into a myopic squint.

"Chief Mate Troxell to you, you landlocked heap of whale blubber."

The old shipmates embraced, then held each other at arm's length.

"Chief mate, is it?" Ou Brock said, holding Troxie at arm's length. "What did you do, spread your pink cheeks for the captain?"

Troxie clapped Kriek on the back and choked out a guffaw. "Listen to the old slug. When I took him under my wing he didn't know enough to piss off the stern. Why, the only reason Ou Brock signed up as ship's cook was he was such a lousy cook he couldn't hold down a job anywhere in Amsterdam. Ain't that so, Brock?" He didn't wait for an answer. "Never seen anybody hated the sea more than Ou Brock. It was cook and puke, cook and puke all the way to Japan. Soon as he got on dry land he swore he'd never set foot on the deck of another ship, even if it meant spendin' the rest of his life among the heathen. Ain't that right, Brock?"

Troxie kept up the good-natured banter between mouthfuls of stew and mugs of Ou Brock's grog, until he had drunk himself into a stupor. Then Kriek slipped out to find the Inn of Eternal Blossoms. According to the Father Vicar's instructions, this was where he would find a Christian woman named Oman who could help smuggle him out of Hirado. How, he didn't know. Considering the security around the island, whatever method she used would have to be ingenious.

The island was small, so it wasn't long before Kriek found the inn he was looking for. Like most Japanese structures, it was a depressing shade of gray. Over the front door there was a *noren*—a dark blue curtain hanging down to about waist height. It was split in the middle, with bold white characters on each side advertising the name of the inn. Next to the entrance, in a tiny room just large enough to accommodate a single reed tatami, a young woman in an elaborate kimono knelt behind a wooden grille, smiling demurely at passersby. A couple of Japanese tradesmen stopped to chat with her, but out of fear of the pox, no Japanese was permitted to patronize a Hirado whore. A sailor dressed like an Englishman came out muttering phrases of butchered Japanese to a woman who kept smiling and bowing as he staggered off down the street.

Kriek crossed the street and went inside. He was immediately greeted by a woman of indeterminate age who politely, but firmly, whisked him into another room, where two other women stripped him of his clothes so quickly and efficiently that he barely had time to voice a protest. It didn't matter. They weren't listening anyway. While he was busy covering his private parts, they were busy removing his boots. As soon as that was done, he was drenched with a bucket of hot water, and the bathing got under way. Kriek decided it was useless to resist. This is Japan, not Portugal, he reminded himself as he stepped into the deep tub of steaming water. He closed his eyes and felt his body loosen as they scrubbed and rescrubbed his hair.

Somewhere in another part of the inn he could hear the plaintive plucking of a strange-sounding stringed instrument. *"Kore wa nan desuka?"* he asked, pointing to his ear. It had been a long time since he'd spoken any Japanese, and he wondered how he sounded.

"The music?" one of the attendants asked.

"*Hai*," he said, pleased that he'd been understood.

"It's the *shamisen*," she responded. "Do you like it?"

"Very much." He didn't know if the woman playing the three-stringed instrument was good or not, but there was such intimate sorrow in her fingers that he felt her loneliness like his own. Memories of Maria returned again to torment him.

Now that they had him in the bath, the two women left him to soak. After a year of being crammed into close quarters with his shipmates, the luxury of this moment of privacy bordered on ecstasy. The tension melted away like snow in a spring thaw. Danger seemed far away.

After a while one of the attendants returned and began drying his hair. When she finished, she waited patiently for him to get out of the tub. He was dried and given a fresh-smelling cotton kimono to wear. This time the woman's ministrations caused him no embarrassment. He asked for a razor and shaved the stubble off his face.

The young woman he'd seen kneeling behind the grille came into the room and asked if she could serve him sake. Kriek accepted with a nod, and she showed him to another room. She kneeled by the shoji screen and slid it open, revealing a room that was bare except for two paper lanterns, a wall hanging with a poem inscribed on it, and a simple flower arrangement. She poured his sake and waited for him to drink.

Kriek studied the young woman's face. She was wearing a light dusting of white powder and her eyebrows had been shaved, the two inked swatches painted high on her forehead as replacements, giving her an expression of perpetual surprise. She wore her hair piled up and fastened in the back with two stays resembling ornate chopsticks. Her full lips were redrawn in crimson to make them appear thinner. Kneeling by his side, she filled his cup the moment it ran dry.

Kriek drank several cups and tried to think of something to say. Sensing his discomfort, the young woman spoke first. "I am told that you enjoy the *shamisen*. Would you like me to play for you?"

"Please . . . *dozo*," Kriek said quickly, then before she

reached the door he asked, "Is there a woman here named Oman?"

Her eyes widened, and she hurried out without answering.

A few minutes later an older woman whom Kriek took to be the proprietress of the inn came into the room. "You are looking for Oman?" she asked with an expression full of reproof.

"Yes, I was told she works at this inn."

"Do you know her?"

"We met briefly," he lied, "the last time I was in Hirado."

"Oman no longer works here," she said curtly.

"Then perhaps you can tell me where I can find her."

"I'm sorry, I don't know."

Something in the way she'd answered him told Kriek that she *did* know, but the information was not going to come cheap. He politely offered to pay if she could find out where Oman had gone. But to his surprise her refusal was as close to an insult as any Japanese woman would dare attempt with a man.

"I'm sorry," she said, "but a bath and sake is all we can offer you this evening. We are so busy. . . ." She bowed abruptly and left the room.

Kriek began to feel desperate. Without help from Oman, finding a way to get to Nagasaki was going to be next to impossible. The Jesuit mission just a few leagues across the bay might as well be on another planet.

The storefront woman brought him his clothes. Kriek held out his cup for more sake, to see what would happen. Real anxiety showed on her face, but she filled his cup anyway before starting to leave.

"Wait," Kriek commanded.

The woman turned. "Please, I must go," she pleaded.

"Not until I finish my sake. I paid for it, and I intend to drink it—all of it." He motioned for her to take her place by his side. Although she looked miserable, she did what she was told.

Kriek picked up the flask of sake and held it out to her, knowing it would be unpardonably rude for her to refuse to drink with him. He poured, and she drank, then he poured again.

"Why am I unwelcome here?" he asked bluntly.

"Didn't Mama explain?" she said, using the sailors' name for the woman who supervised the girls.

"She did, but it wasn't the truth."

"Oh," she sighed. "Maybe I should call her?"

Kriek clamped his hand on her arm. "Stay where you are." The woman looked terrified. "Don't be afraid," he said gently. "I'm not going to cause any trouble for you." He filled her cup again. "You knew Oman, didn't you?"

The woman looked down and said nothing.

"I must see her. It is truly urgent, and I'm willing to pay if you'll help me find her."

The woman looked at Kriek, then glanced toward the door and back to him again. "Excuse me, but Oman must have left before I came to work here." While she spoke, she gestured toward the door, indicating Mama was listening.

Kriek nodded, indicating he understood. He drained the last of the sake, then said, "Hand me my clothes. If I can't stay here, I'll have to find someplace else to spend my money." He took the clothes, reached into his trouser pocket, and took out a handful of silver coins, one of which he pressed into her hand.

As she helped him dress, she whispered in his ear, "Oman is among the *Eta.*"

He was about to question her when the screen slid open. The proprietress smiled at Kriek. "Please come again," she cooed sweetly, as if he had been the model patron.

The storefront woman followed him out into the street. When Kriek bent down to pull on his boots, she whispered, "Meet me here tomorrow at dawn. I'll take you to Oman." Then she went inside and took her place behind the grille.

In the shadows across the street a baleful-looking samurai was watching him. Kriek made a show of weaving down the street. He didn't look back, but he knew he was being followed. When he turned the corner, he ducked into an alley and crouched behind a stack of sake barrels. The samurai hurried past. Kriek waited a few minutes, then stepped out into the street and was almost knocked over by Troxie.

Troxie threw his arm around Kriek's shoulder. "I've been looking all over for you. What's the idea of doing your whorin' without me?"

"Looked to me like you were more interested in sleeping

off the schnapps than womanizing, so I took matters into my own hands, so to speak."

Troxie slapped him on the back. "Well, my boy, was it worth the wait?"

"Maybe you ought to ask those three girls back at the inn."

"Three!" Troxie boomed out. "Three is all you could handle after a year at sea?" Troxie dragged him off down the street. "It's time we got down to some serious whorin'."

Troxie took him to a place where he claimed his sexual prowess was legendary. Before they went inside, he stopped Kriek and asked if he'd really been with three women. Troxie looked worried.

Kriek shook his head sadly and held up one finger. "I just didn't want you to be ashamed of me." It was obvious from the relief on Troxie's face that he'd said the right thing.

"Well, my boy, don't let it worry you. You're still young." Troxie grinned. He had started the voyage with a molar, an incisor, and a dog tooth. One year and eleven days later only the incisor had survived. He was worried that he had lost his looks.

A half hour after the drinking started, Troxie passed out again. Kriek left him on the floor and went to his room. The women who had been serving them spread out a futon on the floor. Kriek flopped down on the bedding and pretended to be hopelessly drunk. The woman waited until he began to snore, then she slipped out of the room. Kriek said his prayers and tried to fall asleep while the sound of lovemaking permeated the paper walls. Sleep was a long time coming.

Just before dawn Kriek left the inn and went to the corner to wait for the storefront woman to join him. When she arrived, Kriek couldn't believe it was the same person. Without her makeup she looked to be barely more than a child. She identified herself as Tomi, explaining that Oman was her friend. They had both come to Hirado from the island of Oyano, near Shimabara.

The *Eta* section of Hirado was the junkyard of Japanese society. In sharp contrast to the fastidiously neat structures that formed the heart of the city, the nameless *Eta* lived in dilapidated hovels slammed tight together to conserve every scrap of lumber. The less fortunate slept in the streets and alleys, finding shelter where they could when the weather turned bad. The air was foul with the stench of rotting animal flesh, their skins stretched and drying in the sun. The *Eta* existed to deal with death. Since touching a dead animal was taboo for a Japanese of any rank, the disposal of carcasses was left to buzzards, crows, worms, insects, and *Eta*. Leather goods, made from the skins they collected, constituted their sole source of outside income. The *Eta* were total outcasts, doomed by birth to live as non-humans. There was no way out.

They found Oman lying in an alleyway, her face hidden under a tattered rag that had been stretched out over a drying pole to make a patch of shade. Her shabby kimono had worked up to her thighs, revealing two painfully thin legs caked in filth and stained with dried menstrual flow. A swarm of blowflies pumped and sucked at the open sores on her swollen ankles.

"This is Oman?" he asked, unable to believe that someone so young could look so old.

"*Hai*," Tomi rasped.

Kriek kneeled down and pulled the hem of her kimono over her knees. She did not stir. "Oman," he said softly. "I'm a priest."

When she did not respond, he drew back the rag that partly covered her face. Her mouth was open, her breathing quick and labored. The dark tongue that protruded between her teeth was too large for her mouth. Several flies were feeding on the viscid discharge around her eyes. Kriek used the rag to wipe her face.

When she opened her eyes, she searched his face like a person trying to adjust to a bright light after a long time in darkness. She tried to form a word, and it came out thick and dry, like water being sucked down a drain.

"Rest now, daughter," he said to her. "Don't try to talk."

"Padre," she muttered, gaining some control of her swollen tongue.

Kriek made the sign of the cross over her, saying, "*In nomine Patras, et Fili* . . ."

Oman grabbed his hand. "No!" she rasped. "Stop." There was fear in her eyes.

"Oman," he said gently, "you are dying, I want to give you the last rites of the Church."

"No . . . please," she pleaded. "I am afraid."

"Don't be afraid. Our Lord taught us there is nothing to fear from death."

"Not death . . . I want to die," she said.

"Then what do you fear?"

Oman gazed at him, gathering her strength. "I fear . . ." She fought for a breath. "I fear your god."

"But there's nothing to fear from God. All of us have sinned against God. Just ask His forgiveness and your sins will be washed away."

"I have not sinned against God. God has sinned against me."

"I don't understand . . ."

"I took your god . . . into my heart. My father sold me. . . . Still I loved God." She closed her eyes, and when she opened them again, they seemed to glow with an inner light. "I helped the padres . . . and I was caught. . . . I prayed to God, and told them nothing. In prison the Chinese pox wrecked my body. . . . Still I loved God. One day they came and told me that a padre I had helped . . . betrayed me. I was sent to live as *Eta*. I will die *Eta*, but I will not die Christian. . . . Your god is too cruel."

"God is not cruel. It is life that is cruel," he said with deep conviction. "God loves you."

"Have you suffered, Padre?" she asked.

"Not the way you have."

"When you have . . . then speak to me of God's love." Like a lantern that had run out of oil, the light in her eyes sputtered, then faded to nothing.

Kriek placed the dirty rag over her face, and recited a prayer for the dead.

Troxie was standing a few feet behind him, listening to Kriek's Latin, unbelieving. He might have killed him on the spot if he'd been able to comprehend the enormity of his friend's treachery without asking for some kind of explanation.

"You! Jan Kriek!" he called out.

Kriek's fingers froze at his forehead. With agonizing control he finished making the sign of the cross.

"Face me, you Papist bastard!" Troxie yelled.

Kriek turned. Troxie's face was red and full of hatred. "She was a Christian," Kriek explained in the most matter-of-fact tone he could muster.

"And you're a God-cursed Papist spy. Can you deny that?" he snarled.

Kriek's mind was racing through lie after lie, but something told him it was going to be futile. Troxie knew what he had seen. Any attempt to compound the deception with another deception could only make a bad situation worse.

"I'm not a spy," he said, deciding to let Troxie steer the course of the confrontation.

"Not a spy!" he laughed derisively. "Maybe you prefer *traitor* then?"

"Does worshiping God in a way that's different from you make me a traitor?"

"It does when Papists sink Dutch ships and kill honest Dutch sailors."

A small crowd had started to gather to watch the spectacle unfold.

"What are you going to do?" Kriek asked.

Troxie fingered the hilt of his knife. "I've got to kill you."

Kriek said nothing. He sensed that Troxie was looking for anything that would overcome his affection for him and fuel his resolution to go through with his threat.

"Are you a priest?" Troxie asked.

"I'm a Catholic."

"Those were a priest's words you were spoutin'!"

"I swear I'm not a spy."

Troxie squinted at Kriek. "Whatever you are, the only thing I'm sure of is you're a liar . . . and a damned good one."

Troxie pulled his knife and started for him. Kriek waited for him to come close, then dove at his feet, knocking him over. As Kriek tried to scramble to his feet, Troxie snatched one of his ankles and brought him down. They rolled in the dirt and Troxie came up on top. Putting all his weight behind the hilt of his knife, Troxie began to press the blade down toward Kriek's chest. Just as the point touched his skin, Kriek saw Troxie's eyes bulge and heard him gasp. The knife dropped out of his hands and he went limp.

Kriek rolled Troxie off his chest. A dagger was sticking out of his kidney. Tomi was staring down at him, a look of horror on her face. The crowd had become noisy. They were screaming and shouting and pointing their fingers at her.

Kriek grabbed Tomi by the hand and pushed his way

through the crowd. Looking over the heads of the people around him, he could see that the clamor had attracted the attention of two samurai standing guard at the gate that led out of the *Eta* section. He veered down a side street, and the crowd followed after them, shouting and gesturing to the samurai, who were trotting toward the commotion.

Kriek tried to pick up the pace, but Tomi's legs, trapped inside her kimono, made speed impossible. But the crowd was growing, providing a buffer between them and the samurai.

They wove their way through side streets and narrow alleyways. The tight confines thinned out the crowd, but each time Kriek glanced over his shoulder, there was always someone following close on their heels. His clothing and towering height made it impossible for him to evade detection. Wherever he went, the *Eta* stopped and stared at the curious foreign *yabanjin* dragging a young woman along after him.

Kriek kept moving, elbowing his way through the packed streets of the *Eta* fish market until he came to the edge of a cliff that overlooked Nagasaki Bay. Now that the *yabanjin* and his woman had no place to go, the mob that had been trailing behind stopped, formed a half-circle around them, and waited in a high state of excitement to see what would happen when the samurai caught up.

Kriek looked down at the water below. It was a long drop from the cliff to the bay, and there were great rocks jutting up out of the foam. He turned to Tomi, whose frantic eyes told him that she already knew what he was contemplating.

"I can't . . ." she gasped, clinging tightly to his arm.

"Tomi, you know what will happen if they take you."

She nodded. For her it had come down to a simple choice. Die at the hands of the *bakufu* or leap off the cliff to an almost certain death. The ghastly dilemma paralyzed her will.

The first of the two samurai broke through the crowd and drew his long sword.

"Jump!" Kriek yelled at Tomi. When she hesitated, he gripped her arm and leapt off the cliff, pulling her with him.

Kriek's aim was good. They hit a spot between two large rocks, and fortunately for them the water there was deep. However, the concussion jarred his hand loose, and when he came up he saw that Tomi was foundering. He caught a handful of her long hair and dragged her behind one of the tall boulders.

"Are you all right?" he asked.

"*Hai,*" she sputtered gamely.

With Tomi clinging to his neck, Kriek worked his way from rock to rock, careful to keep out of sight of the crowd gathered at the edge of the cliff. When he was sure they were far enough away to escape from the water undetected, he swam ashore. There they came across a small crevice in the cliffside. Tomi stripped down to her rose-colored undergown and laid her water-soaked outer kimono in the sun to dry. She twisted her hair like a length of dark cloth, then squeezed into the crevice beside him.

"I'm sorry I involved you in this," he told her.

"I'm a Christian too," she said. "I'm glad I was able to help you. But I'm frightened, and I want to go home."

Kriek was soaking wet too, but he wrapped his arm around her to share what body warmth he had. "I'll do my best to get you there," he promised, knowing in his heart he had no idea how he was going to keep the promise. He sat quietly and prayed for a miracle.

They hadn't been there long when a young *Eta* woman carrying a market basket heavy with fish and vegetables came down the beach and stopped at the water's edge. She lifted the brim of her straw hat and peered out at the bay. Kriek could see that she was watching a small fishing boat tack into the cove.

The woman tied up her ragged kimono and waded out to help beach the boat. She put her basket down and the fisherman got out and took her in his arms. They talked briefly, then went off down the beach together and disappeared among the rocks.

"Ask and ye shall receive," Kriek said happily.

The beach was deserted. He was making up his mind whether to make a dash for the boat or move out cautiously, when Tomi pointed out two men coming down the beach. He pressed his body back into the crevice, making himself as small as possible as he watched the men trot up to the boat and look it over. The older man said something that sounded angry, but Kriek couldn't make it out. Then they began following the couple's footprints down the beach.

"The young fisherman is with an *Eta* girl," Tomi whispered. "There's going to be trouble."

"Let's go," Kriek said, taking her hand. Crouching low, they ran for the boat. He put his shoulder to the prow and heaved. The boat eased out a few feet. "Get in," he told her. Another push and he had the boat floating free.

"They're coming!" Tomi warned him.

He looked back and saw three men racing toward him. Kriek gave a mighty shove and the boat shot away from him. Half swimming, half wading, he finally managed to grab onto the gunwales and scramble aboard just as their pursuers reached the water's edge. Using the oar as a pole, Kriek pushed off for deeper water.

The lead swimmer was strong, and he was closing fast. Kriek leaned into the pole, but the gap between them was narrowing. Another push. A hand flashed out of the water, snatching at the oar and barely missing. Seized by a rush of panic, Kriek swung the oar over his head and slammed it down on the swimmer. The impact was heavy and solid. Kriek saw the swimmer's arms stop flailing and watched his body slide below the surface of the water.

He stood still, peering at the spot where the swimmer had gone down. A sudden sense of his own capacity for violence filled him with self-loathing. He realized that in a moment of panic all his priestly ideals failed him and his instincts had become those of a cornered rat. But worst of all he knew that the instant he'd struck, he had meant to kill.

"Padre!" Tomi alerted him as the other swimmers drew closer. Getting no reaction at all, Tomi grabbed the oar out of Kriek's hands and started paddling furiously for deeper water.

Kriek was just about to plunge in the water when he noticed that the others had given up the chase and were diving at the spot where the injured man had disappeared from sight. Since it was fairly shallow there, the divers were able to locate him without much difficulty.

Kriek took heart and turned his attention to rigging the sail. As soon as the unfurled sail caught the breeze and bellied out, Kriek looked back at the shore. To his immense relief he could see that the man he hit was crouched on his knees, coughing up seawater.

A small crowd had gathered around him. One of the fishermen pointed at the boat, and several men ran off down the beach. It was clear to Kriek that they were going for another boat to resume the chase. Soon he would have to find out just how good a sailor he had become.

Nagasaki seemed far, far away.

By late afternoon they were still trailing him, about fifteen hundred yards astern, matching him tack for tack and gaining. The pursuit boat was carrying a little more sail, and Kriek knew if he broke for the mainland he'd get there just a few minutes ahead of them. Once on land where could he run? Where could he hide?

So, with no tenable plan in mind, he held his course. He was running due south, parallel to the coast. Off the port side Tomi pointed out the mountain peaks of Kyushu, tall and elegant, running down the length of the coast like exposed vertebrae. Among the many fishing boats he spotted one larger vessel of an unusual cut, propelled by ten oars that protruded from her sides like legs on a waterbug. She moved steadily, if not gracefully, to the rhythm of a bare-chested drummer. Tomi identified her as a Tokugawa ship. Watching her lumber along, it wasn't hard to understand why Japan had never become a sea power.

It took only a second for the idea to gel. If what he had heard about the Japanese dread of the open sea was true, he had a chance. The wind was blowing out to sea, steady and strong. Kriek jerked the rudder hard, swinging the small craft into the wind, to make them think he was making for land. As soon as they duplicated his tack, he jerked the rudder hard alee, spinning her around one hundred and eighty degrees. The sail emptied, lufted momentarily, then took the full force of the wind. The wind hit harder than Kriek had expected. He heard a heavy crack as the boat lurched ahead, and the mast pitched forward. The wooden support at the base of the mast had split, but was holding. He was running with the wind now, the speed rattling every seam in the boat, threatening to shake her apart.

Kriek glanced over his shoulder. The other boat was just coming about. The maneuver had been costly, but he'd managed to gain some valuable time. The damage to the mast had impaired his maneuverability. He knew that if they kept coming, sooner or later they'd have him. It all turned on how far they were willing to chase him, and whether or not the damaged mast could take the strain.

The sun, huge and red, was sitting on the rim of the ocean. Kriek aimed the prow directly into the sun, locking the tiller under his arm. His mouth was parched and his stomach empty. When he looked back, they were still coming.

He kept his eyes on the sun as it slid slowly into the sea, pulling the twilight in behind it. After it disappeared, a crimson wash splashed across the horizon and darkness hovered overhead. Soon he'd have the night as an ally.

The pursuit boat was close enough for Tomi to make out the features of the men who manned her. Two of them were carrying spearlike *naginatas*. Another was fitting an arrow into a bow. The archer stood in the prow and drew a bead on Kriek's back.

"Get down!" Tomi shouted.

Kriek ducked just as the arrow whistled over his head and pierced the sail. He kept his head down and watched the wind widen the hole into a rip. The bigger it got, the more speed he would lose. He knew it wouldn't be long before they overtook him.

"Look!" Tomi cried out.

Kriek turned and saw the pursuit boat starting to come about.

"They turned back!" he shouted, then closed his eyes and gave thanks to God for Japanese fear of the open sea.

As he was praying, a sudden gust of wind split the canvas sail end to end. The tip of the spar dropped into the water, throwing Kriek forward against the mast, shattering the damaged supports. The mast groaned and toppled into the sea.

Recovering his balance, Kriek realized that Tomi had fallen overboard. She'd grabbed the spar and hung on. Quickly he pulled her back into the boat.

Although he said nothing to her, his hopes had collapsed with the mast. Miles from shore, adrift in a vast sea with no fresh water and half a pail of fish chum, Kriek pondered his fate. Perhaps this was God's punishment for striking out at the fisherman, he thought. Yet he could not make himself believe he was destined to die in senseless anonymity on a fishing boat in a foreign sea. Had God created him and shaped his life for this? It seemed ridiculous. More than that, it was ugly. Adversity, pain, suffering, and death in all its ingenious forms could be borne so long as it contained a shred of meaning. He could accept being struck down, dashed to pieces in a fit of divine rage. But this! This was divine indifference.

While Kriek agonized, Tomi sat by the jagged stump of the mast, quietly preparing herself for the ordeal that lay ahead. Unlike Kriek, she felt neither bitterness nor remorse. This was just one more moment inside a lifetime of shapeless moments that came from someplace over the horizon. Tomi took one of the bait fish out of the bucket and opened it with her fingernails. She smiled and offered a piece to Kriek. Her smile made him feel ashamed.

The night became thick with clouds. Not a single star was visible to gauge the drift of the boat. All he knew was that the current was taking them somewhere—or nowhere.

After five days at sea Kriek's boat had drifted just a few leagues away from where the Black Ship was standing at anchor. Under orders from the Father General, Captain Francisco Nunes was waiting for Lord Arima to rendezvous with the ship and take his daughter back to her home. Nunes's patience was beginning to wear thin. For the third night in a row a dinghy had left the Black Ship at dusk to cruise along the coastline off Shimabara Peninsula, flashing a prearranged recognition signal to alert Lord Arima that his daughter had returned. A few hours before first light the dinghy returned, and for the third time there had been no response to the signals.

With each passing night Maria's disappointment was becoming more difficult to suppress. To make matters worse, the captain's resentment over her presence on board his ship was rapidly turning into open hostility. So when he came to her cabin to report what she already knew, Maria was prepared for the worst.

"My lady," he said in more solicitous Japanese than she was used to hearing from him, "our efforts to make contact with your father appear to be futile."

"Three days is such a short time to begin to speak of futility," she said.

Nunes stroked his goatee, drawing the skin on his cadaverous face tighter against the bone. "I must remind you that there is a limited amount of time I can spend in this endeavor. My primary mission is, as you know, commerce. In the trading business, loss of time is loss of money."

"Is my life to be measured in terms of Portuguese profits?"

"Perhaps the question of how your life is to be measured should be addressed to your father," he replied with an unfriendly smile. "Each night we've sent a Portuguese boat into waters forbidden to us, for the sole purpose of informing your father of your return. Each night our efforts are ignored."

The insult to her father stung, but unlike her Portuguese hosts, she knew how to conceal her emotions. "My father is a cautious man. The risk could be too great at this time."

"Risk? You speak to me of risk? Need I remind you of the dire consequences to the tenuous relations between our two countries if a Portuguese boat is seen navigating in these waters? It seems to me it may be time for *me* to exercise some caution and proceed directly to Nagasaki harbor."

"And how would you explain my presence on the Black Ship to the *bakufu*?"

The captain glared at her. "Suppose we set you adrift before we entered the harbor?"

"In a Portuguese boat?"

"That would present problems, of course," he said, turning away to hide his embarrassment. "The point is," he continued, "this farce cannot go on indefinitely."

Maria thought it might be a good idea to try to relieve some of the pressure. "I appreciate what you are doing for me. I am sure you won't have to wait much longer."

"We cannot wait much longer. Tomorrow night we will make one last run. If we're unsuccessful this time, I'll order the Black Ship into port."

"And what will you do about me?" she asked.

"My duty to my Church and country come before all other considerations."

Maria felt her stomach tighten. She detected a trace of pleasure in Nunes's pig eyes as he voiced his thinly veiled threat. "You haven't answered my question," she said.

The captain studied her perfectly composed face for some indication of strain. It annoyed him when he found none. "Perhaps I'll think of one by tomorrow night," he replied.

After he left, Maria stepped out on deck. The night air was warm and moist. Just over the horizon was Japan—so close, she thought. Closing her eyes, she tried to imagine the fragrant aroma of pine and water lilies and spring rice and freshly turned earth; the sound of frogs and crows and children playing.

The deck was cluttered with crewmen rigging the sails for the predawn run out to sea. Usually she went back to her cabin before the work began and stayed there until night fell. This time she lingered and was subjected to some lewd gestures from one of the deckhands. She turned away. The morning sea had a golden glow. Off in the distance a dark fleck on the water caught her eye. As it drew nearer, she recognized the silhouette of a small Japanese fishing boat.

Maria rushed to the foc'sle, where she found the captain chatting with one of the ship's officers. "Excuse me, sir," she interrupted. Nunes took his time acknowledging her. She pointed off the starboard bow. "There is a fishing boat over there."

The captain squinted. "I see nothing."

"Please, use your spyglass," she insisted.

With infuriating deliberateness he removed his collapsible telescope from its case and peered off in the direction she had indicated.

"So it is . . . so it is," he said, studying the craft.

"Can you see an Arima crest on the boat?" Maria made no attempt to mask her excitement.

"I'm sorry to disappoint you, my lady, but there seems to be no one aboard."

"May I see?"

The captain handed her the spyglass. It was true. The boat was empty. It had probably broken loose from its moorings and drifted out to sea. But where was the mast?

Captain Nunes was preoccupied getting the Black Ship under way, so Maria continued to observe the small boat. As the sky lightened, she thought she saw something move. The longer she watched, the more convinced she became that the boat was not empty. There seemed to be someone lying on its deck.

"Look, Captain," she said, handing him the glass. "I think there may be someone in that boat."

Nunes looked again. This time he held the glass to his eye a long time. When he lowered it, he said to Maria, "You have a good eye. There are two people aboard."

"Where's the sail?" she asked.

"The poor fellows seem to have met with some sort of misfortune, and I'm afraid it's been lost."

Nunes replaced his glass in its holder and gave the order to sail. It took a few minutes for it to sink in. "Are you going to make no attempt to rescue them?" she asked.

"Why should I?"

"Have you considered the possibility that they might have been sent by my father?"

"I have. But I dismissed the possibility as unlikely." He yawned. "Now if you'll excuse me, I must get some sleep."

"Wait!"

Nunes arched one brow. "Are you issuing orders now?"

"I just want to remind you that your direct order from the Father General was to deliver me to my father, safely. As you've probably guessed, I am carrying secret instructions from the Father General. I can only tell you that you are placing yourself and your Church in great jeopardy by failing to carry out your instructions."

"And do my instructions include picking up every Japanese fisherman adrift in the sea?" Both his tone and look were venomous.

"If the men in that boat have come for me, and you let them die, another boat will not come for me before you sail into Nagasaki. I don't know what you plan to do with me, but this much is certain—if anything happens to me, you will answer for it . . . first to my father, then to the Father General."

Nunes slammed his fist into the rail. "Do you dare threaten *me*!" he shouted.

"It's the truth that threatens you, sir."

To vent his fury, he paced the deck. Finally he strode back to her and announced his decision. "I'll do as you ask," he said in a hoarse whisper, "but know this—if you're wrong, I'll set my course directly for Nagasaki. When I reach port you'll be confined below decks, and when I return to Lisbon, you will return with me. The Father General can decide what to do with you then." He turned away, gave the order, and the ship came about.

A dinghy was launched, and a line fastened to the fishing boat. The dinghy towed her alongside the Black Ship. One of the sailors called for a line, and a man's limp body was hoisted aboard. Nunes bent over him. "God's blood," he gasped, "it's the seminarian I left in Macao!"

It was the crew's opinion that the two survivors had drunk seawater and wouldn't last through the day. But by nightfall both of them were still alive. Tomi was being tended by the ship's doctor. Maria insisted on taking care of Kriek herself, and throughout the night continued to bathe his face and parched lips with water. There was only shallow breathing and faint heartbeat, and no other sign of life. Even when she placed the moistened napkin inside his mouth, Kriek did not respond. His jaw remained slack, his eyes closed.

Nunes stopped by to check on him, and told her to give up. "He reeks of death," was the way he put it. Maria understood that the captain viewed Kriek as just another problem that had to be dealt with if he managed to survive. She was determined to pull him through.

He had changed, she thought, staring at his face. It seemed bonier than before, making his angular features even more pronounced. She dabbed his lips with water. Kriek shuddered, and his jaw clamped tight on the napkin. Maria lifted his head and he swallowed once, then again.

"Jan-san," she said. "Jan-san, drink!"

Kriek opened his eyes, looked past her, and closed his eyes again. Maria wet the napkin and put it back in his mouth. Kriek swallowed.

When the ship's bell sounded the next watch change, Kriek's breathing had become deep and steady. The pitcher of water by her side was half empty, and he had managed to swallow at least one third of it. To keep awake, Maria began to sing an old song to herself. When she looked down at him, his eyes were open. This time she knew he was seeing her.

"You are safe now, Jan-san," she said as she wet the napkin and pressed it to his lips. "Just take some more water." Kriek sucked on the napkin. His eyes searched the dimly lit cabin— lighting here, then there, the way bees flit from flower to flower, sampling nectar. "You are on the Black Ship," Maria told him. "We found you drifting in a small fishing boat."

The last thing he could recall was the maddening thirst that finally drove him to plunge his head into the sea and drink. After that there was the nausea, and then . . . a junkpile of disjointed images. "Maria?" He reached out to touch her arm. Her skin felt fine and smooth. She was real.

"*Hai*," she answered. "I'm here."

"Where's Tomi?" he rasped. "The girl . . ."

"She's alive."

Kriek closed his eyes and drifted off to sleep.

"You, Father, I can bury among the crew," Captain Nunes said to Kriek. He pointed his bony finger in the direction of Maria's cabin. "But she and the other girl, that's a different matter. If the heathen search the ship, as they most likely will do, and find them aboard"—he shrugged—"how am I going to explain them away?"

Kriek continued sipping his bowl of bouillabaisse and did not look up.

"I cannot delay any longer," he went on. "Our provisions are running out and I have a mission to complete."

"So do I," Kriek said evenly.

"Your mission is over!" he shouted. "You failed. Need I remind you that your mission was to make passage on a Dutch ship, then infiltrate the mainland by way of Hirado. We both know the Father General never intended for you to come into Nagasaki on the Black Ship."

"The fact is, I'm here now," Kriek said. "It's God's will."

"If you are entertaining any misbegotten notions of jumping ship in Nagasaki, I swear before God that I'll have you put in irons."

"What did you do with the fishing boat?" Kriek asked.

"It's still tied alongside."

Kriek handed his empty bowl to the captain. "Have the ship's carpenter fit her out with a new mast, and I'll take both women off your hands."

"*Hmm* . . . You plan to sail to the mainland?"

Kriek nodded.

"Well," Nunes mused, "I can't say that I find the notion of getting rid of all of you unappealing."

"Under the cover of darkness there's a chance we could make it."

"And if you're caught?"

"Why would the captain of the Black Ship worry about the

capture of a renegade Dutch sailor?" Kriek asked with a wry smile.

"Why, indeed . . . but tell me, Dutchman, how do you intend to explain the presence of Lady Arima if you're caught?"

"How do you intend to explain her presence on the Black Ship if *you're* caught?"

Nunes fingered the point of his goatee a long time before he made up his mind.

"I'll see to it that your boat is ready at sunset," he said, realizing his options were non-existent.

"You want me to leave tonight?" Kriek had hoped for at least one more day to build up his strength.

"I sail for port at dawn. It seems to me that your chances would be better if you left at night, but if you prefer to rest until dawn, the choice is yours."

"We'll leave tonight," Kriek said.

9

Shimabara Bay
Year of the Monkey—1632
Hour of the Ox

All night they skirted the coastline, trying to pinpoint their location. Kriek was sure that he was well south of Nagasaki and guessed that he was navigating in Tachibana Bay. If the captain's hastily drawn map was anywhere near accurate, Hara Castle lay on the other side of the peninsula, in Shimabara Bay. Maria assured him that even at night it would be easy to spot. Her father's castle dominated the landscape overlooking the bay.

So far all they had seen were a few fishing villages which Maria found impossible to identify in the darkness. "Every-

thing looks so different from the sea," she told Kriek. "Even
in the daylight I think I'd have trouble recognizing things."

The calm night was clear and beautiful, but the lack of
wind was slowing them down. Kriek didn't want to be on the
water when dawn came, so he decided to chance leaving the
coastline to make a run across the mouth of the bay. Although
it meant losing sight of land, the time they would save would
be worth the risk.

The breeze was better farther out, and they were starting
to make up time. Maria was puzzled. "Jan-san, all the towns
and villages here are under my father's control. Anywhere we
put ashore will be safe for us. We don't have to sail directly to
Hara Castle."

"Maybe not. But remember, when you left the country was
in upheaval. In the two years you've been away the political
situation could have changed drastically. The sailors who
scouted the shore reported that there are patrol boats flying
the Tokugawa crest all along your father's coast. . . ." Kriek
paused. "I don't want to worry you, but it's possible that your
father is no longer in control of Shimabara."

"Tomi." Maria turned to the girl. "Have you heard anything?"

She shook her head. "Hirado is like another world. We get
no news from the mainland."

"Do you think that is why he didn't come for me?" Maria
asked Kriek.

"It's one possibility among many. Once we've located Hara
Castle, we'll sail on to the closest village. I'll find a secluded
spot to beach the boat and wait there while you go into the
village and assess the situation. If it's safe, we'll go straight to
your father."

Maria nodded. "Perhaps that's wise."

They sailed on. Kriek was becoming concerned that he'd
missed the tip of Shimabara Peninsula, when Maria spotted a
single light glowing in the darkness. Kriek changed course
and headed for the light. As they drew closer to land he
found a place to beach the boat not far from where they'd
seen what appeared to be a bright torch among the trees.

Kriek offered Maria his pistol. "Do you know how to use
this?" he asked.

"This is Japan, Jan-san. It's safe for a woman to go out at
night here."

"I know it's not Lisbon, but I'd still feel better if you took a weapon."

She patted the razor-sharp dagger all samurai women carried in their obi. "I've been trained in the use of the *kaiken*. Please don't worry about me."

Kriek glanced over at Tomi, who was fast asleep in the bow of the boat. "Maybe I should wake her."

"No," Maria said. "She's still weak from the ordeal. Let her sleep."

"Be careful," he cautioned her as she stepped ashore. "If you run into trouble, call out and I'll be there."

Maria walked off down the beach. At the sound of a heavy thud, she stopped short and listened. She thought she could hear the sound of a woman's voice. Moving closer, she heard another thud and caught a glimpse of illumination through the needles of a gnarled black pine. Cautiously she took a few steps into the trees. Although she could not make out what the woman was saying, it was clear from the rhythm of her speech that she wasn't conversing with anyone. It sounded more like an incantation.

Using the trees as cover, she worked herself into a position to get a view of the clearing. She saw a lone woman dressed entirely in white, her hair hanging loose down her back, a metal tripod holding three lighted candles on her head. The woman bent over a small shrine and picked up a thin metal object that looked like a large nail. In her right hand she held a heavy wooden mallet. Maria strained to hear what she was chanting, but the words the woman spoke were in a language Maria had never heard.

Next to the shrine, nailed to the trunk of a large tree, was a straw effigy draped in black. The woman went to the tree, lifted a circular mirror that hung around her neck, and held it up to the straw figure. Something guttural emerged from deep in her throat. From the poisonous tone of her voice, Maria assumed it was some kind of fearsome curse. The woman lifted her mallet and drove another nail into the effigy once, twice, three times. Then her shoulders slumped and she spoke in Japanese. "You can come out now," she said, without turning around. "I'm finished."

Maria stepped into the light, and the woman turned to face her. She seemed to be in her late twenties or early thirties, her face pale and shaped like an inverted teardrop. Beneath long, fine eyebrows, her narrow cat eyes were bright and dark and seemed to shine in the night.

"Who are you?" the woman asked in a tone that conveyed the exquisite boredom associated with ladies of high rank.

"My name is Kiku," Maria answered, using her childhood name.

"Why have you come to Yushima?"

"Yushima?" They had sailed well past the peninsula and come to an island on the other side of Shimabara Bay. "We were trying to find Hara Castle. It was dark. We lost our way."

The woman arched her elegant eyebrows. "We?"

"Yes, my boatman and my maid." She went on quickly. "We saw the glow from your headdress and came ashore to investigate. . . ."

The woman cocked her head slightly, and her lips parted in a wry smile. "How may I serve you, Lady Arima?"

Maria was stunned into silence.

"You've been gone a long time," the woman said. "I barely recognized you."

"I'm sorry . . ." Maria stammered. "Do I know you?"

"We met briefly in Kyoto. You knew me as Princess Yugiri, the wife of Prince Sanjo. Now I'm known as Rendai."

Rendai . . . the sorceress. A name evoked to frighten children. A name that spoke of dark magic, dreadful curses of awesome power . . . a name linked with the night, charging unlit rooms with inchoate fear. It was said that she had no legs and floated on air like a jellyfish on water. She was part man and part woman . . . or neither. She lived forever, dying each year at the autumn equinox in the Hour of the Ox, only to return again bearing new secrets and demands for redress from unavenged souls. Rendai spoke with the dead and saw the future. It was Rendai whom women called on when their honor had been compromised and there was no one else to turn to for revenge.

All her life Maria had heared tales of this priestess, only half believing. Now she was face to face with the legend. The fact that she walked on legs gave her small comfort.

"Excuse me." Maria bowed. "I was young and overwhelmed by the splendor of the Imperial Court."

"You are welcome here," Rendai said. "However, this is a sanctuary for women. Men are forbidden here. Your boatman must not set foot on this land. Go and warn him. I will wait here for your return."

Maria hurried back to the boat and told Kriek that she had met a woman who belonged to a class of diviners called *Ichiko*. It was not completely true, but how could she explain Rendai to a foreigner? Kriek sensed her apprehension and pressed for more details.

"There is nothing to fear," Maria said with as much conviction as she could. "I'm a woman. No harm will come to me."

"Then why are you afraid?"

Maria could not meet his gaze. "I'm afraid of the dark," she said softly, and started off toward the place where Rendai was waiting. Before she entered the woods, she called out to Kriek, "Remember—do not leave the boat!"

Rendai led her through the woods to the mouth of a cave. The sun was up and the rocks around the entrance to the cave were splotched with shadows. The opening was small, but inside, the candlelit cavern was spacious. At the far end a hearth fire burned.

They kneeled on a tatami mat next to the hearth and Rendai set about preparing tea. Watching her go through the familiar motions of making and serving tea had a soothing effect on Maria. Despite the imposing ambience in the cave, she felt her tension slip away.

"There are rumors that your father sent you to the Pope in Rome," Rendai commented, as if they were chatting across a garden wall.

"I have been to Portugal," she volunteered, not wanting to test a lie on Rendai. "I didn't go to see the Pope."

"Ah, is that so." She seemed disappointed.

"I am surprised to hear that my trip appears to be common knowledge."

"Gossip. Mere gossip. But it has placed your father in a most unfortunate position, *neh*?"

Maria decided to be as candid as possible. "I haven't seen my father. I was returning home when we lost our bearings."

"So you don't know what has transpired since you've been gone?"

Maria shook her head. "We thought it best to learn what we could about the state of affairs in my father's domain before attempting to enter the city."

"A prudent decision," Rendai said. "Your father is no longer

master of Hara Castle." Although Maria knew her father was
out of favor with the Shogun, the news of his eviction hit her
hard. "Lord Arima was transferred to Nobeoka, and now
Hara Castle is occupied by a Tokugawa retainer named
Matsukura. He's cut off the income of all the retainers your
father left behind. To survive they've been forced to work
the land with the farmers. The suffering is terrible. Matsukura
has set impossible production quotas. Farmers who fail to
meet the quotas are burned alive, and their women are
stripped naked and strung up by the ankles. The idea, I
suspect, is to break the back of Christianity in Shimabara.
Those who don't renounce their faith have their rice quotas lowered. The message is clear."

"If that is so, why was my father allowed to live? He's a
Christian."

"No longer," Rendai said. "He submitted to Tokugawa
pressure and performed the *fumie*."

"The *fumie*?" Maria gasped. "My father put his foot on the
image of the Virgin?"

"If he hadn't, your whole family would have paid the price.
You've lost most of your land, but at least you still have your
family name."

"I know my father is still a Christian in his heart." Maria
seemed on the verge of tears.

"Probably so," Rendai said. "But I'm sure you can see that
the return of a Christian daughter from the land of the Jesuits
is hardly an occasion for celebration."

"The *bakufu* knows I've been to Portugal?"

"I wouldn't say the government knows, but suspicion is
enough, *neh*?" Rendai refilled Maria's cup with tea. "In case
you're wondering, your father has not betrayed you."

Cold comfort; Maria's heart sank. She knew she could not
endanger her father's life by showing up with no plausible
reason for a two-year absence. There would be too many
questions she couldn't answer, and too many ways for the
bakufu to check out any fabricated story.

Rendai seemed to read her thoughts. "You are in an ugly
situation, Lady Arima. It looks as though you can neither go
out nor come in."

Maria lifted the tea to her lips and sipped. "The tea is
poignant," she said to Rendai. "It is bitter . . . and refreshing."

"It is Japan," said Rendai.

From somewhere in the depths of the cave came the sound of a lusty wail, metallic and insistent. Rendai excused herself and a few minutes later returned with a child at her breast. She cradled the boy in her arm while he suckled. "This is my son," she said.

Maria reached out and touched his dark hair. In profile, his face was astoundingly beautiful. Yet there was something strange about his beauty. He looked to be about two—old enough to be weaned—but when she looked closer, she saw that he had the features of a much older child. Although his cheeks were full, they were not fat, and the back of his head was not as flat as it should have been at that age.

"He's extraordinary," she said, carefully choosing the precise word.

"His name is Shiro." She drew the character *shi* in the air. To Maria's surprise, Rendai had chosen to represent the sound *shi* with the letter meaning 4—an unlucky number associated with death. "He's the reason you're here."

"What?" Maria blurted out.

"It's no accident that you came to this island when you did. It's karma. Your destiny and the destiny of my son are bound together. At first I didn't understand. Now it's becoming clearer to me."

"Will you explain it to me?"

Rendai's jaw set and her face darkened from within. "One afternoon my husband told me that it was time I bore a child. He invited me to join him in his chambers that evening. Although I had come to despise him, I was overjoyed by the prospect of motherhood. I dosed myself with fertility herbs, put on my finest kimono, and went to him at the appointed hour. Seated beside him was a padre. . . ." Rendai closed her eyes for a moment, then began again. "He was robed in black and I remember feeling like a wounded mouse under the gaze of a hungry crow.

"I served sake while they continued a discussion of politics and guns that had begun earlier that day. Suddenly my husband turned to me and asked for my *kaiken*. After I gave him my weapon, he ordered me to disrobe. I begged him not to shame me, but he only became angry and more forceful. I did as I was told, keeping my eyes closed against the humiliation. Without warning I was dragged down on the mat. My husband held my arms while the padre raped me."

Rendai paused to dab away the perspiration that had formed on her face.

Now Maria understood the effigy in black she saw nailed to the pine. It was surely the padre who had fathered her child.

"When I got pregnant, I ran away to this island. Because of my royal blood, I was chosen to learn the sacred mysteries and assume the position as chief priestess of the *Ichiko*."

Maria knew very little about this mysterious band of women. She knew they studied the dark arts and were reputed to have relinquished their bodies to evil demons who rewarded the gift by investing the *Ichiko* with preternatural knowledge and power. And she knew that she feared them.

"So you are not alone." Maria said, resisting the urge to peek over her shoulder.

"No, there are others here. All women . . . except, of course, my son." Rendai clutched Maria's arm. "Take him with you. Let the *bakufu* believe that your father sent you away to save you from the disgrace of bearing a bastard at home. Tell him you could not bear abandoning your son. Beg him to forgive you and accept the child into his family. How could the *bakufu* doubt your story? Your shame is proof of your veracity. What woman would suffer such humiliation except for the love of her child?"

"You are asking me to dishonor my name, forfeit my opportunity to marry and have children of my own . . . You are asking for my life!"

"I am offering you a way to return home and relieve some of the suspicion that hovers over your father's house."

"Is it so easy for you to give him up?" Maria asked.

"It is hard, but he is a male, and this is a sacred place reserved for women. He cannot stay here."

Maria demurred.

"Do this and you will have the gratitude of Rendai forever." Rendai's eyes narrowed dangerously. "Refuse me and you will come to understand why darkness is feared."

It was a good night, moonless and windy. Kriek sat in the boat, his face obscured by overhanging branches. Maria paced on the shore. She was annoyed. Jan-san had been delighted with Rendai's solution. And why not? Was it his name that would be dragged through the dirt? Would his morals be the subject of street gossip? "Logic be damned!" she fumed aloud to herself. "What would a barbarian know about the honor of a Japanese woman?"

Rendai stepped out of the darkness, her wind-splayed hair dancing around her pale face. When she spoke, her voice was distant and devoid of emotion. "Take him," she said, holding the sleeping child out to Maria. "I have given him a palliative. He will sleep soundly through the night."

Maria took the child in her arms. There was a small bundle of clothes tied to his waist.

"These things I have seen," Rendai told her. The wind swayed the high branches. "You will not keep the boy. He will be reared by others and his name will be celebrated throughout the land. Through him I will be avenged, and"—her voice was barely audible—"he will be the instrument of his own doom."

Rendai turned away and melted back into the darkness.

Within an hour after setting sail from Yushima Island, Maria spotted the outline of Shimabara Peninsula just off the starboard bow. As they drew closer to the shore—close enough to discern the faint silhouettes of thatched roofs in the cloud-shifting moonlight—she and Tomi strained to find some familiar landmark or grouping of houses that would help pinpoint their location. One after another tiny villages drifted by, and each time Maria and Tomi exchanged guesses, but the architectural conformity of the fishing villages defeated them.

Finally Maria recognized a small inn located high on a promontory overlooking the bay. It had once been the site of a Shinto shrine, but now all that was left of it was a large bronze bell hanging inside a rustic pavilion. The rope holding up the back end of the striking log had broken, giving the dangling log the appearance of a finger poised to probe the insides of a cavernous nostril. Neither Maria nor Tomi knew the correct name for the inn, but both of them knew that everyone called it Buddha's Nose.

"The inn is a morning's walk from Hara Castle," Maria told Kriek. "It must be well past midnight. We can spend the night there and leave tomorrow."

Tomi pointed out that it would be unwise for Kriek to go ashore dressed in Western clothes. "Let me go into the village. I should be able to find something for him to wear on someone's drying pole."

It took her only a few minutes to return with a straw-basket hat and a gray kimono that barely reached his shins. Maria showed him how to walk with his knees bent like a male Kabuki actor playing the role of a woman. But after Kriek made a few bumbling attempts to master the gait, Maria came up with the idea of trying to pass him off as a drunk.

When they reached the path that led to the inn, Tomi bowed and thanked both of them for all the kindness they had shown her.

"Are you leaving us?" Kriek asked.

"I'm anxious to start for home." Actually this was only part of the truth. Being in the presence of a refined lady like Maria, a daimyo's daughter, put her under a terrible strain. She didn't know the proper way to speak or act around her. Tomi was frightened of making some social gaffe that would be offensive and bring Maria's wrath down on her and her family.

"Are you sure you're strong enough to travel?" Kriek persisted.

"I slept on the boat, Padre. I feel much better now."

Kriek blessed her with the sign of the cross. "Go with God, Tomi."

She bowed again and shuffled off down the road.

"Wait here," Maria told Kriek. "I'll go inside and make the arrangements."

The inn was small, but it was clean and orderly. Maria was greeted by a sleepy old woman bent double with age and heavy work. After the baby had been perfunctorily admired and clucked over, Maria asked for a room. "My husband is outside."

"Oh?" she said, meaning, Why?

"Too much sake," Maria commented, answering the old woman's unspoken question. "He's not feeling well and would prefer to suffer in private."

"Yes, of course," she nodded, knowing the ways of men.

The old woman hobbled up the stairs to show Maria the room. It was small but adequate. The old woman apologized for the room's humble appearance. "Shall I lay out the futon?" she asked.

Maria told her that she would take care of preparing the bedding. The location of the bath and the privy was explained. Maria made a point of her desire for privacy, and the old woman understood. "I'll leave the tea outside the door," she said, then went off in the direction of the kitchen.

Keeping his hat low over his face, Kriek leaned on Maria and tried to make himself look small as he hurried to the room. "It wouldn't be wise for you to bathe," she said, offering him the sleeping kimono. "I'm sorry, but there might be others there."

Kriek watched as she laid out the bedding. When she finished, he was still standing there, holding the sleeping kimono in his hands.

"What's wrong?" Maria smiled at him. "Are you afraid to undress in front of me?" she teased.

The directness of her question caught him off guard. It annoyed him that she always seemed to know when he was feeling awkward and seemed to take childish pleasure from his discomfort. It was one thing to submit to being stripped to the skin by strangers. But it was quite another thing to disrobe in plain view of a lady, not to mention the very lady whose soft smoky eyes, lilting voice, and spectral grace were driving him mad with desire and making tatters of the paper-thin barrier he had built between his dreams and her overpowering nearness.

"Maria, as a Christian I shouldn't have to remind you that modesty is a virtue," he chided her. The instant it was out of his mouth Kriek knew it not only sounded pompous, but that his words had a counterfeit ring.

The rebuke stung, igniting Maria's fury. "This is Japan, Jan-san," she retorted. "We had a flourishing civilization here while your ancestors were still running naked in the forests and painting themselves blue. We need no lectures on civility from *yabanjin*."

It was the first time Kriek had ever heard her use the derogatory word for foreigners—a word that literally meant barbarian.

This time it was Kriek's eyes that sparked. "Is it civilized for a father to sell his own daughter into prostitution, or for a samurai to hack a prisoner in two just to test the edge of a new sword? Would it be arrogant to suggest that the Japanese practice of wrapping Christian men, women, and children in straw raincloaks and setting them on fire is almost as barbaric as the *yabanjin* sense of modesty?"

For a reason she did not fully understand, Kriek's outburst

pleased her. During the brief time they had spent together, his behavior toward her had been excruciatingly correct, and it had been grating on her nerves. She had been waiting for some sign, the slightest hint, the subtlest word or gesture, to indicate he still cared. Yet he continued to act as if nothing out of the ordinary had ever transpired between them. Maria refused to believe that he had been able to amputate passion like a diseased limb. By provoking his anger, she found out he was at least capable of showing some kind of emotion.

Maria shifted the baby to one shoulder and laid her hand on Kriek's arm. "Forgive me, Jan-san. I had no right to lecture you. It's just that the Japanese idea of modesty is so different. You see, in this country the unclothed body holds little mystery for us. We grow up bathing together, and on a hot summer day it's not uncommon to see men working in their *fundoshi* underwear. I know it's difficult to understand, but we don't think of the unclothed body as offensive. It's lewd behavior that we find shameful."

Kriek put his hand over hers. "There's so much to learn, so much I want to understand."

"Try to empty your mind and listen with your heart," Maria said. "We believe that is the beginning of true understanding." Maria smiled and held Shiro out to him. "I have to change for the bath now," she said, turning her back to him. "If it would help you feel more comfortable, you can look away while I undress."

Kriek cradled the baby in his arms and watched as Maria let her kimono drop from her shoulders to the floor. The soft candlelight molded the lovely curves of her body. Like the first night he saw her at the window, he was unable to look away. She slipped into her sleeping kimono and loosened her hair.

When she returned from the bath, Kriek was lying under the covers. Maria laid the child down on her futon and he began to fuss. Kriek reached out. "Here, give him to me." The boy snuggled against his chest, murmured peacefully, and fell asleep.

Maria poured the tea, and they discussed their plans. It was decided that he would hide out in the mountains during the day and travel the road at night. Maria drew him a rough map showing him how to find the Father Visitor's residence once he reached Nagasaki. In the morning she would set out for Nobeoka.

"Are you afraid?" he asked.

"Not afraid . . ." She didn't finish her thought.

"This thing you are doing . . . it must be very difficult for you."

"*Hai*," she said softly, putting out the candle and lying down beside him.

"I wish there were some other way. You've been through enough already. You deserve better."

"Karma is karma."

"It's strange to hear a Christian speak of karma. Once I tried to convince you that you're free to choose your own path."

"Yes, but choice plays such a tiny part in our lives. It seems to me that accident, pure chance, has much more to do with the flow of our lives than choice."

"You don't believe you have a free will?"

"I suppose so."

"But you're not sure?"

"I'm sure that my free will keeps bumping into your free will and everyone else's free will. It seems to me I spend more time reacting to things than choosing them—I feel like I'm being blown around by the wind."

The boy made a low whimpering noise and burrowed his face into Kriek's chest.

She leaned over and drew Shiro to her. Kriek felt the warmth of her breath on his face, and his hand brushed against her as she rolled onto her back, cradling the child in one arm. Outside the room they could hear the old woman's feet shuffling along the wooden walkway.

Kriek lay on his side, listening to the sound of her breathing and watching the outline of her profile framed against the moonlit paper wall.

"Maria . . ."

"*Shh*." She put her face close to his. "The old woman may be listening."

Kriek slipped his hand into her hair and cupped the nape of her neck in his palm. Maria's eyes widened as he lifted her to his mouth. The kiss was strong and tender and taken with deep conviction. A flood of warmth rushed from his lips to hers, then cascaded through her body. It was strange and good and frightening at the same time.

Maria turned her face away, but Kriek held onto her, putting his lips close to her ear. "Maria, I'm—" He stopped, biting off the lie before it got loose. "I was going to say I was sorry," he whispered. "I'm not."

"Please, Jan-san, don't . . ." she protested, desperate to hear him out, yet more terrified at the thought of what he was going to stay.

"Maria, listen to me. All my life I've been closed up like a musty attic. For the first time, when I met you, light came in. I never expected to see you again, so I can't let you go without telling you this. Whatever happens, one moment was sunlit." He gently lowered her head onto the wooden box pillow. "And no God, man, or Church can take that away from me."

Maria lay still, her lips still tingling from the touch of his lips. Like every young girl, she had asked married women what it felt like to pillow with a man. The answers were always vague and abstract and resolved nothing. "You'll know soon enough," they'd said, followed by the pat on the head, the enigmatic smile, the deepening mystery. But for a brief moment that night she caught a glimpse of the mystery—the feel of his lips on hers, the grip of his hand on her neck. It was all she knew of love, and most likely all she would ever know. And like Jan-san, nothing could ever take that away from her.

The wind had stopped blowing. It was so quiet she thought she could hear the pounding of her heart.

After a night of fitful sleep, a night charged with unresolved tension, Maria and Kriek parted once again and went their separate ways—he to the mountains to wait for nightfall before setting out for Nagasaki, and she to Nobeoka, where her father had taken up residence after being expelled from Hara Castle.

As Maria walked along the road with Rendai's son strapped to her chest, the splendor of the morning began to lift her spirits. The familiar sights and sounds of home were gradually seeping in to fill the emptiness she was carrying inside her heart.

The terraced fields glistened with the iridescent green of early spring. The hillsides were bright as an artist's palette.

On the banks of the mountain streams dogwood and cherry
trees were dropping the last of their pink and white blossoms
in the clear, fast water. The soft motherly breeze was redo-
lent with the scent of juniper and pine and textured with the
sound of grasshoppers and songbirds.

The moon was well past its zenith when she arrived at her
father's villa. Bone tired and coated with road dust, Maria
ordered the captain of the guard to take her directly to her
quarters without waking either the servants or her father.
After a long, luxurious bath she took the child to her room,
and both of them slept the sleep of the dead.

As soon as Lord Arima awoke, the captain informed him
that his daughter had returned home. The news stunned
Arima. Word had reached him of the Black Ship's arrival, but
the Tokugawa had him under such intense surveillance that
he could not risk responding to the signals from the dinghy.
Since it was unlikely that the Portuguese would try to smuggle her ashore, he wondered how she managed to get to
Nobeoka. And now that she was here, he had no idea how to
explain away her sudden return after a two-and-a-half-year
absence. To give himself time to think of a plausible story,
Arima instructed the captain to seal off her room and keep
her in total seclusion until he had a chance to speak to her
privately.

His anxiety changed to relief when Maria told him of her
plan to claim Rendai's son as her own. She would say that she
had gone to Yushima Island to have her baby, but after he
was born, she couldn't bear to give him up and decided to
return home and beg her father to allow her to keep the
child. He would, of course, refuse, and place the child in the
home of one of his retainers.

Lord Arima gazed at his daughter. The baby would effectively blunt the suspicion surrounding her long absence, but
the damage to her reputation would be irreparable. She was
so lovely kneeling there in the soft morning light, it pained
him to think that the story was going to destroy all prospects
of arranging a decent marriage for her. No samurai family of
any stature could possibly consider allowing a son to marry
the mother of an illegitimate child.

"No father has ever had a finer daughter than you," Arima
said with unconcealed affection. "All I have asked of you,
you've done. You put duty ahead of self, and family above

everything. The things you've suffered, you've suffered bravely, without bitterness or complaint." Then he straightened his back and paid her the supreme compliment: "You are a true samurai woman."

Never had she heard anything like this from her father. A look of approval, a nod of the head—simple gestures had always told her all she needed to know. But this! An avalanche of praise! She didn't know whether to weep from joy or embarrassment.

"Let's go into the garden," he said brusquely, as if nothing unusual had transpired.

Except for the trickle of brook water over moss-covered rocks, the garden was quiet. The moon shined down on the surface of the pond, and the air smelled of sea and night flowers.

Lord Arima stopped by the pool to collect his thoughts. "As you can tell," he said, "a great deal has changed since you left."

"What I've heard sounds grim."

"It's worse than you can imagine. The Shogun has his spies planted everywhere. I'm certain every move I make is being reported, every conversation being monitored. Matsukura's death squads roam the countryside, forcing farmers to undergo the *fumie*. Anyone who refuses to defile the image of the Virgin, or even hesitates, is cut down instantly. Those who still practice Christianity, do so secretly. It would be wise for you to do the same."

"I won't renounce the Faith," she said firmly.

"I doubt if you'll be forced to," he said, "since I've already done so."

"I know."

Arima sensed her disappointment, and quickly shifted the subject to his delicate financial position. The late Shogun's edict requiring every daimyo to maintain a residence in Edo and spend at least six months out of the year there was proving to be particularly burdensome for him. "At first I was flattered by the prestigious location of the property I was assigned. Later I realized the intent behind the Shogun's largesse. By putting me among the wealthy and powerful, the cost of building up to their standards put me under terrible financial strain. It became painfully clear that he not only wanted hostages in Edo, he wanted hostages who were too poor to mount any kind of resistance to his authority."

"Don't despair, Father," she said in a hushed voice. "Although Father Sebastio died shortly before I got to Lisbon, one of his students managed to decode your message. The Father General sent him here to try to help."

"What's he going to do?"

"I don't know. He carried sealed instructions. But I'm sure he'll contact you after he reports to the Father Visitor."

Arima frowned. "No, he mustn't come here. It's too dangerous. All Lord Iemitsu needs is to find out I met with a padre, and I'll lose the little I have left."

"Does this mean you've given up? You're prepared to let him turn Shimabara into a slaughterhouse?"

Arima didn't think it would be prudent to tell his daughter about the meeting he'd had with Father Alcala and Prince Sanjo. At this point ignorance was the best protection he could offer her. Still, the look of betrayal in her eyes stung. "Remember, my daughter, in this dreamworld, things are not always as they seem."

Kriek made it to Nagasaki without incident. Finding the Jesuit mission proved to be more difficult than he had imagined. Each house and each building had a number, but numbers were assigned according to when they were constructed, rather than where they were located. He didn't want to risk asking directions, so he wandered the streets at night until he stumbled on to it.

The area was thick with Tokugawa samurai, who made no secret of the fact that they were there to watch the Jesuits. The only people he saw go into the mission were vendors, selling produce and fish. Kriek studied their habits from a distance. About a dozen vendors were gathered at the door soon after first light. A young Japanese in a cassock inspected their wares, then invited a few in and sent the rest away.

The next morning Kriek merged with the crowd waiting at the door and managed to slip inside without being detected by the watchful samurai. Once inside he quickly discovered the reason for the Father General's distress about the quality of the reports he was receiving from the Father Visitor. The old priest had suffered a stroke. The left side of his body was useless, and his speech incomprehensibly slurred. The young

Japanese curate claimed to be able to interpret some of his mutterings, but Kriek suspected that a good deal of the curate's interpretation was little more than educated guesswork.

Frustrated, he received permission from the Father Visitor to read the instructions himself. What he read in the letter shocked him. Kriek was to track down Alcala, order him to turn over to him whatever arms he had stockpiled and return to Lisbon on the first Black Ship out of Japan. Kriek was to conduct the negotiations with the *bakufu*, using the leverage of the guns to secure concessions from the Shogun, with the ultimate goal of ending the persecution of Christians in Japan. Kriek was also authorized to assure the Shogun that there would be no further meddling in Japanese political affairs by the Jesuits.

But the most stunning comment came at the end of the letter. The Father General's language was blunt.

> *We cannot permit one of our Jesuit brothers, regardless of how well intentioned, to shape policy for the Society of Jesus. Father Alcala must be stopped before he provokes the slaughter of thousands of innocent Christians. If for any reason he cannot be persuaded to obey these orders, his life is forfeit. It will be Jan Kriek's duty as a soldier of Christ to see that the threat is terminated by whatever means necessary.*

Over dinner the curate filled Kriek in on the declining influence of the Church since the death of the former shogun. He painted an extremely gloomy picture. "Not long ago the whole island of Kyushu was a safe haven for Christians. Lord Matsukura has changed all that. Many believe his cruel taxes are nothing more than a thinly veiled attempt to drive the farmers to rebellion in order to justify their massacre. Keep clear of his samurai and you'll be safe. The farmers will offer you all the assistance they can."

"How do I find Alcala?"

The curate shrugged. "We've been trying to locate him for a long time, with no success. All I can tell you is that he's probably on Shimabara Peninsula, or one of the nearby islands. I recommend that you use Oyano Island as your base. It's too small to attract Matsukura's attention, and almost everyone there is Christian. You will be safe there—for a time."

10

Edo
Year of the Monkey—1632
Hour of the Snake

Okubo's breathing was still shallow, but not as labored as it had been a few hours before. Jubei took it as a good sign.

In the cell there were only shades of darkness, but it no longer disturbed him. Days and nights seemed to blend together, and sleep came and went in no regular pattern. It was hard to get a fix on time. Jubei leaned his head back against the cell wall and tried to remember how long he'd been there. A month? More?

There was one bamboo-barred window just below ceiling level. Steep overhanging eaves kept the narrow window in constant shadow. Okubo claimed he could tell the difference between sunlight and moonlight by the texture of the darkness at the window. Jubei remained skeptical, but since being right about it seemed to matter to his cell mate, he deferred to Okubo's perception.

The monotony was punctuated by two events. Twice a day they were served a bowl of watery millet flavored with a slice of pickle. The routine was always the same. A guard rapped on the cell door, a sliding panel opened, and they passed their bowls out to be filled. Okubo's bowl was always the first to be returned. "It's the guard's way of honoring my seniority," Okubo joked. Jubei knew it had more to do with who got the poison.

The cell they shared was not much bigger than the one he left. It was longer than it was wide by half a body length. When both of them slept at the same time, they stretched out head to toe to keep from breathing stale air in each other's face. Although the window provided no more ventilation than light, it did provide plenty of flies—drawn by the slop bucket, which saturated the cell with the stench of human waste. Fleas, lice, and other unseen vermin ran riot over their skin, gorging themselves on blood to nurture eggs that grew into ravenous adults that in turn gorged themselves on more blood and laid more eggs in an endless cycle of torment.

Jubei reached inside his kimono and flattened a flea with his forefinger. He rolled it back and forth against his skin to tangle up its legs, then expertly crushed it between his fingernails. As Jubei scratched the fresh itch, he thought of the many years Okubo had languished in this hellhole—the foul conditions, the solitude, the interrogations and torture, the execution of his family, and now a poisoning. He lived through it all, and kept on living. Why? He remembered something Okubo told him when he was suffering his first few days of confinement. "Hang on," Okubo said to him, "you'll get used to it. It's possible to get used to anything if it goes on long enough."

Jubei considered Okubo good company. Listening to Okubo tell stories to pass the time, hearing his richly textured voice, generated the same sense of awe he felt in the presence of a master with the skill to make the extraordinary appear effortless. Takuan did it with weapons, Okubo with words. His gift for story eased the pain and relieved the grinding tedium. When the poisoning started, Jubei could barely contain his anger. Okubo had suffered enough! The cost of earning Okubo's gratitude was coming too high. He wanted to tell Takuan to stop, but there was no way to contact him. Despite the antidote, Okubo hovered on the brink of death.

"Tell them he's dying!" Jubei screamed at the guard who brought the food. No response. The panel slid closed in his face.

Jubei's ear had become so attuned to the sound of Okubo's breathing that now it had become difficult to break the habit of listening. Although he was exhausted, his mind was too restless to let him sleep, so he set about the mechanical task of killing fleas.

Okubo's breathing stopped. Jubei tensed. Then he heard Okubo call his name. His voice sounded farther away than it was. Jubei leaned close to his face. "I'm here," he said softly.

"I know it," Okubo answered. "Your scratching is driving me crazy."

Jubei laughed and patted his shoulder. "At least you're feeling well enough to be cranky. Are you ready to try a little food?" Jubei felt around for his bowl and held it to Okubo's mouth. Okubo tried a couple of swallows, then turned his face away and with some effort managed to hold it down. "More?"

Okubo shook his head.

Jubei lowered Okubo's head to the floor and dipped some water out of the bucket that hung on the wall next to the door. "Open your mouth."

Okubo did as he was told. Jubei poured the last of the antidote on his tongue, and Okubo washed it down with a mouthful of water. The last few times Jubei tried to give the powder to him, he vomited it up in a matter of a few seconds.

"Don't lose it," Jubei told him. "It's all the medicine I have."

Waves of nausea rolled over Okubo, but he fought them off. Suddenly his stomach settled and the abdominal cramps began to subside. An internal warmth spread throughout his body. Okubo found Jubei's hand and squeezed it hard.

"You're feeling better?" Jubei asked.

"Another dose and I might have fought my way out of this pigsty."

The notion made Jubei smile. Whatever Okubo was, he was not a fighter. If man were suddenly given wings, Okubo would be the first to fly. Long and lean and possessed with uncommon grace, his chopstick bones were made for soaring.

Jubei spilled the remaining water out of the ladle and onto his sleeve, then used it to wipe the sweat off Okubo's face. The worst was over. Okubo was going to live. Jubei stretched out on the hard-packed dirt floor and closed his eyes. There was nothing to do now but wait for Takuan to make his next move.

When was Takuan going to fill him in on the details of the escape? How much longer would it be? Jubei made a conscious effort to empty his mind. Trying to figure Takuan out was an exercise in futility. It was always best to expect the unexpected.

"Jubei . . ." Okubo's voice came out of the darkness. "I'm not going to die in this prison. I knew it from the day I was put in here. I can't tell you why . . . I don't fully understand it myself. But I can tell you it was no accident that we were thrown together . . . no accident that you saved my life. For better or worse our destinies are intertwined like threads in a Chinese tapestry. One day we may catch a glimpse of the pattern, and maybe then all this suffering will begin to make sense."

"I don't know if it will make sense or not, but I'm sure the pattern is going to be interesting."

"I hope so. There's nothing an actor hates more than a bad part in a dull play."

Their conversation was interrupted by the sound of the bar being lifted out of the door brackets. The glare from the candlelight at the doorway forced Jubei to turn his face away. A small man carrying a physician's box brushed past two guards and entered the cell. "I was told someone here needs medical attention," he announced.

Jubei's head snapped around. The voice belonged to Takuan. He was standing inside the door, dabbing his nose with a handkerchief. "From the smell of things, it seems I've arrived about a week too late. This is disgusting!" Takuan glanced around the filthy cell and fixed Jubei with a look of revulsion. "How can you live like this?"

"I assure you, *Doctor*," Jubei said acidly, "I'm looking forward to getting out of here . . . soon."

"Yes, yes, I should think so," Takuan muttered. "Excuse me, but I don't have time for banter. Now, which one of you is sick?"

"He is," Jubei said, pointing to Okubo.

Takuan bent over Okubo, examined his eyes, probed his stomach with his fingers, then put his ear to his chest and listened to his breathing. His manner was so expert, Jubei wondered if he had actually been trained as a physician. He asked Okubo a few questions, and seemed satisfied with his answers. "Well," he said, getting to his feet, "you seem to have passed through the crisis. With a little extra nourishment to build up your strength, you should be back to normal inside of a week." Takuan turned to the guards. "See that they both get rice and fish for the next few days."

The guards exchanged looks. "Excuse me, Doctor, but did you say *rice* and *fish*?"

"That is correct," Takuan said sternly.

"For both?"

"Certainly. I don't want the stronger prisoner stealing the weaker man's food."

"*Hai*," the guards responded crisply.

Takuan opened his box and took out a packet of medicine. "Take this," he said to Okubo. "It will control the nausea and help restore your appetite."

With that Takuan left the cell.

"Wait!" Jubei called out. Takuan stopped in he corridor and turned around. "I, ah . . . will you examine me?"

"You look fine." Takuan smiled slyly and the door slammed shut.

Jubei pounded his fist on the floor out of sheer frustration. He had been certain Takuan had come there to pass along some kind of message. Instead he used the opportunity to tease him, leaving him as ignorant of the prospects for getting out as the moment he walked through the door.

11

Edo
Year of the Rooster—1633
Hour of the Horse

Maria spent the rest of the year at Nobeoka, then accompanied her father to Edo, where she planned to stay for the next six months. One of their first visitors was Prince Sanjo. When her father asked her to serve him, Maria protested, but he turned her down. "We may discuss some things too sensitive for anyone outside the immediate family to hear," Arima told her.

The sight of Prince Sanjo made Maria's flesh crawl. The sound of his simpering voice grated on her nerves like fingernails over slate. Everytime she looked at him, she pictured the horror of Rendai's rape. She imagined the leer on his face as he helped another man ravish his wife. Just being in his presence made her feel slimy, as if she were being licked by a dog.

For a while the men gossiped amiably about inconsequential matters. Maria poured a swallow of tea in his cup each time it became empty, and let her mind drift. Word had reached her through the servants that a priest was hiding in the hills of Oyano. It could be Alcala, or it could be Jan-san. No one knew for sure. It would be a long time before she returned to Nobeoka. Perhaps then a trip to Oyano to view the autumn foliage could be arranged. Once there, a few discreet inquiries might turn up the truth.

The subject turned to politics, and Maria adjusted her attention to the conversation.

"I've heard that the talks with the Imperial Court are going well . . . for the Tokugawa." Arima's acid comment was aimed at Sanjo's inept performance at the negotiating table.

Sanjo covered his fashionably blackened teeth with his hand and played the fool. "Hoh, hoh, hoh . . . this poor dolt is simply no match for the Shogun's silver-tongued counselors. Hoh, hoh, hoh."

Arima propped his elbow on his cushioned armrest, took his chin in his palm, and stared balefully at Sanjo. He knew better. "Then we can look forward to no more impediments to Iemitsu's succession to the shogunate."

"Oh, but I didn't say that, did I?" Sanjo said guilelessly. "What is life if not a festival of misfortune, *neh*? Who but the Enlightened One can say what impediments lay in our paths?"

"That's so, but I find it difficult to imagine the shape of any impediment formidable enough to cause Lord Iemitsu serious trouble," Arima said, still probing.

"There are those who have not abandoned the idea of seeing his brother Tadanaga named shogun. And, as you know, desperate men are capable of desperate acts."

"Let's assume these desperate men realize their dream, and Iemitsu is somehow eliminated. How does replacing one Tokugawa shogun with another Tokugawa shogun advance the cause of those who would like to see the power shift away from Edo?"

"Ah, shrewd question," Sanjo said, as if he'd just considered the possibility for the first time. "Actually it might be

better for them if Iemitsu were abducted and held hostage.
It's doubtful that Tadanaga would expend a great deal of
effort to secure his brother's release. In the meantime the
Emperor can hardly be expected to confer the title on either
of the brothers until the rivalry between them is resolved."

"Creating a stalemate that will split the Tokugawa alliance
in two." Arima added, "And plunge the country into another
civil war."

Sanjo took a long-stemmed pipe out of the ceramic tray by
his side. He put a pinch of tobacco in the tiny bowl and fired
it with an ember. Drawing the smoke deep in his lungs, he
exhaled with a sigh of pleasure. "We can thank our Western
friends for three extraordinary gifts—tobacco, firearms, and
Christianity. And how does the Tokugawa respond to these
innovations? Tobacco is banned, firearms are confiscated, and
Christians are persecuted. I assure you the Emperor appreci-
ates the value of these gifts. I can't help wondering how the
Portuguese would react if an opportunity arose to aid someone who was less hostile to their interests."

Maria could scarcely believe her ears. Was Sanjo actually
implying that he was involved in some kind of plot to kidnap
Iemitsu? If so, his motives were clear. Provoke the Tadanaga
and Iemitsu factions into war, then exploit the chaos by
forming an alliance with the Portuguese and Christian daimyos in order to restore power to the nobles.

"The risks are grave," Arima said, his voice barely above a
whisper. "The price of failure is too terrible to contemplate."

"Failure doesn't invent itself. It's the creation of fools who
value luck over hard work and foresight. In any game of skill
no move must ever be taken until every possible counter
move is considered. Even then there's risk. Stupid people
ignore risks and play on as if their opponents didn't exist. The
vast majority of people, however, simply try not to lose. On
the other hand, those who truly understand the game, the
winners, control the flow of the game with superior anticipation and guile."

"Excuse me, Prince Sanjo," Maria interjected, "but you
are speaking like a man who has never been surprised."

"Daughter!" her father growled. "Watch your manners."

"No, please," Sanjo said to Arima, "let her continue. It's a
rare privilege to be instructed by one so lovely."

Arima nodded his reluctant approval.

"It seems to me," she went on, "there is an element of spontaneity in nature that can't be controlled by man."

A fly circled Sanjo's head and lighted on the tip of his nose. He brushed it away with his fan and it landed on his nose again. Maria could not help grinning. Arima glared at her.

"Forgive me, Father, but it occurred to me that the fly was helping to make my point."

"Go on," Arima said, since it seemed Sanjo was genuinely interested in what she had to say.

"That's the element of spontaneity I was speaking of. You see, even one as wise as Prince Sanjo could not have predicted where that fly was going to land. A fly is a simple creature. Think of how much more difficult it is to predict the actions of a man."

Sanjo cocked his head to one side and tapped his fan against his cheek. "A worthy challenge," he mused. "Not one to be taken lightly." Suddenly his hand shot out, snatching the fly that had settled on the rim of his tea cup. "Would you be impressed if I told you I can predict exactly where this fly will go when I release him?"

"I would if he is still alive when you let him go."

Sanjo chuckled. "Fair enough." He took a small gold coin out of his purse and tossed it onto the tatami. "This is where he'll go," he said, tapping the coin.

Slowly, carefully, Sanjo worked his hand open, trapping the fly under a fingernail. First he removed one wing, then the other. Using his folded fan, he guided the fly across the tatami to the coin. Whichever way the fly turned, his escape was blocked. Finally it crawled onto the gold coin. Sanjo looked up triumphantly as he squashed the fly under his thumb. Maria graciously bowed to acknowledge his achievement.

"It is true that the actions of men are more difficult to manipulate," he said. "It requires considerably more patience and skill . . . but I assure you, it can be done."

To Maria's immense relief, her father dismissed her. On her way back to the women's quarters she tried to develop a line of reasoning to convince her father to be wary of Sanjo. The dangers of involvement with such a man were obvious, yet it was evident from the tenor of their conversation that their relationship with each other went much deeper than she had imagined. If asked, what could she possibly say to make him reconsider? Probably nothing. She had an ominous feeling that things had already gone too far.

The full moon, large and low over the Tokaido road, was the color of a marigold. A lone rider urged his chestnut roan to greater speed, sending foot travelers scrambling for the shoulder of the road. It was rare to see horses on the Tokaido, rarer still to encounter a galloping horse. A farmer's wife helped her elderly husband out of the swamp reeds where he had fallen when the horse passed by. She fussed over his clothes while he watched the silhouette of the horseman recede into the center of the moon. "A noble," he muttered to himself. The wife hoisted a pack of vegetables onto her back and followed her husband down the road, toward Edo.

A coat of lather had formed on the roan's neck and flanks, and the dark, sweet scent of horse sweat impregnated Sanjo's robes. He rode on until he came to a gnarled juniper whose back branches had been slashed off by a bolt of lightning. A few yards beyond the tree the thick undergrowth parted, revealing a narrow path. Sanjo followed it up a hill to a small waterfall hidden among the rocks. He dismounted, stripped to the skin, and let the falls wash over him. The horse neighed and fidgeted at the smell of water. Sanjo ignored its pleas. The overheated animal would have to wait until its temperature dropped.

With the powder and paint washed away, Sanjo's face showed signs of hard times. Although his skin was unusually fair, it had the grainy texture of a workingman. There was a ragged scar just below his left eye, and a longer one that spanned his chin. There were scars on his body too, some old, some not so old.

Sanjo lay back in the pool at the foot of the falls, his long hair flowing downstream with the pull of the current. He set his teeth against the chill of the swift water and waited for the discomfort to pass. Overhanging leaves bobbed in an early autumnal breeze. Clouds the color of ripe plums stretched across the darkening sky, and some brighter stars were visible. But the night belonged to the moon. What a night to be young and in love, he thought, and the irony brought a smile to his lips.

Feeling fresh and fine, he climbed out of the water and shook himself like a wet dog. The horse snorted his impatience. This time Sanjo responded. As soon as he was freed, the roan trotted into the stream and drank its fill.

Meanwhile Sanjo took some willow branches and swept the ground clean of hoof marks. When he was satisfied with the results, he backed into the water and led his horse downstream to a place where an extinct tributary had carved a tunnel in the rock. The entrance was just large enough for a horse to squeeze through, but once inside, there was more than enough room to move around comfortably. He lit a candle and went deeper into the cave. Pushing the horse's muzzle away from a grain barrel, he put a few scoops of feed into a pail. "There," he said, patting the horse on the neck. "That should keep you quiet for a while."

On the opposite side of the cave, on a waist-high ledge, Sanjo had stored an arsenal of weapons. There was a spring-loaded spear that passed for a walking staff; a collapsible bow; a blowgun; an array of roped knives, hooks, and garrotes; a collection of blades of all sizes; brass knuckles; and a set of five *shaken*—razor-sharp, star-shaped disks that could be thrown in rapid succession with a whipping motion of the wrist. Sanjo had also stored an assortment of climbing devices, as well as chemicals used to poison darts and manufacture flash-powder grenades and smoke bombs. But he had spurned the use of firearms, preferring the more traditional techniques of *ninjitsu* which had been passed down from father to son for countless generations. However, he had no quarrel with other ninja who found musketry useful.

Sanjo unwrapped his ninja outfit and put it on. Just the feel of the dark cotton against his skin stimulated him like a drug. Excitement smoldered in his guts like a banked fire. His senses sharpened, his breathing deepened, and his lean body felt cat-quick. Nothing charged his being like a moment in the shadows.

Sanjo's fate had been determined for him even before his birth. The leader of the Koga ninja decided it would be useful to plant an agent inside the Imperial Court. It was Sanjo's mother who conceived the scheme that ultimately succeeded in infiltrating a ninja into the royal family. Like all ninja women, Sanjo's mother was especially adept in the erotic arts. She used her extraordinary skills to seduce one of the Emperor's minor sons. As expected, he became so hopelessly enamored that he forged the necessary documents, providing her with the proper pedigree to become one of his consorts. After that the leader of the Koga impregnated her, and when Sanjo was born, the Emperor's son never suspected that the infant was not his own. Sanjo's mother persuaded her lord to install her in a private villa near Koga, where the young ninja prince was initiated into the mysteries of *ninjitsu*. Since early childhood Sanjo had been leading a dual life, but his loyalty to the Koga had never wavered.

When he emerged from the cave the only visible weapon he carried was a long sword which he wore slung across his back like a musket. The rising moon had become smaller and brighter. Sanjo kept to the shadows as he scurried over the rocks to a clearing among a stand of birch. He squatted on his haunches and waited. They were there. He couldn't see them, but he knew he was being watched. Closing his ears to all irrelevant sounds, he remained motionless, alert and calm, his senses acutely tuned to the nuances of darkness.

The first *shaken* came whirling out of the night. He jerked his head to one side and heard it whiz past his right ear. The second and third he blocked with his wrist guards. The fourth embedded itself in the ground at his feet. The last one lodged in his thigh as he somersaulted over his shoulder. Sanjo yanked the missile out of his leg and slammed it into the dirt, infuriated by the realization that a poisoned *shaken* would have killed him.

Someone called out of the shadows, "You're slowing down, old man."

Sanjo gritted his teeth. He waved his comrades out of the woods and set about binding up his wound. One by one, five ninja entered the clearing, bowed, and seated themselves in front of him, to await his instructions.

After several false stops Konosuke spotted the landmark he'd been searching for. He rapped his fan on the screen and the porters lowered the palanquin to the ground. There could be no mistake about it, the blasted juniper looked just as Sanjo had described it to him.

The young man patted his perfectly arranged hair to make certain no strands had broken loose during the trip. Inside the palanquin it was too dark to use his mirror, but without seeing himself, he was convinced that the combination of heat and anxiety had spoiled his makeup. If everything proceeded according to plan, he'd have time enough to make the necessary repairs before Iemitsu arrived.

The door slid open and the elder of the two porters offered Konosuke his hand. Cramped from the long ride, he tried to make his exit as graceful as possible.

"I hope the trip was not too unpleasant, my lady," the porter said politely.

"It was fine," Konosuke responded in his best feminine voice. "Now please fetch the *jubako*," he said as he smoothed out the folds in his kimono. The porter reached inside the palanquin and took out a set of fitted lacquer boxes containing a variety of picnic delicacies. "Oh, yes, the mat too," Konosuke added, almost forgetting.

The old porter smiled to himself. He'd taken a lot of high-ranking courtesans to clandestine rendezvous, but never one as flustered as this. It couldn't be her first time. Maybe she was meeting someone of great importance . . . or could it be that she was sneaking away to meet her true love? Whoever it was, the porter hoped she got her emotions under control by the time her lover arrived. A case of nerves could spoil the magic.

"You couldn't have chosen a lovelier night," he said, just to ease the tension.

"Thank you," Konosuke replied, taking the rolled-up mat from him and tucking it under one arm. "I'm told there are some inns at Kawasaki. You may wait there until you are summoned," he told the porters, following Sanjo's instructions to the letter.

"Would you like me to help you with the *jubako*?" the old porter asked.

"That won't be necessary, thank you. I can handle it."

The two porters waited by the palanquin while Konosuke found the path, and watched as he disappeared into the woods.

"I don't like leaving that girl here alone," the father said to his son.

The son shrugged. "We have our orders."

"She's a strange one."

The two men set off for Kawasaki. At the second turn in the road they were cut down. The ninja stuffed their bodies inside the palanquin and quickly sank it in the river.

Less than an hour later Iemitsu's advance guard arrived at

the juniper. At his command, his entourage was minuscule—just two samurai in the advance party, two in the rear, and one who rode by his side. It had taken all Iori's persuasive powers to get Iemitsu to agree to that number. If Iemitsu had had his way, he and Iori would have made the trip alone. Only Iori's threat to commit seppuku forced him to compromise.

Still, as far as Iori was concerned, the idea of a future shogun traveling down the Tokaido for some romantic interlude with only five guards to protect him was beyond absurdity—it was insane. It was irresponsible. It was willful. And it was totally in character. Iori hoped beyond hope that the sheer outrageousness of the situation would mitigate the danger. Tajima had done him no favor by assigning him to guard the heir, he thought.

Although Iemitsu had barely spoken a word to him since they slipped out of Edo Castle, it was evident from his expression that he was feverish with excitement. Whether Iemitsu was exhilarated by the adventure, or inflamed with passion, or both, was a matter of speculation. He thinks with his testicles, Iori thought. Bad enough for a fishmonger, unconscionable for a man who would be a shogun.

Another problem developed for Iori when Iemitsu refused to let anyone go with him beyond the tree. "Please!" Iori pleaded. "At least allow us to scout the area where you're going. Once we're satisfied that it's secure, we'll maintain a discreet distance. But don't deny us the opportunity to do our duty."

"I assure you, I have my reasons," Iemitsu said.

"But my lord, you could be walking into a trap. It's my duty to do everything in my power to safeguard you from—"

"You seem to understand your duty better than you understand your rank," Iemitsu said sharply. "I am the Tokugawa heir, and you are the heir's guard. Your duty is what I say it is—no more, no less. And I say your duty is to obey without question."

Iori fell to one knee. "If you refuse to let me protect you, I can't live with the dishonor. I humbly request permission—"

"Enough!" Iemitsu snapped. "If you are so anxious to cut your belly, wait until your fears are realized. Then you have my permission to commit seppuku. Until that time you will do everything in your power to protect me, regardless of the conditions. Is that understood?"

"*Hai*," Iori said crisply. All his options were gone. As a samurai he knew he had no recourse beyond obedience. Now karma would decide the outcome.

No one else spoke, but condemnation for Iemitsu hovered in the air like ozone after a thunderstorm. His intransigence in the face of Iori's concern for his safety had cost him a healthy measure of respect.

Iemitsu groped for a way to salvage some of his lost prestige without giving in and compromising his privacy. Then it occurred to him that only he knew that the courtesan he was meeting was a boy. Since Konosuke had not yet made his debut as an actor, no one knew his face. Perhaps he *was* being overly cautious.

"Iori, come with me," he said. "The rest of you wait here. When Iori returns, he'll deploy you within easy shouting distance of where I'll be."

The sense of relief among his men was immediate.

Konosuke was busy spreading out the mat when he heard footsteps approaching. He fought to compose himself. He'd never been more terrified in his life. What if the plan fails? he wondered. Lord Buddha, what if it succeeds! His hands and feet had turned to ice. Why had he allowed Sanjo to drag him into this mess? It's too late for second thoughts, he told himself. It's time to draw on acting skills, and pray for a quick resolution.

Iemitsu stopped Iori at the edge of the clearing and gave him a few moments to scan the moonlit area where Konosuke was waiting for him. "She's beautiful, *neh*?" he whispered to Iori. Iori agreed, but his attention was not on Konosuke. Instead he was using every second he had for reconnaissance.

The courtesan was kneeling on a mat in a grassy area about ten paces from the foot of a small waterfall. The stream ran along a low ridge of rock and vanished into a willow grove. Here and there a few scrub pine protruded out of rocks. Behind them, and on each side, the clearing was bounded by woods.

Iori didn't like it at all. "It's the perfect location for an ambush," he said.

"Or romance," Iemitsu countered with a sly grin.

"I suppose so," Iori muttered.

"Just see that the guards keep out of sight. There should be plenty of time to react if I call out for help."

"Don't forget to keep your sword close at hand," Iori reminded him.

"Stop worrying. Try to remember this isn't the first time a man and a woman have met this way." Iemitsu waved Iori away. "Now allow me a moment of privacy," he commanded.

Reluctantly Iori retreated into the woods.

As soon as Konosuke saw Iemitsu step into the clearing, he arched his back slightly and lowered his forehead to the mat. "*Irrasha mase*," he said softly when Iemitsu sat down across from him.

"Konosuke . . ."

He raised his head. The emotion in Iemitsu's voice, the look of unbridled happiness on his face, started a genuine tear in the corner of Konosuke's eye.

"My lord," he said, reaching for Iemitsu's hands.

"I tried to find you."

"I know."

"Why did you leave without a word?"

"I was forbidden to contact you."

"By whom!"

"My adopted father."

Iemitsu shook his head. "I don't understand."

"A family of Kabuki actors needed a son to take the women's roles. Through an intermediary the family arranged to buy my contract from Yoshiwara. For obvious reasons my adopted father insisted on keeping everything quiet. He ordered me to sever all contact with my clients. Sometimes I wonder what he would have said if he had known my only client was you."

"And you are happy?"

"Except for the brief time we spent together, this is the happiest time of my life." Konosuke's eyes glistened with excitement. "All my life I dreamed of becoming an actor. Every morning I wake up afraid I'm still dreaming. Then practice starts and I know it's real. There's so much to learn! I never imagined it took so much work. Right now I'm just studying the basic movements, but Father says I have the gift to be—"

Konosuke noticed Iemitsu's grin, and he looked away in embarrassment. "Forgive me, my lord, I've been chattering like a magpie."

"Like a beautiful, happy magpie," Iemitsu said. "When your note came to me, I felt the same kind of joy. I promised myself that I would never lose you again. Now that I understand the situation, it shouldn't be difficult to negotiate some kind of discreet relationship acceptable to your father. I can't see how he would object to the Shogun favoring his company, do you?"

"My father is no fool."

Iemitsu took the nape of Konosuke's neck in his hand and caressed it gently. "And I will share a pillow with the greatest actor in the land."

Konosuke pressed his lips to Iemitsu's palm. "And I with the greatest shogun."

Iori held his breath and listened. First the locusts stopped, then the crickets. Through the trees he could see the moon-washed clearing and hear the soft murmur of voices. He cupped his hands to his mouth and mimicked the call of a nightingale.

A ninja loosened the garrote from his fourth victim's throat and answered Iori's signal to the dead guard.

Iori rested his back against a tree trunk. The tension was beginning to get to him. Maybe Iemitsu was right. Maybe he was worrying too much. Nonsense! It was his job to worry. Let Iemitsu enjoy his liaison. It would all be over before long.

Startled by a sudden movement in the branches overhead, Iori dove over his shoulder and came up with his sword drawn. A red-faced monkey looked down at him with baleful eyes. Iori guided the sword back into his scabbard and stood there for a moment, glaring at the monkey. Without warning the inside of his head exploded in a bright burst of light, then darkness.

Spent, Iemitsu lay still, his heart pounding high in his throat, his body glazed with sweat. Konosuke felt Iemitsu's stomach rise and fall against the small of his back. Muscles that had gripped and probed with such ferocious insistence had gone slack. The dampness between his legs was beginning to bother him, but Konosuke resisted the urge to slip away and cleanse himself in the cool water of the stream. As he lay in his lover's arms, waiting, he tried not to think of how he despised himself for betraying Iemitsu's trust. Instead he fixed his gaze on the waterfall and told himself that this night marked the end of a lifetime of pain and fear and sadness. This was the final act in a sordid drama that was going to be over soon.

A sudden gust of wind rushed through the treetops into the clearing. Iemitsu shivered and groped behind him for something to pull over them. Finding nothing within reach, he rolled onto his back, opened his eyes, and saw a masked figure staring down at him. Iemitsu lunged for his sword, only to see it kicked away from his grasp at the last moment. A heavy foot slammed down on his wrist, pinning his arm to the ground.

"Guards!" he screamed.

". . . ards," said the answering echo.

He listened for the sound of his samurai hurrying through the underbrush. The woods were quiet.

"They are dead," the masked ninja said, lifting his foot off Iemitsu's wrist. "Except for one."

Out of the woods came two more ninja, dragging a limp body between them. Iemitsu couldn't see the captured man's face, but he recognized the kimono. The ninja stopped a few paces from the mat and let go of him. Iori's head hit the ground with a thud. His hands were tied behind his back.

For a split second Iemitsu considered making a break for the woods, then reality cracked through. They'd cut him down before he got off the mat. The situation was hopeless, and his nakedness made him feel doubly vulnerable. "If you are going to assassinate me, at least do me the honor of allowing me to dress."

Sanjo reached over his left shoulder and drew his sword. One by one he plucked up articles of Iemitsu's clothing with the point of his sword and tossed them to Konosuke. "Help your lord dress, *boy*," he said in his gruff ninja voice.

"*Iie!*" Iemitsu growled, snatching his clothing away from Konosuke. "That boy will not put his hands on me."

"How strange, you seem to take such delight in his touch," Sanjo mocked him.

"Please, my lord," Konosuke cried, "surely you don't think I—" Iemitsu fixed him with a look of undiluted hate, and the lie died in his throat.

While Iemitsu dressed himself, Sanjo turned his attention to Iori. He poked him in the side several times with the point

of his sword. When he got no response, Sanjo turned him over
with his foot and listened for a heartbeat. Satisfied that he
was still alive, he ordered him taken to the stream to be
revived.

After repeated dunkings, they finally managed to bring Iori
around. His head was throbbing and his legs were unsteady,
but he was able to walk back under his own power. In spite of
his wooziness, it didn't take him long to figure out what had
happened. What he couldn't figure out was why he was still
alive.

Sanjo looked Iori over, noted that his eyes seemed clear.
"What's your name?" he asked, testing his lucidity.

"My name's Iori." His tongue felt fat, and his speech came
out slurred.

"What's your position?"

"I am bodyguard to the Shogun." His words were clearer
this time.

"And who is this?" he asked, indicating Iemitsu.

"He is the Shogun."

Not yet! Sanjo was tempted to say—not until the title is
formally conferred by the Emperor. He had already helped
delay it longer than anyone imagined possible, and if everything continued to work according to plan, the investiture
would never take place.

"Well, Iori-san," he said with a smirk, "you have the
unenviable task of returning to Edo Castle with the news
that your future shogun has been abducted. However, you
can reassure the council that no harm will come to Lord
Iemitsu unless we feel threatened. Tell them they will receive a formal list of demands stating our conditions for Lord
Iemitsu's release. In the meantime advise them to do nothing
to endanger their heir's life. Do you understand?"

Iori dropped to one knee before Iemitsu. "My lord . . ."
His eyes were full of desperate questions.

"Do as the ninja says," he told Iori.

"Hai."

"You will explain the full details of my abduction to Lord
Tajima," Iemitsu continued, "and tell him all the blame is
mine. I behaved like a fool." He cut his eyes toward Konosuke,
then back to Iori. "Earlier this evening I gave you permission
to commit seppuku if anything went wrong. That permission
is rescinded."

"Take him into the woods and hold him there until the Hour of the Tiger," Sanjo said to the ninja standing guard over Iori.

After Iori was led away, Iemitsu was blindfolded, bound, and put on his horse. "Your captivity need not be uncomfortable," Sanjo said to Iemitsu, "provided you know how to behave sensibly." He handed the reins to one of the four remaining ninja and watched as they trotted off toward the stream.

Now that they were alone, Sanjo went over to Konosuke and sat across from him on the mat. The boy looked at him like a scared rabbit. "This is your first encounter with ninja, *neh*?" he said in a reassuring voice.

Konosuke nodded, and drew his kimono tighter across his chest.

"You did well, boy. I'm sure Prince Sanjo will be proud of you," he said, confident that Konosuke had no idea who he was really talking to.

"I thought he might be here," Konosuke replied, glancing around hopefuflly.

"Don't you see him?"

Konosuke looked harder. The moon was high and bright. He saw no sign of Sanjo anywhere. "I'm sorry, sir . . . I don't see him."

"Yes, you do."

"Please, sir, don't tease me. I'm very frightened."

"Really? After the way you played your part tonight, I was sure nothing could rattle you. But then you are a professional actor, aren't you?"

"I'm only a novice, sir," Konosuke said, wishing with all his might that this night would pass more quickly.

"Oh, I see you packed a lunch," Sanjo remarked, pointing at the *jubako*. "It would be a shame to let it go to waste, *neh*?"

Konosuke removed the lid from the upper box and held it out to the ninja. Sanjo selected a pair of chopsticks and picked up a tiny dried fish. With his free hand he reached behind his head and undid a knot, letting the scarf that covered his nose and mouth fall away.

Konosuke stared at him. There was something vaguely familiar about the ninja's face, something . . .

Sanjo pursed his lips and spoke in his high-pitched noble voice. "Do I really look *that* different without my makeup?"

Konosuke gasped, "Prince Sanjo!"

"I told you I'd be here, didn't I?"

Speechless, Konosuke pressed his forehead to the mat. Prince Sanjo, a ninja! He didn't know whether to laugh or cry.

Sanjo helped himself to some rice and a paste of sweet black beans. "A bit drier than I like, but nicely flavored," he commented between bites.

"My lord, what will happen to the Shogun?"

"Surely that's no concern of yours."

"It is if he's set free." Konosuke inched closer. His eyes were large and close to tears. "Did you see the way he looked at me? He knows . . . he knows I let myself be used as bait. As long as he's alive I can never be safe. Wherever I go, he'll find me."

Sanjo smiled and patted him on the knee. "I wouldn't worry about it if I were you."

"Then you *are* going to kill him."

Sanjo laid his chopsticks across the edge of the tray, unfolded a napkin, and dabbed the corners of his mouth. "I'm going to kill *you*."

Konosuke clutched his throat and shrank back in horror. "Please, my lord," he begged, "I've done everything you asked of me."

"Indeed you have," Sanjo said, rising to his feet. "And it's only fair to tell you I was impressed by your performance."

Tears streamed down Konosuke's cheeks. "You're teasing me again, aren't you?" Sanjo drew his sword. "Don't kill me!" He prostrated himself at Sanjo's feet. "What have I done?" he whimpered.

"Konosuke, I'm surprised a boy as bright as you would ask such a question. Think of how much you know about me. I live in the shadows. To survive I need darkness, and unfortunately your knowledge of who I am and what I've done illuminates things that can't thrive in the light. So you see, it's not what you've done, it's what you know."

"Then take me with you! Keep me by your side. Never let me out of your sight. Use me as you did before. Didn't I please you? Didn't I give you pleasure?" he sobbed.

"Do you think you could serve me . . . enthusiastically?"

"I will! I promise!"

Sanjo lowered his sword and leaned over the hilt thoughtfully, peering at the boy. "Are you prepared to give up your dream of becoming an actor?"

"I want to live."

"And you understand the consequences of betraying me?"

"I will never betray you!"

Sanjo nodded decisively. "Gather up your things and come with me," he said.

Konosuke threw his arms around Sanjo's legs and hugged tightly. "Thank you, my lord . . . thank you," he wept.

"Quickly now," Sanjo said sharply. "It's getting late."

Konosuke scrambled to his feet. Without bothering to tie his obi, he set about rolling up the mat. The work was beginning to calm him, but every now and then his body was racked with a convulsive sob.

Sanjo watched for a few minutes. A gifted actor, he thought, as Konosuke placed the top tray back on the *jubako*. There's no telling how good he might have been. Konosuke was fastening the lid when Sanjo took a stride forward and cut off his head with one clean stroke.

As he wiped down the blade, Sanjo wondered if the attempt to free Okubo was going as smoothly.

During the first few months of his imprisonment, Jubei had been restless, anxiously anticipating some sign from Takuan that escape was imminent. As the hours bled into days, days into weeks, weeks into months, and months into seasons, Jubei gave up trying to keep track of time. What began as an irritation became an outrage. Hadn't he done everything that was asked of him? When Takuan told him to keep on playing the role of a drunkard, he did it. Later, when his father was looking for a way to get rid of certain people he suspected of disloyalty to the Shogun, he agreed to pose as a common bandit—robbing and sometimes killing anyone his father identified as an enemy of the peace. He had done everything they asked of him without objection, and endured the shame without complaint. For what? To rot forever in a putrid prison cell!

For the first time since he had been confined to the cell, moonlight had spilled through the window, projecting a grid on the opposite wall. "Amazing," Jubei said to Okubo, "how a simple patch of light can lift the spirits."

Okubo was adjusting his position under the moon grid when a large shadow darkened the square of light. Okubo looked up and saw what appeared to be a head at the window.

"Okubo?" a man whispered.

"*Hai*," Okubo responded.

"We've come." The head disappeared from the window.

"Who was that?" Jubei asked when the shadow fell away.

"The light was behind him. I couldn't make out his features."

"But you *do* know who's come."

"I know."

If he intended to volunteer any more information, the impetus was broken by the sound of masonry being chopped away.

It's just like Takuan to spring a surprise on me, Jubei thought, but the prospect of finally getting out of the cell blotted out all bitterness. Probably Takuan figured the escape would look more convincing to Okubo if it caught me unawares, he reasoned. Just wait and react, he told himself. What could go wrong?

The scraping stopped. Once again the head appeared at the window. "Get in the corner against the outside wall," he ordered. "There's going to be an explosion, then make your escape."

They both crouched in the corner, covering their heads with their arms. "Stay close to me," Okubo told Jubei. "I'll make sure no harm comes to you."

The night was ripped by a thunderous explosion. Debris ricocheted off the walls and the cell was turbid with dust. Groping along the face of the wall, Jubei found a gaping hole. Reaching back, he grabbed Okubo's arm and pulled him along and through it. Outside, the air was laced with the pungent aroma of spent gunpowder. A thick cloud of smoke drifted over the open courtyard.

"Get down!" a voice called out to them. Jubei fell to the ground, but Okubo kept walking forward in a daze. Jubei lunged at his knees and brought him down. A second explosion tore out a section of the bamboo stockade. Over the clanging of the alarm bell, Jubei heard the sound of guards shouting. "Run!" someone yelled, and Jubei sprang to his feet.

Okubo was crawling off in the wrong direction. Quickly Jubei scooped him up and slung him across his shoulders. Off to his right he heard the staccato clatter of swordplay. Jubei started for the stockade on a dead run, and slammed into a guard coming from the opposite direction. The guard went sprawling, but somehow Jubei managed to keep his feet.

Two ninja with horses were waiting on the other side of the fence. There seemed to be a moment of confusion as they looked at Jubei and exchanged puzzled glances.

"Put him on the horse with me," Jubei snapped. "Okubo's in no condition to ride." Without waiting for a reply, he leapt into the saddle and pulled Okubo up behind him. "Hold on," he shouted to Okubo. No reaction. Jubei reached back and pulled his arms around him. Using his obi, he lashed Okubo's wrists together. "Go!" Jubei yelled to the ninja. They took off with Jubei following close on their heels.

Keeping off the roads, they rode hard through woods and marsh, across rain-swollen streams and up steep hills, until they came to a ramshackle farmhouse in the middle of nowhere. The shorter of the two ninja dismounted and went inside. The other one stared at Jubei, saying nothing.

Jubei untied Okubo's hands and helped him off the horse. His legs were shaky, but his eyes seemed clear. "Are you all right now?" Jubei asked.

"I don't remember much, but thanks for getting me here . . . however you did it."

It was apparent that the farmhouse had been abandoned for some time. The yard was overgrown with weeds and the roof was coming apart. Clumps of thatch lay where they had fallen, and bushes were cluttered with small pieces of windblown straw. But the air was a miracle of purity, lightly scented with pine, and it was good to breathe.

So, Takuan had used ninja, Jubei mused. Interesting. Obviously Takuan wanted to convince Okubo that the ninja had been sent to rescue him rather than Jubei. How this ploy served to advance Takuan's strategy wasn't clear, but it was going to be fascinating to watch events unfold. He had done his part. Okubo trusted him, he was certain of that much.

Inside, a craggy-faced ninja sat on the edge of the pit hearth, stirring dead ashes with his foot. His shoulders seemed to sag as he listened to the shorter ninja's description of the escape. He didn't like what he was hearing.

"No one told us there was another man in the cell with Okubo," he concluded defensively.

The chief frowned. He'd known nothing about it either. Sanjo's operations were usually flawless; things rarely went wrong. But this time Sanjo's informers had blundered badly, leaving him with a problem. He had been ordered to deliver Okubo to Sanjo's villa, no one else. Perhaps the solution was not as complex as he had first thought. Still, having to make a decision that might not meet with Sanjo's approval rankled him.

"Why didn't you kill him?" the chief asked, wishing he'd been presented with a dead body instead of a decision.

"At first we didn't know which one was Okubo. Neither one of us had ever seen the man. By the time we found out, it was too late to do anything about it."

"What do you mean, *too late?*" The chief's carbon eyes flashed.

The ninja started to explain about Okubo's infirmity, but the chief cut him short. "Bring them in," he said wearily, then raised his scarf over the bridge of his nose and stared at the door.

Prison has taken its toll on the man, the chief ninja thought as Okubo came in the room, leaning on his cellmate for support. He remembered him as a robust man with peculiar eyes that always made him seem on the verge of laughter. Now his cheeks had collapsed and his vacant eyes were sunken and yellowed. The other one, the one with the eye patch, looked as if he had fared much better. He was filthy, but retained an appearance of vitality despite the privations of prison.

"How does it feel to be free again, Okubo?" the chief asked, pointedly ignoring Jubei.

Okubo sank to the floor and propped his back against the wall. "It's been a long time," he said with undisguised bitterness in his voice.

"So, so," the ninja muttered impatiently, then turned his attention to Jubei, who was watching him with open curiosity. "And you." He rudely pointed his finger at Jubei. "What's your name?"

"I'm called Jubei," he answered, pretending not to notice the slight.

"You carry yourself like a samurai. Is it an affectation or do you have a family name?"

Jubei wondered why he was being goaded. Since he had no answer, he decided to play along. "My family name is Tajima."

"Jubei . . . yes, your father is the sword instructor for the Shogun, *neh*?"

Jubei nodded.

"Isn't he also one of the Lord Iemitsu's counselors?" Suspicion narrowed his eyes.

"So I hear." Behind him, muscles tensed and the room seemed too quiet. "But I'm afraid I don't pay much attention to my father's career."

"Jubei was disowned after a fight with his father," Okubo added, hoping to defuse the mounting tension.

"There are fights, and then there are fights," the ninja said with heavy skepticism. "Some are serious . . . some are convenient."

"This one cost him his eye," Okubo countered. "Is that serious enough for you?"

The chief made a quick motion with his hand, and instantly the other two ninja had Jubei's arms pinned to his sides.

"What are you doing!" Okubo protested.

Without so much as a glance at Okubo, the chief went directly to Jubei and lifted the patch off his eye. He looked at the scarred socket and said, "Now I'm convinced you lost an eye. The rest remains to be seen."

Jubei was beginning to feel uneasy. There was something a little too convincing about the ninja's performance. Why was he raising the spectre of collusion between Jubei and his father? Was it a clever test of Okubo's trust in him? If so, Okubo was giving them the kind of response they were looking for. Still . . .

"Why were you imprisoned?" the chief asked.

Jubei told him the cover story.

"So your father kicked you out, and you turned to a life of crime, is that what you're saying?"

Jubei decided it was time to push back. "It's not my fault that I happened to be in the cell with Okubo when you came for him. If you've got doubts about me, let me go and I'll be on my way."

"I've got a better idea," the ninja said. "One that carries less risk. If you're the common criminal you say you are, I can save the *bakufu* the trouble of executing you, *neh?*"

Okubo struggled to his feet and stepped between them. "You will not kill this man!" he growled. "I owe him my life."

"Sorry, but I'm afraid you have no say in this matter."

"Don't I?" Okubo was trembling with rage. "Let me remind you of something you may have forgotten. There is only one reason why I wasn't left to die in jail. I have certain invaluable information, information the person who retained you must have. I swear to you, if Jubei dies, the information dies with me. I don't think the man who sent you would want my will put to the test."

The ninja measured Okubo with his eyes. All his instincts told him it was no bluff. Okubo was right—he was not prepared to challenge his resolve. Why not let Sanjo handle this? he thought. After all, the rescue went fine; it was Sanjo's planning that had broken down.

"Are you prepared to deliver your ultimatum to *my employer?*" he asked with a smirk.

"I am." Okubo's response was resolute.

"Well then, you'd better get some rest. We'll take you to him in the morning."

"I'm looking forward to it," Okubo said. "It's been a long time, and we have a lot to talk about."

The realization hit Jubei like a hammer. The escape had not been a ruse! *We'll take you to him in the morning.* If these ninja were Takuan's agents, they wouldn't be taking Okubo anywhere! They would simply release Okubo and hope he would lead his former prisonmate to the gold. But instead both of them would be taken to the man behind the escape, someone whom Okubo had dealings with in the past, someone the ninja were afraid to cross.

Then it hit Jubei that this was exactly what Takuan and his father had been waiting for. Neither one of them had ever had any intention of putting the original plan into effect! A murderous rage engulfed him.

The chief ninja ordered Jubei tied to a support post for the night. "I'm sorry to discomfort you," he said to Jubei, "but it's better than being dead, *neh?*"

It was a long steep climb to Hie Shrine—well over a hundred steps from the street to the top of the hill. Panting heavily, Tajima pushed himself harder. The exertion felt good, and the pain in his side temporarily took his mind off Jubei's plight.

Reaching the top, he sat down on a bench and wiped the sweat from his face and neck. Below him the tiled roofs of the houses rose up like waves in a dark sea. It was past midnight, the Hour of the Mouse. There were a few stragglers wandering the streets now that the drinking places had closed, but most of the city was asleep.

After his fatigue had passed, he started up the path toward the shrine. Gravel crunched underfoot like dry snow, and wind chimes turned the breeze into music. The cheerful tinkling grated on his nerves the way ebullient morning chatter affects a hard drinker.

Outside the shrine barrels of sake had been stacked one on top of the other—presents to the gods from hopeful suppliants. Tajima tossed a handful of coins into the offering box, clapped his hands twice to get the spirits' attention, and he bowed his head in prayer.

"I am Lord Tajima, counselor to the Tokugawa," he announced, so the spirits wouldn't think him presumptuous enough to expect them to recognize him on sight. "I've come on behalf of my son, Jubei. He's suffered much at my hands, and now he's in grave danger. I humbly beg you to watch over him and keep him from harm. I ask this not only for his sake, but for the sake of the clan I have sworn to protect."

He hoped his last statement would not be taken as an offensive exaggeration of his own importance. It had been an honest rendering of his opinion. If the gods disagreed with his assessment, well, they were gods and he was only a man. Tajima was satisfied that he had said what he meant, but just to be on the safe side, he tossed another handful of coins into the box as he left the shrine.

Takuan's cold-blooded reaction to the escape had rankled him. "Think of it," he had told Tajima. "Jubei may be in a position to get at the heart of the conspiracy. If he's clever enough, he could learn more than we ever dreamed possible."

"Forgive me if I'm wrong," Tajima responded in arch tones, "but isn't that the reason you kept postponing the escape?"

When Takuan chided him for letting his emotions blind him to the unique opportunity this situation offered them,

Tajima lost his temper. "He's not a piece of meat!" he snapped. "He's my son."

"What was he the day you nearly killed him?" Takuan asked pointedly.

Takuan's tasteless rejoinder had caught him off guard. The remark would be tolerated, but not forgotten.

Still, after the heat of the moment dissipated, Tajima had to admit Takuan was not far off the mark. The situation did hold real possibilities. What was done was done. He could do nothing to undo the past.

Halfway down the path he heard the sound of footsteps coming fast. Since it seemed to be only one person, Tajima kept walking. With his left hand he tilted his scabbard into position and pressed his thumb against the underside of the swordguard.

A woman broke around the bend in full stride. Although he couldn't make out her face, Tajima recognized his daughter by the compact way she moved.

"*Chichive*," Akane called out, running up to him. Her face was flushed and her breathing was heavy, but not labored. "Iori sent me to find you. Something happened and he needs to talk to you right away."

Tajima took her by the shoulders. "He was guarding the heir. Did something go wrong?"

"I don't know," Akane said. "All I can tell you is that he's been injured."

"Who? Iori or Iemitsu?"

"Iori," she answered quickly. "That's why he sent me instead of coming himself."

"How badly?"

"I saw some blood on his collar, maybe from a head wound, but he seemed to be all right."

All right! If it was true, then it was the only thing that was *all right*. Tajima felt like his world was coming apart at the seams.

As Tajima jogged through the empty streets, he tried to steel himself for the worst. One look at Iori's face and he knew his preparation had not been in vain. Something awful had happened.

He hustled Iori off to his private quarters and listened to the stupefying tale of Iemitsu's abduction. For a long time afterward the two men sat across from each other, lost in their own private misery. Neither one spoke. Iori stared at the floor. Tajima stared into the middle distance as storm-tossed thoughts bobbed on the surface of his mind.

Finally Iori broke the silence. "There must have been something I could have done to prevent this," he said abjectly, "but even now I can't think of anything."

Nor can I, Tajima thought. "You were put in an impossible position. Lord Iemitsu knows there are predators out there stalking him, waiting for the first sign of weakness to move in for the kill. Yet he chose to flaunt his weakness, and it brought him down. There's no need to blame yourself."

Although it was left unstated, Iori understood Tajima's predicament. It was he who would have to report to the council and accept responsibility for Iemitsu's indiscretion. Many on the council resented Tajima's rapid rise to power and might seize the abduction as a golden opportunity to get rid of him. It was going to take all his considerable wiles to survive this fiasco.

Tajima was already grappling with a larger problem. Regardless of his fate, once word of Iemitsu's abduction leaked out, the Tadanaga and Iemitsu factions would be at each other's throats. It would only be a matter of time before the fragile peace shattered, plunging the empire into chaos again. Unless . . .

"Iori, you say no one survived but you?"

"*Hai*." He nodded briskly.

"And you reported directly to me?"

"*Hai*," Iori responded crisply.

"Then we are the only ones who know the truth." Tajima stroked his mustache. "The odds are against us, but if I can invent a credible story to explain the heir's absence to the council, it would give us a little time to search for him, *neh*?" He leaned closer to Iori. "Are you able to travel?"

"I'm prepared to leave at your command."

Tajima did not want to send him out alone in his condition, yet it was too delicate a matter to entrust the assignment to anyone else. Since Jubei had been away, Iori had become like a son to him. Tajima thought for a moment, and realized he had another option. As the personal bodyguard of Iemitsu's sisters, Akane had been able to provide him with a great deal of useful information. However, the situation he was facing left him precious few options. The time had come to take her out of the women's quarters, expand her duties, and make her into a full-fledged agent.

"Take Akane with you," he said to Iori. "Explain everything to her. She will help you search for Lord Iemitsu."

Iori got up to leave.

Tajima stopped him at the door. "Sooner or later the truth will come out. You may have a day, two days, even a week. If that time comes before you find Lord Iemitsu, keep on searching, but do not return to Edo. I won't be in a position to protect you, or any member of my family."

"I understand," Iori said. "Shall I send Akane to you before we go?"

Tajima shook his head. "There's no time to spare. We all have things to do."

The ninja wore large basket hats over their heads, with narrow slits in the front for vision—the kind of hats popular with itinerant monks and other travelers who had to walk long distances through bug-infested areas. They were also useful for those who preferred to travel incognito.

For the most part they kept off the main roads, sticking to poorly defined paths and tiny trails that wound through the forests. One of the ninja lagged far behind. The chief walked in front of Jubei and Okubo, and the big ninja walked behind them. Jubei guessed the other one was somewhere ahead, acting as an advance scout.

Despite the constant twists and turns, Jubei observed that their general thrust was westward. He saw nothing that looked familiar, no landmarks to help him get a more precise fix on where he was. Throughout the night he had tried to construct various scenarios so that he could formulate several plans of action, depending upon what evolved when they reached their destination. But the paucity of specific information thwarted any hope of coming up with viable options. All his attempts to get Okubo to divulge additional information about where they were headed and who they were going to see had been deftly deflected. Jubei knew he was going to have to wait and see what developed, then rely on his instincts to pull him through.

By mid morning Okubo was so exhausted that it took all his concentration to put one foot in front of the other. Jubei hooked Okubo's arm over his shoulder and did what he could to keep him moving. In less than an hour Okubo was no longer capable of picking up his feet. His full weight was on Jubei and his toes were dragging in the dirt.

"Unless you're planning on delivering a corpse," he called to the lead ninja, "you'd better stop for a while."

The chief looked back at Okubo and decided to take Jubei's advice. They found a resting place near a stream. Jubei held Okubo by the hair while he lay on his belly and drank. Later on the captors produced some dried mackerel. The fish was dark and salty, and when they finished all they were given, Jubei took Okubo back to the stream and they both drank again.

The short rest and the food and water put some strength back in Okubo's legs. He gamely refused Jubei's offer of help and started off on his own, using a stout shaft of driftwood for a walking staff. But it wasn't long before he was back on Jubei's shoulder.

From the position of the sun over the trees, Jubei reckoned it was near the Hour of the Ram when they stopped again. The advance scout was waiting for them by a tall bamboo hedge. He and the leader had a brief conversation. When it was over, the leader returned and put a blindfold on Jubei.

As he followed along, holding onto the ninja's obi, Jubei noticed that the path became smooth, and he could hear the crunch of gravel underfoot and smell the distinct fragrance of garden flowers. He guessed he was being led through a residence of some sort, and when the gravel changed to paving stone, knew he'd been right.

He was separated from Okubo and taken to a room saturated with heat and humidity. Even before the blindfold was taken off, Jubei realized he'd been put inside a bathhouse. Overhead a network of bamboo lattice vented the steam and received a little sunlight. Except for the huge tub that dominated the enclosed space, the small room was empty.

The ninja wrapped his knuckles on the wall. "You were brought here because the stout lumber in these walls should discourage any ideas you might have about breaking out. I advise you to be patient and hope your luck holds." He stepped out the door. "By the way," he added, "don't be shy about using the bath. You smell foul."

The door slammed shut. A heavy bolt slid into place.

Jubei stripped down and rinsed his body by dipping water out of the tub with his cupped hands. He took his time, savoring the thought of immersing himself in the steaming bath. Little by little the accumulated grime gave way, flowing in rivulets down his body and out through the slats in the floor. Finally he lowered himself into the tub and let the scalding water work its magic.

Meanwhile, inside Sanjo's private quarters in the mountain villa, Okubo was pleading Jubei's case.

"I appreciate your loyalty to your former cellmate," Sanjo said, "but considering the stakes, don't you think it might be wiser to eliminate any possibility of mischief, no matter how remote it might seem at the time?"

"Jubei has a reputation as an excellent swordsman—"

"I'm not surprised. His father, Lord Tajima, is a renowned sword instructor." Then he added, "As well as a distinguished member of the Tokugawa council."

"His father has disowned him."

"So I've heard."

"And you don't believe it."

"My dear Okubo, whether I believe it or not is irrelevant. Whether he is a fine swordsman or not is also irrelevant. What matters to me, and I daresay should matter to you, is only one thing: is the life of one man, however worthy, worth taking a chance on jeopardizing the dream we've risked so much to realize?"

"Since we're speaking of risks, Prince Sanjo, I'm prepared to put the execution of my family, the revocation of my family name, and five years of torture and imprisonment up against anything you might have suffered to accomplish our goals."

"Forgive me if I sounded callous. No one has lost more than you. That's why I'm bewildered by your passion for bringing an outsider into our inner circle. Especially one whose family is so closely tied to the Tokugawa. You see, if you are wrong about this . . . Jubei, then every sacrifice you've made could vanish in a puff of smoke."

"I'm not talking about bringing Jubei into our inner circle. All I ask is that he be accepted as my personal bodyguard. I owe the man my life."

"And if I refuse your request?"

"You know the consequences."

"I want to hear *you* say it."

"I am the only man alive who knows where the gold is hidden. If Jubei dies, I will take the secret to my grave."

"Well." Sanjo clapped his hands together. "It seems to be settled then."

"Jubei lives?"

"He lives. But you won't be offended if I keep him locked up until I leave for Edo? You see, although I find it amusing that your new bodyguard is the son of a Tokugawa counselor, I don't share your unqualified trust in him."

"Agreed."

"Excellent." Sanjo helped Okubo to his feet. "I'm sure you'll want to relay the good news to your friend. Then I suggest you eat a hearty meal, take a long bath, and get a good night's sleep. We have a great deal to talk about once you've had some time to rest."

"I'm deeply grateful to you." Okubo bowed solemnly.

"I only hope your faith in this man is not misplaced."

12

Tokaido road
Year of the Rooster—1633
Hour of the Rooster

After a day of searching for clues to Iemitsu's whereabouts, Iori and Akane met again at sunset at the place where Iemitsu had been captured—Iori from the west and Akane from the Tokaido. Their moods were uniformly gloomy. Iori reported that he'd run across a woodcutter who hadn't seen or heard anything unusual that night. When he showed the woodcutter a *shaken* he had found embedded in a tree trunk not far away, the woodcutter shrugged it off, saying that the woods were full of ninja. "I don't bother them," he had told Iori, "and they don't bother me." That was as much as Iori had learned from him.

"On the way back I picked up some hoofprints on the bank of the stream, but lost them in the rocks along the foothills," he told Akane. "It may be a good idea to concentrate our efforts there tomorrow, unless you uncovered something."

She shook her head. She had spent the day questioning travelers and checking out the way stations along the Tokaido. "Everybody saw something," she said. "Suspicious-looking monks, farmers who didn't look like farmers, pilgrims dressed in the wrong kind of clothes for traveling, a small band of performers who were so untalented they had to be frauds . . ." Akane bit into a rice cake she had bought at one of the inns. "The entire population of Edo couldn't have followed up on all leads I got today."

A voice came from out of the rocks overhead. "Want some help?"

Iori and Akane sprang to their feet and looked up. Partially concealed in a cleft between two boulders, a young man with a headful of uncooperative hair and a face like a monkey peered down at them. He looked so comical that in spite of her surprise, Akane couldn't help smiling.

"What kind of help?" Iori called up to him.

"You're looking for the young lord the ninja dragged off, aren't you?"

Iori was so stunned, all he could do was nod.

"Then I can help you." With that he leaped out of the rocks, did a complete flip in the air, and landed on his feet a couple of paces from where they were standing. "I am called Saru, a trained acrobat," he said proudly. "The name was given to me by my former master, the famous sword swallower Giroemon, who coined the name to describe my acrobatic skills. At first I didn't like being called Monkey. Who wants a name like that? So I tried to get him to call me Nekko—the cat. But he insisted that Saru had more crowd appeal, so I accepted the nickname, and now I'm used to it."

Akane wondered if Saru realized his nickname described more than his acrobatic skills.

"So Saru," Iori said, "you say you saw our lord abducted."

"That I did, that I did. I was sitting right up there where you saw me, watching your lord and that boy go at it!" He shot a sheepish glance at Akane. "Beg your pardon *ojo-san*, but I'll tell you something," he rambled on, "that boy looked more like a girl than a lot of girls I've seen. And believe me, traveling acrobats get to see plenty of girls."

"If you don't mind," Iori said gruffly, "we're only interested in what happened to our lord."

He cocked his head and scrutinized Iori's face, "Say, aren't you the one the ninja let go?"

"You've got good eyes," Iori said.

"You bet I do!" He pointed to his beady eyes. "Saru doesn't miss a thing."

"Look," Akane pleaded, "if you know something that can help us find our lord, please tell us. We don't have time to chat."

"I know where they took him."

"Where?" They both said at once.

"Now wait a minute," Saru said, backing off a few steps. "I took a pretty big chance following those ninja. I did it because I figured the information might be worth plenty to the people who came looking for him. Now you're here . . . I'm here . . . what's your offer?"

Iori reached out to grab the lapel of Saru's *happi* jacket and ended up with a handful of air. With blinding speed Saru had executed a back flip and was running for the rocks. "Come back," Iori shouted, "we'll work something out."

Saru stopped, then approached them gingerly. "Don't try that again," he warned.

"Name your price," Iori said to him.

"I'd say from the look of your lord he ought to be worth at least . . . one hundred *ryo*. That should keep me comfortable for quite a while." Saru pursed his lips in an attempt to look shrewd. "A hundred *ryo*, that's my price."

"Done!" Iori agreed quickly. Too quickly.

"Now, of course, if you'd like me to lead you there, well . . ." Saru scratched his head. "That'll cost you another hundred *ryo*."

Realizing he had made a tactical error, this time Iori asked for a few moments to discuss it with Akane. "We've got to haggle or he'll keep this up all night," he whispered. Akane nodded and shouted at Iori, loud enough for Saru to hear, "No! It's outrageous. Not a *zeni* more."

Saru watched them argue and began to feel better about

his offer. After a few minutes of haggling and posturing, they finally settled on one hundred fifty *ryo*.

"How long will it take you to get it here?" Saru asked.

Iori's hand went to the hilt of his sword, but Akane grabbed his wrist before he could draw.

"Listen to me, Saru," she said. "You know we can't take the time to go back to Edo for the money. Agree to take us there now and we'll double the money."

"How do I know you'll pay?"

"How do we know you'll take us to our lord?"

"I keep my word!"

"And so do I," Akane said. "When we return, I'll stay with you as a hostage until the money is delivered." Saru demurred. "You've shown yourself to be a shrewd business-man, Saru." Akane stared hard into his eyes. "Refuse this offer and we'll be forced to continue our search without you. And then," she added, "you'll have lost everything."

"Triple!" he shouted.

Akane would have been glad to settle for a hundred times the amount, but she turned her back on him and walked away.

Saru saw his dreams collapsing. "All right, you win," he said. "But believe me, I'm not a man to trifle with."

Jubei couldn't get enough to eat. The more they brought him, the more he ate. The rice was new rice, fluffy and moist and white as early snow. The miso soup was pungent with aroma. The fish tasted like the sea, and the late cucumbers and sweet potatoes had not lost their firmness and flavor.

Jubei couldn't be sure whether the long period of depriva-tion had tricked his palate or the food was really that good. "Good is good," said the laconic serving woman when he put the question to her. Although she was obviously under orders to keep the conversation to a minimum, she made no attempt to mask her wonder over the prisoner's stupefying appetite.

After he had cleaned every morsel of every dish she'd served him, Jubei leaned his back against the tub, folded his hands over his distended belly, and took his first real look at the woman who'd brought the food. In the half light of the bathhouse it was difficult to determine her age. Taken sepa-rately, her features were comely, but the total effect was spoiled by emotional neglect. Jubei had seen more vitality expressed on the faces of stone statues. She wore the extinguished look of a professional victim.

If his undisguised scrutiny affected her in any way, he couldn't detect it. She went about her job of tidying up just as though she were there by herself. When she finished stacking the dishes on the tray, she slid it to one side and returned his stare. "My name is Yoshie," she said. "I've been assigned to wait on you. I'm twenty-one years old. I'm not a virgin." She might have been a foot soldier making a field report to a commanding officer.

"My name is Jubei," he said in the same matter-of-fact tone. "I'm not a virgin either." He had hoped for a smile, and got none.

"Shall I prepare your futon?" she asked. Jubei nodded, and she spread his bedding out on the wooden platform that ran around the base of the tub. "If you wish to pillow with me, I'd like your permission to bathe now," she said flatly.

"What?"

She reproduced the same statement, only a little slower and a little louder this time.

"Well," he sighed, "if it's really *that* important to you."

There was a long silence while she puzzled it out. "Important to me?" she said at last. "I don't understand."

"It's clear that you've fallen desperately in love with me. Even though I'm exhausted I want you to know I'm not a cruel man. I won't force you to go away unfulfilled."

"Forgive me, but why are you talking like this?"

"Like what?"

"Like . . . a crazy person."

Jubei burst out laughing. "Crazy?" he said when he caught his breath. "Here you are alone in a steaming bathhouse with a one-eyed samurai who's been locked up so long he doesn't know what day it is . . . you stuff him full of exotic food and offer yourself to him like another sliver of mackerel, and then ask him if *he's* crazy!" He wiped away a stream of tears that spilled out of his good eye. "We're all crazy!"

Yoshie picked up her tray and backed out the door.

Iemitsu, who was being held in the west wing of the villa—out of view of Sanjo's quarters—had just stepped out, accompanied by two guards. Once in the morning and once after the evening meal he was taken out of his room and allowed to stroll through the garden. He heard peals of laughter coming from the direction of the bathhouse.

"Someone seems to be enjoying himself here," he commented sardonically to one of the guards. There was something familiar about the quality of the laugh—a careless freedom to it that titillated his memory like a fragment of an early morning dream. But the harder he clutched at it, the more elusive it became. "Who is it?" he asked, not expecting an answer.

"Another prisoner," one of the guards said, feeling that imparting that much information was nothing more than innocuous chatter. Then he added, "It's nobody important."

When his time in the garden was up, Iemitsu returned to his room, still haunted by a half-formed recollection. He opened the screen and gazed at the bathhouse, which was partially obscured by garden foliage. Stop trying to remember, he told himself, and maybe it will come to you.

In the east wing of the villa Sanjo was putting the finishing touches on the document to the council announcing Iemitsu's capture. It was a subtle piece of work, casting suspicion on Iemitsu's younger brother, Tadanaga. After all, who else but Tadanaga would benefit from his brother's ruin? Leaving the document unsigned and couching all the demands in terms of *we*, implied a conspiracy vast enough to tar anyone who ever had a grievance against the Tokugawa.

Sanjo read it over and smiled. Unless he had badly misread Lord Tajima's character, the announcement was going to catch the council completely by surprise. No doubt Tajima would be clever enough to keep the news of Iemitsu's capture away from the council as long as he could. And because of this, Sanjo was convinced that Tajima would become the first casualty in a war destined to return the nobles to power—if, and only if, he didn't lose his grip on destiny's throat.

The keys were planning, patience, and merciless determination. So far everything was proceeding in season. Sanjo mentally ticked off his accomplishments. He had Iemitsu, he had Okubo, and he would have Arima very soon. Arima's financial problems had forced him to give serious consideration to Sanjo's request for his daughter's hand in marriage—an arrangement that would help secure the loyalty of her unreliable father. Alcala was already obligated to him, and as soon as Okubo told him where he hid the gold, Alcala would have the money he needed to buy more guns. It had all the majesty of *go*, a game of enticement and entrapment—a game at which he was very good.

Okubo was proving more difficult to manage than he anticipated. Over dinner that evening Sanjo lightly touched on the subject of gold. Each time the door was opened, Okubo refused to come in. Perhaps holding on to the secret had become reflex—a habit so ingrained that it was hard to break, even after the reason for guarding it was gone. Or it could be that Okubo was harboring doubts about his value to the operation once the secret was revealed. Sanjo decided that it would be necessary to come up with a tactic to win Okubo's trust.

"Can I trust you?" Sanjo asked Okubo after the dinner dishes had been cleared away and they were alone in the room.

Okubo raised his eyebrows. "After five years of silence, I'm surprised that you could ask such a question."

"I'm sorry," Sanjo apologized, "and what I'm about to reveal will place another burden of secrecy on you that you may not want to hear."

"I think—"

"Please," Sanjo interrupted, "before you answer, there are a few things I want you to consider. We've progressed much further than you can imagine. We've entered into a critical phase where one slip, one miscalculation, will bring everything crashing down around our ears. It is precisely because you have already given so much that I make you this offer. Take a portion of the gold, enough to keep you comfortable for life, and go far away from here. Live out your remaining years in peace and watch events unfold from the safety of your home. After all you've sacrificed, I can't find it in my heart to ask for more."

Okubo exhaled slowly. He knew himself to be a dreamer. Sanjo was a man with the capacity to convert dreams into reality. He stood in awe of his brilliance, his remorseless energy, even his ruthless ability to get things done. Up until this moment he'd never imagined that Sanjo could experience a human emotion, let alone compassion. Yet there it was—a side of Sanjo's nature he'd never seen.

"I would be lying if I told you I'm not tempted," Okubo said. "And if I had known how things were going to turn out for me, I doubt if I would have had the courage to make the

same decision I made then. If I began to regret now, I'd just
be wrong twice. Besides, nothing has really changed, has it?
Christians are still being brutalized by the Tokugawa. How
could I justify backing out now?"

"Some would say you've done enough."

Okubo shrugged. "What's enough?"

"That's the question I'm asking you."

Okubo smiled. "Well, when I find out, I promise you'll be
the first to know."

Sanjo leaned forward. "For the sake of all of us involved,"
he said without a trace of mirth, "I hope you mean that."

For the next half hour Okubo listened in rapt silence while
Sanjo ran through the details of every event that had transpired during his imprisonment, omitting nothing of significance. He spoke of Arima's commitment to provide them
with a safe sanctuary to raise and train an army. He detailed
Alcala's efforts to win the support of the Portuguese military
authorities in Manila. "So far, they've shown very little
enthusiasm for getting directly involved in a war against the
Tokugawa. However, they seem to be more than willing to
provide us with the armament we need, so long as there's a
profit to be made." He ended by telling Okubo about Iemitsu's
abduction, and explained the political benefits he expected to
reap from the capture of the Tokugawa heir.

"Now you know everything," he said to Okubo.

Okubo executed a deep bow. "I congratulate you on the
scope of your accomplishments."

"You made it possible. Without your contribution, all our
efforts amount to nothing more than a prelude to chaos. Gold
has the power to bring chaos under control. Gold means
guns and armies and food to feed our armies. Without your
gold, our ship is dead in the water." Sanjo bowed to Okubo.
"You are the one to be congratulated."

The moment had arrived. Okubo knew Sanjo was going to
press him to produce the gold. It was no longer possible to
evade the issue. Anxiety tightened his throat. Surrendering
the information made him expendable, laying him open to
treachery. Suddenly he felt ashamed. What reason had Sanjo
given him for suspecting treachery? Hadn't he offered him a
way out if he chose to take it? Hadn't *he* made *himself*
vulnerable by confiding in him? Refusing to divulge the loca-

tion of the gold would constitute an unforgivable insult to
Sanjo, wrecking the bond of trust between them.

"You're telling me you've reached the point where you
need the gold to proceed."

Sanjo nodded.

"Then tell me how much you need, and I'll get it for you,"
he said, improvising a dodge that might work to his advantage.

"No," Sanjo answered sternly.

"No?"

"Two reasons. You are an escaped criminal. How far do
you think you would get before someone recognized you and
turned you in to the *bakufu*? I doubt that they would waste
any more time trying to extract information from you. The
chances are excellent that you'd be summarily executed."
Sanjo took a sip of tea. "Which leads me to my second point.
If anything happens to you, the gold is lost, and with it any
prospect for success. That, my friend, is a risk we can no
longer afford to take. I want to know where the gold is
hidden."

Sanjo's logic was irrefutable. It came down to one simple
question: Did he trust Sanjo?

"I'll draw a map tonight," he said. "You'll have it in the
morning."

"Excellent." Sanjo beamed. "Plan to stay here until a suitable place can be found to hide out. In time it will be less
dangerous for you to travel the roads."

Sanjo thought about inviting Okubo to stay for a game of *go*,
but changed his mind. Matching wits with Okubo would be a
bore. He's too easy, he thought. Much too easy.

Fresh from her morning bath, her hair dressed with the
juice of wild vine, her skin tingling from an application of
araiko, Maria held her breath while the maid adjusted the
padding used to straighten out her curves.

"Your waist is too small, your breasts too big," her maid
grumbled. "This body was never meant to fit in a kimono."
Partly out of habit and partly out of a desire to ward off
vanity, Yoshino tried hard to cover up her admiration for her
mistress's beauty with a litany of complaints.

"Look, Yoshino," Maria said as she slipped her arms through
the sleeves of her sky-blue undergarment, "someone's coming."

"Where?" Yoshino squinted to focus her myopic eyes.

"By the fish pond."

Yoshino eased the door closed, leaving just enough of a crack to peep out. Even with poor eyesight she could identify the man coming toward them. "It's your father," she said, clearly annoyed that he had not given them advance warning.

"Yoshino, I'm not dressed!"

Without seeming to hurry, Yoshino slipped the white silk mid-garment over her shoulders, then the plum-colored kimono. The obi was wound and tied, and after some deft tugs at the collar, Maria was ready for the outer robe. She was seated, fanning herself, when her father appeared at the door.

"*Chichive*," she said, bowing low, "I'm honored by your visit, but I'm afraid you've caught me unprepared."

"Yes, I know," he said as Yoshino prepared a place for him to sit. "I have to attend to some urgent business in Osaka, and I wanted to see you before I left. There are some important matters we need to discuss."

"Bring Lord Arima some tea," Maria said to Yoshino.

Arima waited until the door slid closed behind her before he continued. "As you know, I've had considerable difficulty finding a suitable husband for you. I blame myself for passing up the many opportunities for excellent arrangements when you were younger. And now so much has happened—rumors about the child you brought home with you, concern over the family's ties to Christianity, which you stubbornly refuse to renounce publicly, our financial difficulties, and so on. I don't need to tell you that with each passing year the problem is compounded."

Maria nodded. Several times since her return from Lisbon her father resurrected the same speech. She had come to accept it as his way of apologizing for assigning her to the ranks of the unmarried. Each time her answer was the same: "*Chichive*, please don't fret over me. I lead a full life as mistress of your house. I'm content serving you as long as you need me." It seemed to assuage his guilt, at least until the next time he experienced an attack of conscience over his failure to find her a husband. She had no reason to suspect that this time would be different.

Arima had racked his brain to come up with some way to lubricate his announcement, but he knew no matter how adroitly he presented the arrangement, Sanjo was going to be a bitter dose for her to swallow. There was nothing to do except get it over with as quickly as possible. He took a deep breath and plunged in.

"Although I've never mentioned it to you, there's been a long-standing offer of marriage that must be given serious consideration. I've postponed making a final decision out of deference to, ah . . . certain reservations you might have about this particular arrangement. But," he hurried on, "I can assure you I've given a good deal of thought to this matter, and I think in the end you'll agree that, although it may seem imperfect in certain respects, the advantages outweigh the disadvantages by a considerable margin."

"Who is it?" she asked, feeling drowned in verbiage.

"He's a man of high rank," Arima said curtly. "Surely you don't think I'd marry you to anyone beneath your station, do you?"

"*Chichive*, please just tell me his name."

"Prince Sanjo," he said as casually as he could.

The expression of horror on her face chilled him to the marrow. Her mouth tried to form words, but no sound came out. He'd expected resistance, but this . . . this was revulsion. She looked physically ill.

Arima reached out to take her hand, and she shrank back as if he'd moved to strangle her. "Stop it!" he shouted. "This is too much. You're acting like a child. What's wrong with you?"

"You're my father," her voice cracked. "You know what kind of man he is. I told you what he did to his former wife, and yet . . ."

"Listen to me," Arima said gently. "All men have certain eccentricities when it comes to, ah . . . pillowing. Surely you've heard the women speak of things like that."

"Eccentricity! You call forcing your wife to pillow with a stranger eccentric? I call it inhuman. Prince Sanjo is nothing but a vicious pervert!"

"My child, don't be so quick to judge. No man is without faults," he pleaded. "Talk to the other women, they'll tell you as much."

Maria glared at him in utter disbelief. A swirling fury raged inside her. Hot tears filled her eyes, but she refused to weep, refused to give in to the sob that welled up in her throat. Over

and over a single question raced through her mind: Why?
Why? Why?

Arima sat across from her, his hands clenched at his sides,
waiting for the tempest to break. He'd never seen her like
this. The valiant effort to maintain her composure in the face
of the terrible blow he'd delivered, and the awful look of
betrayal in her eyes tore at his heart. But there was no
turning back now. Inviting Sanjo's infamous wrath was simply
not an option he could afford to entertain. All he could do
was appeal to her sense of family loyalty and pray that her
solid character would eventually overcome her grief.

"No one knows better than you how perilous our financial
situation is. Tokugawa taxes have put us on the brink of ruin.
The Shimabara farmers are starving. There's no more to take.
I was forced to listen to Prince Sanjo's offer—"

"And will I bring a good price?" she asked bitterly.

"And do you think you are the first daughter who tolerated
an unhappy marriage to help her family out of financial difficulty?" he retorted sharply.

"*Chichive*, I'm not being selfish. I've never refused anything you've asked of me. Believe me, if it would help, I'd
marry a merchant . . . anyone, anyone with enough money to
pay our debts. But not Prince Sanjo. I'd rather die."

"I forbid you to talk that way!" He ground his fist into his
palm. "You will not put your personal likes and dislikes ahead
of your duty to your family. There will be no more talk of
merchants. There will be no more talk of death. Where is
your pride? You are samurai!"

"Yes, samurai," she said softly. "We sneer at merchants
who peddle their wares in the marketplace and kill them if
they don't bow properly when we pass by. We take away the
farmers' rice and let them sell their daughters into prostitution to keep from starving to death. And now, when you tell
me you're going to sell my body to the highest bidder, you
remind me that I am samurai." A tear broke free and trickled
down her cheek. "And you ask me, 'Where is your pride?' "

"Let me assure you that there are far deeper factors than
money involved in this arrangement," Arima said coldly.
"Things I'm not able to discuss with you right now. But
believe me, there is great change on the horizon. The winds
are shifting, and only fools and madmen set their sails against
the wind."

Arima got up to leave. Maria opened the door for him, and he saw Yoshino kneeling outside with the tea tray on her lap. Her head was bowed, but he could see that she was sobbing.

"I won't make my final decision until spring." Arima put his hand on Maria's shoulder. "You may feel differently by then," he said, but his voice lacked conviction.

Maria passed the rest of the morning gazing out into the garden, her cupped hands resting lightly on her lap, her head slightly bowed, her shoulders stooped, as if her center had given way and she was collapsing in on herself. Random thoughts and feelings presented themselves uninvited, then wandered away like neglected guests. Each time Jan Kriek emerged, Maria tried to catch hold of him, but she seemed to lack the strength of will to hold on tight enough to keep him from slipping away. Even this caused neither pain, nor sorrow, nor anger. She felt numb, disconnected from the world—like a kite whose string had snapped in a sudden gust of wind.

Yoshino stayed close by. The tea she poured for Maria had gone cold, the bowl of rice and pickles on the tatami untouched. Maria seemed lost in a fog, responding to Yoshino's attempts to reach her with somnolent nods, as if Yoshino's voice were coming from far away.

Finally, out of sheer frustration, Yoshino grabbed her hands. "Cry! Scream! Break something!" she pleaded. "Don't just sit there and let your spirit shrivel up."

The two women's eyes met, but Maria remained silent.

"Maybe you need to rest," Yoshino said tenderly. "You might feel better after a little nap." She took the futon down from the cupboard and spread it out on the floor

When she began to undress her mistress, Maria waved her away. "Give me some time to myself," she said.

Yoshino hesitated at the door, then did as she was told.

Maria opened the lacquered box that held her private treasures. She thumbed through the pages of her journal and found the pressed sprig of cherry blossoms she had picked the morning she and Jan-san parted. Time had stolen the scent, but the delicate pink color remained. She read the poem she had written:

Spring went off with the blossoms that left the trees
But I shall pick them up, for they are mine.

* * *

Okubo brought Sanjo his answer the following morning. At
dawn he came to Sanjo's quarters with a map indicating the
location of the gold.

"Sake barrels!" Sanjo chuckled with admiration. "You smuggled gold out in sake barrels and had them delivered to an
obscure shrine in Oyano." He folded Okubo's map and tucked
it away inside his kimono. "I must congratulate you. Who
would ever think of inspecting a gift to the gods?"

"Each of the thirty barrels is one-quarter full of gold dust,"
Okubo said. "I added enough sake to convince anyone who
handled them that there was actually liquid inside."

A servant announced that the porters had arrived with
Sanjo's palanquin and were awaiting his pleasure.

"So, you'll be leaving for Edo now," Okubo said.

"Soon," Sanjo answered, dabbing a little more rouge on his
lips. He inspected his blackened teeth in the mirror and
traced his finger lightly over a spray of age lines at the corner
of his eye. "As the maidens say, I must be spending too much
time gazing at the moon," he commented, referring to the
popular notion that moonlight caused wrinkles.

Okubo replied with a familiar line of poetry.

> "With flowers that fade, with leaves that turn, they
>   speak
> Most surely of a world where all is fleeting."

And Sanjo answered:

> "In a world where no one can be sure of the morrow,
> I grieve for him who did not live out the day."

"Ah," Okubo said, "Ki-no-Tsurayuki's poem on the death
of his cousin."

"How delightful to trade poems with a literate man," Sanjo
said. "It serves to remind me how much I despise returning
to Edo. Life is so coarse there. It's like wallowing in dirt."
He adjusted the peak of his ceremonial cap and collected his
katana from the sword rack. "But before I leave," he said to
Okubo, "I want to show you the east garden at dawn."

The shoji screen facing the east garden was illuminated with
a rosy glow. "Come," Sanjo said, motioning Okubo to join
him. "The effect is extraordinary."

He opened the screen and Okubo stopped, frozen in his tracks. Tatami mats had been laid out on the garden path. On each side three ninja were kneeling. The morning sun cast a pink hue over the white silk runners that covered the mats.

"Seppuku?" Okubo rasped, unbelieving.

"Execution would hardly be appropriate, considering all that you have contributed, *neh*?"

"Why?"

"Come now," Sanjo said in a patronizing tone, "don't force me to demean your intelligence with an explication of the obvious."

"I demand an explanation!" Okubo's indignation had momentarily dismantled his shock.

"As you wish," Sanjo sighed. "From the moment you were captured, you became a magnet, a compass needle pointing the way to the gold, the guns, and on to the very heart of the conspiracy. My security, and the security of all of us who remain in the shadows, has been irreparably compromised."

"So after years of silence, you still don't trust me," Okubo said with disgust.

"My dear Okubo, you're not listening to me. It's not a matter of trust. It's really much simpler than that. It's your misfortune to be the only identifiable link in a chain that connects the Tokugawa with us. Remove the link and the chain is broken. I'm truly sorry. You've performed admirably, but—"

"But now I'm expendable."

"Why don't you view yourself as an actor who has played out his role? Deliver your final lines with grace and dignity. Exit and let the play go on."

Okubo looked out over the garden. Everything was still. Multicolored leaves, damp with dew, glimmered like freshly minted coins. The path to the reflecting pool had been swept clean, and the surface of the water was dark vermilion. A stone lantern cast a soft light over the moss that grew in the shade of an ancient plum tree. A strange peace enveloped him, and he suddenly felt vast. It was an uncommonly lovely morning.

The voice of a long forgotten teacher came back to him. *How can the wind be cold? The wind is not cold. The rain is not cold. You are cold.* Only he could spoil the moment now.

Okubo lifted his chin and walked to the head of the mat.

He kneeled facing the sun and bowed to the witnesses. Sanjo positioned himself on Okubo's left side and requested the honor of acting as his second. Okubo agreed, instructing him not to strike the killing blow until he lowered his head.

While Sanjo dipped water from the stone basin and cleansed his sword blade, Okubo composed his death poem. It occurred to him that as a Christian, suicide was a mortal sin, damning him to eternal hellfire. For a moment the thought disturbed his composure, until he remembered that the killing blow would come from Sanjo's sword. Surely God could not fault him for choosing to die with dignity.

Okubo crossed himself and said a prayer to Jesus, the one god who could understand his desire to die well. Then he took up the writing brush and paper that had been left by his side. With firm, bold strokes he put down the lines of his final statement to the world of men.

No bridge am I, to see others safely across.
And why have I passed a life like a long, long bridge.

He set it aside and opened his kimono to the navel. At his signal one of the ninja stepped forward and offered him a tray bearing a dirk with the hilt wrapped in white silk. Okubo poised the point over a spot just above his pelvic bone. He set his teeth against the pain and yanked his hands toward him, plunging the blade deep into his abdomen. Sanjo raised his *katana* over his shoulder. Okubo opened his eyes as the initial pain abated. The first full rays of sunlight burst through the branches. It was beautiful to see.

Okubo tightened his grip and drew the razor-sharp blade across his belly, fighting hard to keep from gasping. Flecks of light danced in front of his eyes. Waves of nausea began to threaten him. Mustering the last resources of his will, he twisted the knife blade and jerked the hilt up toward his solar plexus. His head dropped forward. Sanjo struck before Okubo could lose his balance and fall.

Sanjo picked up Okubo's severed head by the hair and held it out for the witnesses to identify. "Look at this and remember how a brave man dies," he said.

At sunrise Saru stopped them at an overgrown graveyard

near the ruins of a farmhouse. "This is as far as I go," he told them. "The villa you're looking for is just over that knoll."

The knoll he pointed to had been clear-cut. Nothing higher than a stump stood between them and the hilltop.

"Is this the only approach?" Iori asked.

"Well, there's a lake on the other side of the villa, but it's too big to swim, and I guess you don't want to come in by boat." Saru chuckled. "Only way you're going to get there is to take the main road in. At least you've got some trees along the sides for cover."

"How did you get in?" Akane asked.

"I never said I went in."

"Then how do you know there's a villa in there?" Iori snapped.

"See that big boulder over there?" East of where they stood was another hill, a good distance from the road. "Well, I climbed up to that rock and took a look at the place. All I could see was the roof of the main house and some outbuildings. There's a good-sized wall that runs around the place. But if you make it that far, you've got some cover once you get inside."

Akane got Saru to draw a picture in the dirt. After studying the details for a few minutes, she came to the conclusion that it was hopeless to try to sneak in during daylight.

Iori disagreed. "It's risky, but not impossible. Saru says there's a stream running along the side of the road. Maybe the bank will give us some cover. It might even be deep enough to swim." He turned to Saru. "Is it?"

"It wasn't where I crossed over, but I remember seeing a lot of big rocks in the streambed."

"They'd give us some cover, wouldn't they?" he asked Saru.

"The ones I saw would, but who knows what you'll run into farther downstream. If you want my advice, listen to the girl and wait until it gets dark to make your move."

"Well, I'm not asking your advice!" he lashed out at Saru. "Besides, if it hadn't been for you lagging behind, we'd have made it here before first light."

"I can't help it if I've got little legs," Saru replied, fending off Iori's cut. "I was built for acrobatics, not long-distance running."

Iori threw up his hands in disgust. "The point I'm trying to make," he said to Akane, "is that we don't have the time to be overly cautious. Who knows what's happening in there? We may be too late already."

"And if we're not, rushing in and getting ourselves killed isn't going to help anybody."

"Enough!" Iori barked impatiently. "We're up against ninja. Their element is darkness. Also, this is their terrain. They know every nook and cranny. At least if we go in now, we can use our eyes against theirs. That makes the odds a little more even." Akane nodded thoughtfully. "And the last thing they'd expect is for anyone to try to penetrate their defenses in daylight."

"Get down!" Saru hissed. Everyone sprawled on the ground. "Look, coming down the road."

Through the trees they could make out a troop of guards on the road. Keeping low, they scrambled behind the broken-down foundation of the farmhouse and peeked through the cracks in the mortar.

As the column drew closer, they saw a palanquin swaying between the two files of soldiers wearing the uniforms of the Imperial Guard. The palanquin was borne by four porters rather than two, a sure sign that the occupant was a court noble.

"So," Iori said after the procession had passed by, "the nobles are involved in this."

"Or the ninja are using a court palanquin to move your lord from place to place," Saru speculated.

Akane shook her head. "I don't think they'd risk moving him around on the roads. If he's alive, he's still in there."

Jubei finally had enough light to read Okubo's note. Okubo had left it with the serving woman, instructing her to deliver it only if he didn't return before she brought Jubei his breakfast.

Jubei held the note up to the light that filtered through the bamboo vents. Although the characters were small, Okubo's strokes were beautifully executed and easy to decipher.

My friend—

If you are reading this note, you will know that I am dead, killed by the very people whom I protected with

*my silence. I feared my usefulness would end the moment
I revealed the location of the gold I took from the
Tokugawa mines, so I gave them a false map to test their
response. Since I am betrayed, what hope do I have that
the cause I served would not be as easily betrayed?*

*You are the last person I can trust. Here is the true
map to the gold. Please see to it that the gold is used to
help relieve the suffering of my Christian brothers and
sisters. That is my final request.*

You must escape. Time is short.

Okubo

Jubei folded the note. And I will betray you too, my friend,
he thought, just as the others have. And I will tell myself that
I did it for some higher purpose, just as the others have. "So
now you know that the last man you could trust has deceived
you," he said out loud to Okubo's spirit. "I did what I set out
to do. I won your friendship through guile, and I used it to
get at your secret. But who really won? You died believing
you had a friend you could trust. I live on knowing that I had
a friend who trusted me, and I used that trust to gut his
dream. It may not help to tell you this, but I feel cheap. And
it may not help to tell you that you became like a brother to
me, but it's true." Jubei slipped the map inside his obi.

With Okubo dead, Jubei couldn't think of any reason why
he would have a better chance of surviving. He had to figure
a way to escape, and quickly.

Jubei looked up at the bamboo vents. During the night he
had managed to work three of the bars loose. A fourth would
give him just enough room to squeeze out. But doing it at
night and doing it in the daytime were two different things.
Still, given the situation, there wasn't much choice. If he
made it, it was going to take a spectacular piece of luck.

Standing on the edge of the tub, Jubei leaped and caught a
bar with one hand. He felt it begin to give, and quickly
snatched another with his free hand. Then he pulled himself
up, forced a leg through a space in the bars, and locked his
leg in. Suddenly he froze. From his perch he could see the
ninja guard listening outside the door. He watched the guard
draw his sword and carefully slide the bolt out of the hasp.
The door burst open and he rushed in, assuming an attack
crouch a few paces inside the door.

Jubei held his breath as the ninja scanned the dark corners of the bathhouse, looking for some sign of his prisoner. Then he seemed to focus on the tub. He inched forward, his sword cocked over his right shoulder. Jubei waited until he reached the very edge of the tub, then pushed off, smashing into the startled ninja's chest before he had a chance to set his sword. He heard the ninja's head thud against the rim of the tub and felt his body go slack under his weight. He listened. The ninja wasn't breathing.

Jubei grabbed the sword, dashed to the door, and pushed it shut. He sat with his back against the door, waiting for the sound of onrushing footsteps. Everything remained quiet—no shouting, no alarm bells, nothing.

He eased the door open a crack. Two servant girls were carrying baskets of laundry along the veranda of the main house. A gardener was absorbed in trimming a boxwood hedge. He saw no sign of other ninja.

Jubei undressed the dead ninja and put him in the tub, balancing the back of his crushed head against the rim, as if he were enjoying a morning bath. Then he put on the ninja's clothes, removed his eye patch, and wrapped the lower part of his face with the ninja's scarf.

As casually as he could, he stepped outside and locked the door. The lake was directly in front of him. The villa was on his left and the woods behind him. Jubei chose the woods. He didn't hurry, but his pace was purposeful. About halfway to the first line of trees, he had the distinct impression he was being watched. A subtle glance to his right confirmed his suspicion. A ninja had stepped out of the shade and was staring at him from a small garden close to the villa.

Without seeming to notice, Jubei stopped, looked around, then undid his pants and urinated in the shrubbery. The ninja turned away and joined a man seated on a stone bench. The other man, dressed in a kimono got up and walked a few steps out into the sunlight. Jubei's stomach knotted. The man in the kimono was Lord Iemitsu!

The staggering incongruity of the heir's presence at the villa compelled Jubei to question his own perception. The profile was unmistakable—the way he moved with measured elegance, every gesture charged with self-conscious precision. A second look solidified Jubei's conviction that he was right. It had to be Iemitsu.

Jubei realized that standing and gawking was not moving him one step closer to unraveling the enigma of what Iemitsu was doing here. Further speculation was going to have to be put off until a more propitious time.

When he was sure the ninja was no longer paying attention to him, Jubei did up his pants and slipped into the woods. There were several well-defined paths to follow, but he avoided them, choosing instead an untrammeled route through the underbrush. The ground was strewn with dried winterkill, forcing him to pick his steps carefully, to keep from making too much noise. The going seemed excruciatingly slow, but he kept his patience.

Then he discovered that the woods had been booby-trapped with an elaborate web of trip wires, probably connected to some kind of alarm system. He wondered how many times he had barely missed treading on a wire. Once again the mysterious force Takuan called *haragei* had guided his footsteps. It had taken him a long time to come to the realization that his uncanny ability to sense danger was more than mere happenstance. Time after time Takuan had forced him to rely on this gift, and little by little Jubei had come to the certain knowledge that his perception was not limited to the five senses. Jubei closed his eye, took a deep breath, and began to listen with his whole body, just as Takuan had taught him.

When he started moving, Jubei picked his way through the maze of wires slowly and carefully, but with utter confidence. Eventually the intense effort began to cause his thighs to tremble, playing havoc with his balance.

A small stack of rocks overgrown with mulberry bushes provided him with some concealment while he rested. He hadn't been there long when the quiet was jolted by the sudden rush of wings. A covey of spooked quail raced overhead and disappeared among the trees. Jubei gripped the hilt of his sword and listened.

Stillness.

After a while the hush gave way to the mating urge of cicada and the territorial squabbles of assorted birds. It took a little longer for his heart to pump out the excess excitement.

Jubei was just about to push on when he thought he caught a glimpse of movement in the area where the quail had been nesting. Something had disturbed the light pattern streaming through the leaves. He focused on the area and saw it again.

This time he could make out a definite shape. Someone was coming toward him.

Jubei eased his sword out of the scabbard, deadening the sound with his thumb and forefinger. He adjusted his breathing to minimize body movement.

The undergrowth parted slowly and a man stepped into the tiny clearing a stone's throw from where Jubei was hiding. When the man lifted his head to look around, Jubei got the second surprise of the morning.

"Iori," Jubei called out in a stage whisper, quickly squirming out of his hiding place. Iori gaped at the ninja. In his excitement, Jubei had forgotten how he was dressed. He pulled the scarf down and revealed his face.

Iori stared at him in disbelief. "Jubei?" he said.

Jubei sheathed his sword and went to him, half wondering if he was in the grip of some persistent, lifelike dream. First Iemitsu, now Iori. None of it made any sense at all.

"I thought you were in jail," Iori said, seizing one of a multitude of perplexing questions jangling around in his head.

"I was until a few days ago, but that's another story. What are you doing here?"

"We're looking for Iemitsu."

"We?"

"Your father sent Akane and me out to find him." He glanced over his shoulder. "She should be here any minute."

"I just saw him."

"Iemitsu?" Jubei nodded. "Then he's still alive!"

Jubei took Iori by the shoulders. "Tell me what happened."

Iori gave him a condensed account of the kidnapping and the subsequent events that led them to the villa.

When Akane saw Jubei, she asked no questions. She threw her arms around his neck and held him tightly. Jubei stroked her hair and said to them, "Put aside all your questions for now. I'm working for Father, and I've been working for him a long time. Now let's concentrate on finding a way to free Iemitsu."

Jubei sketched the layout of the villa in the dirt. "It's a good bet they're holding him here." He indicated the spot where he had seen Iemitsu. "That's the west wing. Over here," he pointed to the shore line, "I saw a fishing boat tied up. We'll never make it back through the woods moving fast because of all the boody traps, so the lake's our best chance.

"How many ninja are there?" Akane asked.

"I don't know. I was locked up the whole time."

"Worrying about it won't change anything," Iori said to Akane. "We'll just have to take whatever comes our way."

"There's one more thing you ought to know," Jubei said. "My escape is only going to make things harder for us. As soon as they discover the ninja I killed, the security around the compound is going to be fierce."

Suddenly Jubei leaped to his feet. He spotted a man sitting on the limb of a tree, listening intently.

"Saru!" Akane said. "What are you doing here?"

"I've got an investment to protect," he replied. "And from where I sit, things don't look too good."

"He's the one who showed us the way," Akane explained to Jubei.

Saru dropped to the ground, hardly making a sound when his feet hit. "It seems to me you need a diversion, *neh*?"

"What kind of diversion?" Jubei asked.

"Suppose I ran around the woods tripping all the alarms. What do you think the ninja would do?"

Jubei peered at the strange little man thoughtfully. "It might draw them off."

"Might! What self-respecting ninja could resist a tasty morsel like that?" Saru grinned his idiot grin.

"You'd be willing to do that?" Iori asked.

"For another hundred *ryo* I would."

So they started off, leaving Saru behind to stir up a commotion at the precise moment the sun reached its apex. Since Jubei had already covered the ground ahead of him, he took the lead and the others followed, stepping where he'd stepped.

They approached the compound without incident. Jubei could come up with only one plausible explanation for the lack of ninja activity—perhaps when the serving woman came back to clean after breakfast, she mistook the ninja in the tub for him. Assuming he was bathing, she might have taken the tray and left without uttering a word. Considering her disposition, Jubei viewed it as a distinct possibility. If so, lunchtime would be the moment of truth.

Nearing the west end of the villa, they took up positions within sight of each other. Because of his ninja attire, Jubei would go in first to try to locate Iemitsu. At his signal the rest would follow. When they had Iemitsu, they would make a dash for the boat.

At noon the alarms went off. Gongs thundered, bells clanged, and ninja ran everywhere. There were more of them than Jubei had imagined—maybe forty or fifty. They gathered in the courtyard, got their instructions, and took off on a dead run down the main path through the woods. Apparently the trip wires were set to pinpoint the precise area of intrusion, since the ninja gave every indication of knowing exactly where they were going.

However, enough of them remained behind to be troublesome. Jubei jogged past the first two he came across, drawing only perfunctory glances as he passed. The next ninja he saw was pacing back and forth on the veranda outside the west wing. He fixed Jubei with a malevolent stare and ordered him to stop.

"Where are you going?" he snarled.

"What?" Jubei said, walking up to him.

"I said where—"

Before he could finish restating his question, Jubei drew and cut him down. With a powerful shove of his foot, he rolled the ninja off the veranda and into the bushes.

Taking up the dead ninja's post, Jubei mimicked his mannerism of pacing around. The screens were closed tight. Inside one room he heard voices. Jubei slid the screen open slightly and saw a group of serving women huddled together in animated conversation. Moving on to the next screen, he stopped and listened. The only sound was the faint click of chopsticks. Then he heard a familiar voice. "The tea is cold," Iemitsu complained.

"*Gomen nasai,*" the serving woman apologized, and he heard her shuffle toward the door.

Jubei timed his steps so that he passed by just as the screen was drawn back. Two ninja were standing on each side of Iemitsu, who sat cross-legged on the tatami, picking at his lunch.

The serving woman took no notice of Jubei as she scurried off down the veranda. He drew a deep breath and charged into the room. He killed the closest ninja with a swift overhand cut, dropped to one knee and caught the other one under the arm with a sweeping backstroke. The sword fell out of the ninja's hands and he staggered backward, finally collapsing through the shoji screen on the opposite side of the room.

It all happened so fast that Iemitsu was still sitting upright with his chopsticks poised in his hand when Jubei pulled down his scarf.

"Jubei!" he shouted.

Jubei picked up a sword and handed it to Iemitsu. "Follow me," he ordered, disregarding all formality. Iemitsu did as he was told.

They stepped over the fallen guard and went out through the hole in the screen. Fortunately for them, the back veranda was deserted. "Go into the garden and wait by that oak tree," he told Iemitsu.

Jubei stuck two fingers in his mouth and let go a long shrill whistle. When he saw Iori and Akane break into the clearing, he waved his sword at them, raced back into the room, emptied the brazier onto the floor at the base of the paper screen, then blew the embers into flame. As soon as he had a blaze going, he hurried out to join the others.

"Look out!" he shouted at Akane.

A ninja who had just rounded the corner of the house fired two *shaken* at them in rapid succession. Jubei picked off the first with the blade of his *katana*, but the second embedded itself in Akane's shoulder blade, spinning her around. She clutched at Jubei's sleeve as she dropped to one knee.

In a blind rage Iori charged at the ninja, who quickly ducked out of sight.

Jubei jerked the star-shaped missile out of Akane's back. She gasped, and Jubei lifted her to her feet. "Does it burn?" he asked, fearing that the *shaken* had been treated with poison. Akane shook her head. "Is your arm getting numb?" he persisted.

"Stop worrying about me!" Akane snapped. "It's only a flesh wound."

Jubei nodded. If the *shaken* had been poisoned, by now Akane would have been in serious agony.

Iori ran up to them. As soon as he saw Akane back on her feet, a look of immense relief came over his face.

"Go!" Jubei shouted, and they dashed ahead through the garden, toward the waterfront. Smoke billowed out behind them, partially covering their escape.

As Jubei had hoped, the fire set off a panic among the

servants, triggering confusion and chaos. They poured outside, getting in the way of the pursuing ninja. With everyone running from the fire or to the fire, it was difficult for the ninja to pick out the right people to pursue.

It was a different story when they got to the lakeshore. Six Ninja were standing by the boat, waiting with drawn swords.

"Stay here," Jubei said to Iemitsu, whose face had lost all color.

The ensuing battle was furious. The ninja were unbelievably agile, leaping high in the air, twisting, turning, slashing. But at close quarters, ninja swordplay was no match for theirs. One by one the ninja were cut down, until Iori was engaging the last man.

"Get Iemitsu on the boat," Jubei shouted to Akane as he ran to Iori's aid. The ninja had slashed Iori's thigh, and he appeared to be in serious difficulty.

Jubei circled behind the ninja, forcing him to give ground. As Jubei closed in on him, he realized it was the same ninja chief who had wanted to kill him that night at the farmhouse. Jubei cocked his sword over his right shoulder and unleashed a lightning barrage of cuts which the ninja chief barely managed to fend off. Then Jubei switched to the left attitude and closed again. This time the ninja held his ground. Reaching inside his sleeve with his free hand, he came out with a fist full of metal fragments and flung them at Jubei's face.

Instantly Jubei snapped his head to one side, taking the worst of the spray on his blind side. When he turned back to meet the attack, the ninja was halfway down the beach.

Jubei let him go. He helped Iori on board, then pushed the boat out waist deep and scrambled over the stern. Akane passed him a long pole, and Jubei got the boat a good distance from the shore before the lake bottom gave out. The sail was useless in the dead calm, so they took up the paddles and pressed on. In the distance they could see a group of ninja watching helplessly from the shore.

No one except Iemitsu escaped unscathed. Jubei looked the worst. The entire side of his face was drenched in blood, but the tiny gashes were superficial—painful, but not threatening. At Akane's insistence Jubei thrust his head into the water and washed the blood from his face.

Akane's back had stopped bleeding and she was concentrating on Iori's thigh wound, which turned out to be more

serious than anyone suspected. The gash was large and deep.
He had already lost a lot of blood and was losing more. What
concerned Akane most was the pumping action of the wound.
She had been able to slow down the bleeding by applying
pressure to a point just below the groin, but she couldn't get
it to stop. She made a tourniquet with her obi, using her
kaiken to twist it tight.

Iemitsu had already shredded his cotton underwear and
was helping Akane attend to Iori's wound. To her relief, she
discovered that the artery had not been completely severed.
She took a needle out of her medicine bag and threaded it
with a hair from her head.

"Sit still," she said to everyone.

When the boat settled she wiped out the wound with a
wet cloth, dabbed it dry, and began the intricate work of
sewing the artery together. It took several tries before she
got it. Slowly she loosened the tourniquet and watched the
blood flow in. The spurting had stopped.

"Don't move," she said to Iori as she bandaged his leg. "It
should hold until we can get to a real doctor."

Iori never heard her. He had passed out a few minutes earlier.
Akane cradled his head in her lap and lifted the damp hair off
his brow. She studied his face. The pallor of his skin and the
fine sensitive features made him appear more an artist than a
swordsman. It amazed her that Iori could be so fearless in
combat, yet so painfully shy around women. It had taken him
months to work up the courage to speak to her, and months
more before he could start a conversation without blushing.
Although he had never dared to express his feelings openly,
Akane was certain that he had fallen in love with her. The
knowledge troubled her deeply because of the terrible secret
she kept locked away in her heart. Akane knew she was
incapable of giving herself to any man until she succeeded in
exorcising the shameful, all-consuming desire she felt for her
own brother.

"You handled yourself well, my sister," Jubei said with
unconcealed admiration.

Akane looked up at him and smiled, but didn't trust herself
to speak.

As the afternoon shadows began to lengthen, a light breeze
skimmed over the surface of the lake. Jubei set the square-
rigged sail, the wind took it, and he put the paddles away.

Nearing a small promontory they heard a shrill voice cry out, "*Oi!* Over there. *Oi!*" A small figure with stumpy legs was jumping up and down at the water's edge, frantically waving outsized arms.

"It's Saru," Akane said, waving back.

Without waiting for the boat to change course, Saru plunged into the lake and swam toward them. When he got close enough, Jubei offered him the pole and Saru grabbed it gratefully. Huffing and puffing, he clung to the side of the boat, too exhausted to climb aboard.

"Am I glad to see you!" he sputtered. "They almost got me."

"Are you all right?" Akane asked.

"I am now," he replied, his beady little eyes sparkling with delight. "You're looking at a rich man."

The following morning Sanjo presented himself to the Shogun's council with a signed document from the Emperor, stating his willingness to formally recognize Iemitsu as Shogun. "As soon as Lord Iemitsu fixes his mark to this agreement, I'll return to Kyoto and begin preparations for the investiture," Sanjo said to the stony-faced council members.

Tajima accepted the scroll and promised to return immediately, with the document executed by the heir.

"Excuse me, Lord Tajima," Sanjo said, "but as you know, it's necessary for a member of the Imperial Court to witness the signing—in keeping with tradition, you understand."

"Yes, of course," Tajima replied. "Let me see if Lord Iemitsu is disposed to comply with your request."

After Tajima had left the room, Sanjo studied the faces of the individual counselors, looking for signs of the strain they must be feeling after receiving the ransom note earlier that morning. Each one was doing his best to mask his anxiety, but the brittle silence in the room gave away their collective tension. Sanjo wondered what kind of excuse Tajima would offer to explain Iemitsu's inability to appear at the meeting. While he waited for Tajima to return, Sanjo mentally rehearsed his reaction.

Nothing he prepared had anticipated what happened next. The door slid open and Iemitsu entered and took his place on the dais. Sanjo's deep bow had not been executed quickly enough to cover up the flicker of shock that Tajima saw in his eyes.

Sanjo listened but barely heard the brief statement Iemitsu made before the council. He watched but barely saw Iemitsu take out his official chop and stamp his mark on the document. Beneath the layers of powder, behind the painted smile, Sanjo's mind was groping for answers in a sea of uncertainty. How could this happen? What had gone wrong?

He returned to Kyoto in a black funk and immediately demanded a full accounting from the chief of the Koga ninja. He was told that those responsible for the security of the villa had been denied the honor of seppuku and summarily executed. He was told that Tajima's son Jubei had been instrumental in the escape, told the identities of the others who had penetrated his defenses in broad daylight, and discovered that his villa had burned to the ground.

However, it wasn't until a few weeks later that the true dimensions of the disaster became apparent. Sanjo's agents, who had been sent to Oyano to recover the gold, returned with the news that the shrine indicated on Okubo's map had never existed. Of the forty or so casks of ceremonial sake they found at other shrines on the island, not a single one showed the slightest trace of having contained any gold dust.

For the first time in his life Prince Sanjo caught a powerful whiff of his own fallibility. It was a time for reevaluation, he decided, not capitulation. Tajima had proved himself to be a worthy adversary, and Jubei would bear watching. Although the opening advantage belonged to them, the game was far from over. There were still ways to sow seeds of chaos. Sooner or later the Christians would be driven to rebellion. If the farmers could be trained and supplied with firearms, and if enough Christian daimyos could be persuaded to commit their samurai, and if the Portuguese could be drawn into the war, then there was still hope. It all turned on finding the gold.

Sanjo knew his biggest mistake had been doing away with Okubo before he actually had the gold in his hands. But who would have believed that after all that Okubo had been through, he was prepared to die without revealing his secret to anyone? Sanjo thought he had won his trust. Then it occurred to him that the only one Okubo really trusted was Jubei. Was it possible . . . ?

Ironically it was the same question, in a slightly different context, that Tajima had put to his son after Jubei's return to Edo. "How was it possible?" Tajima asked, scowling at a tattered piece of rice paper with nothing but dark smudge marks on it. "You actually *forgot* Okubo's map was in your obi when you waded out into the lake?"

"I'm afraid so," Jubei answered, but his response did not betray the slightest indication of contrition. "Just as you forgot that your son was locked away in a filthy cell for nearly a year."

Tajima knew this moment would come. The longer he had allowed Jubei to languish in prison, the more difficult it had become to justify his inaction. Leaving the whole matter in Takuan's hands had been a convenient device for abdicating responsibility. Tajima knew he could have pressured Takuan, even insisted upon going through with the original plan to arrange an escape for Jubei and Okubo. But the truth was, both he and Takuan realized that sooner or later someone would try to free Okubo, and once that happened, Jubei would be in a much better position to gain access to the kind of invaluble information Tajima needed to combat the forces in league against the Tokugawa.

"If you want sympathy from me, you have it." Tajima fired his long-stemmed pipe and drew tobacco smoke deep into his lungs. "But if you want me to apologize or tell you that I regret not freeing you sooner, I cannot." He vented his lungs, blowing the smoke out through his heavily stained teeth. Tajima aimed the stem of his pipe at Jubei like the barrel of a gun. "In spite of the mental lapse that cost me the map, you were able to rescue our lord, the man I've sworn to protect with my life. Seen in that light alone, a year of imprisonment is not too great a price to ask from my son."

Jubei pushed the pipe away from his face. "It was luck," he snapped back. "Nothing but dumb luck. What if they never came for Okubo? What if Iemitsu had been taken to some other place? Would that year—or however long you might have left me there to rot in that cell—have been too much to ask?"

"Ah, but they *did* come, and Iemitsu *was* there when you arrived. Was it just 'dumb luck,' or could it be that the gods had a hand in it? Who can say for sure why things turn out the way they do. All I can tell you is that I've made a commitment to help save this land from chaos, and for me that's an ideal that's larger and more important than the preservation of one individual life—even the life of my own son."

Jubei got up and slid open the door. His gaze fell on the wind shadow at the far end of the garden. All around the great rock, trees and flowering shrubs were bobbing and thrashing in wind. But inside the wind shadow's shelter the garden was at peace. It was the kind of serenity Jubei longed for and had only been able feel during moments of mortal combat, and it troubled him deeply.

"*Chichive*." Jubei turned to his father. "As difficult as it is for me to say this, perhaps the time I spent in that cell with Okubo was good for me. The darkness forced me to look inside, and I began to see things in a different light. I began to see that ideals are the easiest things to come by. People are full of them, even when they're facing one another across a battlefield. It seems to me now that a good question is a much rarer thing than a good answer. Every Japanese child learns to ask how, what, who, where, and when . . . but from the moment we're born, the one question we're taught to avoid like poison is any question beginning with the word why. It's a dangerous word that eats away at the mortar of a society held together by obedience, and I think the discovery made me a dangerous person."

Tajima arched his eyebrows. "Are you saying I can no longer trust you?"

"You are my father and the head of my family," Jubei answered. "I will not betray you. But if you want me to go on serving you, you must understand that I'm looking for something besides blind obedience to guide my path. I may never find it, but I want you to know that the search has begun."

PART TWO

13

Oyano
Year of the Dog—1634
Hour of the Dragon

It was hot—the kind of day that breeds flies.

In the shadow of the gorge the heat was tolerable. At the spot where Kriek decided to try his luck, the river was wide and deep. "This is where the big trout live," he told the boy.

"How do you know?" Shiro asked, his fawn eyes bright with curiosity. Like all bright boys at five years of age, Shiro's waking hours were punctuated with question marks.

Kriek beamed at the boy. Never in his life had he seen a more lovely child. The blend of Rendai's subtly sculptured beauty and Alcala's sharp, avian features had produced a comely amalgam of East and West. It was more than the elegant lift of his cheekbones, more than deep, dark eyes that seemed to have no bottom to them, or the fine head of wind-tossed hair that pitched and rolled to the nape of his neck like rumpled threads of silk. Shiro's beauty radiated from within and seemed as natural as warmth from a fire. But it was the kind of fragile beauty belonging to things easily broken.

Sometimes when they traveled the road together, people they met would remark on Shiro's exotic features, and they would invariably ask if Shiro were his son. Kriek always made a joke of it, saying that it was like asking if a warthog could sire a lamb. It always provoked a round of good-natured teasing, for no people on earth appreciated the art of self-depreciation more than the Japanese. Yet there was some truth behind the joke. There was not much delicacy in Kriek's weather-beaten face. Exposure to the sun and wind and rain had cut deep fissures around his eyes, and a meager diet consisting mostly of millet had collapsed his cheeks. As a precaution against detection, he kept his hair dyed black. Over two years of living among people who were forced to slave in rice fields, growing crops they were forbidden to feed their starving families, had also taken its toll on his spirit. More than once young children whose only image of a Westerner was that of the crucified Christ, had mistaken him for Jesus, come down from the cross.

"Look up there." Kreik turned Shiro toward the waterfall and pointed out a faint rainbow spanning the vapor that collected in the gorge. "If you were a nice fat trout, wouldn't you want to make your home under a rainbow?"

The boy nodded enthusiastically. When he saw the way the padre was grinning, Shiro knew he'd fallen for a made-up story. "But fish don't care about rainbows," he retreated.

"How do you know that?" Kriek asked, turning the tables on him.

"Because fish wear their eyes here." He put one finger on each temple. "They'd have to swim on their sides to see the rainbow," he concluded triumphantly.

"Good point," Kriek conceded, "but if that's true, how do they see waterbugs swimming on the surface?"

Shiro thought for a moment. "I don't know, Padre. How do they?"

"I don't know either." Kriek tussled his hair and beamed at the boy. "But I do know a question when I hear one."

"Anyway," Shiro said, glowing with pride, "rainbows are a good sign. I'm sure we'll have luck today."

Kreik sat down on the bank to bait their hooks. In some mysterious way being close to Shiro made him feel closer to Maria. The day she left the inn with Shiro strapped to her breast, he never dreamed he would ever see either of them again. Then, by a strange twist of fate, Lord Arima had sent Shiro to the home of Watanabe Kozaemon, a good Christian who was also the chief farmer of the Oyano district—the very place where Kriek had begun his search for Father Alcala.

At first Kriek spent all his time and energy tracking down each and every rumor that came to him about Alcala's whereabouts. Once or twice he had actually come close to finding him, only to discover that Alcala had moved on just a short time before he arrived. Certain that Alcala was well aware that a brother Jesuit was trying to locate him, Kriek came to the conclusion that he was engaged in an elaborate game of hide and seek with the elusive Alcala—a game the renegade priest was winning.

After a time Kriek had become so absorbed with ministering to the impoverished Christians of Oyano that his unsuccessful attempts to locate Alcala no longer seemed significant. The reports he smuggled into Nagasaki had never provoked a response from his superiors. Kriek was beginning to think that the Father General's interest in Alcala had waned.

The fishing was good. Shiro hooked and lost so many fish that Kriek quit counting. Still, between them they had accumulated a string of seven plump trout. When the gorge filled up with shadow, Kriek told Shiro it was time to go.

"One more try," the boy begged.

Kriek impaled another worm on Shiro's hook, taking care that the metal was completely covered and enough of the worm was free to entice the trout with some tantalizing wiggles. Then he gathered in the string of fish and took them to a sandy spot where he gutted them and packed them away in a basket, using layers of wet grass to keep their meat cool and fresh.

He turned and saw Shiro running toward him, his bamboo pole bent under the weight of the biggest catch of the day. Soon Shiro's fish had been cleaned and cut into bite-sized chunks. Kriek arranged the translucent pieces of flesh on a lily pad. The raw trout was cool and fresh. It was gone in a matter of minutes.

"And now for a special treat," Kriek announced. Wrapped inside a bandana were two rice balls. Shiro's eyes widened. Rice was reserved for samurai. The farmers subsisted on millet and sometimes wheat or barley, in scarce supply because the rice quota was so great that there was very little acreage left for growing anything else.

Although pilfering from government supplies was punishable by death, it was not uncommon for the authorities to reward the chief farmer for meeting his quota by turning a blind eye to a small amount of skimming. As chief farmer in Oyano, Shiro's adopted father had chosen to abstain, out of sympathy for the plight of his tenants. Watanabe Kozaemon still managed to find a way to feed his wife and adopted son. But for Shiro rice was an unimaginable treat.

It was the last of a small supply Kriek had raised in a tiny paddy near his hideout in the hills. He watched Shiro as he bit into the rice ball and discovered the pinch of *shiso* he'd put inside for flavor. The expression of unabashed delight on his face made Kriek laugh out loud. Shiro looked like a ground squirrel with a load of nuts in his cheeks.

After dinner they shouldered their fishing poles and started for home. Side by side they wound through the terraced paddies. The rice stalks were heavy with grain, and the twilight was vibrant with the sound of frogs and crickets. Gnats and ravenous flies buzzed around their heads and swarms of mosquitoes searched for exposed skin. Kriek pulled his wide-brimmed hat as low as he could to discourage the insects, but there was nothing he could do about his ankles. Although the *hakama* pants he wore had been made especially for him, they were still too short. The length of his legs simply defied the imagination of the woman who made his clothes.

Lost in make-believe, Shiro's bamboo pole became a flag flying Lord Arima's insignia. Safe in an impenetrable cocoon of divine protection, he was marching forward, impervious to the arrows that whizzed past him. Grown men cried out and dropped at his feet, but he—Lord Arima's young bannerman— kept moving ahead. The spectacle of his bravery inspired his comrades, and little by little the tide of the battle shifted to Lord Arima's favor. And when the battle was won, victorious samurai gathered around and chanted his name—"Shiro! Shiro! Shiro! The tiger of Amakusa!"

His moment of glory was interrupted by an urgent need to relieve himself. He asked Kriek to wait while he rushed to one of the tubs on the side of the road that the farmers used to collect fertilizer for their crops.

Overhead a lone hawk circled in the gathering darkness. The way he tightened his spire, Kriek knew he was on to something. Suddenly the hawk's wings collapsed and he plummeted below the crest of the hill. Seconds later he reappeared with something furry clutched in his talons.

"What were you looking at?" Shiro asked.

"A hawk."

Shiro scanned the sky. "Where is he?"

"He's gone." Kriek told him about the kill. "He's headed home now."

They walked along in silence. Kriek noticed that Shiro seemed to be brooding over something unresolved.

"Padre," he said after a time, "when you saw the hawk dive, whose side were you on?"

"Whose side?"

"The hawk or the animal he caught?"

"A strange question." Kriek thought it over for a moment. "I guess I just watched what was happening. I don't remember taking sides."

"You didn't feel *anything?*"

The disappointment on Shiro's face forced Kriek to reconsider his answer. Yes, maybe he had felt something. A twinge of anticipation when the hawk dropped out of sight, a surge of excitement when he came up full. "It seems I was rooting for the hawk," he said.

The boy accepted his answer with a nod of his head, as if to say, "I thought so."

"Wait a minute," Kriek said to Shiro. "Aren't you going to tell me what you think about it?"

"I always hope they'll miss." Then his face brightened. "Sometimes they do."

Before they rounded the last bend on the outskirts of Shiro's village, Kriek stopped and sent the boy ahead to scout the road. It was nearing harvest time. Patrols from Hara Castle kept a watchful eye on all the farm villages at this time of year to make sure yields were accurately recorded so nothing could be held back.

Shiro came running back with the information that the road was clear.

When Kriek turned the corner he was surprised at how right the boy had been. The road was empty. The fields were deserted. There was no activity around the outlying farmhouses. Strange. The rice was at a critical stage. Recently the farmers had been working from morning to night, fighting insects by dipping straw brooms into a mixture of hot whale oil and vinegar and splashing it over the plants. Even if they had quit early, there would still be plenty of cleaning up to do.

Shiro noticed too. "Where is everybody?" he asked.

"Maybe there's some kind of festival in town," Kriek said, thinking out loud.

"Oh, I hope so."

Shiro broke into a trot and Kriek lengthened his strides.

Unlike European towns, Oyano village was a celebration of
conformity. The tightly packed houses were indistinguishable
from one another. Identical thatched roofs sloped down to
identical overhanging eaves which projected over identical
verandas. At the north end of town there was an abandoned
structure that had belonged to a sake maker whose business
failed when his family daughtered out. Except for a black-
smith and a cooper, everyone else in Oyano farmed the land.

Inside one of the houses a baby was crying. Otherwise the
street was quiet. Kriek caught Shiro's arm, slowing him down.
Something was wrong. Gloom had settled over the village
like a fog.

Near the center of town the street curved. Just to be safe,
Kriek waited while Shiro checked the south branch of the
street. In a few seconds Shiro returned. He stood in the
center of the street waving his arms. "Padre!" he shouted,
and Kriek winced at the boy's indiscreet use of his title.
"Come quick! It *is* a festival."

At the far end of town Kriek could see a large crowd
milling in front of the granary. Three or four torches were
blazing, but it was difficult to make out what was going on.
Only the torchlight suggested a festival, nothing else. No one
was beating a drum, clashing cymbals, singing, dancing, or
laughing.

"Wait," Kriek called to Shiro as he started off down the
street on a dead run. A few heads in the back of the crowd
turned. There was a low murmur. More heads turned, and a
young woman came out of the crowd, walking briskly toward
them. As he got closer, Kriek saw it was Tomi, the young
woman who had helped him escape from Hirado. She had
been living with her parents since returning to Oyano.

"Go home!" Tomi pleaded in a hoarse whisper. "Take Shiro
with you. It's not safe here."

"What's wrong? What happened?"

"This morning Watanabe Kozaemon announced Lord
Matsukura's new rice quotas . . . even higher than before.
The farmers demanded that he go to Hara Castle and beg
Matsukura for relief."

"Matsukura!"

Tomi lowered her eyes.

Kreik didn't say anything more, but his blood ran cold at the
thought of Shiro's stepfather trying to reason with the mon-

ster who had been sent from Edo to stamp out Christianity in
Lord Arima's provinces.

"But that's not the worst of it," Tomi went on. "While he
was at Hara Castle some hotheads broke into the granary and
took a bale of rice."

"Where is Watanabe Kozaemon now?"

"He and his wife are locked up inside the granary. Some
officer from Hara Castle is in there with him. Everyone's
waiting to find out what's going to be done. It's an ugly
situation. Everybody expects trouble."

Their conversation took place out of Shiro's hearing. He
was chafing to get closer to the gathering to see what was
going on. How could the padre stand there and chat when
there was so much excitement just down the street? Finally
Shiro ran over to him and stood close, hoping to get noticed.

". . . standing guard in front of the granary," Shiro overheard Tomi tell the padre. "Probably waiting for more troops
to get here."

Kriek eyed the restless crowd. Pent-up fury had transformed the peaceful little village into a seething volcano
about to erupt in a self-destructive spasm of frustration. It was
like experiencing historical déjà vu. Governments—all governments—test the tensile strength of the people by taking,
taking, taking in tiny increments until the bond between
rulers and the ruled is stretched to the breaking point. Like
patient oxen the people stick their collective necks in the
government yoke and pull their load. Day after day a little
more weight is added to the cart, until the animal can pull no
more and stops. Out comes the whip. Driven by fear and
suffering, the animal strains against the harness. When the
tether snaps, the result is anarchy. Sooner or later anarchy
becomes unbearable and another bond is fashioned. Necks go
back in the yoke, the wagon is loaded, and the whole process
starts all over again. It's the nature of the two beasts, Kriek
thought. It's inertia against inertia to the end of recorded
time.

Shiro tugged on Kriek's sleeve. "Padre, can we go see?"

Kriek sat down on his heels and took the boy by the
shoulders. "Look over there"—Kriek pointed to the crowd—
"and tell me what you see."

"A lot of people standing around," he said. "Some torches . . ."

"You see what the men have in their hands?"

Shiro squinted against the failing light. "Tools," he said. "Sickles and . . ."

"Mattocks," Kriek said, supplying the name of the implement that was half ax, half pick. "Yesterday they were tools. Tonight they're weapons. Do you understand what I'm saying?"

Shiro wasn't sure, but he knew he had been wrong about the festival. It was too quiet. Nobody seemed to be having fun. "Is there going to be a fight?"

"I hope not, but just in case there is, I don't want you here."

Shiro's face fell. "Do I have to go home?" Up till now all his battles had been imaginary. The thought of missing a real fight made him feel wretched.

"No, not home." If the ax fell on Watanabe Kozaemon, it would fall on his wife and son too. "Go to my place in the hills and wait for me there." Shiro's eyes got big and his lower lip began to quiver. Kriek was not about to waste any more time arguing. "Do as you're told," he commanded, and Shiro reluctantly started off, glowering over his shoulder as he went.

Locked inside the granary, Watanabe sat with his wife by his side. She busied herself picking loose threads and imaginary pieces of lint off his kimono. Instead of reprimanding his wife for fussing over him, he let her continue, understanding she needed an excuse to stay close to him.

The officer who had arrested them paced back and forth, repeatedly peering out through a crack in the door. His inability to control his nerves disgusted Watanabe. It was unseemly for a samurai to behave so shamefully in front of his prisoners. But good retainers had been hard to come by since the carnage at Osaka Castle.

Watanabe's audience with Matsukura had gone just about as he expected. In his capacity as chief farmer of Oyano, he had done his duty. Summoning all his dignity, he had laid the farmers' petition for relief before the appointed lord of Hara Castle. He remembered the icy glaze over Matsukura's hooded eyes as the lord listened to his speech.

When he finished, Watanabe handed over the formal petition. A sardonic smile creased Matsukura's face when he noticed that all the farmers' names had been written in a circle, to prevent him from identifying the ringleader. Without asking questions, without even pretending to ponder the matter, Matsukura rendered his decision. The new quotas would be temporarily rescinded to allow him time to examine the validity of the farmers' claims. However, to prevent this act of magnanimity from being misinterpreted as an act of weakness, a small price would have to be paid. Since the chief farmer had shown himself incapable of maintaining discipline in Oyano, a new chief farmer would be named, and Watanabe—along with his wife and adopted son—would be publicly executed the following morning.

Bows were exchanged, and Watanabe was escorted back to Oyano under guard and locked in the granary.

But the discovery of the theft, together with the nasty mood of the mob outside the granary, had muddied the waters, leaving the officer in charge dangling between the hammer and the anvil. He had his orders, but attempting to carry them out was tantamount to suicide. The farmers had armed themselves, and his troops were outnumbered ten to one. Seizing on the granary incident as his excuse, he sent one of his men back to Hara Castle to seek clarification from Matsukura. All he could do now was pray that he had made the right decision and he would not be ordered to proceed without reinforcements.

Full night came on. Out in the street the mob was becoming increasingly restive. Little by little the phalanx of guards had been forced back, the butts of their spearlike *yari* braced against the wall, their razor-sharp points just one step away from the farmers in the front ranks.

Kriek circulated through the back of the crowd, urging restraint. "Keep calm," he whispered to anyone who would listen. "Violence breeds violence," he said. No one refuted him. No one paid much attention either. "Christ taught us to love our enemies," he told a recent convert, and saw the young farmer look up at him as if he had just pronounced decapitation the best cure for a headache. Kriek began to feel foolish. Pious homilies were not going to defuse the situation. The spectre of a bloodbath loomed large.

It began as a distant rumble, freezing the milling crowd like a sudden blast of arctic chill. Everyone stood still and listened. Horses. Heads turned south. Fists tightened. The officer in charge heaved a sigh of relief. Watanabe stared straight ahead. His wife's shoulders slumped. Jan Kriek retreated into the shadows.

Matsukura's samurai rode in and positioned themselves at the rear of the crowd. All wore armor, their half helmets shaped like tortoise shells and emblazoned with the Tokugawa hollyhock insignia. The brim of one flared helmet, however, was decorated with a silver crescent. That rider dismounted and boldly waded into the crowd, never altering his pace, never doubting that the hostile sea of farmers would part before him. No one got in his way. He reached the granary at the same time the door opened.

"Matsukura-sama!" the stunned officer gasped, and dropped to one knee. He had not expected his lord to involve himself directly in this incident.

Matsukura strode past him without a word and approached the condemned man, who bowed solemnly. "Welcome to Oyano," Watanabe said with magnified dignity.

"I'm beginning to think the farmers of Oyano are out to test my will. Wouldn't you agree?"

"The farmers of Oyano are hungry, my lord. They are just trying to survive."

"Survive?" He snorted. "Look outside. Tell me how good their chances of survival are right now."

Watanabe looked and said nothing. Despite Matsukura's bluster, he doubted there would be a slaughter if the farmers managed to keep their heads. Even a martinet like Matsukura could understand that you don't cut off the hand that feeds you. Where would he find good farmers to replace them?

Matsukura ordered a platform made out of bales of rice. The work was completed quickly. Refusing assistance, he mounted the rice bales and snapped open his war fan. "I am Lord Matsukura of Hara Castle," he boomed out in a voice meant for a much larger gathering. He waited for the murmuring to die down. "Farmers of Oyano, you have been betrayed." Matsukura paused, searching the upturned faces for anyone bold enough to lock eyes with him. It thrilled him to see how easily their defiance crumbled under his gaze. "Rice was stolen from this granary . . . the fruit of your arduous labor, the life's blood of the samurai . . . pilfered by thieves. No," he corrected himself, "rats and mice are thieves. Men who steal rice from the mouths of samurai who fight and die to protect you . . . are not thieves. *They are traitors!*" he shouted. Then he added in a voice barely above a whisper, "And treason must never go unpunished.

"When word of the break-in reached me, I rushed here to assess the situation personally. And what did I find? I found the good farmers of Oyano gathered in the street with sickles and mattocks in their hands. At first glance a suspicious man might have interpreted what he saw as an act of rebellion, and slaughtered the lot of you without a second thought. But fortunately your lord is not a suspicious man. I prefer to think that the farmers of Oyano gathered here to protect the granary from further pillaging by outside marauders. Of course," he smiled sweetly, "if I've misconstrued your intentions, I hope someone will be kind enough to disabuse me."

Kriek held his breath. Everywhere Matsukura looked heads dropped, throats cleared, and feet shuffled. Not a word was spoken.

"Good," he said after an excruciating wait. "As a reward for your efforts, the new quota will be lowered to only one extra *koku* from each family.

Watanabe grimaced. Matsukura had cleverly taken away most of what he had given back. And who among them would dare complain now? In a single stroke Matsukura had virtually wiped out the tiny gains he bought at the cost of his life. He reached out and took his wife's hand.

"Now go to your homes," Matsukura concluded, "and pray to your Christian god that this harvest is a good one."

Matsukura remained there with his feet planted wide apart and his arms folded imperiously across his chest as the street cleared.

Kriek watched from the safety of darkness as Matsukura deployed his troops in a semicircle in front of the granary. Some heavy pieces of lumber were dragged into the street, and though it was difficult to see what was happening, from the sound of hammering Kriek concluded that something was being built. The workers called for more light. When additional torches were lit, Kriek saw three crosses under construction—two large crosses, and a smaller one.

"God have mercy!" Kriek uttered under his breath. Crucifixion was an age-old tradition in Japan, but after the introduction of Christianity it had become the preferred form of execution for the followers of the crucified Christ. When he overheard one of Matsukura's men report that a search of the village had failed to turn up Watanabe's adopted son, Kriek breathed a sigh of relief. For the moment at least Shiro was out of danger.

He watched as Watanabe and his wife were led out of the granary and stripped naked. He saw their arms lashed to the crossbeams and watched the crosses lifted into place. Neither one made a sound. Watanabe squirmed against the strain. His wife held still, keeping her eyes shut against her shame. A few soldiers exchanged some lewd remarks about her desiccated breasts, and someone told them to shut up. Watanabe said something to his wife. She lifted her head and looked at him, gazing into his eyes as long as she could before her head fell forward on her sunken chest.

The small cross was set between them.

A surge of helpless rage washed over Kriek. There was nothing he could do to save them, nothing even to relieve their agony, except . . .

"Watanabe Kozaemon!" his voice rang out of the shadows. "I won't let them get Shiro!" he shouted defiantly, and dashed off into the night.

Shiro's knee hurt. It was too dark for him to tell if it was bleeding. He touched the sore spot with his finger. It wasn't damp or sticky, so he guessed the fall hadn't broken the skin. It hurt anyway. And it was cold up in the hills. He hugged his knees and thought about the warmth of his mother and wished he were home. Why had the padre yelled at him? He hadn't done anything wrong. His stepfather wouldn't have acted like that. He'd have taken him by the hand and led him home. Or maybe he'd have let him stay.

The wind rustled the leaves overhead. Shiro drew his knees tighter to his chest. There were blankets and a futon inside the rude hut where the padre lived, and sleep was bearing down so hard on Shiro that it made his body ache. But he stubbornly fought it off, partly because the more miserable he felt, the easier it was to feel sorry for himself, and partly because he was scared to fall asleep in a strange place. The padre would be ashamed when he came home and found out how wretched he had made him, Shiro thought. He didn't want to miss that moment.

Kriek found him fast asleep under the tree outside his door. He collected an ember from the banked fire and made a flame to light his candle. When he had his futon arranged, he picked the boy up and lay down with Shiro's head nestled on his shoulder.

Suddenly Shiro sat up and looked at Kriek through eyes wide with strangeness.

"It's all right," Kriek murmured softly. "Go back to sleep now." He tried to draw the boy to him, but his little body stiffened.

"I want to go home," Shiro whimpered.

"Not now. Sleep here tonight."

"Where's my mother?"

"She knows you're with me." Shiro looked bewildered. "You're not afraid, are you?"

"A little."

"Come on, lie down next to me. I'm cold."

This time Shiro let Kriek hold him. Reaching across his chest with his free hand, he ran his fingers through Shiro's hair, lifting it up and letting it fall, just as his mother had done to him long ago. He thought about the first night the baby Shiro lay in his arms. He remembered Maria's serene face next to him, and hung on to the image as long as he could before sleep took him.

"Padre . . . Padre . . ." The urgent voice invaded Kriek's dreams. He felt a cool hand on his cheek, and opening his eyes saw Tomi hovering over him. "Padre," she said in a taut whisper, "get up. They're coming."

Kriek rolled up on one elbow, keeping Shiro locked in the crook of his arm. "Who's coming?"

"Matsukura's soldiers."

He sat bolt up, jarring Shiro out of his deep sleep. "How did they find out? What happened?"

She glanced out the open door. "Please, there's no time. We must get out of here!"

Kriek quickly collected a few of his possessions and hurried outside. In the pre-dawn darkness he counted five—no, six torches moving along the path below. The only option he had was to make for higher ground.

"Come on!" He grabbed Shiro's hand, but before they had gone any distance at all the drowsy boy had fallen twice. "Here." Kriek handed Tomi the bandana containing his books, crucifix, and several articles of clothing he had thrown together. Then he hoisted Shiro onto his back and carried him piggyback up the hill.

They kept up an exhausting pace, trotting then walking briskly through the early morning hours and into full dawn, only stopping briefly at certain vantage points to check the route below. Although he saw no activity along the path, Kriek was certain Matsukura's men were still coming. Having ordered Shiro's execution, Matsukura was not the kind of man who would rest easily knowing it had not been carried out. The only question in Kriek's mind was how far behind the soldiers were. That probably depended on the amount of time they had wasted searching in and around his hut. So the three of them pushed on, looking for an opportunity to get off the narrow mountain path. Although he could tell from Tomi's brightly flushed face and wobbly legs that she was exhausted, she never lagged behind or asked for rest.

The higher they climbed, the more rugged the terrain became. It would have been better to have left the path earlier, he thought, at a place where the hills had been sculpted with a lighter touch. But it was too late for second guessing. Besides, the blunder might work to their advantage if Matsukura's soldiers thought the same thing.

Their chance came about three quarters of the way up the steepest hill in the Oyano range. Just off to the side of the path, a full body length down, a narrow ledge ran under a protruding lip of overhanging rock. How far it ran was impossible to tell by leaning out over the rim. Kriek surveyed the ledge and found a place where it seemed possible to climb down with a little assistance from above.

"Look, Tomi," he said, "I'm going to slide over the edge on my belly. I need a hand to keep me stable. Just let go when I'm ready to drop to the ledge. Can you do that?"

"*Hai*," she said.

They grasped each other's wrists and Kriek bellied out over the rim. Gripping the rocks with his left hand, he was able to take the bulk of the strain off her. "Now," he said, and Tomi let go. The drop was a little farther than he had figured, causing him to stumble backward. Tomi gasped as he teetered precariously close to the edge before regaining his balance.

From where he stood he could see that the ledge maintained a fairly level grade for twenty or thirty paces, then sloped downhill for a short distance, leveling out again until it disappeared around a bend. As much of it as he could see was wide enough for two people to walk side by side.

"Wait here," he called up to them. "I won't be long."

The going was easy, and he made the bend in a matter of minutes. What he saw there was more ledge cutting deeper into the hillside and running a long way to another bend. It was narrower, but there was still enough room for them to negotiate the trail if they went single file. It was worth a try.

Luck was with them. They hadn't made it to the first bend when they heard the sound of pounding footsteps overhead. Kriek pressed his back against the cliff and offered up a silent prayer of thanks. At the speed Matsukura's men were traveling, the three of them wouldn't have had a chance if they had kept to the original path.

If his choice needed any more vindication than that, he got it when they rounded the second bend and discovered that the ledge showed no signs of petering out. In fact it widened to the point where all three could walk abreast, but since Tomi wouldn't think of committing the indiscretion of walking alongside a man, she lagged a few steps behind, taking in the view as calmly as if she were out for a morning stroll.

Shiro, on the other hand, was in a high state of excitement. To him this was an adventure beyond anything his fertile imagination had yet conceived. Men preparing to fight in the streets of his village, a scary night away from home, running from soldiers along mysterious trails leading who knows where—Shiro knew he was harvesting experiences destined to make him the envy of every boy in Oyano. Even the slight pain in his knee lent nobility to his exploits. Just to enhance the drama he threw a little more effort into his limp.

Kriek noticed Shiro's limp and realized that out of his own nervous energy rather than real need, he had been pushing them hard. It was almost noon, and they hadn't stopped once to catch their breath.

He came across a depression in the face of the cliff and decided to stop there to take advantage of the shelter it offered. The cleft was deeper than he thought at first glance. The steep angle of the roof made it appear much shallower than it actually was. The floor sloped down gently, and after several steps inside it was still impossible to make out where the floor and ceilings of the hollow came together.

Shiro wanted to go exploring, but Kriek stopped him.

"You've had a hard morning," he explained. "We've got more traveling ahead of us. I want you to take a rest." Shiro swore he wasn't tired. "Maybe you aren't, but I am. Besides, it's too dark to go poking around back there. And I don't want you to get lost."

Kriek found a level spot and stretched out with his hands behind his head. Tomi sat down next to him. "Does Shiro know?" she said softly, leaving the obvious part of her question dangling.

"No, I haven't told him anything about the crucifixion." Kriek looked up at her. "Are they. . . ?"

Tomi shook her head. "It always takes a long time. The suffering is terrible."

"How did they find out about Shiro and me?"

"I don't know. My father overheard them giving directions to the soldiers. He sent me out right away."

"I'm sorry you got caught up in this." Tomi leaned back and closed her eyes. Her face had paled with exhaustion. "We're both thankful for what you did," he added.

"I know," she said, meaning it wasn't necessary to put it into words.

One of the first things he had learned from Maria was the Japanese disdain for articulating emotion. She'd told him that translating emotion into words carries with it the suggestion that the other person lacks the sensitivity to interpret feelings without help. "Words are always cheap substitutes for the things they represent," Maria once explained. "Nothing becomes more real because you can find a word to describe it."

Shiro came over to Tomi and laid his head in her lap. Soon his breathing deepened, and Kriek saw that he'd fallen asleep. Although there had been no time to formulate any long-term plans, one thing was certain—returning to Oyano anytime in the near future was out of the question. Nor was seeking shelter with a Christian family in another village a viable alternative. It would be unconscionable for him to ask a family to risk annihilation by giving them sanctuary. Locating a secluded place to hide out until Matsukura put an end to the hunt seemed to be the only possible answer.

"Tomi," he said quietly, so as not to wake the boy.

"*Hai*," she whispered.

"Stay here with Shiro. I'm going ahead to see what's out there. I'll be back within the hour."

Not far away the ledge wound around the hillside and opened into a small glen where wild fruit trees were growing along the bank of a narrow, quick stream. The water was cool and clean. Kriek took a long drink and then set out to explore the grassy meadow. It was a lovely place, shielded on all sides by towering hills. Next to a tall stand of bamboo he discovered stalks of wild rice growing among the cattails. He was ecstatic. It was as if he had stumbled on to the Garden of Eden. He couldn't wait to show Tomi.

"It's a perfect place to hide," he told her as they approached the glen. "There's good water and plenty of things to eat."

"And at night we can take shelter in the cave," she said, swiftly calculating all the possibilities the site offered them.

"Tomi, Shiro and I will be safe here for a while. No one knows you were the one who warned us. The sooner you return home, the less danger that anyone will suspect you helped us get away."

Tomi shook her head. "I can't go back."

"Why?" he asked. "I'm sure we can find a pass that leads to the lowlands from here."

"It's not that." She looked down at the ground. "There's barely enough food for my brothers. An unmarried daughter is a heavy burden, especially now, when no father in Oyano can afford to let a son bring a new wife into the family. When my father sent me out to warn you . . ." Tomi swallowed hard. "He told me not to come home."

Kriek's eyes flashed. "He said that!"

"Please, Padre, he's not a bad man."

"Tomi, your father sold you into prostitution. Now he's thrown you out. At some point . . ." Kriek just shook his head.

"Try to understand," Tomi pleaded. "I'm the youngest of three daughters. My father needed sons to help him with the farm, but he never took out his bad luck on his wife or daughters. He worked from morning till night, and we had enough to eat. Then my mother bore him a son, and one year later, another. It was a happy time. Then the great drought hit. One of my sisters died and the other one got married. Still there wasn't enough food for the four of us.

"I remember the day my father came home with the news that the farmers' petition for lower taxes had been refused.

For a long time he stayed out in the fields alone, crushing clods of dry soil in his hand. Later that night he called me to him and explained that the family couldn't survive the year unless he leased me to a brothel in Hirado. I was thirteen, and I didn't know what a brothel was, but I knew I was afraid to leave home. Still, I can remember feeling proud that I could do something for my family. And I can remember how hard he fought against the tears when he told me."

"I didn't know," Kriek murmured.

Tomi looked up at him, her dark eyes brimming with hope. "Padre, please don't send me away."

"Shiro is still a little boy," he said to her. "He needs a woman to look after him. I'd be grateful if you stayed."

14

Kyoto
Year of the Dog—1634
Hour of the Rabbit

Snowflakes.

Some the size of butterfly wings fluttered among wet black boughs of maples and oaks, elms and cherries, crab apples and plums, tumbling down one on top of the other, until every forked twig bloomed.

Children caught some on sheets of colored paper. Some vanished in a liquid instant. Some lingered on, to *oohs* and *ahs* of wonder.

It whitened fields and dusted lightly traveled roads, collected on thatched roofs, then tiled roofs and the walls of the Imperial Palace. And finally even the streets of Kyoto succumbed to the persistence of the falling snow.

Maria looked up from her sewing and listened. The intense

quiet outside her quarters alerted her senses. She opened her door and saw the garden filling up with snow.

Yoshino shuffled into the room and promptly scolded her mistress for letting in the cold. "Will you come away from there, my lady, before you freeze us both to death."

"Make some hot tea," Maria said, ignoring her plea.

Yoshino thought about pressing her point, but Maria's tone of voice persuaded her to turn her attention to the tea. It saddened Yoshino to see the change in her mistress since her marriage to Prince Sanjo. All the laughter and joy had gone out of her life. At first Yoshino had been terrified that she would go through with her vow to commit seppuku if her husband tried to touch her. She recalled the panic she experienced the first time Sanjo ordered her mistress to his sleeping chamber, and remembered the look of grim determination on Maria's face as she went out the door, and the blank stare when she returned. To her immense relief, Yoshino learned that Sanjo had demanded nothing of her except that she remain in attendance while he cavorted with some boy. That night Yoshino used up three sticks of incense before she finished giving thanks to the gods.

Yoshino poured the tea and brought the cup to Maria.

"Look, Yoshino." Maria gestured toward the cherry tree just outside the door. "Is that something hanging on the limb?"

Yoshino pulled down on the corners of her eyes to bring them into focus. There, dangling from a string tied to the largest branch, was a note folded in the shape of a bow. "My, my," she clucked, "it looks like you've finally attracted an admirer."

"Stop teasing and get the note," Maria said. "I'm sure it's intended for you."

"Not likely," Yoshino grumbled. "Any suitor interested in me would be too old to climb a tree."

"Will you hurry!"

It took all the stretch Yoshino could muster to reach the note. After a few tugs the string broke and she brought it inside. "Close the door," Yoshino said. "Sometimes they spy on you to watch your reaction."

"That's ridiculous," Maria muttered, but she couldn't resist the impulse to take a quick peek at the garden. "It must have

been there for some time," she said. "There are no footprints
in the snow."

"Aren't you going to open it?"

Maria kneeled by the brazier and unfolded the note:

To Lady Sanjo—

> *Word had reached me that the son I entrusted to your
> care has come under the influence of a Jesuit. If this is
> so, I consider your marriage to my former husband
> sufficient punishment for this betrayal. However, I in-
> tend to find the Jesuit and take my revenge.*
>
> *Rendai*

Which Jesuit was Rendai talking about, Maria wondered—
Alcala or Jan-san? Either one of them could have come across
the boy. What if Jan-san had found him first? Was Rendai's
hatred reserved for Alcala alone, or did it extend to all
Jesuits?

Maria felt a deep pang of dread. The thought of harm
coming to Jan-san stirred emotions she thought had atro-
phied. Some way had to be found to warn him. Recalling that
Sanjo was off on one of his mysterious excursions, she realized she could use the opportunity to visit her father in
Nobeoka. Leaving without her husband's permission was a
very dangerous thing to do, but she had no choice.

"Yoshino, start packing my things," she commanded. "We're
leaving for home."

"*Hai!*" Yoshino flew into action. She had no idea what the
note was about, but it had worked like a tonic. Although she
couldn't say her mistress looked happy, at least the fog had
lifted. It had been a long time since she'd seen her eyes with
that much life in them. Yoshino was dying to get a peek at
the note. She kept an eye out to see where Maria put it.

It was also snowing in Edo. The curved surface of the
Nihonbashi Bridge had become treacherous to negotiate. Some
dim-witted city laborer had scattered ashes down the center
of the bridge to improve the footing, failing to take into
account that anybody who wanted to make it over the hump
had to use the side railings for support.

A crowd of people had gathered at the foot of the bridge to

watch hapless travelers lose their footing and come careening down the slope in a wild variety of undignified poses. A great cheer went up when one young lady came down on her back, scooping snow up her kimono as she slid along. By the time she reached the bottom, there was so much snow packed in her kimono that she had to be raised like a roofbeam.

It was such a comical sight that Jubei couldn't help chuckling along with the others. The young woman laughed too. Jubei looked again. The laugh belonged to his sister.

"Akane!" he called out, pushing his way through a bunch of onlookers. She saw him coming and grinned sheepishly. "Nice slide," he said.

"I don't need compliments, I need help." She motioned him closer. "There's a couple of baskets of snow between my legs. I can't get it out, and I can't strip off my kimono."

"What do you want me to do?"

"Pick me up and shake me."

Jubei got her in a bear hug, raised her off the ground, and jiggled her up and down. Akane kicked her legs, and clumps of snow began dropping out of the bottom of her kimono. The crowd clapped and cheered each time a fresh deposit hit the ground. Jubei started laughing so hard his feet slipped out from under him and he went over backward, landing in the snow with Akane on his chest. They both lay there, helpless with laughter.

"Where have you been?" she chided him when they finally managed to get up. "I've been looking all over for you."

"Just wandering around, breathing in cold air and blowing out steam," he said. "After all this time I still can't stand being cooped up for very long."

"I know," she said. "Saru says you're hardly ever in the tavern."

It was true. Although Saru had given him a comfortable room over the tavern which he bought with his reward money, being locked up for so long left Jubei with a lot of residual restlessness that needed to be walked off at odd hours. It had been almost a year since his escape from prison, and he still felt like a bird who suddenly found the cage door open. It wasn't good enough knowing that he could go out the door any time he wanted—he had to do it, over and over again.

Akane passed on a message from Tajima instructing Jubei to go to the Honjo waterfront district and look for a boat bearing the mark of the fabric merchant, Mitsui. Someone would be there to meet him. She didn't know who it would be or what the meeting was about. "But you'll have to hurry," she said. "Father wants you there within the hour."

He hadn't seen much of his father since he got back to Edo. Tajima still thought it wise to keep him at arm's length. However, he had expanded Jubei's role by putting him in charge of a select group of trusted agents who had worked for the Tokugawa in the past. They were scattered throughout Edo, each one possessing a certain skill that could be useful to Jubei. One was an expert in explosives, another poison, another forgery, another arson, another tunneling, and so on. Most did not even know who the others were. But those at the core did—Akane and Iori. Saru's tavern served as their unofficial headquarters.

Until recently Tajima had kept them fairly busy. Akane had spent a few months posing as a servant in the house of a daimyo suspected of trying to secretly rally support for Iemitsu's younger brother, Tadanaga, who had been exiled to a remote castle in Suruga, where he was studying the sutras and waiting for Iemitsu to concoct an excuse to order him to commit seppuku. When Akane uncovered no evidence of any collusion to report to her father, Iemitsu flew into a rage and demanded that Tajima recall her and find some other way to get rid of the daimyo. It took all of Tajima's persuasive powers to convince Iemitsu to bide his time.

Coping with Iemitsu had become increasingly difficult since his formal installation as shogun. The abduction had had a profound effect on him. He'd become reclusive, and irrationally suspicious of everyone around him except Tajima. However, even Tajima's considerable influence had not been sufficient to prevent Iemitsu from banning from the investiture ceremony certain powerful daimyos he suspected of harboring a preference for his brother. As a result an important opportunity for healing old political wounds had been carelessly squandered.

As for Jubei, Tajima had assigned him the job of ridding Edo of the White Hilt Mob. Working with Iori and Saru, Jubei organized a small band of *ronin* to challenge the mob for control of the streets. At Tajima's orders the *doshin* stood aside and let the two rival gangs fight it out. After a few clashes, the ranks of the White Hilt Mob had become seriously depleted. In a desperate effort to reverse the tide, the chief of the White Hilt posted signs around Edo challenging Jubei to a duel. They met at dawn on the dueling ground where Jubei had lost his eye. Those who witnessed the duel were stunned by the ease with which Jubei dispatched his adversary, a formidable swordsman whom many had considered invincible. The humiliating defeat broke the spirit of the White Hilt Mob. A short time later the gang disbanded, and the former members went their own separate ways.

Jubei found the boat he was looking for tied up to a wharf in front of the huge Mitsui warehouse. It was a large seagoing vessel cut in the European mold. He had never seen anything quite like it. She carried no armament that he could see, but there were gunports along the side, something he had never seen on any other merchant vessel, large or small.

A plump cheerful-looking man greeted him at the gangplank. "Welcome Jubei-san," he said, bowing deeply in deference to Jubei's samurai status. "I am the merchant Mitsui. It is an honor to place my ship at your disposal."

Jubei thanked him and boarded the ship. Paper lanterns strung on a line from the wharf to the rigging illuminated the deck. Except for Mitsui the ship looked deserted.

"Your friend is waiting for you in my cabin." He gestured toward a door located in the aft section of the ship. He bowed again and hurried off down the wharf.

Jubei slapped the flat of his hand against the door and stepped back. The door opened.

"*Sensei!*" Jubei exclaimed.

Takuan frowned at him. "Rélax," he said, "I'm not going to hurt you."

It was the first time Jubei had seen him since his last visit to the cell, when he'd posed as a physician. Jubei was taken aback by the changes in him. Takuan seemed to have shriveled. His skin was sallow, almost the color of candle wax; there were large brown spots on his bald head; and although he wore the same wry grin, it seemed as if the magical fuel that fired his eyes was running low.

Still, Jubei couldn't pass up the opportunity to get in a jab at Takuan for doing nothing to help him escape from jail. "I guess you know you almost got me killed," he grumbled.

"Are you going to stand out here and quarrel with me, or come in and feel sorry for yourself where it's warm?"

The cabin was small and sparsely furnished. Takuan sat down on a cushion in front of a window set with small panes of leaded glass. Jubei laid his long sword on the tatami and sat cross-legged on the cushion opposite him.

The old man scooped a measure of green tea powder in a cup, whisked it into a hot froth, and offered it to Jubei. "Here," he said, "maybe the bitter taste will remind you that all of life is bitter."

Jubei just shook his head and took the tea.

Takuan raised his cup. "And I'll join you"—he took a sip from his cup—"just to show that I forgive you."

Jubei choked. "Forgive *me!*"

Takuan lifted his eyebrows slyly. "The map," Takuan reminded him.

Of course, the map. Jubei nodded. "I have to admit it wasn't my finest hour."

"You have a genius for understatement," Takuan said sardonically. "Your finest hour indeed."

This time Jubei raised his cup to Takuan. "Shall we call it even, *sensei?*"

"Why do I let you take advantage of my good nature?" he sighed.

They shared smiles.

"At least we know the gold won't fall into the wrong hands," Jubei rationalized. "That's something."

"Do we?"

"If we can believe Okubo, the secret dies with him."

"How do you know he died? Did you see his corpse?"

"When he didn't show up I assumed—"

"Assumptions are the parents of surprise, *neh?*"

"Then you think Okubo may still be alive?"

"Who knows?" Takuan shrugged. "But ask yourself if you would have eliminated Okubo before you made sure that the gold was where he said it was."

"People make mistakes," Jubei answered.

"Certainly *some* people do," Takuan said pointedly. "However, that's just another assumption we can't afford to make."

"It seems a little late to start worrying about it. If they know where the gold is, don't you think they'd have it by now?"

"You're forgetting one important thing. They think you know where the gold's hidden. If you were smart, you might leave it there to bait a trap. The possibility could make them wary enough to bide their time before going after the gold."

"Sooner or later they're bound to figure out that the spot's not being watched."

"Exactly." Then Takuan abruptly changed the subject. "What do you think of this ship?" he asked.

"I don't know anything about boats, but this one seems . . . well, different."

Takuan explained that Mitsui had it built by Portuguese shipbuilders in Manila. "While he was there, Mitsui stumbled across some interesting news. It seems some Jesuit has been smuggling small groups of Christian *ronin* in and out of the Philippines. According to Mitsui, Portuguese regulars have been training them in the use of firearms. Apparently there's an enormous stockpile of muskets stored in a warehouse in Manila. Rumor has it that some weapons have already reached Shimabara, but the bulk of the guns won't be released until this padre pays in gold."

"Okubo said in his note that he wanted the gold to help his fellow Christians," Jubei replied. "Maybe that's how he intended to use it."

"What else do you remember about the note?"

"Only that he was afraid the ones who betrayed him might also betray his cause."

"Okubo may have been a misguided idealist, but nobody can accuse him of being naive." Takuan thought for a moment. "How much do you remember about the map?"

"The gold's somewhere in the hills near Oyano village. That's all I can recall. I just glanced at it."

As Takuan fixed another cup of tea for them, he said, "That whole area—Oyano, Amakusa, Shimabara—all of Lord Arima's territories, is a hotbed of revolt. Matsukura has his hands full squashing one rebellion after another. Your father wants you and the others to go to Oyano and pose as wandering *ronin*. If a full-scale revolt is brewing, sooner or later somebody will try to hire you as retainers. Take them up on the offer and find out what you can about the situation. In the meantime scout the area for the gold. Who knows, you might get lucky."

Jubei dipped his head to indicate both comprehension and compliance. "When do we leave?"

"This ship is leaving for Nagasaki the day after tomorrow,"

Takuan said. "Mitsui has been kind enough to provide you with transportation."

"What's Mitsui's role in this?"

"He's a businessman, nothing more, nothing less. He's helping us because war is bad for business. It's as simple as that."

Jubei drained his cup and got up to leave.

Takuan stopped him at the door. "One more thing," he said. "If you happen to run into that Jesuit, kill him."

"*Hai*," Jubei said in a voice barely above a whisper.

Something in Jubei's voice—the intonation, or maybe the lack of intonation—alerted Takuan. "Jubei," he asked, "what's bothering you?"

Jubei thought for a moment. "I'm getting very good at killing people."

Takuan raised his eyebrows. "Isn't that a strange thing to bother someone who's chosen the way of the sword?"

"*Sensei*, I've gained a lot from you, and I'm grateful. You kept me blindfolded until I learned to hear. You stopped my ears with wax until I learned to see. Each time you took something away from me, sooner or later something always bubbled to the surface to take its place. I was like a snake shedding old skin, only to discover there was bright new skin underneath. But in the process of becoming an efficient killer, I gave up something that hasn't yet been replaced. I think you called it *passion*. You told me that passion was the flaw that cost me my eye. You said passion is the thing that makes a man vulnerable. That may be so, but *sensei*, it's also the thing that makes a man a man. While most men kill out of anger, fear, or moral outrage, I kill because I'm good at it. That bothers me."

"I suppose it would make things a lot easier if our enemies— the enemies of peace—had nasty-looking fangs and ate babies for lunch. It's too bad life's never that simple. The fact is, you're doing the right thing. It's not necessary to get excited about it."

"Don't worry, I'll do my duty."

Jubei shut the door behind him.

The snow had changed to rain.

After Jubei finished relating the news to the others, Saru invited everyone downstairs for sake. It was to be their first formal operation together, an occasion which the irrepressible Saru seized on as justification for a spontaneous celebration. Steaming bowls of rice were handed out, along with sheets of dried seaweed, yellow pickled radishes steeped in water and rice bran, and to everyone's amazement, octopus, squid, and slices of fresh-caught sea bream.

Saru was running around directing, exhorting, browbeating his employees like a *hatamoto* in the heat of battle. His sweatband drooped down over one eye, and his boisterous shouting could be heard out in the streets. In each hand he wielded a jug of hot sake, personally seeing to it that no cup ran dry.

He spilled some on Jubei's hand, and Jubei accused Saru of being drunk.

"Drunk!" Saru protested. "Can a drunk do this?"

He sprang in the air and came down like a high diver, catching and balancing himself on both hands. Then he lifted one arm and demanded that Jubei put a full cup of sake on the tatami below his head. When it was done, Saru lowered himself to the mat, picked the cup up in his teeth, drained it dry, and flipped backward, landing on his feet.

Everyone whooped and cheered except Iori, who called it a cheap theatrical stunt. "Anybody can do that trick with a little practice," he teased Saru.

Saru challenged him to duplicate it. The others joined in, taunting Iori to make good on his boast.

"I've got a better idea," Iori said. "Bring me three beans and I'll show you something you can tell your grandchildren about."

"Beans!" Saru bellowed out to the kitchen.

Iori selected three from the handful that the cook brought him. He gave them to Akane. "You know what to do?" she nodded. "Stand back," Iori warned, waving his arms like a swimmer doing a breaststroke. His knees were slightly flexed, and he let his hands dangle loosely by his sides.

Akane's hand shot up and the beans lifted off her fingertips. Iori drew and sliced the first bean in half on the way up, got the second bean on the way down, and caught the third bean on the side of his sword just before it hit the floor. He flipped the bean to Saru and took a deep bow.

"I saw a drunken *ronin* in Sendai do the same trick using mosquito eyes," Saru scoffed.

They all laughed and agreed it was worth another cup of sake.

As the celebration grew more boisterous, Saru called on everyone to provide some entertainment. The cleaning woman did finger tricks, fashioning her hands in the likeness of a fox, a crane, an owl and a frog. One of the serving women stretched her elastic face into an hilarious assortment of grotesque configurations, ending up with a spectacular rendition of the hideous face of the god Nio, the protector of the other Shinto gods. Then Akane sang an old mountain song.

Sweet and sorrowful, it told the story of a pair of lovers separated by a vast lake. Every night they would go to the shore and sing to each other across the water. One night, when the torment became too much to bear, they swam out to the middle of the lake and finally embraced. Realizing that neither one had the strength to swim back to shore, the god of the lake transformed them into nightingales to preserve their beautiful songs.

Jubei glanced at Iori, who had been visibly moved by her song. Along with everyone else close to Iori, Jubei knew that he was desperately in love with Akane. His instincts told him Akane knew it too, but for reasons of her own always pretended not to notice.

When Jubei's turn came, he asked everyone to write down a secret on small bits of paper he passed out. He had them put the folded pieces of paper inside a bowl, and announced that he would use mystical power to reveal the secrets. Selecting one from the bowl, he pressed it to his forehead and closed his eyes in concentration.

"Itaro," he said to the cook, "you are secretly keeping a woman in the Akasaka district."

"That's right!" the cook exclaimed, shaking his head in apparent bewilderment.

Actually the cook was the only one who was *not* mystified by Jubei's powers, because he was in on the trick. Jubei had taken him aside earlier and told him to listen to whatever he said and agree that whatever secret he revealed was indeed his secret. This would give him the excuse he needed to open the note he was holding and read it. While everyone thought Jubei was simply verifying Itaro's secret, he was actually reading someone else's note. That way he could always keep one step ahead. One after another Jubei mystified them with his uncanny powers.

The last note belonged to Akane. When Jubei read what she had written, his stomach clutched. He glanced at her, and she looked up at him with a smile in her eyes.

"It, ah, seems that Akane is, ah . . . in love."

"Is that true?" Saru gasped.

Akane raised her palms in a gesture of surrender. "If Jubei says so, it must be true."

Iori looked as if he'd just been hit with a hammer. The rest cheered and toasted her with sake. Saru clapped Iori on the back, jolting him out of his stupor. Quickly recovering, Iori joined in the merriment.

Saru pulled his *happi* jacket over his head like a bridal hood and did a riotous parody of Akane on her wedding day. He minced and fanned himself frantically, and shot lustful glances at Iori. Everyone laughed to exhaustion.

In a moment of quiet Jubei leaned over to Iori and asked him where he learned to handle a sword like that.

"My father, Musashi, taught me that trick when I was just a young boy," he answered.

"He must have been an amazing swordsman!" Jubei said. "Someday I hope to meet him."

Jubei asked a few more questions about his training, but he sensed Iori was responding to his questions the way a man toys with food when he has no appetite. Jubei stopped in mid sentence and invited Iori to tell him what was on his mind.

"I guess you don't know how I feel about your sister. . . ."

Jubei maintained a straight face. "If I had to make a wild stab at it, I'd say you were in love with her."

"Is it that obvious?"

Jubei nodded.

"Well, then you probably know what's bothering me."

"I wouldn't go that far."

"What if the one she's in love with isn't me?" Iori asked.

"Who else would it be?"

"That's what I wanted to ask you."

"Look, my friend," Jubei said, giving Iori's neck a playful squeeze, "don't you think it might make more sense to ask Akane that question?"

"You're right!" Iori replied, slapping his hand on his knee. "I'll do it."

Jubei filled Iori's cup with sake, and Iori tossed it down with singular determination.

The cook and the cleaning woman had fallen asleep on each other's shoulders. Akane was bent over Saru, mopping his forehead with a wet handkerchief. He was lying on his back with his eyes wide open, his face a ghostly shade of gray.

Jubei got up and closed Saru's eyes. "It looks like the party's over," he said to Akane.

"It's too late to go home," she replied. "Do you mind if I stay here tonight?"

Iori's face fell.

"It's all right with me, but Iori can see you home."

"No need for that," Akane said, going toward the stairs.

Jubei looked at Iori and shrugged as if to say, "Life's like that."

After Iori left, Jubei put out the lights and went up to his room. His bedding had been laid out for him, and Akane was sitting on her futon, taking her hair down.

"You're a cruel woman, Akane," he said. "You must have known Iori wanted to talk to you."

"Did he?"

"This may be hard to believe, but he's worried he may not be the one you're in love with."

Akane settled her head in the concave arch of the wooden pillow and pulled the thick covers up to her chin. "He's not," she said.

Then who? Jubei almost asked, but at the last moment resisted the impulse. He leaned over and blew out the candle, then began undressing in silence. Her reponse hit him like a sudden blow to the stomach, and like a fighter who had been hurt, he tried to hide the extent of the damage.

During the long days and nights of his imprisonment, Jubei had discovered a disquieting truth: He discovered that being deprived of fresh air and sunlight, clean water and decent food, was much easier to bear than the separation from Akane. Before, when went off to study with the warrior monks of Hiei, he had missed his sister. But this separation had been different. He not only missed her, he longed for her with an intensity that bordered on physical pain. At times his dream spirit went to her uninvited, and when he touched her, she moved him in ways no brother should ever be moved by a sister. The forbidden nature of his desire troubled him deeply, but in spite of his guilt, he knew he could not force himself to let her go. So he kept her close, and her nearness helped him through the horrible ordeal.

After his escape, he saw that Iori had fallen in love with her. It took him a while to reconcile himself to the idea that another man shared his love for Akane—a man who had every right to expect her to return that love. Little by little his genuine affection for Iori had eased the pain to tolerable levels.

And now this!

Jubei knew that all he had to do was ask her to name the man, and she would do it. Instead his jaws tightened around his silence. Sooner or later he would have to ask, but that moment would have to wait until he got a firmer grip on his emotions.

As the silence in the room lengthened, Akane's nerve began to fail her. The tension between them was almost palpable. She was certain Jubei had guessed where the conversation was leading. At best Jubei's silence could be interpreted as an admonition to go no further, at worst, it was an expression of disgust beyond words. Akane shuddered at the thought of how close she'd come to sharing her darkest secret with him. She closed her eyes. The moment of truth had passed and surely would never come again.

15

Oyano
Year of the Dog—1634
Hour of the Monkey

Yoshino was miserable. She was cold, her buttocks ached from hours of continuous bouncing on the saddle, and her stomach felt queasy after the ferry ride to Oyano. Making matters worse, her mistress seemed oblivious to her suffer-

ing. By the time they reached the outskirts of Oyano village,
she was too worn out to keep up her litany of complaints.
What good did it do, anyway? she wondered. Maria had been
in a daze ever since she found out that a padre answering Kriek's
description was living somewhere on the island of Oyano.

The information had not been easy for Maria to come by.
Matsukura's reign of terror had turned the peaceful farming
districts of Shimabara into a seething hotbed of hatred, mistrust, and violence. The countryside was in such turmoil that
the usually reliable underground network of communication
among Christians had broken down. Trust had become as
scarce as food. There were times when Maria had all but
given up hope of ever finding Kriek. To keep her spirits up,
she consoled herself with the notion that Rendai was probably having as much trouble locating him as she was. But deep
down Maria knew she was fooling herself. Rendai was no
ordinary woman—she possessed powers far beyond anything
Maria could imagine. All she could hope for was to somehow
reach Kriek before Rendai did.

Earlier that morning, before Maria had awakened, an old
farmer appeared at the inn where she and Yoshino were
staying. Yoshino immediately recognized him as one of the
gardeners who had worked for Maria's father before he'd
been evicted from Hara Castle. He told her that he had once
carried a letter from a padre in Oyano to the mission in
Nagasaki. Although he could not remember the padre's name,
he had never forgotten his strange violet eyes.

As they rode along now, Yoshino silently cursed herself for
passing the information along to her mistress. A single flame
of smoke rose high over the fields beyond the village. Maria
had been watching it for some time, wondering what was
burning, and led them into the village to find out.

Except for two guards at the granary, the village was deserted. When she questioned them, they told her that the
townspeople had gone to help fight a fire at one of the
farmhouses.

Yoshino begged her to stop for tea.

"Is there a teahouse nearby?" Maria asked one of the
soldiers.

"Teahouse!" he snorted. "You're lucky if you can find a tea
leaf in this godforsaken village."

"I can't go one step farther," Yoshino groaned.

Maria rode on in the direction of the smoke, and Yoshino reluctantly followed.

Along the sides of the road villagers were returning home, carrying empty buckets in their hands. Their soot-blackened faces showed both wearinesss and defeat. Some managed a bow as she passed by, others merely nodded their heads and stared at the strange sight of a samurai lady traveling through the countryside escorted only by her servant. She thought about stopping someone to inquire about Kriek, but changed her mind when she saw scant evidence of friendliness in their eyes.

She found an elderly farmer sitting on an overturned bucket, gazing at the smoldering ruins of his farmhouse. His wife and two sons were poking through the embers in a futile attempt to recover anything the fire had left behind. Maria dismounted and approached the farmer, who seemed not to notice her. Yoshino used the opportunity to warm herself by a burning timber.

"I'm sorry about your house," she said with genuine feeling.

The old man nodded, and continued peering at the destruction in silent grief. His face was dark with soot, and both hands were swathed in grimy bandages.

Seeing a samurai lady standing next to his father, the elder son, a nervous looking young man in his late teens, rushed over to head off any breach of etiquette that might bring more trouble down on his father's muddled head.

"I am Yosuke, first son of the farmer Kusuke," he said, bowing formally to Maria. "Please forgive my father's behavior. He's not himself today."

"*Iie*," Maria responded, "I'm the one who needs forgiveness for bothering your father in his moment of sorrow."

"You are very kind," Yosuke said, bowing again.

"What happened?"

"A small band of marauders came to the village in search of food. When they found the granary guarded, they attacked my father's house instead, killing one of my brothers and stealing the seed rice." Maria made the sign of the cross, and Yosuke did the same. "Before they went away," he continued, "they set fire to the house."

"Why?" she asked, horrified by the wanton cruelty of the act.

"Why not?" the old man muttered. "What use is a farm-house when there's no seed to plant?"

"It's a warm place to live," she said.

The old farmer shook his head. "*Iie*," he corrected her, "it's a warm place to die."

"Who are these marauders?" she asked the son.

"Mostly farmers who couldn't grow enough on their land to survive. To keep from starving, they left their farms, joined up with *ronin*, and began raiding government storehouses. When Lord Matsukura reinforced the guards, they turned on the farmers."

"Why doesn't Lord Matsukura send soldiers here to hunt them down?"

"It's not just Oyano, my lady," he said. "It's all of Shimabara. Lord Matsukura barely has enough troops to guard the storehouses."

"What will you do now?" Maria asked.

Yosuke looked down at his feet and did not answer.

"Tell her!" his father ordered.

"We will have to go into the hills."

"And!" the old man snapped.

"And find a gang to join," he said contritely.

"And the circle widens," she said, more to herself than to the father and son. "May God have mercy on us all."

Beyond caring, the old farmer stared up at Maria. "Who are you?" he asked bluntly.

The son winced at his father's indiscretion.

"My Christian name is Maria." Then she added, "I'm the daughter of Lord Arima."

Hearing that, the farmer rose and bowed deeply. "Your father is well thought of here in Oyano, my lady. How may I serve you?"

"I'm searching for a padre who I was told is living on this island. It's very important that I find him. There's reason to believe he's in grave danger."

"I'm afraid you're too late," the old man replied. "Lord Matsukura found out he was hiding here the night they crucified our chief farmer and his wife. My daughter warned him, and he took Watanabe's son with him into the hills."

It was the first she had heard of Shiro's parents' execution. "Then they may still be alive!" she cried.

"The soldiers came back without the padre, or his head. Most people believe he's hiding somewhere in the hills."

"I have to find him."

"Please," the farmer pleaded, "don't think about going into the hills alone. It's more dangerous than you can imagine."

"Since you're going into the hills," she said to the old man, "let me accompany you."

"My wife and I would make poor bandits at our age," he replied. "No, we'll die here in the village where we were born."

Maria understood. "What about your sons?" she asked. "I would see that they were well rewarded for their services."

"Two farmboys wouldn't provide you with much protection. . . ."

"I am going, with or without an escort," she said with fierce determination.

"Give me a moment alone with my sons, please."

Maria joined Yoshino, still toasting her hands over the timber, and watched the farmer huddle with his family. After a while the mother hugged each of her sons and squatted down by her husband's side. They both stared at the ruins of their home.

Yosuke and his younger brother came over to Maria. "We have no weapons," Yosuke said. "All our tools were lost in the fire. But if you insist on going into the hills, we will do our best to protect you."

Maria started toward the father to thank him.

"Please," Yosuke gently implored her, "they want to be alone now."

As Maria and Yoshino mounted their horses, the mother turned to look at her sons, but her husband merely stared into the fire. The wind shifted, momentarily shrouding the old couple in a pall of smoke. When it cleared, Maria saw the farmer's wife dab her eyes with the hem of her sleeve.

The *ronin* who led the raid was followed by two pairs of farmers trudging along with a bale of seed rice slung on a pole between them. The farmers—in their straw hats, straw capes, straw leggings, and straw sandals—resembled the effigies of evil spirits that farmers often paraded around their fields as a charm against locusts. Despite the chill, the *ronin* wore a loose cotton jacket and trousers. There was a thick stubble of beard on his face, and it had been months since he'd shaved his forelock. If it hadn't been for his haughty strides and double swords, it would have been hard to imagine that this samurai had once commanded a cavalry unit at Sekigahara, the pivotal battle which established Tokugawa supremacy throughout the Sunrise Land.

When they stumbled on to Kriek's abandoned hut, the *ronin* called a halt to the march. The grateful farmers dropped their burdens and sank down to rest as the *ronin* went inside the hut to look it over. He found some bedding there, several candles, an iron cooking pot, and not much else except a few pieces of rice paper covered with strange ink marks. He used the paper to start a campfire.

"We'll spend the night here," he said, reaching inside his flea-ridden jacket to scratch.

"What if the villagers come after us?" one of the farmers asked.

"That's what lookouts are for," he said contemptuously. "You'll each take three-hour shifts." He tossed the cooking pot to the nearest one. "Get some water and start the rice." To the one sitting next to him, he ordered, "You gather up some dry wood." To the next, "You hide the rice." And to the last farmer, "You take the first lookout." Then he went into the hut and lay down.

Earlier that same morning Tomi had gone down to the brook to fetch water and found a skin of ice on the still surface where the reeds were growing. She felt a twinge of guilt. The half-day trek to her sister's house in Mikamura for winter provisions couldn't be put off any longer. Winter was coming on earlier and harder than she could ever remember, and Shiro had already developed a worrisome cough.

Despite the hardships of living out of a cave, these past five months with Shiro and Kriek had been the happiest time of her life: foraging for berries and wild rice in the warm afternoon sun, sharing Shiro's joy when he returned from a day of fishing with a few infant trout for their dinner, weaving reed mats by the fire while the padre told wondrous tales of faraway places. After years of thinking of herself as a burden, Tomi finally felt needed. She did her best to hide her happiness from the gods, for fear they might be tempted to take it away from her.

Tomi stopped at the mouth of the cave to catch her breath and let the abdominal pains subside. They had become more frequent lately, often catching her off guard. Once or twice Kriek had noticed her distress and asked her about it. "Just woman trouble," Tomi had answered, promptly putting an end to his questions. Although she hadn't lied to him, she hadn't told the truth either. The "woman trouble" was pregnancy. It was one of the reasons her father had asked her to leave home. She was afraid if she'd told Kriek, he might not have taken her in. So far she had been able to conceal it from him, but in a few months . . . Tomi made up her mind to tell him after she got back from Mikamura.

Dusk was collecting in the eastern sky.

"It will be dark in about an hour," Yosuke said to Maria. "If we hurry we can make it to the padre's hut before nightfall."

"A hut!" Yoshino cried out to Maria. "Haven't I been a faithful servant to you? Why are you bent on killing me?" She moaned. "Surely there has to be an inn somewhere on this island."

"There's a small inn in Mikamura," Yosuke told her, "but that's a day's journey away."

Yoshino burst into tears. Maria reached out and took her hand. "Bear with me, dear Yoshino," she said. "Try to think of this as an adventure."

"If I don't die of the ague," she sniffled, "your husband will kill me for letting you go through with this madness."

"Tomorrow, I promise we'll stop at the inn. You can have a hot bath and a good meal, *neh*?"

Yoshino muttered something and rode on in misery.

The lookout ran into the camp and woke the *ronin*. "Two women on horses and two men on foot are coming right up the path," he said breathlessly.

"Are the men armed?"

"I don't think so. They look like farmers."

The *ronin* wiped his hand over his beard. "Horses, huh?"

"One of the women is samurai. The other one is probably her servant."

"A samurai lady escorted by farmers!" The *ronin* scratched his scruffy beard. "Go back and keep watch on the road, in case anybody else is coming. The rest of you stay out of sight until I give the signal."

He sat down cross-legged in front of the fire and waited. It wasn't long before he heard the clip-clop of hooves coming closer.

As Yosuke approached cautiously, the *ronin* bent over the cooking pot, pretending not to notice their arrival. Maria slipped her *kaiken* out of its sheath and handed it to Yosuke. He advanced a few steps closer. The *ronin* looked up from the pot, his features distorted by the flickering firelight.

"Welcome," the *ronin* called out cheerfully. "I was just about to have some dinner." He waved to Yosuke. "Why don't you and your friends join me?"

Yosuke glanced back at Maria. He looks rough, but seems friendly enough, Maria thought, also noting that he was outnumbered. She nodded to Yosuke and dismounted, walking her horse into the clearing to hand the reins to Yosuke's brother.

The *ronin* squinted through the flames. "What have we here?" he said as Maria stepped into the outer reaches of firelight. "A samurai lady out for a ride in the hills at this late—"

"Stop!" Yosuke yelled at Maria, recognizing the *ronin*'s face. She froze in her tracks. "He's the one who burned our house!"

As the burly man slowly got to his feet, Yosuke positioned himself between Maria and the *ronin*. "Get to your horse," he rasped, and Maria began backing up.

The *ronin* drew his sword. Yosuke's knees were trembling, but he held his ground. Suddenly the *ronin* let go a bloodcurdling shriek, leapt over the fire, and charged at Yosuke.

Yoshino screamed. Her horse reared and she went tumbling over its flanks.

Yosuke never had a chance. It was *kaiken* against *katana*, farmboy against samurai. A sweeping stroke sliced across Yosuke's midsection, dropping him to his knees. The reverse cut decapitated him. Yosuke's younger brother let go of the reins, fell to his knees, and covered his face with his hands.

Snorting and stomping, Maria's horse nervously refused to come under control. Unable to mount, she turned to run and found herself face to face with one of the *ronin*'s sickle-wielding cohorts. The others closed in around her.

Then Maria saw Yoshino lying on the ground, her eyes open but her jaw hanging slack. Maria bent down and raised her head. Yoshino's hair felt wet and warm. "Yoshino!" Maria cried out, staring at her hand, which was dripping with blood from the back of Yoshino's crushed skull. The *ronin* loomed over Maria ominously, then abruptly shifted his attention to the horses, leaving Maria alone with her fear and sorrow.

Once the horses were restrained and secured, he ordered the boy tied to a tree. While his men rushed around, putting everything back in order, the *ronin* remained with the horses—stroking their necks, speaking to them in a soft soothing voice.

Maria clung to Yoshino, refusing to surrender her lifeless body to the renegades.

"My lady, your servant is dead," one of the men said, appealing to reason.

"Get away!" Maria snarled.

The *ronin* left the horses and walked over to her. "Let the men bury her," he said to Maria.

"Murderer!" she hissed.

The *ronin* looked over each of his shoulders, pretending to be searching for the person she was accusing of murder. "A servant fell off a horse and died. A farmer threatened a samurai with a *kaiken*, and he died. What crime has been committed here? What law has been broken?"

"Thank you for reminding me," she sneered. "I almost forgot that the privilege of murdering farmers and servants is a precious part of our samurai birthright."

The *ronin* reached down and snatched open her kimono, exposing the cross that hung between her breasts. "*Soka*," he said, exposing a smile, "let me also remind you, Christian lady, it's a little hypocritical for one outlaw to lecture another outlaw on morality."

"Let me remind *you*, *ronin*, there is a difference between worshiping Jesus and murdering innocent people."

"I'm sure Lord Matsukura would be fascinated to hear your sermon."

"He might also be fascinated to hear that the daughter of Lord Arima was abused by a *ronin*."

"You are Lord Arima's daughter?"

"*Hai*."

The *ronin* bowed deeply. "And I am the Shogun," he replied sarcastically. With that he jerked her to her feet and pushed her inside the hut. "Look at you," he said, reaching out to touch her. "There's blood all over your kimono." Maria shrank away. "Take it off," he barked. "Now!"

Jubei and the others had passed the night in the abandoned sake brewery at the west end of Oyano village. When the fire broke out they joined the rest of the villagers in a futile attempt to extinguish the blaze. By late afternoon the farmhouse had burned to the ground and everyone returned to the brewery to clean up and eat.

Saru noticed Maria and Yoshino riding by, but it was Akane who recognized the lady as Lord Arima's daughter. She had once visited the house of the daimyo where Akane had been posing as a servant. "She's married to Prince Sanjo," Akane informed them.

No one could understand why the wife of a noble would be traveling through Oyano with only one servant and no military escort. The puzzle intrigued Jubei so much that he decided it might be worthwhile to follow her at a discreet distance. So when they finished eating, Jubei, Akane, Iori, and Saru set out on foot after her.

It was an easy matter following the trail of hoofprints that marked the way. The temperature of the horse droppings indicated that they were about half an hour behind.

As a precaution Saru volunteered to scout the road ahead. While the rest walked along at a leisurely pace, he scrambled over rocks and through the scrub pine along the side of the road. A short time after dusk he reached a spot that commanded a good view of the road below. Looking back he could barely make out the moonlit figures of his comrades rounding a bend in the distance. He was just about to move on when he heard the sound of someone crashing through the underbrush. Saru ducked behind a boulder and waited.

The lookout, panting heavily from his dash back through the woods, took up his vigil. No sooner had he settled in than he spotted movement out on the road. Crouching low, the lookout inched out to the edge of the rocks and began counting—one, two, three . . . Unsure of whether this was the only group coming, he waited longer than he should have, giving Saru time to creep up behind him.

Saru set himself and delivered a devastating kick that caught the renegade farmer square in the buttocks, launching him out over the rim of the rocks. He tumbled down the steep slope, bouncing off tree trunks and rocks, and hitting the road like a sack of vegetables.

Saru tested a few descents before he found one he could negotiate all the way down to the road. Without bothering to waste time checking out the condition of the unfortunate farmer, he sprinted back to Jubei to relay the news.

Jubei was furious. "How do you know the man you kicked over the cliff wasn't one of the farmers with Lady Arima?"

Iori jumped to Saru's defense. "He was probably one of the bandits who burned out the farmer and stole his seed rice."

"*Probably* is not good enough!" Jubei snapped at Iori. Then he said to Saru, "In the future kill only out of necessity, never out of convenience. Do you understand?"

"I understand," Saru answered, taken aback by the vehemence of Jubei's admonition.

"Now Saru, you and Iori go back the way you came. Akane and I will take the road. It looks less suspicious if we travel as a couple. Try to keep us in sight, and let us make the initial contact."

Akane and Jubei walked along in silence until they came to the place where the farmer lay sprawled in the dirt. Akane put her ear to his back and listened. "He's dead," she said.

Jubei rolled him over with his foot, looked at his weather-beaten face, and saw that he was too old to be one of the farmer's sons. Jubei looked up, saw Saru watching him from the rocks, and waved at him. Saru waved back, immensely relieved.

"I'm afraid Lord Arima's daughter's stumbled into some trouble," he said to Akane as they started off at a quicker pace.

"Then Saru was right," she replied.

"No. He was lucky."

They reached the clearing undetected. Huddled around the fire they could make out three men dipping their hands into a pot and stuffing their mouths with rice. "Listen," Jubei whispered. Akane could hear the faint sound of a woman sobbing. It seemed to be coming from inside the hut. Jubei gestured toward the shadows, where he saw the silhouette of someone against a tree, just behind the three men who were eating. Akane peered into the darkness, but couldn't make out what Jubei had seen there. With a hand gesture he signaled her to wait, his skin tingling in anticipation of danger.

The three farmers were so engrossed in their food that Jubei got within spitting distance before they reacted. All three leapt to their feet, leaving their weapons lying on the ground.

"*Kon ban wa*," Jubei greeted them casually.

The sobbing stopped, too quickly.

"Who are you?" the one farthest away asked as he bent down to pick up his sickle.

"Just a traveler." Jubei let them watch his eye roam to the tree where the farmboy was tied.

"You'd better look for some other place to stop," the one with the sickle snarled. "This place is taken."

"Is that rice I smell?" Jubei asked, sniffing the air.

The other two picked up their weapons, giving the spokesman a charge of confidence. "Can't you see you're not welcome here?"

Jubei pointed to the boy bound to the tree. "Is that how you treat unwelcome guests?"

The three men began to fan out around him, balancing their sickles in their hands. Just then Jubei heard a muffled cry in the hut, followed by silence. He squatted down, scooped some rice out of the pot, and tasted it. "A little sticky," he said, "but edible."

The *ronin* popped his head out of the cloth flap that served as a door to the hut. His face was badly scratched and his ear was bleeding. When they saw him, his men held their ground. He stepped outside carrying his sheathed sword in his left hand. He was bare-chested, dressed only in his trousers. For a moment he said nothing, measuring Jubei with his eyes.

"Why are you here?" he asked.

"I want the samurai lady."

The *ronin* lifted his chin and narrowed his eyes. "The only lady here is my wife."

Jubei was completely surrounded now. "Let me see her," he said.

"She's inside the hut."

"Tell her to come out."

"She's sleeping."

"You're a liar."

The *ronin* smiled. "Announce your name before I kill you."

"Inu Goroshi," Jubei said, meaning Dog Slayer.

"*Soka*," he murmured, "you wish to die a joke."

"If you don't want your men slaughtered, tell them to lay down their weapons."

The *ronin* laughed. "I'll say one thing for you, Inu Goroshi, you have a high opinion of yourself."

"No," Jubei said. "But I have no taste for wasting lives." He raised his right hand slowly, and Saru and Iori emerged from the shadows into the firelight.

The *ronin* quickly assessed the situation. It was difficult to tell in the dim light, but he guessed that the person standing behind the one-eyed samurai was a woman. Although she was dressed in men's clothing and wore a wide-brimmed traveler's hat pulled down low over her eyes, there was something about the way she carried herself that seemed decidedly feminine. Of the two others who's just stepped into the light, only one wore the two swords of the samurai. The small one, with the face of a monkey, was unarmed. Based on this cursory observation, the *ronin* judged it to be a fairly even match.

"We fight," he said, drawing his sword.

The night rang with the clash of steel against steel. The *ronin* was good. He moved swiftly for a big man, trading and blocking blow after blow. Jubei was unaware that behind him three renegade farmers already lay dead on the ground. His concentration was absolute. The *ronin* saw a strangeness come to his eye, a piercing stare that seemed to see everything, and nothing. It unnerved him.

The *ronin* swooped in low and Jubei sprang over his sword, but the *ronin* recovered in time to deflect Jubei's combination counter.

Then Jubei switched to his left-hand grip and advanced on the *ronin*. He saw the familiar trace of confusion come to the *ronin*'s eyes. Jubei struck three lightning blows and the sword spilled out of the *ronin*'s hand. The *ronin* took two steps backward and sat down hard, his fingers clutching his sliced abdomen. As he looked up at Jubei, a puzzled expression showed on his face, then he shut his eyes and toppled over on his side.

A faint light inside the hut diluted the darkness around the edges of the curtain covering the door. Jubei stood to one side and listened. The hut was deathly quiet. He tore down the curtain, paused for a second, then stepped inside. A single candle flickered in the corner, illuminating the figure of a woman lying naked on a pile of clothes. Her eyes were closed. There was blood on her face and upper body, but the slight rise and fall of her breasts indicated she was still alive.

"Akane!" Jubei called out as he bent over Maria. There were two fist-sized bruises on each side of her neck, where the carotid arteries feed the brain. Aside from that his cursory examination revealed no apparent wounds. Akane quietly entered the hut and knelt down beside him, feeling for a pulse.

"It looks like he used a blood choke," Jubei said, showing Akane the bruises on Maria's neck.

Akane agreed. "Her pulse is strong," she said. "She's in no real danger."

Jubei stood up. "I'll get some water."

The blood Akane cleaned off Maria's face and chest was not her own. However, Akane discovered that the blood between her thighs was. She had been brutally raped.

The cold water began to revive Maria. She stirred, then opened her eyes. Akane talked to her while she worked, using her voice like a soothing balm. Little by little the terror in her eyes dissipated, replaced by standing pools of tears. Maria shivered. Akane found a shabby quilt on the floor and covered her up. Maria reached out for Akane's hand and pressed it to her cheek. Her silent agony tore at Akane's heart. She cradled Maria like a baby and rocked her gently.

Outside Jubei fed the fire while Iori and Saru ate from the pot of rice. The surviving brother sat next to Jubei. Neither one of them felt much like eating.

"What will you do now?" Jubei asked him.

"I don't know," the farmboy said. "My brother and I came into the hills to join up with a *ronin*." He poked at the fire with a stick. "I'm not much of a fighter, but if you'll have me, I'll stay with you."

"Your place is with your father," Jubei told him. "He'll need your help in the planting season."

The farmboy looked at Jubei in surprise. "You mean you're not going to keep the rice?"

"We're not thieves," Jubei said. "We came to Oyano because we heard there's a Christian army forming here. There's not much work for *ronin* these days. We take what we can get."

"Everybody's heard those rumors," the boy said, referring to the Christian army. "But most people pass it off as a story to keep Christian spirits up."

"What do you think?"

Whenever anyone, especially a stranger, raised that question, it was unwritten law among the farmers to scoff at the notion. But this one-eyed *ronin* had saved his life, given back his father's rice, and avenged the deaths of his two brothers. The only way he could think to repay him was to tell the truth. Besides, there was something about this man who called himself Inu Goroshi that engendered trust.

"I believe it's true," he said. "On the other side of the Oyano range there's a small village called Mikamura. My eldest sister married a farmer from that village. Once when she returned home for a visit, I heard her say she'd seen a valley not far from Mikamura where men were being trained for war. The truth is, my brother and I were headed there when we were captured."

"What were you doing with the lady?"

"My father asked us to escort her."

"Where?"

Jubei's questions were beginning to make him uncomfortable. "Please, sir," he said, "it wouldn't be proper for me to talk about her business. I hope you're not offended by—"

"I'm not," Jubei said quickly. "In fact I admire your sense of discretion."

Jubei got up and stretched. He had noticed Saru sitting off by himself, looking unusually somber. After checking on Maria, he picked a spot near Saru and began preparing a bed of pine needles. When he had it the way he wanted it, Jubei lay back with his fingers locked behind his head and gazed up at the clouds.

"Was tonight the first time you killed a man?" he asked Saru.

"*Hai*," Saru answered after a moment's hesitation.

"What did it feel like?"

"I didn't give it much thought at the time," he said.

"And how do you feel about it now?"

"Jubei." Saru shifted toward him. "I thought I was helping out. What do you want me to say?"

"I want you to say you hated it."

Saru didn't say anything for a long time. Finally he turned the question back on Jubei. "How do you feel when you kill?"

Jubei shut his eyes. "I don't," he said in a voice that was barely audible.

"You don't what?"

"Feel."

Tomi shifted the sack of provisions she got from her sister from one shoulder to the other and started the long climb toward the cave. Her legs were heavy and her back ached, but she refused to slacken her pace. She was almost home, she told herself, leaning into her burden and plodding on. Despite the chill, she was perspiring heavily. Her damp undergown clung to her legs.

The journey to Mikamura had taken more out of her than she was willing to admit. Her sister had noticed her exhaustion and begged her not to leave until she had a few days rest. She might have, if it hadn't been for a powerful urge to get back, a need as strong as it was inexplicable.

"Tomi!"

She lifted her head and saw Shiro racing down the hill, his little arms and legs churning like a pinwheel. Dropping her sack, she put her hands out to catch him. Shiro leaped into her arms. She whirled him around, then collapsed on the path.

The boy chuckled merrily and scrambled to his feet. Tomi lay still. Her eyes were open, but only the whites showed. Her face was very pale, especially around the mouth.

"Tomi?" he said, reaching down to touch her shoulder. "Tomi?" she didn't answer. Shiro hugged her tight. "Please, Tomi, get up!" he pleaded.

Her cheek was cool and moist. The quick rise and fall of her chest told him she wasn't dead. Was she fooling him? he wondered, and stood up. "Tomi, you're scaring me."

Then he noticed that her feet and ankles were streaked with blood.

When Kriek heard Shiro's shrieks, he dropped the bowl he was carving and rushed out of the cave. As soon as Shiro saw him coming, he yelled, "Come quick!" then dashed back down the path.

Kriek chased after him and caught him by the arm. "What's wrong?" he said to the frantic boy.

"Tomi!" he gasped. "She's dying!"

Kriek found her lying where she'd fallen. He parted her kimono and saw that her undergown was soaked with blood. "She's weak from loss of blood," he told Shiro, who was standing behind him, weeping. "She fainted."

"Did I hurt her?" Shiro sobbed.

"No, it's not your fault," he said, gathering her up in his arms. "All grown-up girls bleed at certain times. It's natural." Shiro looked puzzled. "Get Tomi's sack," he told him. "I'll explain it to you after we get her back to the cave."

Kriek laid her down on the reed mat next to the fire and covered her with one of the blankets he found in her pack. After a few minutes of sponging her face with cold water, Tomi began to stir. Her eyelids fluttered and she looked up at him with the uncomprehending stare of one who wakes up in a strange place.

"I'm glad you're back," Kriek said to her in his most reassuring voice.

"What happened to me?" she asked weakly.

"It's your time of the month," he explained, not knowing the Japanese word for menses. "You lost a lot of blood and fainted."

Tomi turned away and covered her face with her hands.

"There's nothing to be ashamed of," he said, stroking her hair. "You just had an accident, that's all." Kriek noticed that her shoulders were trembling. Having never found himself in this kind of situation, he was at a loss for the right words to comfort her. For someone growing up in a culture where taking a bath was viewed as a social event, Tomi had always been unusually modest about her body—never undressing or bathing where she could be seen. "I'll warm some water for you," he said.

Tomi clutched his arm. "Don't leave me!" she begged. Her tear-glazed eyes were filled with fright.

"Tomi, tell me what's wrong."

"I'm afraid." Her voice was small and childlike.

Kriek smiled and grasped her hand. "Listen to me, Tomi. You took a long trip at a bad time. You were exhausted, and probably lost more blood than usual. As soon as you eat something and get a little rest, you'll feel better." He wiped away her tears with his thumb. "There's nothing to be afraid of, is there?"

"You don't understand," she said. "This isn't my monthly *seiri*. That stopped long before I came to you." Tomi could see comprehension taking hold.

Kriek laid his hand on her stomach. It was distended, but not huge. "Why didn't you tell me you were pregnant?" he asked, stunned by the revelation.

"I was afraid you wouldn't let me stay with you," she said. "I didn't have any other place to go."

"Is that why your father sent you away?" he asked in disbelief.

Tomi nodded. "Don't blame him, Padre. There wasn't enough food as it was. Another mouth to feed . . ." Her voice trailed off.

"God help us," Kriek mumbled, shaking his head.

"Are you angry, Padre?"

"Not with you," he said tenderly, lifting aside a damp strand of hair that lay against her cheek. "How many months?" he asked.

"I think seven. I'm not sure, though."

"Does the blood mean the baby is coming?"

"I'm not sure what it means."

"Have you had pains?" He probed her stomach lightly with his fingertips.

"Not many," she said. "On the way back I had to stop twice when it got too bad to walk."

Although Kriek was trying not to show it, a terror as cold as an ice storm was building inside him. Under the best of circumstances he was hopelessly ignorant about the mechanics of childbirth, and from the look of things, the circumstances couldn't have been worse. All he could do was pray that Tomi's condition would stabilize, giving him time to find someone competent to come and help her.

"Do you think you can tell me what to do if the baby starts to come?" he asked.

Moved by his transparent effort to appear calm, Tomi smiled wanly. "Don't worry, everything seems to happen naturally. All you have to do is cut and tie the cord, then clean the baby."

"Is that all?" It was hard to believe it could be that simple.

Kriek was certain she was forgetting something critically important.

"It is . . . unless something goes wrong," she said.

"Nothing's going to go wrong," he told her with such unassailable conviction that she almost found herself believing it. "Rest now." He tucked the blanket under her chin. "As soon as the water's hot, I'll get you cleaned up."

"Is Tomi going to die?" Shiro asked as they prepared the water for her bath.

"No," Kriek said. "She's going to have a baby."

"Good," the boy said, profoundly relieved. "Should I get some more wood for the fire?"

After Shiro left, Kriek helped Tomi out of her clothes. The amount of blood absorbed by the undergown alarmed him. Except for the bulge above her lap, Tomi was pitifully thin. He silently cursed himself for being so unobservant, and set about the grisly task of cleaning her legs.

Before he was finished he had used three large bowls of water. He rooted through the sack she'd brought from Mikamura and found two more heavy blankets, which he piled on top of the shivering woman. Using the last of the water, he started a thin rice gruel cooking over the fire. When it thickened to a milky consistency, Kriek added some dried *shiso* for flavor.

Tomi had dozed off. Considering the blood she lost, he decided that food was more important than sleep at this juncture, so he woke her and held her head while she sipped the gruel. "How's my cooking?" he asked.

"Delicious," she fibbed, and politely refused seconds.

After only one bowl of hot gruel, Kriek thought he detected a trace of color returning to her cheeks. Although she was still shivering, the back of her neck was warming up. Just as he was laying her head back down, the first contraction hit.

Tomi groaned. Her knees came up and her heels ground into the reed mat. Color rushed back into her face. Her jaw muscles quivered as she bore down on the pain. Not knowing what else to do, he gripped her hands and waited for the savage assault to abate. When Tomi finally drew a breath, she took gulps of air in jerky spasms. Her eyes were rolling in their sockets like a spooked horse.

"Stay calm, Tomi," he said in a soft, insistent tone. "Breathe deep. It'll pass soon, soon." Kriek kept up a litany of encouragement until the contraction relented.

When it was over, Tomi seemed to crumble. Beads of perspiration raised on her forehead. Her breathing was quick and shallow, and all the color had drained from her face. Kriek lifted the blankets aside. The area under her hips was soaked with blood. Remembering a small bolt of cotton material he had seen in the sack, he tore off a piece large enough to make an absorbant pad and put it between her thighs. Dear God, he thought. How many more of those can she take?

As he dried the sweat from her face, Tomi looked up at him like a bewildered child. Kriek struggled to think of some way of responding to the unspoken question in her eyes, some way of wringing meaning out of her pain, some way of convincing her that her agony was not an act of inexplicable sadism perpetuated by a cruel God on the mothers of His children.

"Padre," Tomi said so softly that he had to lean close to hear. "Please say the 'Ave Maria' for me."

Kriek translated the prayer from the Latin so Tomi could hear the meaning of the words.

Hail Mary, full of grace, the
Lord is with you.

Her lips moved soundlessly along with his.

Blessed are you among women
and blessed is the fruit of
your womb, Jesus.

Tomi closed her eyes.

Holy Mary, mother of God, pray
for us now, and at the hour of
our death.

As she lay there listening to the sonorous drone of his voice, twilight images drifted by like cotton-soft clouds, enveloping her spirit in contentment so palpable that it almost hurt.

Deep into the night Kriek watched over her while Shiro paced the floor like a caged animal. Every sudden move, every uneven breath, touched off spasms of helplessness inside him. He would stroke her hair and whisper things to her until her restlessness eased and her chest rose and fell in a steady rhythm again.

Near dawn the calm shattered. Tomi lurched and groaned, and clutched at her belly. It went on and on with a ferocity that made the first siege seem petty by comparison. Shiro stood over them looking on in silent despair. Kriek could feel her grip on his hands weaken, and still her cramped abdominal muscles refused to loosen. Tomi threw her head back and let go a long, pathetic moan that tore at his soul. Then it passed.

As she lay there trembling, he thought he heard the sound of gushing water beneath the blankets. Pulling the covers aside he saw her thighs awash in a pinkish fluid. The lumpy outline of an unborn child showed under her collapsed belly. Her water had broken and the bulges were moving.

"Get some more water," he said to Shiro. The boy stood there in a daze, his hands over his stomach. "Shiro!" Kriek barked sharply. "Water!" Shiro took a few steps backward, then turned and ran from the cave.

"Is it coming?" Tomi asked as he lifted her off the soaked bedding.

"Not yet, but soon . . . I think."

Kriek was wrong. The contractions began coming in swarms, but there was nothing to indicate that Tomi's baby was any closer to being born. Being too weak to assume the proper squatting position by herself, Kriek kneeled behind her, his arms locked around her to hold her upright. And when each onslaught was over, he would check to see if there had been any progress. Each time she would look at him, and each time he would shake his head and Tomi would close her eyes to wait for the next assault.

There was so little he could do. If only he could think of some way to relieve her suffering and give her strength to fight on, he thought. How much more of this could she take? Then he remembered.

"Stay with her," Kriek said to Shiro when he returned from the creek. "I'll be back soon."

It seemed like eternity before he emerged from one of the

several shafts that fed into the deeper recesses of the cave.
He returned carrying a pot of sake he had drawn from one of
the thirty casks Shiro had discovered in one of the interior
rooms during one of his caving expeditions. Neither he nor
Tomi had been able to guess why all that ceremonial wine
had been stored there, but whatever the reason, Kriek viewed
it as a godsend.

When the pot was heated, he poured some of the steaming
rice wine into a bowl and held it to Tomi's lips. She drank it
down, feeling the warmth radiate out from the walls of her
stomach to the tips of her frigid limbs. Kriek started to pour
another bowlful when he noticed that the bottom was fouled
with a coating of some kind of grit. He wiped it out with a
cloth and filled the bowl again. This time Tomi took only half
the sake and turned her head away. Kriek drank the remains.
The last sip contained more particles of grit. He spit it back
into the bowl and examined it under candlelight. It looked
like fine grains of golden sand.

Tomi's labor pains started again.

Unable to force himself to stand by and watch any longer,
Shiro wandered outside and covered his ears with his hands
to shut out the sound of Tomi's misery. He knew the padre
was doing everything in his power to save Tomi, but deep
down he understood that it was not enough. If only his
mother were here, he thought, she'd know what to do.

Then a bold idea struck him. He could use the same path
Tomi had taken up to the road. Once he got there, he
thought he could make it to Oyano village before nightfall
and bring his mother back to help Tomi. The padre had told
him that going back to the village was dangerous, but he
wasn't afraid. Anyway, who could blame him for trying to
save Tomi's life?

Burying the dead took most of the morning. Maria gave
Yoshino's horse to Kosuke's son, and he left for home with his
father's seed rice and his brother's corpse lashed to a makeshift travois.

Insisting that she was fit to travel, Maria managed to convince Jubei to escort her as far as Mikamura.

"Suppose you don't find this padre?" Jubei asked as he
walked along beside her horse.

"He's here in Oyano somewhere," she said. "I'm certain of that. Sooner or later I'll find him, or he'll find me."

Maria knew her answer wasn't an answer at all—it was wishful thinking. She hoped Jubei wouldn't press her any further, because she was incapable of projecting her future past the next bend in the road. The rape had left her numb and befuddled. Finding Kriek had become an obsession, and like all obsessions, it sprang from a fear of losing the last toehold on the precipice of sanity.

By early afternoon Shiro had only gotten as far as the place where they had climbed down to the ledge to escape the soldiers. The path out of the glen had taken him up to the road, but it had also taken him in the opposite direction he wanted to go. He was thirsty and leg-weary and still faced a long walk to the village. Doubts began to creep in that he could actually make it there before nightfall.

He was resting on a rock when Jubei and the others came around the bend. Since they weren't soldiers, they posed no threat. If they look friendly, Shiro thought, I'll ask for a drink.

As they approached, he jumped down from the rock and ran up to the pretty woman riding the chestnut mare. Shiro bowed and politely asked her for some water. Maria passed down the bamboo water tube she carried on her saddle. He took a couple of big mouthfuls and glanced up to see if he had taken too much.

"Go ahead," Maria said kindly, "drink all you want."

Shiro thanked her and slaked his thirst. Maria stared at the boy's exotic face while he drank. He handed the tube back to her, then reached up and touched her horse's neck. The horse jerked his head up in the air, and Shiro quickly apologized.

"How old are you?" Maria asked.

"I'm five . . . almost six," he said, counting himself one year old at birth.

"And your name?"

"Shiro."

Maria slid down from her mount and took his hands. "Tell me your father's name."

"Watanabe Kozaemon," Shiro said proudly. "Chief of the Oyano village farmers."

"You mean your stepfather, *neh?*"

Shiro nodded his head. "I don't know my real father," he said, feeling a little deflated.

"This is the boy!" Maria cried out to Jubei. "The one with the padre!"

"Who are you?" Shiro asked, fearing he'd revealed too much to a stranger.

"A long time ago the padre and I brought you here from another island. You were too young to remember."

Shiro's eyes lit up. "You're Maria!" he exclaimed. "The padre told me about you."

"Where is he?" she asked.

"He's with Tomi," he answered. "She's very sick. I'm going to Oyano village to bring my mother back to help her."

Tomi? Maria wondered if it could be the same girl who escaped from Hirado with Jan-san.

"What's wrong with her?" Maria asked.

"She's trying to have a baby, but the padre says it won't come."

Maria kneeled down and took Shiro by the shoulders. "You must take me to them."

"I'm going to get my mother," he said stubbornly.

"There may not be time, Shiro. Take me there," she insisted. "I may be able to help her."

Shiro fidgeted for a moment, then made up his mind. "The quickest way to the cave is down here," he said, pointing to the ledge below the road.

Jubei called Akane and Iori aside. "Take Lady Arima's horse and go to Mikamura. Find out what you can about the existence of a Christian army. I'll take Saru with me, and we'll join you at the inn later."

As Maria struggled along the ledge, the thought of actually coming face to face with Jan-san after all these years of separation tested the tensile strength of her resolve. She had tucked him away in the virgin womb of her imagination—untouched by time, unchanged by any event outside of her control—and now her fantasies were about to run headlong into hard reality. The prospect both thrilled and and frightened her.

Jubei was also preoccupied with thoughts of the padre. Was this the Jesuit that Takuan told him to kill? If so, he had probably stumbled onto the epicenter of the Christian conspiracy. Despite Takuan's order to kill him on sight, Jubei made up his mind not to do anything precipitous. For one thing, he was curious about this padre's connection with the Arima clan. For another, he was interested in observing one of these notorious Jesuits close up.

Shiro led Maria to the cave entrance, and for a moment she stood there, holding him by the hand. Shiro looked up at her, his little-boy eyes full of hope and sorrow. Together they made their way down to the floor of the cave, her heart pounding heavily.

"Padre," Shiro said, "I brought someone to help."

Kriek turned and saw a woman in the dim cavelight. Her face was familiar, like something out of a dream. "Maria?" he said, too drained by exhaustion to trust his own eyes.

"Jan-san," she responded, taking a few steps closer. She reached out and touched his stubbled cheek. "It *is* you."

The feel of her fingertips dispelled any notion he had that she was a figment of an overwrought imagination. "What are you doing here?"

She told him about meeting Shiro on his way to Oyano village. "The rest can wait until later. Let me see the girl."

Kriek pulled the blanket off Tomi's limp body. Maria probed her abdomen with her fingers, then asked him to lift Tomi's hips so she could check the progress of the birth. The expression on Maria's face confirmed Kriek's worst suspicions.

"When did the pains start?" she asked. "And the water, when did it break?" Kriek told her. "Has she been bleeding since the beginning?" Kriek nodded. "How long has it been since you last saw the baby move?" He couldn't recall.

Maria laid her ear against Tomi's chest. She had to listen a long time to pick up the faint sound of her heartbeat. Realizing time was short, she took Kriek aside and gave him the grim news.

"She's very weak, and the baby seems to be twisted inside her. It's hard to tell exactly how it's wedged, but I don't think it can be forced out."

"Isn't there anything we can do?"

"I've heard of experienced midwives somehow manipulating the unborn baby into the proper birth position, but I'm afraid even if I knew how to do it, it's already too late."

"Too late?"

"She's used up the last of her strength. Even a perfectly normal delivery would be too much for her now."

"Maria . . ." His voice broke. "What are you saying?"

"If we act quickly, we may be able to save the baby."

"What about Tomi?"

"We'll have to cut her womb open and take the baby out."

Kriek bristled. "You mean butcher her like a sow?"

"Jan-san," she pleaded, "please listen to me. Whatever we do, or don't do, Tomi is going to die. Don't you understand? Nothing can change that."

He whirled around and pounded his fist against the cave wall. "No!" he bellowed. "I won't let you kill her." Then he sank to his knees and covered his face with his hands.

Maria kneeled in front of him and gently pried his hands apart. "Jan-san, during all these hours you were by her side watching her suffer, didn't you pray for it to be over? Didn't you wish for some miracle to end her agony?"

"I prayed for simple compassion, for some sign of pity for that girl." Kriek shook his head. "I didn't ask for a miracle," he said bitterly.

"Perhaps death is the miracle that puts an end to suffering," she said to him.

"Death!" he sneered. "That's the Japanese solution to every problem. Tax the farmers to starvation. Kill them if they can't pay. Kill them if they protest. Kill them if they run away. Kill them if they turn to God for help. I'm sick to death of killing! What kind of land is this?"

"I don't know," Maria said. "I'm not wise enough to tell you why there is cruelty and injustice in the world, but I *can* count. One life saved out of two is one more than none. If you care about life as much as you say you do, stop complaining and do something useful."

Kriek glared at Maria, and Maria glared back.

A low moan cut through the silence. Kriek closed his eyes and his head dropped. "You're right, Maria," he said wearily. "Let me go to her alone," he said.

Maria lifted his face with her hands. She gazed into the burned-out pits of his eyes. Without another word she rose and took Shiro out of the cave.

There was barely enough energy left in Tomi's ravaged body to fuel the next contraction. It was over almost as soon as it had begun.

"Tomi, you are dying," Kriek said, gripping her hand.

"*Hai,*" she whispered.

"Are you afraid?"

Tomi shook her head.

He made the sign of the cross over her and gave her the last rites.

"You have been like a good wife to me, and a good mother to Shiro. We will miss you, Tomi."

"I will miss you, too." Her eyes filled with tears.

Kriek combed her hair with his fingers. "You look beautiful," he said, and Tomi forced the glimmer of a smile. "Now close your eyes. It's time to sleep."

After a few minutes by her side, he went out to find Maria. She was standing with Shiro and two strangers. One wore an eye patch, and the other was a small man with an odd-looking face. Kriek gave them only a cursory glance and told Maria to come with him.

"Do you know what to do?" he asked as they approached the place where Tomi was lying.

"I know what has to be done."

Kriek nodded and put his hand out to her. "Give me your *kaiken*." Maria handed him her dirk, and he kneeled down beside the sleeping girl. Kriek lifted the blankets off her chest, placed the point of the dirk over her heart, and summoning all his resolve, drove it deep into her breast. Tomi shuddered once and lay still.

Maria took the dagger out of his hands and quickly made an incision across the dead girl's abdomen. Kriek turned away and waited while Maria worked to extract the baby.

It became quiet. "Is it over?" Kriek asked without turning around.

"The baby is dead," Maria answered. "Strangled by its own birth cord."

Kriek found Shiro sitting at his favorite fishing spot, his arms around his shins, his forehead resting on his knees. He sat down beside the boy and draped his arm over his shoulders, trying to think of a gentle way to break the sad news. What had *his* mother said when she told him his father had died? Kriek asked himself. Something about "sitting among angels at the foot of God's throne" and "walking on streets paved with gold." It all sounded very beautiful, but he remembered it hadn't done much to ease the terrible loss he felt. So he stared at the sunstruck surface of the brook and said nothing.

It was Shiro who finally broke the silence. "Tomi liked to sit by the willow and weave," he said. "I think we should bury her there."

"It's a fine place."

"I'm trying not to cry," Shiro said, blinking back tears.

"So am I," Kriek confessed.

Then Shiro began to weep, and Kriek held him tight. When the boy's sobs subsided, he looked up at Kriek and asked the question Kriek had been dreading. "After we bury Tomi, will you take me home to my mother and father?"

Unwilling to conceal the truth any longer, he told Shiro what had happened to his parents. "So you see, it wasn't just me they were looking for the night Tomi came to warn us. It was you too. That's why I couldn't take you home."

Shiro broke away from him and started to run. Kriek caught up with him by the willow tree. There was a look of terror on the boy's face. "Let me go!" he yelled.

"Listen to me," Kriek said, gripping his arms. "You're safe with me. I won't let anything happen to you."

"No!" He tried to jerk free. "You're going to die!"

"How do you know that?"

"Because I love you."

16

Mikamura
Year of the Dog—1634
Hour of the Rooster

Akane arrived at Mikamura well ahead of Iori, who was coming behind on foot. She had expected to find a sleepy farming village like Oyano, but instead the streets were swarming with people. Groups of haggard-looking farmers gathered in front of boarded-up houses. Several *ronin* had built a fire in the street. They looked up from their gambling game as she rode by. A noodle vendor was hawking his wares. Children watched her with grimy fingers in their mouths.

A beggar woman sidled up to Akane. "Three copper *zenis*," she cried out.

Akane reined in her horse and took three *zenis* out of her obi. "Where's the inn?" Akane asked, offering her the coins.

"Keep going. It's at the far end of town."

A drunken brawl was in progress outside the inn. Two men had their swords drawn, but judging from their advanced states of inebriation, Akane concluded that the only danger either one of them faced was a self-inflicted wound. A mob of *ronin* surrounded them, laughing and yelling out encouragement to whichever buffoon had captured their fancy.

Akane dismounted and went inside to look for the proprietor. After repeated attempts to rouse somebody proved futile, she gave up and went back outside.

She saw a middle-aged man leaning against the wall of the inn, his bushy gray hair tied up like a bottlebrush. He was watching the fight through half-closed eyes. Akane suspected he was drunk too, but decided to approach him anyway, in the hope that he might be reasonably coherent.

"Excuse me," she said politely. "Can you tell me if there's anyone around to rent me a room?"

"You're new here, aren't you?"

"That's right," Akane said, relieved to see a pair of clear eyes looking out at her from under droopy lids.

"The owner of the inn took his family and went into the hills."

"Who's running the inn?"

"They are." He nodded toward the mob of ruffians milling around in the street.

"I don't understand."

"All these *ronin* came here because they heard some padre was trying to raise an army. When they found out there was no money to pay for their services, they drifted into the village. It seems things got a little rough for the innkeeper's tastes, so he left for Nagasaki."

"I see," Akane said. "Is that what brought you here?"

"No. I've given up the way of the sword. I spend my time writing and painting. Now and then I come down to the village to pick up a few supplies. It may be hard for you to believe, but Mikamura used to be a pleasant place."

"When I rode in, I saw a lot of farmers wandering around the streets. What are they doing here?"

"Some are villagers who had their homes taken over by *ronin*. Some drifted here from other villages when the soldiers came to collect taxes they couldn't pay. Some came to be a part of the great Christian victory over the forces of darkness," he said with a wry grin.

"Are you talking about a Christian revolt?"

"I'm not, the padre is."

"Where can I find this padre?"

"If I were you"—he tilted his bottlebrush tuft toward the street—"I'd worry about your horse first."

A stocky *ronin* with a shaved head was circling Maria's mare, appraising her with the critical eye of a Sakai horse trader.

"Who's that?" Akane asked.

"From what I can gather, it's the new innkeeper," he said sardonically.

Akane stepped down from the veranda. "I understand you're the one I should talk to about lodging at the inn," she said to the bald *ronin*.

The *ronin* cast a sidelong glance at Akane and bent over to check the mare's hooves, ignoring her altogether.

Rankled by his rudeness, Akane stepped up the volume. "I asked you—"

The *ronin* cut her short. "This your horse?"

"It is," Akane said.

"Fine animal. Where'd you steal it?" he sneered.

Summoning all her self-control, Akane let her shoulders relax. "I need a room, two if you have them."

"Certainly, *Ojo-san*," he answered, stressing the word *girl* to show that her man's attire had not fooled him. "But they won't be cheap." he added, adopting the solicitous tones of a merchant.

"How much?"

"Let's see." He stroked his beard stubble. "I think an even trade for this horse would be fair."

Akane just laughed and started for the horse. A younger *ronin* jumped out of the crowd and blocked her way. "I'm going to tell you one time," she said softly. "Move!"

"Listen to this!" the young *ronin* yelled out to his cronies. "Just because the girl dresses like a man and carries man-sized swords, she thinks she can order me around like a man. I guess I'll have to teach her some manners." No sooner had his hand touched the hilt of his sword, then Akane drew and sliced it off at the wrist. The mob murmured, but the young *ronin* never made a sound. For a few seconds he stood there, staring at his severed hand. Then he fainted.

Two of his friends rushed out of the crowd with their swords drawn. The first one to reach her made a wild slash at her head. Akane ducked, came up behind him and dropped him with a lateral cut across his back. Seeing that, the other one approached more cautiously. As Akane fixed her attention on him, the bald *ronin* began creeping up behind her.

"Behind you!" the bottlebrush *ronin* shouted and moved to help, though armed only with a staff.

"Stay out of this, old man!" the bald *ronin* yelled at him.

"I agree with the young lady," he answered calmly. "Your prices *are* too steep."

With her back protected, Akane finished off the other *ronin* in short order.

A teenage boy who had been hanging around the mob ran to the bald *ronin* and whispered something in his ear. "Are you sure?" Akane heard the *ronin* say to the boy. The boy nodded his head vigorously. The *ronin* took a step backward and sheathed his sword. "You didn't think I was serious," he said to the bottlebrush *ronin*. "A horse for a room . . ." He slapped the horse on the rump. "What a joke!" He backed into the crowd.

Akane looked at the stranger standing next to her. "What was that all about?" she asked. "Do you know what the boy said to him?"

"Maybe he warned him not to fight you."

"It wasn't me he was worried about—it was you."

"I think you underestimate your skill with the sword, Akane."

Stunned by his use of her name, Akane asked how he knew who she was.

"I recognized your sword style," he said. "Only Lord Tajima's daughter would have had the opportunity to learn it so well."

"Do you know my father?"

"When I was younger we were close friends."

"May I ask your name?"

"Musashi," he said, withholding his family name—Miyamoto.

"Musashi?" She was awestruck. "Not the legendary swordsman?"

Musashi bowed to her. "I'm surprised to hear you refer to me as a legend—I'm not dead yet."

"So that's what the boy told the *ronin*!" Akane clapped her hands together. "No wonder he was scared to death."

"When you see your father again, please convey my regards."

"Musashi-sama, please wait." Akane smiled at him. "Now I have a surprise for you."

"A surprise?"

"Your son Iori is traveling with me. He's coming on foot and should be here soon."

Shiro refused to come into the cave until Tomi's body had been removed. Although Kriek understood his apprehension, the idea of exposing Tomi's remains to carrion did not sit well with him. So a compromise was struck. Until a grave could be dug, she would be kept in the back of the cave where the casks of sake were stored.

"Sake!" Jubei said when Kriek solicited his help.

Misinterpreting his excitement for thirst, Kriek told Jubei that someone had used the cave to store about thirty casks of

ceremonial wine. If Jubei had no qualms about drinking sake
intended for the gods, he was welcome to drink his fill. In
fact, Kriek told him, one cask had already been tapped.

Jubei and Saru traded glances. Could it be that these were
the very casks they were looking for? Was it possible they
had stumbled on to Okubo's gold? Jubei had a vague recollection that the number of casks Okubo indicated on the ruined
map was thirty. The one thing he did remember clearly was
Okubo's rendering of a lotus blossom, which was the identifying mark on the casings.

With Kriek leading the way, Saru and Jubei followed,
carrying the young woman's corpse in a blanket. The passageway was tight, but after a sharp turn to the right they came
upon an opening leading into another room. When they
entered, the light from Kriek's candle revealed the casks,
stacked one on top of the other around the walls of the room.
Each one was wrapped in woven straw and decorated with
the mark of the lotus blossom. Jubei could hardly believe his
good fortune.

"This is the one I opened." Kriek said, showing them the
cask with a wooden tap jutting out of the bunghole. He
handed Jubei an iron teapot and one of the candles. "Take as
much as you want, but it might be a good idea to strain it
through a cloth. I found some grit in the bottom of the pot."

"There's no need to stay with us," Jubei said to Kriek.
"Just leave a candle. We can find our way back."

After Kriek left them, Jubei told Saru to give him the
hajimaki tied around his head. Using Saru's headbands for a
strainer, he filtered out a handful of gold dust. Saru looked at
the gold, then at Jubei.

"The padre doesn't know anything about it," he said.

"There's a lot *I* don't understand, but I think I know a way
to clear things up."

"How?" Saru asked.

"I'm about to throw out a minnow to see if I can catch a
mackerel."

Kriek and Maria were deep in conversation when he and
Saru came back with a pot of sake. Jubei detected a shift in
the tone of their discussion, indicating to him that his presence had redirected their conversation.

When the sake was heated, Jubei brought the pot over to
them and offered to pour. More than a day and night without

sleep had taken its toll on Kriek's body, but his mind refused to slow down. Thinking the sake might help restore some kind of reasonable equilibrium, he gratefully accepted a bowl.

Without waiting to be asked, Jubei sat down next to them, took out Saru's *hajimaki* and held it out to Kriek. "I believe this belongs to you," he said.

"It's not mine," Kriek said, thinking Jubei meant the *hajimaki*. "Where did you find it?"

Jubei untied the knot and dumped a glob of wet gold dust into Kriek's palm. "In the sake," he said.

This time Kriek took a close look at the grit. Taking a pinch he held it up to the candleflame. A shiny paste coated his thumb and forefinger. He turned his eyes toward Jubei. "It's gold," he said.

"The sake's laced with it," Jubei told him. "There must be a fortune in those barrels."

"Okubo's gold!" Maria said, remembering the widely circulated story about the missing gold.

"That's right," Jubei agreed, to the surprise of both Kriek and Maria. "Okubo told me the gold was stashed in sake barrels in Oyano. I didn't know where."

"Who are you?" Kriek demanded. "How do you know Okubo?"

"My name is Jubei. I was Okubo's cellmate in an Edo prison. We escaped together and Okubo was killed. Before he died he told me about the gold and asked me to see to it that it was used to relieve the suffering of his Christian brothers and sisters."

Kriek rotated the bowl between his palms and gazed down at the swirling wine. "And did he tell you how that noble goal was to be accomplished?" Jubei shook his head, and Kriek continued. "Okubo had fallen under the influence of a charismatic Jesuit who was plotting to convert all of Japan to Christianity by force of arms. This priest, Father Alcala, had a vision. Perhaps you've heard of his prophecy." Kriek looked up at Jubei, who again shook his head. "Alcala believed that God had chosen him to crush the heathen. He predicted that when the time was ripe, God would send him certain signs—a great light would appear in the western sky, the earth would tremble, and flowers would bloom out of season. Then a godchild would be sent to lead the Christian forces to victory, and all of Japan would receive Christ as their king. Okubo's gold was to be used to finance this holy crusade."

"And you, Padre . . . do you believe in this prophecy?" Jubei asked.

"I believe that Alcala's grandiose schemes can only lead to a Christian genocide." He turned to Maria. "The Father General sent me here to stop Alcala, then do what I could to convince Christians that violence and war were no solutions to the problem."

"What *is* the Father General's solution?" she asked Kriek.

"He believes that the survival of the Church in Japan depends on cooperation. Accommodation with the Shogun, not conflict. As an act of good faith I was ordered to turn Alcala's weapons over to the *bakufu*, along with whatever remained of Okubo's gold, in return for a pledge to end the persecution of the Christians."

Maria was incredulous. "Disarm the Christians and leave them defenseless in exchange for a *pledge*! If he thinks that such an 'act of good faith' would soften the heart of the Shogun or transform a monster like Matsukura into a lamb, then he must be a blind fool!"

"Maria, I can forgive the Father General's ignorance. He's never been to Japan. He has never seen the horrors with his own eyes, never lived among the farmers and shared their misery and terror. But I have been here too long and seen too much to delude myself into thinking that the Shogun is prepared to accept anything less than the total annihilation of Christianity in Japan. Alcala and all the meddling priests before him have poisoned the well. I believe that leaving the Christians defenseless in the face of certain extermination is as morally irresponsible as Alcala's mad dreams of conquest. So I petitioned the Father General for permission to try to convince Alcala to give up his mad idea of a crusade, and to use the weapons he's accumulated for self-defense only."

"And how did he respond?" she asked.

"There's been no response."

"Then what do you plan to do?"

"That remains to be seen. As a Jesuit I took a vow of obedience. Until I hear from the Father General, my original orders still stand. But as a man I can't bring myself to obey orders that I know will result in the slaughter of thousands of innocent Christians." Kriek's shoulders slumped as waves of fatigue rolled over him. "It's a terrible dilemma, and I guess the feeble attempts I made at locating Alcala were just an easy way to avoid facing the moment of decision."

How strange, Jubei thought. There seems to be no way for a foreigner to reconcile his differences with his lord and still retain his dignity. Without the option of seppuku, this poor padre was reduced to just two choices—both equally intolerable. He could either dishonor himself by breaking his oath of obedience, or live with the shame of doing something he believed was morally repugnant.

For Jubei and any samurai, seppuku was a dignified way of expressing loyalty and disapproval in the same noble act. Yet Jubei had heard that Western people viewed ritual suicide as an act of unspeakable barbarism. Apparently they considered life without honor easier to bear than death with honor, he concluded. Whatever the reason, he was glad he'd been born in a civilized land where breathing was not the ultimate value.

"I'm not a Christian," Jubei admitted, "but my friend Okubo was. I know he wanted the gold to be used to relieve the suffering of his Christian brothers and sisters. If you can assure me that you'll honor his last request to me, I will relinquish all claim to the gold and turn it over to you."

Kriek was not sure whether Jubei's offer was a blessing or a curse. "I want you to know that whatever decision I make, I won't use the gold for the purpose it was originally intended."

"Okubo is dead and can't answer for himself, but I believe his goal was to save Christian lives."

"Then I can give you my word that I'll do everything in my power to see to it that his wish is fulfilled."

Saru, dumbstruck by Jubei's largesse, shot him a disapproving look and stalked out of the cave. Jubei ignored him and leaned closer to Kriek. "It seems to me, having control over the gold gives you a powerful lever to pry concessions out of Alcala."

Kriek nodded. "That's true. Perhaps now he'll listen to reason." He mulled over the possibilities for a moment, then came to a decision. "As soon as Tomi is buried, I'll make a serious effort to track him down. After I've found him, I should have a clearer idea of what to do."

"One favor . . ." Jubei said. "I ask that you allow me to

serve you as a guard. By protecting you, I'll be honoring my obligation to Okubo."

Kriek dropped his head in a bow. "Okubo was truly fortunate to have a man like you for a friend."

Maria smiled warmly at Jubei, then turned to Kriek. "Jan-san, you are exhausted," she said tenderly, laying her hand on his arm. "Please try to get some sleep."

"There's so much I want to ask you," he said, fighting to stay awake a few moments longer.

"Rest now," she insisted. "I'll be here when you wake."

Jubei excused himself and went outside to join Saru. The instant Jubei appeared at the entrance, Saru leapt down from the rock and caught him by the arm. As soon as they were around the bend and safely out of earshot of the cave, Saru said, "Am I crazy, or did you just turn over the Shogun's gold to his enemies?"

"Calm yourself." Jubei grinned. "You can't catch a badger unless you bait the trap, *neh*?"

"But you already have this padre, and a fortune in gold! What more do you want?"

"I have no quarrel with this padre. He's not involved in any conspiracy against the Shogun. I'm going to let him lead us to Alcala. Once we find him, it's my guess that it won't be long before the scent of gold lures our real enemy out of hiding—the one who took Iemitsu captive and killed Okubo."

"Then what happens to the gold while we're out looking for Alcala?"

"It stays here."

Saru wrinkled his brow and peered up at Jubei through his eyelashes. "I don't like the idea of leaving all those kegs here unprotected."

"I don't either. That's why you won't be going with us when we start for Mikamura tomorrow. I want you to stay behind and keep an eye on the kegs."

"By myself?"

Although he had no reason to mistrust Saru, the thought of leaving him alone with that much gold for very long made Jubei feel uneasy. "Only for one night. I'll have Iori pick up some supplies and join you here."

"Good idea!" Saru grinned slyly. "I don't know what's worse, my weakness for gold or my weakness for sake."

* * *

Iori's reunion with his father was a joyous event. The three of them—Akane, Iori, and Musashi—sat on the floor of the inn, drinking and talking through the afternoon. Word had spread about Musashi's presence at the inn. Out of deference to the legendary swordsman, all the *ronin* had cleared out of their rooms, leaving the place at Musashi's disposal. Once in a while a pair of curious eyes would peep in through a hole in the sliding door, but no one had the temerity to disrupt his privacy.

During the early hours Akane listened quietly as Musashi and Iori filled each other in on the directions their lives had taken since they went their separate ways. After more than ninety successful duels Musashi said he had accumulated so many enemies who were obligated to avenge the death of this or that member of the family, that he decided to retire rather than go on slaughtering the hapless relatives of prior challengers who felt obligated to seek revenge. "I am a swordsman, not a butcher," Musashi told them. "Besides, I had learned all I could from dueling." It was stated as a simple, incontestable fact, and coming from Musashi, it did not sound in any way pretentious. "It's not enough to master the outer techniques of kendo—the physical movements. I wanted to understand the inner aspects, the attitude, the state of mind that generates victory not only in duels, but in all human endeavors. I'm struggling to see beyond rules, beyond style, and into the essence of winning."

"And have you seen, *Chichive*?" Iori asked.

Musashi smiled at the look of eager anticipation on Iori's face. "I've caught a few glimpses, my son . . . just glimpses." Iori looked so disappointed that Musashi felt compelled to go on. "There are beautiful lies and ugly truths. And if reality is too ugly to bear, most people will discard it in favor of illusion. This is the strategy for defeat. But if you learn to look at a beautiful lie without being seduced by it, and stare at an ugly truth without blinking, then you have a strategy for winning."

For Akane it was as if Musashi were speaking directly to her. *Ugly truths . . . beautiful lies*—his words hurt in a way he could never imagine. Ever since she'd been old enough to grasp that her feelings for Jubei went far beyond natural sibling affection, she had been living the beautiful lie, unable to face the ugly truth that her romantic fantasies were noth-

ing more than a twisted perversion of love. To think how
close she came to opening her heart to him the night of Saru's
celebration—only Jubei's reluctance to pose the question, "If
not Iori then who?" had saved her from the shame of con-
fessing her love to him. She felt wretched.

Musashi told them what he knew of Alcala's activities in
the hills north of Mikamura. "I've never really seen him, but
I've heard he has a few guns and very little money," he said.
"From what I can gather, Alcala's been training farmers in
the use of firearms. There's a rumor that the coalition of
Christian daimyos that promised to support him against the
Tokugawa is beginning to unravel. Apparently Alcala made
some extravagant commitments he couldn't keep. Still, more
farmers are flocking to him every day. Some say his forces
number in the tens of thousands."

"Here on Oyano?" Iori asked, unable to believe Musashi's
estimate.

"I heard the main force is massed on Shimabara Peninsula," he replied. "They say Oyano is only used for training."

"For a recluse," Iori said, "you certainly have access to a
lot of information."

Musashi admitted that he was only semiretired. "In exchange for permission to live here in seclusion, I agreed to
serve Lord Arima as a retainer. All he asks is that I keep him
informed of any activities that might be of interest to him,
and that's what I do." He flashed a wry grin at his son. "Even
a living legend has to eat."

Musashi's comment reminded everyone that they were
hungry. Akane offered to see if she could find something to
cook. As she got up, Iori laid his hand on her arm and asked
her to wait.

Akane noticed that Iori seemed uncharacteristically agitated as he cleared his throat and said, "I asked you to stay
because there's something I want to discuss that involves the
three of us." Musashi raised an eyebrow and listened attentively. "I think you know I have great respect for you. . . ."
He cleared his throat again. "And I have other strong feelings
too, about you." Musashi repressed a smile. "Meeting my
father here came as a great surprise to me, so I didn't have
time to prepare you for this, but since he has to leave soon
and I don't know when I might see him again, I thought it
might be a good idea to use this opportunity to . . . You see,

he knows your father, and if it's all right with you, I'd like to ask him to see if he can, ah . . . with your permission, arrange a marriage . . . between us."

So the moment had arrived, she thought. What did it matter that she wasn't in love with Iori? He was a good man. Perhaps in time she could come to love him. In any case it was time to get rid of destructive illusions, she told herself.

Instead of lowering her eyes, as she should have, Akane looked at Iori without blinking. "If the arrangement is acceptable to our parents, I'd be honored to be your wife."

The radiance from Iori's face could have started fires.

Akane tried to smile, but only the muscles moved. A dense gloom settled over her spirit. Instead of relief, she felt like an unfaithful wife who'd made a calculated decision to deceive her husband. She knew it made no sense, but abandoning her dreams of Jubei was like betraying a sacred trust. One day she might get used to the idea of sharing her pillow with Iori, but for now she was incapable of sharing his joy—unable to dance on Jubei's grave.

Musashi rotated his finger in the air. "Circles inside circles inside circles," he mused as he gazed at Akane. "Did your father ever tell you it was I who recommended that Takuan bring you to the Tajima family after the fall of Osaka Castle?"

Akane stared at him in total bewilderment. Not knowing how to answer, she just shook her head.

"Well, it's true," Musashi said warmly. "When Takuan found you among the ruins, he brought you to my tent. He asked me if I could recommend a good family to rear you. I told him I could think of no better samurai to bring you up than Lord Tajima, your adopted father."

Akane's jaw went slack. "My adopted father?"

Musashi glanced at Iori, then back to Akane. "You didn't know you were adopted?"

The revelation hit her like a hammer. She felt lightheaded. "No . . . I never . . . no one ever told me," she stammered.

Musashi reached out and took her hand. It was as cold as ice. "I'm sorry," he apologized. "I didn't know. I shouldn't have spoken."

"My real father . . . who is he?"

"Takuan wouldn't say, but I suspect he never would have rescued you if you weren't special in some way."

"It doesn't matter!" She squeezed his hand, her heart

nearly bursting with joy. "It's not an ugly lie!" she blurted out. "It never was!" Tears spilled down her cheeks. "Thank you!" she choked. "Thank you . . ."

Musashi had no idea how to respond. He glanced over at Iori for help, but he could see that his son was as baffled by her unexpected reaction as he was. Iori stared down at the floor and fidgeted with his fingers as Akane hurried out of the room.

At precisely that moment the first of a swarm of small earthquakes hit the island of Oyano.

The Oyano earth tremors had everyone on edge.

"It's the sign!" Word spread throughout the Christian encampment like wildfire. "It's the sign!" Pulses quickened. "It's the sign!" Mothers gathered their young ones to them. "It's the sign!" Farmers tied pieces of white cloth to bamboo poles and milled around the valley. "It's the sign!" Eyes cut to a hilltop where a solitary figure in a black cassock stood framed in the dying light.

Out of sight, just over the western horizon, a minor geological event of major significance was taking place. Great plumes of steam and sulfurous gases were rising from the cone of a freshly roused volcano. A fever sweat was building beneath the inland sea, sending shivers along the earth's spine. Vast quantities of magma leaked out of rifts extending from the base of the volcano, raising the temperature of the seawater. Offshore winds absorbed the warmth, and bathed Shimabara Peninsula in balmy breezes, stirring the sap in hibernating trees and fooling heat sensitive vegetation with a false promise of spring.

Father Alcala peered into the twilight with a calm that bordered on ecstasy. In spite of Prince Sanjo's blunders, in spite of weak-kneed allies, inadequate money and armament, in spite of the resistance of the Church fathers, he knew to the core of his soul that God had not abandoned him. The fulfillment of his prophecy was at hand.

In the valley below him a host of Christian refugees gravitated to the foot of the hill where they gazed up at the padre who had heard God's promise to lead them out of their misery. Thousands of white banners fluttered in the night wind. A fierce-eyed woman in a shabby cotton kimono worked her way through the throng. Someone thrust a banner in her hand. She took it and pressed forward.

Partway up the hill a phalanx of burly *ronin* blocked her advance. "That's far enough," one of them said firmly.

"I want to see the padre," she insisted. "Let me through!"

"Get back!" He menaced her with the blunt end of his *yari*. "Can't you see he wants to be left alone?"

The woman stepped back, muttering a curse between clenched teeth. For days she had waited for the padre to show himself, and now the man she had come to kill was only an arrow's flight away. But deep inside she knew that even if she had a bow, even if she had a clear shot at him, she wouldn't take it. It was not enough to end his life. Alcala must understand that the instrument of his death was Rendai!

It was well past the sixth canonical hour when Alcala knelt down to say vespers.

Rendai watched the breeze play with the coiled tendrils of his hair, and she remembered the dark hollows of his glazed eyes, the flared nostrils, the moisture, and the foreign stench on her body. She watched and let the vile memories flood in to quench any spark of human compassion that might enfeeble her will. Remembering had become a ritual of hate, used over and over again to stave off any erosion of resolve.

Alcala made the sign of the cross, lifted his head, and witnessed a sight so magnificent that it took his breath away. Above the rim of the western sea a Pentecostal flame ripped through the darkness, setting the sky on fire. Dogs howled. People stared at the roiling blaze in wonderment. The ground underfoot shuddered. The night air filled with a thunderous rumble, but it was deeper and more terrifying than thunder. Babies cried. Men and women fell to their knees and praised their Lord Jesus Christ, and God, His heavenly Father.

Tears of joy streamed down Alcala's cheeks. It was happening just as he had seen it in the vision. "Oh, dear God," he whispered. "This unworthy servant will not fail you."

After Tomi was buried, everyone except Saru set out for Mikamura. It was late afternoon when they reached town. The streets were packed with people who were afraid to stay indoors because of the earth tremors. Iori was sitting on the steps outside the inn when he spotted Jubei coming through the crowd. He stood up and waved, and Jubei waved back.

While the others were eating, Jubei took Iori and Akane aside and told them everything that had transpired at the cave. Iori was disappointed to hear that he wouldn't be traveling with them, but he understood Jubei's concern about leaving Saru alone with gold. "When I get there it might be wise to drain the casks and put the gold in bags, just in case we need to move it quickly," Iori suggested.

Jubei agreed. "There's a stable here where you can rent some horses. You'll need them if I send word to move the gold to another place."

Then Iori told him about his brief reunion with his father. He passed along the bits and snatches of information Musashi had gathered about Alcala's activities, and gave Jubei a rough map his father had sketched showing the area where they might find the Christian encampment. "My father says there are rumors of a larger force in Shimabara, but since this camp is only a day's journey from here, he thinks that's a good place to begin the search."

Throughout the conversation Akane barely said a word. She stood apart, unable to take her eyes off Jubei. Now that she knew he was not her brother, it seemed to her that she was really seeing him for the first time. The strong cheekbones, the stubborn set of jaw, the way he tilted his head and arched his eyebrow when his thoughts ran deep were all familiar, yet now charged with a freshness that puzzled and fascinated her. Each time he glanced at her, she felt the color rise in her cheeks and quickly averted her eyes, as if she'd been caught thinking out loud.

Jubei was acutely aware of the tension in the air. Something had happened—something both Iori and Akane were hiding from him. Several times during the conversation he sensed that Iori was about to tell him something important, only to back away at the last moment. Taken with Akane's strange behavior, it convinced Jubei that she and Iori had pillowed together. Although he thought he'd come to terms with the idea that sooner or later this day would surely arrive, he discovered that it still hurt.

Iori, who interpreted Akane's mood shift as a natural reaction to the shock of learning she was adopted, decided to keep silent about the marriage arrangement until she had time to resolve the matter in her own way. There would be ample opportunity for her to talk it over with Jubei during the search for Alcala. In time the wound would heal, of that he was certain. Until then he felt content to bask in the afterglow of her promise, and plan for their future.

The following morning Jubei and Akane left the inn and headed north along a narrow road that wound up into the hills. Iori watched them disappear from view, then went inside to make a list of the provisions he needed to take with him to the cave. He was just about to leave when a samurai rode up to the inn with a message from Lord Tajima. Iori recognized him as one of the guards who accompanied Tajima whenever he traveled outside Edo.

The message was brief. Tajima ordered them to abandon the search for the gold and join him at Lord Arima's residence in Nobeoka without delay.

"The others are off in the hills somewhere," he told the messenger. "You could ride out and try to find them, but without a map to guide you, it would probably be a waste of time."

Iori considered the alternatives. He could not disobey a direct order from Tajima, and he knew Jubei did not want him to leave Saru alone with the gold. It occurred to him that under the circumstances the best course of action would be to pack up the gold and take it with him to Nobeoka.

"Return to Nobeoka with this messsage," he said. "Tell Lord Tajima that there's an urgent matter that I must attend to before I can leave Oyano. With luck I can be there by tomorrow night."

After the messenger rode off, Iori wrote an explanatory note to Jubei and left it with the innkeeper, who had returned when he heard that the *ronin* had been expelled. "This is for my friend," Iori told him. "The one with the black eye patch. See that he gets it the moment he gets back." The innkeeper bowed and accepted the coins pressed into his hand.

On his way out of town Iori stopped at a stable and rented four horses—mounts for himself and Saru, the other two horses to transport the gold to Nobeoka.

Saru was in high spirits when Iori reached the cave. He reeked of sake, but his speech was unslurred and his gait stable.

"No more sake today," he told Saru when he finished

explaining his plan to collect the gold dust. "We have a lot of work to do, and a short time to do it."

Saru guided Iori through the twisting passageway that led to the room where the casks were stored. The single candle he was carrying barely dented the dense darkness. "We need more light," Saru said when they arrived at the entrance to the room. "Wait here and I'll bring more candles."

Saru hurried off, leaving Iori immersed in inky darkness so impenetrable that it seemed to have weight.

"He probably thinks this is amusing," Iori grumbled to himself as he groped his way into the room. His hand came against the straw casing of one of the kegs. Running his fingers over it like a blind man, he found a tap jutting out of the bunghole. He tipped the cask and found that it had been drained. Working his way down the stacks, Iori discovered that all of the casks had been emptied. . . .

Seconds later there was a muffled roar. Smoke and dust and chunks of debris belched out of the cave like flames from the mouth of a dragon.

Saru had stolen two powderkegs from a small government outpost on the edge of town, positioned them at the mouth of the corridor that led to the room where Iori was trapped in darkness, laid down a long trail of gunpowder, then touched the candle flame to the powderline and scurried out of the cave.

Now he gathered up the eight sacks of gold he had extracted from the barrels and hidden, and loaded them on the backs of the horses. He took his time, giving the dust a chance to settle. When he finished he went back inside and inspected the damage.

The entire passageway had collapsed into rubble. Massive boulders sealed the route to the room where he had left Iori. From the wealth of devastation, Saru doubted that Iori had survived the initial blast. At least Saru hoped that he died quickly—it hadn't been his intention to bury Iori alive. He'd merely wanted to throw Jubei off his trail by making it appear as if an earthquake had destroyed the cave, killing both of them.

Saru glanced back over his shoulder as he rode away. Yes, he thought, blasting the cave was a stroke of genius. Prince Sanjo had been wise to turn to the Koga ninja for help.

* * *

After two days of winding their way along the dusty roads and rolling hills of Oyano, Jubei and the others arrived at the Christian encampment. Alcala was gone, and except for a few stragglers, the valley was deserted. Jubei learned that Alcala had moved on to Shimabara, where the main force of refugees was massed. The old man who gave them the information said, "The time has come." He was holding a blooming plum branch in his hands.

Events were beginning to outstrip Kriek's ability to keep up with them. He felt like a little dog yapping at the heels of a galloping horse. For good or ill Alcala had acted, while *he* spent his years in Japan as an irrelevancy. Christians were still starved, brutalized, and hunted like animals. Every baby he baptized had been marked for extermination. Yet they came to him, listened to him tell them to love their enemies and turn the other cheek, and they tried to accept their miserable lot as an act of Christian piety. Christ's promise that the meek would inherit the earth began to take on ironic overtones. It seemed to Kriek that the only earth the meek would ever inherit was the soil that covered their graves.

"The old man's right," he said to Jubei. "Whether we like it or not, the time *has* come."

"What are your plans?" Jubei asked.

"We'll spend the night here," Kriek replied, "then leave for Shimabara at dawn."

The old man pointed out Alcala's abandoned hut on the hillside. "There's firewood up there, and a spring too. It should be a good place to pass the night."

Kriek asked him to join them, but the old man declined the invitation, claiming that his legs were too old to carry him up the hill.

"You can ride my horse," Shiro said, meaning Maria's horse.

The old man shook his head. "I'm a farmer," he said with a tinge of pride. "Horses are for samurai."

Kriek offered the old man some dried squid. "I hope you're not too old to eat," he joked.

"No, I'm too old to chew." He flashed a mouthful of vacant gums. "Anyway, tonight I'm going to the Pure Land. No sense in wasting food on me."

"Do you want me to hear your confession?"

"Never had enough spare time to do anything bad," he said. "Besides, I'm not a Christian."

"What are you doing here?" Jubei asked.

"When they took away my farm, I didn't have anyplace else to go. Everybody said the padre didn't care much about a man's religion. He fed anybody who showed up."

Respecting the old man's decision, they left him alone and started the long climb up the hill. Shiro rode ahead. Kriek and Jubei followed, with Akane and Maria lagging behind.

"What's troubling you?" Maria asked Akane when they were out of earshot of the men. Throughout the journey from Mikamura, Akane had seemed preoccupied and distant. Since the night of the rape an unspoken bond of trust had formed between the two women, and it bothered Maria to see her friend drifting away. "Please let me help you, if I can."

Akane desperately wanted to turn to Maria for help, but before she could begin to untangle the threads of her snarled emotions, she had to find a single strand to work on herself. From the moment she learned that she was not Jubei's sister, a thousand scenes had played across her imagination—all designed to convince Jubei to accept her love, all climaxing in rejection and shame. She had no reason to believe that Maria would find her any less ridiculous than she found herself.

"It's hard for me, Maria. I've never been good at putting feeling and words together. And this . . ." Akane bit her lip to keep it from quivering.

Maria took her hand and held it as they walked along. "Don't worry, Akane. We all have secret feelings that we're sure no one but us has ever experienced or could ever understand. And then, when we find a way to share them with someone who cares, we make an amazing discovery. Everyone dreams dark dreams."

"Do you?"

Maria laughed. "I dream of an outcast . . . a barbarian who also happens to be a Jesuit priest. And you dream of your brother. Which dream is darker?"

Akane's jaw fell slack. "You knew?"

She smiled playfully. "Akane, I'm a woman too."

Suddenly Akane found a voice for her feelings. Words flowed in torrents as she poured out her heart. She spoke of her childish fantasies that evolved into confusion and guilt. She told Maria about her decision to abandon the "beautiful lie" and accept Iori as her husband, only to discover that she was an adopted child with no blood ties to Jubei. "I want him to know, but I can't think of a way to tell him without scaring him away."

"What do your instincts say to you?"

"Instincts?" Akane scoffed. "All my life I've lived in a man's world, studying the martial arts. I know more about killing than I know about being a woman. When it comes to the gentle arts, I'm lost. Believe me, Maria, it would be easier for me to devise a strategy to defeat Jubei than to make him love me." She covered her face with her hands.

Maria reached out and pulled them apart. "Look at me!" she said. "I'm no more woman than you are. Being a woman isn't something you study like kendo, it's something you are! Iori saw it and fell in love with you. You are a beautiful woman. Do you think Jubei can't see that?"

"I think he looks at me and sees a sister," she said abjectly. "But there have been moments . . ." She shrugged. "Who knows, it could have been my imagination."

"You're worried about his reaction, *neh?*" Akane nodded.

"Then there's no need to serve him a bigger portion than he can swallow at one time. Just tell him that you aren't his sister, and let that fact sit in his mind like a nesting bird."

Akane stopped and put her arms around Maria. "You are a wise woman and a true friend," she whispered. Maria hugged her, celebrating a warmth as comfortable as home.

17

Nobeoka
Year of the Dog—1634
Hour of the Ram

It was mid December. Cherry blossoms were blooming in Lord Arima's garden.

"How extraordinary," he said to Tajima as he clipped a particularly opulent branch. "My grandfather once told me he saw such a thing as this, but he was very old and often got his memories tangled." He scrutinized the sprig for defects, found none, and walked on in search of two companion pieces for his flower arrangement.

"This island of yours has always been something of a mystery to those of us who live in the north," Tajima said. "Here in Kyushu even nature itself seems to rebel against the natural order of things."

"There's no mystery. Kyushu is just a foolish old woman who powders her face and reddens her lips to see if she can remember how it felt to be young and carefree.

"When an old woman can't bring herself to accept the seasons of change," Arima went on, "it's merely pathetic. But when a leader commits the same error, it's dangerous."

Lord Arima selected a smoothly curved red-bud willow stem and snapped it off at the joint. "You see, the willow's strength lies in its flexibility. While other sturdier trees are ruined by storms, the willow survives . . . not because it resists the wind, but because it doesn't." Arima worked the stem between his fingers to improve the curve. "Yet as supple as the willow is, it still can be broken if it's bent too far."

Tajima had to admire the subtle turn of Arima's mind. By

characterizing his rebellious territories as a "foolish old woman,"
he had acknowledged both the futility and folly of continued
resistance. Then he had gone on to imply that he was prepared to bend to the Shogun's will, if only some way could be
found to do it without losing face. Unfortunately, Lord Iemitsu
was in no mood to compromise.

The two men crossed the stone bridge that led from the
main garden to the moon-viewing room, where Takuan had
remained, waiting for their return. The old monk pushed his
uncooperative body into a sitting position, and the effort left
him light-headed. He fumbled through his medicine pouch
and took out a piece of paper with a sticky substance wrapped
inside. A small pinch of the poppy resin would see him
through the next few hours. Takuan cut off a portion with his
fingernail and let the bitter goo dissolve in his mouth. There
was enough left for one, possibly two more doses. After
that . . .

The opium was taking hold when Arima and Tajima entered the room. Takuan greeted them, then detached himself
from the ruined body that housed his spirit and observed the
scene from a comfortable distance away. It no longer bothered him that he was unable to leave his body without the aid
of the drug. The relentless throbbing at his temples had
savaged his ability to concentrate.

As the dialogue began to unfold, Takuan imagined that he
was viewing two skillful swordsmen engaged in verbal sparring. Each man was handling himself with considerable power
and grace.

Tajima maneuvered under Arima's guard with a surprise
thrust. "I suppose you've heard rumors of your son-in-law's
involvement in a plot against the Shogun?"

Arima did not raise his eyes from the flower arrangement he
was shaping. Only Takuan detected a nearly imperceptible
hesitation in the movement of his hands. "There are always
those who delight in spreading specious rumors. As prudent
men we'd be shamelessly irresponsible if we defamed the
character of a noble of the Imperial Court by giving credence
to such gossip, *neh*?"

"We would, indeed. However, these rumors seem to be
borne out by some rather compelling evidence." Arima put
aside his flower arrangement and gave Tajima his full attention as the details of Iemitsu's abortive abduction were re-

vealed to him. "The description of the palanquin seen leaving the villa where Lord Iemitsu was being held fits one belonging to Prince Sanjo," Tajima said, concluding his indictment.

"I see," Arima replied, realizing that the Shogun would need stronger evidence than that to accuse Sanjo—and by implication, the Imperial Court—of treason. "And have you confronted Prince Sanjo with your suspicions?"

"We're most anxious to hear from Prince Sanjo. The problem is, no one knows where he is." Tajima paused. "It occurred to the Shogun that as his father-in-law, you would be eager to see this disagreeable matter cleared up as soon as possible. The Shogun thought you might be persuaded to help us locate him . . . if only as a sign of your own loyalty."

"So, in the Shogun's mind I'm guilty by association."

"Let's say you can prove your innocence by cooperation."

"You're asking me to betray my son-in-law?"

"Betray?" Tajima raised his eyebrows. "What a strange choice of words. We're asking you to deliver a traitor into our hands. I'd hardly characterize that as an act of betrayal. Unless . . ." Tajima opened his hands, leaving the obvious unstated.

Takuan couldn't help smiling as Lord Arima's defenses began to crumble.

Arima knew he was trapped. If he turned against Sanjo, surely Sanjo would turn on him and reveal his role in the overall conspiracy. On the other hand, refusing to cooperate with Tajima would brand him as a traitor in the Shogun's eyes. Either way he was finished. At least seppuku remained an option.

Takuan sensed Arima's desperation and shrewdly intervened to provide him with a glimmer of hope. He directed his comments to Tajima. "I must say I sympathize with Lord Arima's dilemma. We know Prince Sanjo's capacity for treachery. Suppose out of vengeance he decided to falsely accuse Lord Arima of complicity? What guarantee can we offer him that the Shogun won't take Sanjo's charges seriously?"

Tajima nodded gravely, playing out his part just as they had staged it. "The atmosphere of suspicion is thick in Edo Castle. I can promise Lord Arima that I would advise against accepting Sanjo's accusations, but I can't promise that the Shogun will take my advice."

"Do you have any doubts that Sanjo is the head of the conspiracy against the Shogun?" Takuan asked Tajima.

"None."

"And when the head is cut off . . ."

"The body dies."

Within the bracket of silence that followed, Arima grasped the line Takuan was throwing to him. Agree to help us, he was saying, and in return we'll dispose of Sanjo before he can implicate you in a conspiracy destined to die along with its leader. Arima studied Tajima's face for some indication of his reaction to Takuan's proposal.

Tajima was in no hurry to land his fish. Let him taste the bait before the hook is set, he thought. If Arima only knew the truth. Although Prince Sanjo had been under suspicion for years, never had anyone considered taking him alive. The evidence against Sanjo was too flimsy, and the political ramifications too grave to execute an imperial prince for treason. So Arima was rising to factitious bait.

When Tajima looked at Arima, his gaze was cold and hard. "Will Sanjo's death break the back of the conspiracy against the Shogun?"

"I'm in no position to—"

"Lord Arima!" he cut him off harshly. "I'm talking about saving your life and the lives of your family . . . not because I believe you're innocent, nor because I trust you. But because I want Sanjo. Without him you are nothing. So don't insult my intelligence by playing shadow games. Answer my question."

"The conspiracy will be over," he said in a voice barely above a whisper. "But the Christians will fight to the end. For them it's only a matter of choosing the way they will die."

"Will there be foreign intervention?"

"I once believed the padres' promises. After years of waiting, I've given up hope. They sowed their seeds in Kyushu, then left the crops to rot in the fields."

Tajima took a letter out of the sleeve of his kimono and handed it to Arima. It was marked with the Shogun's seal. "The harvest is long overdue," he said. "You can help convince the Shogun of your loyalty by joining forces with Lord Matsukura. Working together it will be possible to eliminate the Christian threat in Kyushu once and for all. In return you have my word that Sanjo will die without tainting your good name. If you cannot bring yourself to obey the orders of the Shogun, I've been instructed to summarily execute you, confiscate your holdings, and take command of your troops. That is the Shogun's ultimatum."

A long shadow was creeping across the floor of the valley where only a day before thousands of Christians had listened in rapture to Alcala's prophecy of the coming victory over the forces of darkness. When he had finished speaking, they left the valley, following him to Shimabara, where an even larger number of Christian rebels had gathered.

Inside Alcala's abandoned hut Maria had built a fire. The orange embers in the hearth pit shimmered like a pool of iridescent carp. In the half shadows beyond the circle glow, Shiro lay sleeping, his knees drawn up tight to his chest, his lovely face unmarred by troubles. A nearby cricket, addled by the unnatural warmth in the air, kept insisting it was spring.

"Maria, come look," Kriek called to her from somewhere outside the hut.

She whisked the charcoal dust off her hands and ducked through the split *noren* that hung over the doorway. Kriek was sitting on the floor of a small outbuilding that had served Alcala as a chapel. His back was to her, and the setting sun made his flaxen hair shine like a halo. He turned as she came up behind him, and he pointed in the direction of the hilltop where a few days earlier Alcala had witnessed his miracle.

Backlit against the cloud-streaked sun, she saw the silhouettes of Jubei and Akane executing a slow ballet in perfect unison.

"What are they doing?" Kriek asked her.

"It's the T'ai Chi, an ancient Chinese exercise developed by Taoist monks to help their followers find their centers. You see how slowly each movement is done? It takes frightening concentration. Any imbalance will cause them to falter. The secret is *Tsuki-no-kokoro*—a spirit as calm as the moon. Once you have it, the confusion of the world can never throw you off balance."

"It's like a beautiful dance performed outside of time," he marveled. "I've never seen anything so peaceful."

"Watch carefully," she told him. "Try to imagine each

movement speeded up a hundred, no, a thousand times. What do you see?"

What Kriek saw was a series of ferocious kicks, slashes, lunges, thrusts, and punches. "Why did you have to ruin it for me?" he complained.

"Jan-san, you've been living among us for years now, and you're no closer to understanding us than the day you set foot on this shore."

"Then perhaps you'd be gracious enough to enlighten me," he said coolly.

"Was I being too critical?" she asked.

"No," he said, after taking a moment to reflect. "That was my pride speaking. Deep down I know what you say is true. Everywhere I look, I see contradictions inside of contradictions." He gestured toward the hilltop. "Movements designed to maim and kill transformed into a dance of exquisite beauty. Nice people with faultless manners, who wouldn't think of harming anyone until they'd been properly introduced. I know mothers who'd gladly die for their families, then take a newborn girl out back and smother her. I've seen men and women bent double under back-breaking loads because the wheel was one idea no one thought was worth borrowing from China." Kriek shrugged. "These are just a few of the things I don't understand."

"The beginning of understanding is knowing what you don't know."

"Another contradiction."

"That's only because your world is linear and our world is circular. Everything you see is either-or—either good or bad, beautiful or ugly, intelligent or stupid, alive or dead. But in a circular world there are no contradictions. At the moment you're born, do you start to live or start to die? Isn't it possible for a coward to do something brave or a wise man to do something stupid? Haven't you ever hurt someone you loved or felt happy and sad at the same time? For us all this is not only possible, it's natural."

Kriek chuckled.

Maria stiffened. Color rushed to her cheeks. "I'm not very good at explaining—"

"Maria." He lifted her face with his hands. "I wasn't laughing at you. I was remembering the night I was having such a hard time convincing *you* that making the character *jisei* wasn't as easy as you thought it should be." Maria smiled as she remembered. "So please don't be impatient with me if I seem a little slow."

"Do you remember the other things you told me that night?"

This time it was Kriek's cheeks that colored. "There are two things a man never forgets—the first time he declares his love to a woman, and the first time a woman turns him down. In my case both things happened that same night."

"I didn't want to hurt you."

"You only told the truth. I was young and naive enough to think that love conquered all. You say I don't understand the Japanese, but at least now I can see how foolish I was for thinking that the daughter of a daimyo might entertain a proposal of marriage from a common foreigner. I still have my blind spots, but from that time on I stopped seeing Japanese as Europeans in strange clothes."

His attempt to cover his embarrassment with humor didn't have the effect he hoped for. Maria remained somber. It was true that the realities she'd explained to him that night remained unchanged, but it was also true that she had changed. Her marriage to Sanjo had fueled an amorphous discontent with Japanese tradition that had been brewing for a long time. Yet her loyalty to her father, her commitment to duty, had paralyzed her will. She saw herself as the Japanese woman bent double under the weight of a heavy load, blind to the idea that the wheel could be used for anything except pull-toys.

There in the twilight hush, in the shadowy crack between light and darkness, Maria made her decision. Kriek listened as she told him about her unconsummated marriage to Sanjo, her visceral abhorrence of the man, and her anguish before she left to find him. She spoke of the night the *ronin* raped her, and recounted the revulsion she felt as he brutalized her body and spirit.

"It wasn't until that moment that I grasped the full horror of being taken against your will. He was only a stranger. I thought of how much uglier it would be to go back to Sanjo and face the possibility of suffering that kind of intimate horror over and over at my husband's whim. Death has to be preferable to that kind of degradation and shame."

"Maria, you can't—"

She touched her finger to his lips. "No, Jan-san, I won't. After I found you there in the cave, for the first time I caught a glimpse of another way. It was Tomi who showed it to me. When I looked into the face of the dying girl, she looked back at me through eyes that had seen more hardship, more pain and degradation, than I, the daughter of a daimyo, could ever imagine. Yet, Jan-san, there was something else. She glowed with an inner peace, a kind of happiness deeper than anything I'd ever known. Tomi died knowing she'd given herself to someone she truly loved, and at that instant I would have gladly changed places with her, just to feel what she felt. That's when I knew I could do it."

Up to that point Kriek had been able to follow her, but now she'd lost him. "Do what, Maria?"

"Take Tomi's place," she said, "if you'll have me."

Kriek was stunned. "Maria, I . . ." His words were buried in a junkpile of emotions.

"Jan-san," she helped him, "I know a padre is forbidden to marry. But you are still a man. I can accept the same situation Tomi accepted. And I'll bear your children just as she did."

"You think . . . !" Kriek took her hand. "Tomi was pregnant with her child when she came to me."

"Then you never—" He shook his head. "She wasn't your consort?"

"No," he stated flatly. "She stayed with me because she had no place else to go. We were fond of each other, but it was never love."

"Are you telling me that you never knew that girl was in love with you?" she said incredulously.

"I guess at the end I suspected something like that." Maria's dark eyes brimmed with tears. "Maria?" He reached out to her, and she turned away. "What did I say?"

"She loved you so much." She caught the tear that trickled down her cheek on the sleeve of her kimono. "How could you be so blind?"

"Maria, don't you think there are times that it's better not to see?"

"Once I might have thought so, but no more." She looked directly at him. "Right now nothing is more important to me than making you see all the things I feel for you. If you send me away, at least you'll do it knowing that I love you."

The way he gazed at her, the searching, the faint suggestion of vulnerability, the intensity building behind his strange violet eyes, resonated down to the core of her being.

Kriek raised himself to his knees, slid his hand behind her neck, and gently, firmly drew her to him. Maria closed her eyes and felt the soft heat of his breath on her face, on her lips . . . almost touching, then touching. As the pressure increased from imperceptible to light to hungry, a miracle of warmth spread through her body, and for a brief moment she felt as light as a willow leaf.

His fingers twined in her hair, and he drew her head back. His lips grazed her cheek and tasted each salty eyelid. "Thou art the seasons of my life." He had unconsciously slipped into his native Portuguese. "The bird's song in spring, the sweet grass of summer, the leaves of autumn, the crystal trees of winter. Thou are all that is beautiful, and I love thee."

Maria barely understood the words, but the sound of his voice transcended language.

"I've waited so long for you," he said in words she could understand.

Maria buried her face in the hollow of his neck and let him guide her down to the mat-covered floor. Her thoughts glided back to the inn where they had spent the night together in agonizing nearness. But this night she didn't resist him. They touched and touched again, until nearness became fullness and fullness became ecstasy. The feel of him inside her body was so different, it was as if she had been taken for the first time.

The ferryman recognized the horses Saru brought to the dock. "I'm sorry, sir," he said. "I'm not permitted to take rented horses off the island. You'll have to leave them here."

"What am I going to do with the sacks they're carrying?" Saru protested.

The boatman eyed the little monkey-faced man suspiciously, convinced that he was trying to use the little sacks as a ruse to sneak the horses off the island. "They don't look that heavy to me. What's in them?"

"Gold," Saru said with a straight face.

"*Nani!*" the ferryman exclaimed.

Saru clapped his hands together and burst out laughing. "I

got you, didn't I?" he clapped the embarrassed ferryman on
the shoulder.

"I suppose you think I really believed you," he grumbled.
"Just toss those sacks on board and you can rent some more
horses on the other side."

Saru responded with a low bow. The ferryman returned
the bow. As his head dropped, Saru brought up his arm,
slamming the butt of his hand under the bridge of the ferryman's nose. The bone fragments that lodged in his brain
killed him instantly.

Saru quickly loaded the horses onto the ferry. When he
reached the middle of the bay, he dumped the ferryman's
body overboard and continued on.

The *otera* where he had been instructed to bring the gold
was in sad condition. All the wooden grave markers lay
broken and decaying on the ground. Farther up the knoll
underbrush had grown up around the granite tombstones. At
the top of the hill, where prominent families had buried their
dead, the taller monuments were tangled in a riot of wisteria
vines. From the look of things, Saru concluded that the *otera*
had fallen on hard times many years ago and the care of the
graves was probably in the hands of a few surviving family
members.

He led the horses up a stone path that led to a small
thatched *shoro* with a large bell hanging inside. The ropes
that held the hammer log had rotted away, so Saru announced his arrival by hitting the bell with a fist-sized stone.
The old bronze still gave off a fine rich tone.

He looked around for the stone lantern and found it at the
entrance to a magnificent bamboo grove. The bare trunks
were evenly spaced and soared to a remarkable height. Their
top limbs intertwined, forming a dense canopy that blocked
sunlight, starving out all vegetation below except for a lush
carpet of spongy moss. Somewhere a trickle of water spilled
into a standing pool. Otherwise the grove was quiet.

"All men are thieves."

Saru tried to locate the source of the voice issuing the ninja
recognition phrase and couldn't see anyone. "And it will rain
tomorrow," he said, completing his part of the signal.

A hand touched his shoulder. Startled, Saru jumped back.

"You're getting complacent, Saru."

"Prince Sanjo!" Saru glanced around, wondering what ninja

had dared to utter the recognition in the presence of an outsider.

"Relax, Saru," he said. "The voice you heard was mine."

"You are—"

"Ninja?" Sanjo finished his question.

Saru slapped his thigh. "I can't believe it. A noble in the Imperial Court! How in the world did you manage that?"

"I didn't, my mother did . . . but that's a long story."

The voice, the eyes—things began to fall into place for Saru. "Then it was you in charge the night we took Lord Iemitsu."

"At the time it seemed prudent to keep my identity secret, even from those of you working for me." That night Sanjo had made certain that Saru and the other ninja had left the area before he lowered his mask. "However, word has reached me that Lord Tajima has uncovered my role in the abduction. Now that I'm too much of a liability to be welcome at the court, there's no longer any reason to conceal my identity from my ninja brothers."

"Since you can't return to Kyoto, will you hide out in Koga for a while?"

"First there are some loose threads to snip." Abruptly Sanjo altered the direction of the conversation. "Did you bring the gold?"

"It's on the horses." Saru explained how he used gunpowder to blow up the cave, along with one of Jubei's men.

"One!" Sanjo complained. "Who escaped?"

"Tajima's son and daughter never showed up. They went off with the other padre to search for Alcala."

"So," Sanjo said through his teeth, as he helped unload the sacks of gold, "more loose threads to cut."

"It was bad luck."

"No, it was sloppy planning."

A short time later Saru mounted one of the horses and prepared to leave. "Now that my assignment's over, I guess I'll pick out some place far from Edo and live off the reward money I got for leading Tajima's search party into your trap. Too bad the trap didn't close, but some good came out of it. You got the gold, and I ended up with a pension from the Shogun."

"And we both learned a valuable lesson, *neh*?" Sanjo slapped the rump of Saru's horse, sending him on his way. "Never underestimate your adversary," he called after him.

Saru waved his hand in the air without looking back. His heart had been beating so hard when he rode off that he was almost convinced Sanjo could hear the thumps. As he approached the first bend he glanced over his shoulder. The road was empty.

Two bends later Saru reined in his horse and dismounted. It took him a few minutes to locate his marker. He took his bearings and marched exactly fifty paces into the woods. Which oak was it? There were two that looked similar.

The first one he checked turned out to be the right one. He brushed away the leaves from the hollowed-out trunk and reached inside. Saru screamed. A spring-loaded trap had crushed his wrist.

"Is this what you're looking for?" Sanjo dragged a sack of gold out of the bushes about ten paces from where Saru was writhing in pain. "Sloppy planning, Saru. It's the little mistakes, those tiny errors in judgment, that always confound us, *neh*?"

Another step closer, Saru thought. The fingers of his free hand tightened around the edges of a star-shaped *shaken*.

"Your mistake was thinking that everyone else is as careless as you are. If you intended to steal some gold, why didn't you keep quiet about your find and take it all? After you sent word you found the gold, the roads were watched day and night. In fact I followed you to this very spot. I stood right over there and watched you hide the gold."

Saru's hand shot out, and just as Sanjo had done so many times in practice, he deftly dodged the missile. Before Saru could reach for another, Sanjo stepped on his hand, pinning it to the ground.

"And another thing," he said. "I knew exactly how much gold Okubo put in those casks."

Sanjo drew his sword and finished Saru off with one quick cut.

"All men are thieves," he said as he cleaned the edge of his sword.

On the other side of the hill, where Akane and Jubei had been exercising, the low moon cut a swath across the surface of a small lake. Although a chill had returned to the air, the prospect of a night swim in December was too inviting to resist. They raced down the hill, building up body heat. With antelope strides Akane easily outran Jubei, and was out of her clothes and into the water before he reached the shore. The spring-fed water was so frigid it took her breath away. It was all she could do to keep from bolting out of the lake.

"Is it cold?" he called out to her.

"No," she lied, knowing if he had any idea how icy the water really was, he would never get in. "The heat wave's turned it into bathwater." She bit down hard to keep her teeth from chattering.

"Ah," he said, rubbing his hands together. "It's too good to be true."

And you'll know how right you are the second you hit the water, she thought. Akane lured him on with a great show of swimming, splashing, and diving.

It seemed forever before he had his clothes off and climbed out on the overhanging rock. He was about to test the water with his foot when Akane stopped him with a challenge. "A race to the other side!" she shouted.

Rising to the bait, Jubei executed a long arching dive off the rock. When his head popped out of the water, his one eye showed a lot of white and his howl echoed off the hillsides. He was out of the water and onto the bank so fast, Akane was certain there were parts of his body that never got wet.

When Akane climbed out, he was using her undergown as a towel and muttering dark curses. Akane knew it wouldn't do any good to complain about getting her undergown wet, but she did it anyway.

"Stop carping," he snapped, "or I swear I'll throw your carcass back in that torture chamber."

His threat gave her pause, so she left off teasing him and dried herself with her bandana. She was covered with goose bumps, and the nipples of her breasts were hard as copper coins. Compared with the freezing water, the night air felt sultry. Spreading her kimono out on the ground, Akane lay back, letting the naked chill escape unimpeded.

It had been a long time since Jubei had shared a bath with Akane. She was no longer the gangly adolescent—all legs and hips. Age had sculpted her into a fine-looking woman with long, graceful curves. He marveled at the subtle play of light and shadow on her skin.

Although her eyes were closed, Akane was not unaware of his interest. The moment hadn't been contrived to attract his attention, but if the sight of her body pleased him, then she was glad.

Jubei broke off his stare, rolled over on his back, and tried to shift his concentration from Akane to the sky. Bathed in the steady glow of the moon, the night was very still, holding its breath as if waiting for something to happen.

"Jubei . . ."

He turned toward her and braced his chin in the palm of his hand.

"What have you decided to do about Alcala?" she asked.

"I'm going to follow him to Shimabara."

"Will I be going with you?"

"No," he said. "Everything seems to be coming to a head faster than anyone anticipated. I have a strong feeling that all of Kyushu is about to explode. If Alcala unleashes his holy war, our plans could fall victim to events we may not be able to control. For that reason we need to get the gold off this island as soon as possible. Tomorrow I want you to leave for Mikamura. Check at the inn to see if there are any messages for me, then go out to the cave and tell Iori and Saru to take the gold to Nagasaki. You can ride ahead and make arrangements to have it shipped back to Edo."

"*Hai*," she said, but her response was limp.

"Is something bothering you?"

"I know it doesn't make sense, but taking Okubo's gold makes me feel like a thief."

"I know," he said. "I have the same feeling."

"I'm having a hard time believing that these Christians are the monsters the Shogun thinks they are. Even a mouse will fight back if it's tormented long enough. And it seems to me the Christians of Shimabara have had more than their share of torment from the *bakufu*."

Jubei nodded in agreement. "Placing the blame for all the unrest on the Christians is like blaming muddy streets for the rain."

"What do you plan to do when you meet Alcala?"

"I don't know yet. That's why I have to see him and hear what he has to say."

"Jubei, don't go!" she pleaded. "It's just a feeling—"

He gently pinched her lips shut. "You're going to catch cold," he said softly, lifting a wet strand of hair off her face. He laid it across the nape of her neck and let his hand rest on her bare shoulder. For an instant it was as though the night had wrapped them in a cocoon, and nothing existed beyond the place where they lay.

Suddenly an image of her lying next to Iori ruined the moment. He let his hand drop from her shoulder and rolled over on his stomach. Why was it impossible to rid himself of this unnatural desire for his own sister? he wondered. Why did her spirit continue to haunt his dreams?

"Jubei," she whispered. "You don't remember my birth, do you?"

He thought for a moment. "No, you weren't born in Edo. All I can remember is Father bringing a baby girl to my room when I was about four years old. He said, 'This is your sister. Her name is Akane.' That's all I remember."

"That was after Father returned from the Osaka campaign, wasn't it?"

"I think so."

"Where was Mother while he was at Osaka?"

"She stayed home, of course."

"Think about it, Jubei. I was born in Osaka while Mother was with you in Edo."

"So Father must have had a consort in Osaka. Strange . . . I wonder why he never told me you were my half sister."

"Because I'm not."

The moment had arrived. Akane felt strange, almost giddy. Over and over she had rehearsed the scene in her imagination. How would Jubei react when she told him the secret she had learned from Musashi? One version had Jubei outraged at the deception; another pictured him as simply bewildered. But in each case the result was always the same. He would look into her eyes and suddenly see a woman where he had once only seen a sister—a woman whose love for him ran deeper than dreams. Then he would reach out to touch her—touch her in a way she had imagined so many times before—and would say to her, "I love you Akane. I've always loved you."

Or when the fear gripped her heart, she would see his eyes turn to ice. He would look up at her and see just another woman—a woman devoid of charm, no more alluring or mysterious than a well-worn cloak.

Or worse yet, he would merely shake his head in dismay and reassure her that she would always be his sister, if not in blood, at least in spirit. And the weight of his magnanimous generosity would squash her like a bug.

Akane was determined to press on. Rejection, disgust, rage—even pity would be preferable to living out her life in emotional limbo.

She began by telling Jubei the story of her encounter with Musashi in the inn. The words kept coming, drawing her closer and closer to the moment when nothing would stand between them but the naked truth.

Jubei listened in amazement.

"So you see," she concluded the tale, "I am not your half sister . . . I'm not your sister at all."

Dormant emotions exploded inside him like dry leaves in a sudden blast of wind. His first instinct was to grab her in his arms and be done with the deception that had been tormenting him for so long. But on reflection he realized that his passion for her would appear so twisted, so perverted, that the very sight of him would surely repel her. "It can't be!" he said. "All these years—"

"It's true." Akane's heart was pounding high in her throat.

Without warning, Jubei leapt to his feet and started for the woods. Akane threw her kimono around her shoulders and ran after him.

She found him standing with his forehead pressed against the trunk of a tall pine. She came up behind him and touched his shoulder. His muscles tensed.

"Jubei, why did you run from me?"

"Leave me alone!" His voice was tight with strain. Akane stood her ground. "Please," she implored. "Tell me what's wrong."

Jubei turned around. Akane was stunned by the look of anguish on his face. He gripped her with his hands, but it was his gaze that held her fast. He seemed to be looking deep inside her, searching for something to grab on to, something to keep him from losing his balance.

As she stared back at him, she saw the storm begin to subside. When he finally spoke to her, the harshness was gone from his voice.

"No more lies," he said with quiet resolve. "For a long time I've hated myself for feeling things for you that no brother had a right to feel for his sister. When I looked at you, I saw more than just a beautiful woman—I saw a woman that I wanted with every fiber of my body."

"Jubei, I—"

"Wait," he cut her short. "Let me finish. Maybe somehow I knew you weren't my sister. Maybe there's something in the blood of real brothers and sisters that keeps them from being attracted to each other . . . I don't know. All I can tell you is that I love you now, and I think I've always loved you."

"Hold me, Jubei. Hold me tight." She closed her eyes and felt his arms enfold her. "I'm afraid to open my eyes," she whispered, then dug her fingers into his back for the sheer pleasure of it. "I dreamed this so many times before, but this time it's real!"

Jubei could scarcely believe what he was hearing. "Are you saying . . . ?" The words stuck in his throat.

Akane opened her eyes and looked up at him. "I always pretended, but I never really believed . . ." Akane turned away and drew her kimono closed.

"You're frightened, aren't you?" Jubei asked.

"The truth?"

"No more lies."

Akane took a deep breath. "Even now . . . even knowing what I know, when I look at you I see the only man I could ever love." Akane shut her eyes. "And . . ."

"And it feels wrong when I hold you," Jubei said, completing her thought.

"I'm sorry," she said softly.

"It's only habit . . . after all those years of guilt and denial. We've both lived in a lie for so long, it's going to take a while to get used to the truth."

"Will it take long?"

"When the time is right, I think you'll know."

"Are you sure?"

"Sure enough to wait and see."

Jubei put his arm around her and felt a warmth spread through him like strong wine. There was nothing left to do but savor each moment as it passed.

Throughout the night they lay close together on the soft

moss. Sometimes they talked. Sometimes they listened to the
wind and watched the moonlight through the pine needles.
When morning came, they woke in each others arms.

For both of them a new day had never held more promise.

Nothing of what transpired in the night passed between
Akane and Maria, not because they were keeping secrets
from each other, but because words were superfluous. The
moment their eyes met, everything that mattered was instantly exchanged. As they walked along together in the dawn
blush, Maria slipped her hand inside Akane's hand and their
fingers intertwined.

At the fork in the road Akane and Maria said their good-
byes, consoling each other with promises of a quick reunion.

Jubei lingered behind for a private moment with Akane.
"Wait for me in Nagasaki," he said. "I'll join you there as
soon as I can."

For a moment she was tempted to try to get him to change
his mind and let her catch up with him in Shimabara, but she
knew his mind was made up, and she didn't want to insult
him by implying that he made frivolous decisions.

"*Hai*," she said crisply. "I understand."

Incapable of public displays of affection, they both stood
there, aching to hold each other.

"You'd better go now," he said to her.

"Be safe, Jubei."

Jubei watched her until she disappeared from view, then
rejoined Kriek, Maria, and Shiro, to continue the search for
Alcala.

It was a half-day journey to the seaside. The salt air was
tinted with the aroma of simmering noodles in the fishing
village. After a steady diet of dried squid, the thought of hot
udon was too tantalizing to pass up. They followed their noses
to the noodle vendor's shop and ate their fill.

The old woman who served them said they would have to
hire a fishing boat to cross the bay to Shimabara. "Some
horse thief murdered the ferryman and took his boat," she
said in a things-have-come-to-that tone of voice. "Are you
going there to join the rebels?" she asked.

"We're looking for the Christian padre," Jubei said.

"He went over on the first boat. The rest followed after
him. It took all day and night to get that mob of farmers

across the bay. Must have been a couple thousand of them. You'll be lucky if you can talk any of the fishermen into making another trip."

The only fisherman they found on the beach was sitting on the hull of his boat, mending a net. He grimaced when Jubei approached, having made up his mind to refuse any more trips to Shimabara. But seeing that he was dealing with a *ronin*, the fisherman decided to make an exception, though he was not happy about it.

They sailed west toward the tiny island of Yushima, then due north. Maria watched the great granite walls of Hara Castle slide by in the distance. She thought of earlier times and younger dreams. Happiness for her had taken on a different form than the little girl who had lived in that castle could have ever imagined.

To the fisherman's amazement, the one-eyed *ronin* insisted on paying for the trip. In a gesture of gratitude, he warned him to be careful. "Heard a rumor that Lord Matsukura himself left Hara Castle with nearly every samurai who's not out putting down food riots. You might be safer back on Oyano." Jubei thanked him for the warning and assured him they would keep their eyes open.

The fisherman beached his boat in a remote spot south of Shimabara City. "Matsukura keeps a small contingent of troops in town to protect the castle. They don't go outside the castle very often," he said. "But safe is safe, *neh*?"

They followed the road south for about an hour and came across a breathtaking sight. Below them, on a plain between two low ridges of hills, thousands and thousands of men, women, and children were milling about, waving white banners. Kriek looked at Jubei. "I think we found Father Alcala," he said.

Actually locating Alcala turned out to be a frustrating ordeal. Everyone they talked to had a conflicting opinion about Alcala's whereabouts. Eventually they were directed to a large farmhouse separated from the teeming throng by a picket line of surly-looking guards.

"Tell Father Alcala a Jesuit brother is here to see him," Kriek said to the nearest guard.

After a moment's hesitation, the guard did what he was told.

Shiro, who was astride Maria's horse, saw a padre dressed

in a long black cassock coming out of the house. "Here he comes," he told Kriek.

Alcala came halfway to the picket line and stopped. "Let the padre through," he called out to the guards. They stepped aside, and closed ranks quickly, blocking the others' path, after Kriek passed through.

"They're with me," Kriek said brusquely. The guards glanced at Alcala, who indicated his permission to let them pass.

"You must be the famous Father Kriek." Alcala smiled broadly and offered his hand. "I've heard a great deal about you."

Alcala had the quick, cautious eyes of a street fighter. "And you must be the elusive Father Alcala," Kriek said. There was no warmth in his grip.

"Elusive?" he chuckled. "Yes, it's the one quality that's kept me alive all these years."

"And out from under the authority of the Church," Kriek added.

All trace of Alcala's good humor vanished. "I suppose you've been sent here to rectify that."

"I've come to talk."

Jubei listened intently. The strange language they were speaking had a liquid texture, like the sound of boiling gruel. Although he couldn't understand a word, he could see that something Kriek was telling Alcala had broken through his wariness and captured his interest. He heard Kriek mention the word *sake*, and guessed he was talking about finding the gold. His name was mentioned, and Alcala looked him over, then turned back to Kriek. Something else was said. Alcala stared at Maria with undisguised curiosity. Jubei wondered if he had told him who she was. As Kriek continued to speak, Jubei could see Alcala stealing glances at Shiro. Suddenly Alcala said something that brought fire to Kriek's eyes.

"The boy isn't *my* son," Kriek snapped. "I'm told he's *yours*."

"Mine!"

"According to Prince Sanjo's former wife, you fathered this child."

The conversation stopped.

The boy began to squirm under the padre's intense gaze. Then Shiro saw Alcala's face start to light up, taking on the look of rapture that comes to some men who have had too much to drink.

From far away came the mournful call of a trumpet shell. Alcala turned away and looked up at the hills. A second blast—closer this time. Then a hush fell over the valley.

"I'm afraid we'll have to continue this conversation later," Alcala said to Kriek. "Lord Matsukura is about to attack us."

"What!" Kriek exclaimed, appalled at Alcala's nonchalance in the face of an impending disaster.

"From what I can gather, the promise of slaughtering thousands of Christians in one stroke was too tempting for Lord Matsukura to resist. I'm sure he expects us to flee in panic, but we plan to disappoint him. This time we stand and fight."

Out on the plain Kriek could see farmers running in all directions—a few with swords, but most wielding makeshift weapons.

A young boy ran out of the farmhouse with a sword in one hand and a Portuguese infantry helmet in the other. He gave them to Alcala.

"Would you prefer to fight with us or wait in the farmhouse until the outcome is decided?" Alcala had framed his question as a challenge.

"Neither," Kriek said, refusing to be goaded. "I'll wait here."

Alcala donned his helmet. "If you change your mind and decide to fight, there are weapons inside."

Kriek turned to Maria. "Take Shiro inside and wait there until the battle is over," he ordered.

"No!" Alcala shouted. "My son stays with me."

"Are you crazy!" Kriek grabbed the boy's arm. "He's only five years old!"

"God will protect him," Alcala said his eyes burning with utter assurance.

A volley of musket shots rang out, followed by the thunderous din of hoofbeats. The vanguard of Matsukura's cavalry broke onto the plain. They were riding directly at the farmhouse, slashing their way through a sea of farmers, who fell on them with scythes and sickles and mattocks and shafts of sharpened bamboo. Horses reared; some stumbled and fell and got up again, always riderless. Closer and closer the riders came, leaving a wake of dead behind them.

Jubei drew both swords. Maria took out her *kaiken* and braced her feet. Alcala positioned himself between Shiro and the onrushing cavalry.

The farmers refused to break. They swarmed on Matsukura's samurai like ants on a worm. Women fought and fell beside their men. Children snatched up dropped swords and charged into the fray. The noise was deafening. Horses whinnied, and screams of the dying mingled with the battle shrieks of warriors. Steel clashed against steel. Gunfire crackled. The ground shook under pounding hooves.

Several cavalrymen made it through the ranks and raced up the hill. Jubei held his ground and cut three of them down with lightning strokes. More followed, and more. Inspired by Jubei's valor, the *ronin* guards who had fallen back closed in. One of them leaped at a horseman and pulled him down. They both landed at Kriek's feet. The *ronin* was stunned. Matsukura's samurai recovered quickly and raised his sword for the kill. Kriek snatched Maria's *kaiken* out of her hand and plunged it into the samurai's neck. Then he picked up the dead samurai's sword and waded into the battle.

Foot soldiers followed the cavalry into the field and desperately tried to hold formation against the weight of the farmers' numbers. It was like trying to stave off an avalanche. Their ranks cracked, then broke into isolated pockets of resistance. Back to back the small circles of samurai imploded as human walls caved in on them.

No one knew exactly when the battle ended. Cries of pain and rage and grief and exaltation continued long into the night. But by sunset the issue had been decided. Matsukura was dead, his head impaled on a pole just below the farmhouse. The bodies of his men were stacked one on top of the other like cordwood. The air was rank with the stench of human waste and the sweet smell of blood.

Kriek wandered the battlefield, blessing the dead, stopping here and there to pray over the wounded. Physically and emotionally exhausted, he ignored Maria's pleas and forced himself on. He came across a woman cradling a child's dismembered arm in her arms. She said it was her son. He saw a boy, not much older than Shiro, trying to carry his wounded father on his back. Names were being yelled out. Bodies were being overturned and inspected. Weapons were being collected. And somewhere, someone started to sing. Other voices joined in, and the song grew and grew until it reached into the far corners of the battlefield.

Faces turned toward the farmhouse. Those who could, began walking in that direction. Torches were lit and white banners carried to the base of the high rock where Alcala was standing. A great cheer went up, and another. Kriek was too far away to hear what Alcala was saying, but he could see Shiro being lifted high in the air. *"Tendo!"*—godchild—the cry went up. Alcala raised Shiro again. *"Tendo!"* New voices picked up the cry. *"Tendo!"* Again and again, until the roar became deafening.

"So," Kriek said to Maria, "we've brought Alcala the godchild he's been looking for."

Rendai, who had been stalking Alcala for weeks, never strayed far from where he was. She had seen and heard everything. When she saw the boy's exotic and beautiful face, she wondered. When she heard Alcala say that the *Tendo*'s name was Shiro, from the island of Oyano in the Amakusa district, she knew.

The padre had used her, and now he was using her son. Silently she called on gods whose terrible powers belonged only to Rendai.

Arima stayed long enough to welcome Akane into his home, then made an excuse, leaving Tajima alone with his daughter. Although Arima was curious to find out what urgent matter had compelled her to insist on seeing her father before taking the time to bathe and change her grimy clothes, he retired to the privacy of his room and began composing the letter he was planning to send to Maria.

"Is Musashi still here?" Akane asked, recalling that he'd told Iori he had business to conduct with Lord Arima.

"He is," Tajima answered, puzzled by her question. "Would you like me to send for him?"

Akane nodded. *"Hai."*

"Musashi told me he had inadvertently revealed the secret of your adoption. What's done is done, and I don't care to embarrass him further by allowing you to bring the subject up in his presence. However, if you wish to discuss the marriage arrangement, it can surely wait until you've made yourself more presentable."

"Chichive." Her lip quivered. "Iori's dead."

Tajima clapped his hands twice, a servant appeared, and he was sent to find Musashi.

While they waited, Akane brought Tajima up to date on everything that had transpired, up to the moment she arrived at the cave. Then her voice cracked, and she asked his permission to wait until Musashi arrived to finish.

Tajima told her what he had learned of Prince Sanjo's involvement in the plot to abduct Iemitsu. "Lord Arima has agreed to cooperate with us. He's sent Sanjo a message asking him to come to Nobeoka. We're waiting for his response."

Musashi appeared at the door, his hair still damp from the bath he had just left. Akane bowed to him as he entered and sat down on the tatami across from her. "This is quite a pleasure," he said. "I hadn't expected to see you again so soon."

"I'm afraid I've brought sad news," she said, feeling the tears begin to well up in her eyes.

Akane explained that she had gone to the inn and read the note Iori left for Jubei after Tajima ordered them to meet him at Lord Arima's villa. "I hurried out to the cave," she said, "hoping to catch them before they set out for Nobeoka. When I got there, I found the cave in ruins.

"At first I thought it had collapsed during an earthquake, but as I probed deeper into the cave I could detect the faint odor of spent gunpowder. I thought perhaps they had taken the gold out and blown up the cave to bury the casks, but I couldn't be sure, so I kept searching just in case I was wrong.

"I was almost ready to give up when I heard a scraping sound deeper inside the cave. Following the sound, I managed to work my way through some narrow gaps, and then I saw something move in the dim candlelight. I pressed forward and saw the point of a sword jutting out of a crack in the rubble.

"The boulders were too large to budge, so I grasped the sword point and jiggled the blade. Someone pulled the sword back. I shouted into the opening and got no answer. I tore at the rubble and managed to widen the hole to the size of a fist. I thrust my arm into the hole and felt another hand touch mine."

Akane bit into her lower lip to control the trembling, and after a short pause continued the story. "Iori called to me from behind the wall of rock. He said that the explosion had shattered his eardrums, and he asked me to identify myself by scratching out my name on his palm. I couldn't ask him anything, all I could do was listen. His voice was very weak, but he managed to tell me that Saru had taken the gold and blasted the cave, leaving him trapped inside.

"I ran outside to find a pole—something I could use to pry the rock away. When I found something I could use, I went back and reached into the opening to let Iori know I had returned. His hand was limp and I could find no trace of a heartbeat in his wrist."

Akane buried her face in her hands. "I tried," she sobbed, "but I couldn't get his body out."

Musashi stared straight ahead, silently sharing Akane's agony. He turned to Tajima. "Who is this . . . Saru?" Musashi spoke his name like a curse.

"He could be a common thief," Tajima replied. "But it's my guess that he's an agent working for Prince Sanjo."

Arima blew the ink dry and folded his letter.

A cloud passed over the face of the moon. The breeze quickened.

He thought about closing the screen, and decided against it. Even though most of the blossoms had fallen, and the few tenacious ones remaining made the flowering fruit tree look half dressed, it was still better than staring at a blank panel. He hoped to get it over with quickly, but just in case, he shifted his position closer to the brazier.

The tone of the letter pleased him. It was the sort of thing a mother would show to her children and say, "This is the kind of man your grandfather was." And they would see a wise and loving father strong enough to admit mistakes, but too proud to beg for forgiveness. There were traces of nobility in the letter, even tragedy. "My grandfather dreamed great dreams," he could hear them saying. "And at the most profound moment in his life he died alone." Yes, it was a fine letter.

Arima took his short sword off the stand and laid it across his lap. For a while he sat there with his eyes closed, composing himself. But his mind refused to be still. It raced around in a mad search for inappropriate thoughts. The longer he sat there, the worse it got. First his hands got clammy cold, then his right leg went to sleep. Arima slammed his sword down on the tatami, got up and limped around the room. All the while the letter lay on the floor like an indictment.

Then he remembered he had forgotten his death poem. It was inside the lacquer chest he kept in the overhead cupboard.

Arima read it and decided it had been written too long ago to capture the essence of this particular moment. So he sat at his writing stand and started composing a new statement.

Sanjo, who had slipped into the compound undetected, was observing him from the garden. He found Arima's lame attempts at suicide amusing.

On the second try Arima appeared to be the picture of determination. The sword was jerked out of the scabbard. His kimono was snatched open with authority. Up came the hands, the point of the sword poised over a spot just to the left of his navel. Sanjo watched intently. Suddenly Arima's eyes popped open. He realized he had forgotten to wrap the blade in white silk. As soon as he had the error corrected, he started again. Arima set his jaw and squeezed his eyes shut, but for Sanjo the effect was ruined. Arima's hands were shaking uncontrollably.

"So it's come to this," Sanjo commented from the doorway.

Startled, Arima dropped the sword like a poison snake. "You shouldn't have come here!" Arima gasped.

Sanjo slid the door closed behind him. "Then why did you send for me?"

There was something about the way the question was posed that made Arima believe Sanjo already knew the answer. Still, he could not bring himself to tell the whole truth. Instead he related a sanitized version of the story, leaving out any reference to his deal with Tajima. "They must have guessed I'd try to warn you. So they stayed on, waiting to see if you'd show up."

"I see," Sanjo said, pretending to believe him. "Lord Tajima is a very clever adversary."

"No," Arima said. "It was stupid of me to act so impetuously. I should have known that he was using my loyalty to set a trap for you."

"Anyone can make a mistake. It's your intentions that matter, *neh*?"

Amazed by Sanjo's gullibility, Arima decided to push the

deception a little further. "As soon as I realized what Tajima had in mind, I wanted to warn you to stay away." He lowered his eyes abjectly. "But they were watching me too closely, and I was afraid a messenger might lead them to you."

"I understand," Sanjo said, hating Arima for having the audacity to try to sell him such indigestible tripe. Nothing about him was genuine—not even his laughable attempt at seppuku. Does a man who is seriously contemplating suicide waste his time inventing self-serving lies? "I'm curious," he pressed Arima. "What brought you to the decision to commit seppuku?"

Arima sighed deeply. "I'm both a dreamer and a practical man. When I saw our dreams for a Christian Japan fall to pieces, the only practical choice left to me was seppuku. I can't stand alone against the Shogun, and I can't participate in the slaughter of Christians to earn the Shogun's trust." He did not bother to mention that he learned his own daughter was among the Christians he would have to slaughter. Nor did he mention that her marriage to Sanjo had put him permanently outside the boundaries of the Shogun's trust. "So I've chosen the way of the samurai."

"Then allow me the honor of acting as your second," Sanjo said, drawing his sword.

Arima blanched. "I couldn't ask you to do that. You're in grave danger here. For your own sake I insist that you leave at once."

"And leave you to die a long and horrible death without the benefit of a friend to administer the final cut?" Sanjo raised his sword to the striking attitude. "I couldn't live with the shame."

Arima was trapped. If he called out for assistance, Sanjo would murder him. There was nothing to do but perform the act with dignity, and be grateful that it would all be over with quickly.

Sanjo exulted at the defeat in Arima's eyes. "Your courage will always be an inspiration to me." He handed him the short sword and set his feet.

Arima knew he would have to stab himself quickly to keep his hands from shaking. The instant the point entered his abdomen, he planned to drop his head for the killing blow.

Arima took a deep breath and drove the sword deep into his abdomen. Searing pain shot through his innards. His head

dropped. Hurry! He continued holding his breath to keep
from screaming. What's he waiting for, the lateral cut? Summoning every iota of will left to him, Arima twisted the blade
and prepared for the extention of the ritual cut. He felt like
he was going to vomit. "Now," he gasped as he started the
pull across his abdomen.

Sanjo smiled. Slowly he put his sword back into its lacquer
scabbard and walked to the door, pausing long enough to
watch comprehension register on Arima's face.

"Sanjo!" Arima shrieked as his head hit the floor.

His cries touched off a wild flurry of activity throughout the
villa. Arima's retainers poured into the compound, reinforc-
ing positions along the stone walls. Torches were lit, gongs
sounded, officers shouted instructions, and search parties
combed the grounds in teams of three and four.

A discarded kimono was found in a rain barrel, but Sanjo
had vanished without a trace. His escape mystified everyone
except Takuan, who knew exactly where Sanjo was.

Unrelenting pressure from the walnut-sized tumor growing
at the base of his skull had blurred Takuan's vision, upset his
balance, and converted the inside of his head into a raging
inferno. Incapable of enduring the agony any longer, he had
swallowed the last of his opium. When it began to take effect,
he wandered into the garden, found a quiet spot among the
rocks next to the fish pond, and settled in, accepting the
poppy's mercy with gratitude.

Startled by Arima's cry, he had shifted the focus of his
attention from the tiny beads of moisture collecting on his
eyelashes to the door where Sanjo was standing. He saw him
sheath his sword and duck into the shadows by the corner of
Arima's room. Takuan tried to get to his feet, but discovered
that his body would not submit to his will.

Realizing that something needed to be done, Takuan made
up his mind to try to escape from his body and let his dream
spirit follow Sanjo. It was a technique that only he and a
handful of other ninja had mastered. The secret was finding
the twilight crack between sleeping and waking, then choosing the precise moment to slip out with consciousness intact.
It used to be easier, he complained silently. Finally he saw
the opening he had been waiting for, flexed his will, and was
instantly out of his body, hovering over the spot where his
flesh remained.

Rising higher over the garden, he saw Sanjo strip off his kimono and stuff it inside a rain barrel. Taking note of the Koga-style ninja outfit Sanjo was wearing under his outer garments, Takuan realized that the Koga had infiltrated the Imperial family. He couldn't help being impressed.

Takuan followed Sanjo to the pond, where he watched as Sanjo selected a fat *ashi* reed and fashioned it into a long breathing tube. Making barely a ripple, he eased into the water and disappeared among the reeds.

Letting his dream spirit drift out over the pond, Takuan peered down through the murky water and saw Sanjo lying on the bottom with a rock balanced on his stomach. He could hear the faint whistle of air being drawn in and out of the breathing tube. Sanjo was forcing his metabolism lower and lower, bringing himself to within a whisker of death. Takuan knew Sanjo could remain submerged for days, if necessary.

Takuan decided it was time to return his dream spirit to his body so that he could reveal Sanjo's hiding place, but the sight of his own dessicated body propped up against the rocks filled him with a deep sadness. For an instant he thought he caught a glimpse of the dead Shogun peeking at him from behind his left shoulder. The sight filled him with wonderment and peace.

So, my lord, he thought, now you know it's true. A ninja *can* see death over a man's left shoulder.

Takuan glanced back at the pool and briefly considered trying to reenter his body, but somehow he understood it would not be possible this time. He took one last look at the worn-out heap of skin and bone that had been his home for so many seasons. It's not much to look at, he mused. But I have to admit it served me well.

In the distance he saw a brilliant white light that seemed to beckon him closer. The conflicts and passions of the world seemed far, far away. Takuan started toward the light with no regrets.

Meanwhile, in the silent depths of the pond, Sanjo pondered his future. Like a heavy-footed implacable beast, the Tokugawa clan was plodding on toward absolute control of Japan. The first Tokugawa shogun had brought the daimyos to their knees. And now his son was choking the life out of them. The last of the proud and independent daimyos were scrambling to Edo to curry favor before they lost the little they had left. Nobles who once ruled the land now cowered behind painted screens, selling out their birthrights for scraps from the Shogun's table. Only the Christians, a pitiful collection of half-starved rabble armed with a few muskets and some farm implements, stood between the Tokugawa and unchecked power.

Where were the Portuguese? Sanjo wondered. Where were their guns and soldiers? Where was the much vaunted armada? Had it all been a figment of Alcala's overactive imagination? Or had the Shogun seduced them with promises of trade?

Whatever the reason, the unholy alliance was in a shambles. Never again, he resolved, would he make the mistake of putting his fate in the hands of foreigners and incompetent fools. With guile, and gold, and ninja support, he'd find a way to make the foundations of Tokugawa authority tremble!

18

Shimabara
Year of the Dog—1634
Hour of the Boar

When Matsukura's dead were counted, it was evident that only a few samurai had been left behind to defend Hara Castle. Using the overwhelming advantage of their numbers, the Christian forces could breach the great granite walls and occupy the castle. Once inside the safety of the fortress they would have access to Matsukura's store of weapons and food, which they needed desperately to have any chance of surviving the onslaught that was sure to follow. In spite of the advantages of storming the castle, without the proper siege equipment the cost in Christian lives would be incalculable.

It was Kriek who came up with an idea that resolved the

predicament. "No one inside the castle yet knows of Matsukura's defeat. When he rode out of the castle, not one person who stayed behind ever dreamed that a poorly armed, half-starved collection of farmers could defeat Matsukura's samurai. So why not give them the victory everyone inside the castle expects? Suppose we dress our best fighters in uniforms taken from Matsukura's dead samurai and send them to Hara Castle. If my guess is right, the guards will open the gates for them, and before they realize their mistake we'll be inside."

The next morning three thousand farmers disguised as Matsukura's troops marched on Hara Castle, and just as Kriek had predicted, the gates were thrown open and the Christian forces charged inside. By noon the battle was over. The occupants of the castle town were turned out, and the rest of the Christians streamed inside.

News of the fall of Hara Castle spread like wildfire. When Jubei did not appear, Akane asked Tajima for permission to go to Shimabara to look for him. Like everyone else, Tajima had been stunned by Matsukura's crushing defeat. Anxious to take measure of the situation, he thought Akane's relationship with the padre she called Kriek might put her in a position to provide him with valuable information about the rebellion, so he let her go.

The roads were packed with Christian refugees streaming into the castle from every province in Kyushu. The victory over Matsukura had touched off smaller revolts throughout the southern island. Day after day the Christians poured into Hara Castle—old men, young men, women and children—bearing their belongings and all the looted rice they could carry in sacks on their heads. Awash in a sea of humanity, Akane felt as if she were being swept along by a tsunami.

The castle grounds were teeming with people, and the streets were jammed with late arrivals who had been unable to crowd into one of the hundreds of abandoned buildings that made up the castle town. Large groups of women were gathered around the wells, patiently waiting their turn to draw water. Others lined up outside the granary, where the daily ration of rice was being portioned out. Children scurried around in search of firewood while the men who weren't busy fashioning makeshift shelters were preparing for the castle's defense.

Akane made her way through the winding streets to the central donjon, the tallest structure on the castle grounds. It dominated the surrounding buildings the way Fuji-san humbled the lesser mountains. She hoped to find Maria or Kriek there, thinking they might know where Jubei could be found.

Getting to the main entrance proved no easy matter. The courtyard was full of people who had gathered to catch a glimpse of Shiro. "*Tendo! Tendo!*" the chant began, and before long Shiro appeared at one of the third-story portals. A great cheer went up as Shiro shyly waved. A moment later Maria came up behind him, rested her hands on his shoulders, and looked out over the enraptured assembly below.

"Maria!" Akane called to her when the noise died down.

Maria scanned the crowd, and when she saw Akane waving, her face brightened. "It's Akane!" she told Shiro, and both of them waved back. "Come join us," Maria shouted down to her.

Akane tried to work her way forward, but her attempt was frustrated by the density of the crowd. "I'm looking for Jubei," she shouted over craning heads. "Where is he?"

"He's at the dock." Maria gestured toward the waterfront. "Come back when the crowd thins."

It was almost sundown, and the last of the fishing boats were unloading their catches. At the far end of the pier she spotted Jubei leaning on a piling, watching the fishermen hoist baskets of bream and yellowtail onto the dock. He seemed so engrossed that she decided to see how close she could get before he noticed her coming.

Jubei felt the strange sensation at the back of his neck that always put him on guard. He laid his left hand on the hilt of his sword, then turned quickly.

Akane stopped a few paces away and scowled at him, but her eyes were smiling. "You ruin all my fun," she complained. "Just once I'd like to be able to surprise you."

"This is enough of a surprise for one day." He beamed at her. "I thought you'd gone to Edo with the gold." Sorrow came to her face like a cloud passing over the sun. He took her hands and drew her closer to him. "What's happened?"

"Let's walk on the beach," she said. "There's much I have to tell you."

Jubei listened intently to the litany of horrors that had taken place in his absence, his jaw muscles tightening with each new revelation—Saru's treachery, Iori's brutal murder, Arima's seppuku, followed by the escape of the man who had manipulated this tragic sequence of events like a Bunraku puppet master—Prince Sanjo.

Almost as an afterthought Akane mentioned the death of the monk Takuan. To her astonishment the news visibly staggered Jubei. His reaction was not unlike a warrior who in the rage of battle had unexpectedly taken a mortal wound. If he hadn't reached out and braced his hand on a rock, he might have fallen.

"Takuan, dead?" he rasped.

"I thought you hardly knew him," she stammered, perplexed by the depth of his grief.

"He was my teacher, my master . . . my tormentor," Jubei answered in a voice barely above a whisper. "And although he couldn't say it, I know he loved me."

Jubei turned and leaned his forehead on the damp face of the rock. Akane came up behind him, wrapped her arms around his waist, and laid her cheek against his back. For a long time they stood there, neither one uttering a sound.

Finally Jubei spoke. "Something important happened to me," he said. "Something only Takuan would have understood. It happened while I was fighting alongside the farmers at Shimabara. For the first time in my life I felt something in battle. For the first time my head didn't go cold. I found myself fighting not just to win, not just to survive, but with passion! I fought beside old men and women and children, some no bigger than Shiro. And when it was over, there were tears streaming down my cheeks. Don't ask me why, it just happened."

A chilly gust of wind came in off Shimabara Bay, tossing a loose strand of hair across Jubei's face. Akane took it in her fingers and tucked it behind his ear.

"All our lives someone else has chosen our enemies for us," he said. "It was never a question of right or wrong, it was always a matter of duty, nothing more. I think this time I truly listened to my own voice and saw with my whole being, just as Takuan said I could. And when it happened, I saw the carnage all around me with crystal clarity. I saw the lives of women and children, farmers and samurai, spent like cheap copper coins . . . squandered by a padre with a twisted vision of conquest and a shogun who confuses justice with might, compassion with weakness. The wastage will go on until one or the other has no coins left to spend . . . unless I can find a way to end it."

Akane, like Jubei, had looked into her heart and found sympathy for the plight of the Christians. Although she doubted that anything could be done to prevent more bloodshed, at least Jubei was willing to try.

"I don't know where this new path leads," she said, slipping her hand in his. "But wherever it goes, I'll be by your side."

By the beginning of the new year nearly forty thousand Christians had come to Hara Castle. In addition to the food they brought with them, three hundred *koku* of rice were found inside the castle granary. With careful rationing it was estimated that there was enough food to sustain everyone for about forty days.

The armory yielded five hundred muskets, bringing the total amount of firearms to just under fifteen hundred. Musket balls were in short supply, and so was gunpowder. But there were plenty of bows and arrows, and more were being made every day. Still, though they could probably withstand the siege that was sure to come—unless the Portuguese authorities in Manila could be convinced to come to their aid—Hara Castle was nothing more than a holding pen, waiting to become an abattoir.

"They cannot turn their backs on us now!" Alcala slammed his fist on the writing table. "No matter what their present posture is toward the Shogun, there are thousands of Christian lives at stake. If we die here, all hope of a Christian Japan dies with us. But if our superiors act according to God's will, if they send us men and supplies, all of Japan will fall into the embrace of the Mother Church. Christians everywhere will take heart and rise up against the heathen Tokugawa. Total victory is within our grasp! To deny us now is to deny our Lord Jesus Christ! And their souls will fuel the fires of Hell!"

Kriek listened, still unconvinced that Alcala's grandiose vision of a Christian Japan was anything more than a pipe dream. However, with Portuguese assistance the odds were better than even that the island of Kyushu could be taken and held. There were certainly enough ships in the Orient to command the seas around Kyushu. Portuguese firepower was overwhelming, and Portuguese officers knew how to use it with maximum effect. Once the farmers had been armed and trained, even the vast armies under Tokugawa control would be at a decided disadvantage.

The battle at Shimabara had resolved any doubts that coexistence with the Tokugawa was possible. Kriek had seen men, women, and children cut down, harvested like stalks of rice. He had felt his own horror turn to rage, and rage to violence. And when it was over, when the uncounted Christian bodies were interred in a mass grave, the requiem mass had been said, and samurai blood had been washed out of his clothing, his anger remained. Shimabara had transformed him into a killer beyond remorse. Guilt over his love for Maria faded to insignificance. Could taking love from a woman be more offensive to God than the taking of life?

"Then go to Manila and plead our case before the bishop," Kriek advised Alcala. "If it's gold they want, we have enough to satisfy their appetite."

"The gold is gone," Jubei informed them.

"Gone?" Kriek replied.

"One of the men we left behind betrayed us. He killed a trusted friend and took the gold!"

The long silence was broken when Kriek turned to Alcala and said, "That means you'll have to make your appeal to the Church fathers on moral grounds." It was evident from the tone of his voice that Kriek doubted that morality carried the same weight as gold.

"With or without gold, this time I will be heard." Alcala's eyes sparkled. "As God is my witness, I won't let them abandon us."

Among the boats along the seawall only one was large and sturdy enough to attempt the long ocean voyage to Manila. Kriek and the three fishermen who agreed to crew the boat inspected the rigging and hull. It was determined that with minor repairs she could make it, barring bad weather and high seas. Since there was no time to waste, work started immediately. By morning the boat could be ready to sail. Kriek remained there to oversee the repairs.

At Alcala's request, Jubei accompanied him back to the

central donjon. Several times along the way Alcala stopped to chat with people who called out to him, asking his blessing.

"What is your name, daughter?"

"Miyo, Padre."

"Are you married, Miyo?"

"*Hai*. My husband is training with the guns."

"Do you have children?"

"*Hai*. My son is helping his grandfather with the fishing nets. My daughter is hulling rice."

"Where are you staying?"

"My clan was assigned a place in the west stables."

"And who made the assignment?"

"Oh, the head man from our village."

"Do you have everything you need?"

"*Hai*, Padre. Our headman sees to our needs."

"God bless you, daughter."

All around them the castle grounds were teeming with activity. Several groups of men were practicing archery. Others were learning to load and sight muskets. A *ronin* was teaching a class of farmers the art of kendo. Nearby, a wiry farmer was demonstrating "empty-hand" fighting, a technique for self-defense the farmers perfected after their weapons were confiscated during the Great Sword Hunt.

"They look quite effective," Jubei commented, clearly impressed.

"Reckless samurai who made the fatal mistake of underestimating the effectiveness of the empty hand lie in unmarked graves throughout Kyushu."

Akane met them as they arrived at the donjon. She told Jubei that she would be with Maria and would wait there until he was finished talking to Alcala.

Jubei followed the priest up the winding stairs to a sparsely furnished room with a commanding view of the castle grounds. The two men sat across from each other. Alcala lit a long-stemmed pipe and drew tobacco smoke deep into his lungs.

"Jubei, you are no ordinary *ronin*," he said, exhaling a long thin stream of smoke, then laying the pipe down by his side. "I've seen you in combat. The elegance of your sword style is, to risk a pun, a cut above anything I have ever witnessed." Jubei bowed his head to acknowledge the compliment. "One thing puzzles me. Why is a samurai of your extraordinary skills without a master?"

"I'm a student of the sword. I had a master—not a daimyo, but a monk who was a very great teacher. He taught me to suspend thought and rely on instinct, and my instincts have led me down a solitary path."

"Jubei, what do your instincts tell you about our chances for success?"

"How do you define success?"

"A Christian Japan."

"It's too late for that. While you padres were fighting among yourselves, the first Tokugawa shogun was uniting the country. At one time you had a monopoly on firepower, but you gave it away for trading concessions. A moment ago we watched a smaller, weaker man defeat a larger, stronger man by using balance to overcome strength. This is the same principle the Shogun used against you. By shifting his favor back and forth between the Spanish, the Portuguese, the Dutch, and the English, he kept you off balance until you stumbled and fell. Now that you are down, the Tokugawa will never let you get to your feet again."

Alcala nodded thoughtfully. "It's true. We made a few mistakes, but with God's help all things are possible. Don't you agree?"

"Padre, I agree that all leaders have one thing in common—they make the mistakes and their followers pay the price. There are forty thousand Christians out there who never forged a clandestine alliance, never negotiated a trade deal, never schemed for territory or power or anything that didn't belong to them. All they did was accept the teaching of a god you call Jesus. And because leaders like you used their simple faith to advance secret visions of power, their dead bodies will become another monument to one more charismatic leader's bad idea."

"If you believe that, why are you here?"

"I came to kill you."

Alcala sat frozen in his spot, his eyes reflecting the bewildered intensity of a man who had just been awakened from a deep sleep. "Who are you?"

"I am the son of Lord Tajima, chief counselor to the Shogun."

"And Father Kriek, what is his role in this . . . assassination plot?"

"He knows nothing."

"So you duped him too."

"Just the way you duped those poor farmers out there."

Not a trace of fear or panic showed on Alcala's face. Suddenly he burst into laughter. "How extraordinary! An executioner who lectures his victims on the sanctity of life. As soon as you're finished with me, I suppose you'll report to the Shogun and deliver the same inspirational message to him. If your eloquence holds up, perhaps you'll move the Shogun to call off this butchery."

"That is exactly what I intend to do. But I need your cooperation to have any chance of success."

"My cooperation! I thought you said you were going to kill me."

"I'll either leave this room with your cooperation or your head. Either way your dreams of conquest are over."

"I'm listening."

"Go to Manila and convince your superiors to sign a pledge formally stating that neither you nor any other Portuguese padre or soldier will set foot on Japanese soil without the direct permission of the Shogun. In exchange for this pledge I will try to convince the Shogun to grant the Christian rebels total amnesty."

"And if you fail?"

"If I fail, you and your followers are no worse off than before. You see, by letting you go I can use the threat of Portuguese military intervention as a stick to prod the Shogun toward compromise."

"Suppose I betray you. Suppose instead of convincing my superiors to surrender to your demands, I convince them to fight."

"Padre, in the long history of the Sunrise Land no foreign power has ever been able to take and hold one small piece of Japanese territory. We fight among ourselves, but we resist foreign invaders with a ferocity that dampened even Genghis Khan's appetite for conquest. I can't believe that the Portuguese could succeed where the Mongols failed."

A look of despair came over Alcala. "God spoke to me, Jubei! He sent me signs to guide me. He promised a Christian victory. You saw the faces of the farmers. They believe it too!"

"If it's so," sad Jubei, drawing his sword, "then your God won't allow me to end it for you with one blow." The silver-blue blade loomed over Alcala's head. "You've had your victory. You defeated Matsukura and took Hara Castle. Perhaps the final victory will be an end to the persecution of Japanese Christians. The time is now. Make your decision."

Alcala's lips were moving in silent prayer. Jubei laid the edge of his blade across the back of his neck. Alcala shivered.

"I will go to Manila," he said softly.

"And . . . ?"

Alcala swallowed hard. Jubei put more pressure on the blade. "And I'll petition my superiors for a pledge of nonintervention."

"Swear it before your God."

Alcala clasped his crucifix in his hands. "I swear it."

All day long Rendai carried water and food to the workmen who were fitting out Alcala's boat. When work ended she slipped into the hold and concealed herself among the cargo.

Soon, she thought, the waiting will be over.

She curled up into a tiny ball and went to sleep.

Jubei took Alcala to the boat and waited on the beach until he saw the sail disappear over the horizon. Then he returned to the central donjon and went to the room where Akane was waiting with Maria and Kriek.

Akane watched their faces as Maria and Kriek listened to Jubei explain who he was and how he planned to appeal to his father on behalf of the Christians, and if necessary, take the matter directly to the Shogun. "Now that Alcala is gone, you speak for the Christians here on Shimabara," he told Kriek. "Without your support I can go no further."

After a long silence Kriek got to his feet and embraced Jubei. As he gripped Jubei's shoulders, he said something in a voice too low for Akane to hear, and it moved Jubei to return the embrace. Akane could hardly believe her eyes. It was an astounding display of affection—a gesture she had never seen any Japanese man make. Yet Jubei had done it with such genuine emotion, it seemed natural.

When Jubei and Akane left the donjon, the winter sun had already set. The warm spell was passing, and there was a sharp chill in the night air. Akane was glad she had put her *hakama* trousers on over her kimono.

During the long walk to the gate, Akane was afraid to speak

for fear her voice would reveal the depth of her feelings. The gods are jealous of those who love too much, she thought as she followed Jubei, matching him stride for stride.

Just out of sight of the castle they passed through an orchard of plum trees. The arthritic branches were bare, but the ground beneath them was thick with fallen blossoms. In the bright moonlight it looked like a dusting of new snow.

Akane caught Jubei's arm and tugged him to a halt. "Let me fix that scraggly hair," she said, reaching up to undo the string that held his topknot in place. She arched up on tiptoe, laying the full length of her body against him.

Jubei grinned and put his arms around her. "You never used to fix my hair like this," he teased.

"Maybe that's why it took you so long to realize you weren't my brother."

Jubei swept her up, carried her into the orchard, and put her down on the blanket of blossoms. For a long time they lay together, whispering, holding each other, letting their long-suppressed desires quicken.

"Akane . . ."

"*Hmm?*" She picked a plum petal out of his hair.

"I won't be going to Nobeoka with you."

"What!"

"I decided to stay here at the castle." He handed her a letter he had composed for his father. "Give this to Father. Try to make him see the situation in its true light. If that fails, ask his permission to take the proposal to Iemitsu."

"And if he refuses?"

"Remind him that Iemitsu promised us direct access to him."

"But Jubei, even if I get to see the Shogun there's no guarantee that I'll be able to persuade him to call off the siege."

"That's why I'm staying behind. My presence here should strengthen your argument for restraint. As long as his son's in Hara Castle, Father might have second thoughts about ordering an all-out assault, *neh*?"

"It's too dangerous. What if Alcala goes back on his word and the Portuguese intervene? You'll be caught in the middle."

"Kriek is convinced that Alcala's militant views are out of favor with the Church."

"But he also believes that the Church can't stand idly by

while practically every Christian in Japan is exterminated," Akane reminded him.

Jubei broke off a tiny branch with a single plum blossom on it and brushed the petals lightly over her eyelids, her cheeks, her lips.

"When we have all this behind us, I'm going to take you to a quiet place where the summers aren't too hot and the snow's not too deep in the winter. We'll open our own kendo school. When I'm too old to teach, I'll sit in a shady place and watch our sons conduct classes."

"And you can put on a sour face to let them know that the students of today are only a sorry imitation of the great swordsmen of your time."

"That's right," Jubei said. "And our children will think we're bored with each other because we don't talk much, but at night when it gets cool, we'll push our futons together and sleep very close."

"Even in the summertime."

Jubei thought that over for a moment.

"You said the summers wouldn't be too hot," she reminded him.

"That's true." He smiled, imagining their bodies locked together in spite of the summer's heat. "I almost forgot why the climate was so important to me."

The smile faded from his lips as he gazed down on her lovely face. He put his hand behind her neck and lifted her close to him, so near to his mouth that she could feel the warmth of his breath on her lips.

"Akane, I ache for you," he whispered. "I need you, now."

Her breathing deepened. "*Hai*," she said softly, closing her eyes. "There is no more distance between us."

Jubei eased her back, pillowing her head on the carpet of fallen blossoms. Then he opened her kimono and took her, gently but firmly pressing himself against the maddening warmth between her pale thighs—slowly at first, and when the pain that was not pain suddenly ended for her, their lovemaking became more intense, more frenzied, until total abandon engulfed them.

Akane was taking air in gulps, as if drowning in a sea of bliss, and when Jubei reached the moment of thunder and lightning, sensations beyond anything she had ever known exploded inside her and she felt her body shudder again and again.

They lay together in the dark stillness of the orchard, their chests heaving in unison. Akane buried her face in the hollow of his neck, fearing that her heart could burst with love.

When Akane arrived at Nobeoka, and gave Jubei's amnesty proposal to Tajima, he exploded in rage. "Who is he to negotiate terms for the Shogun! It's bad enough that Jubei disobeyed my orders and let the leader of the revolt walk out of the room alive, but he actually had the audacity to send him to Manila!"

"He swore a holy oath—"

"A holy oath!" Tajima shouted. "What is a holy oath to somebody who presided over the slaughter of three thousand samurai? These padres have been lying and scheming to take control of this land since the first Jesuit laid eyes on the heathen Japanese. And you shame me by believing a padre's 'holy oath.'"

"Suppose he keeps his word—"

"Suppose he doesn't!" Tajima cut her off. "The thought of Portuguese warships cruising up and down the coast bombarding our cities at will makes my blood run cold." Tajima leapt to his feet and turned his back on Akane.

"Perhaps this is a decision the Shogun should make," she said, and saw Tajima's back stiffen. "Let me go to him and present Jubei's case."

Tajima spun around. "Are you mad? When the Shogun finds out what Jubei's done, he'll order us both to commit seppuku!" He smoothed the oiled hair at his temples with the palms of his hands, an unconscious gesture Akane recognized as a sign that he was seriously troubled. "The Shogun has ordered me to take command of Lord Arima's troops and lay siege to the castle." He massaged his temples, trying to keep his anger under control. "How many rebels occupy Hara Castle?" he asked icily.

"The best estimate is forty thousand."

"Farmers?"

"Except a handful of *ronin*."

"What about arms?"

"They have the weapons they captured at Shimabara and

whatever they found stored in the armory. I can't give you the exact number."

"Food?"

"Perhaps forty or fifty days."

"Jubei's seen them fight," he said, taking a little of the edge off his voice. "What was his estimate?"

"He told me that they fight like men with nothing to lose. What they lack in training, they make up in ferocity. No one doubts that the castle can be taken, but the cost is going to be staggering."

Tajima smoothed his hair again. "I'm afraid I agree," he said, sitting down across from Akane. The very idea of samurai dying at the hands of *farmers* filled him with revulsion. It would upset the natural order and shake the foundation of the rigid Japanese class structure. What did it matter if a samurai killed five or ten farmers before he fell in battle? It would only be remembered that a samurai had been defeated by some nameless farmer, and the greater the numbers, the greater the stain on samurai prestige. "I tell you Akane, Arima's samurai have no stomach for this kind of battle. I never saw such wretched morale among soldiers. I suspect many of them are Christian sympathizers. In fact I'm certain of it. If I hadn't threatened them and their families with the Shogun's wrath, they might have refused to fight."

Akane sat quietly, letting Tajima's despair simmer.

"The logical choice is to starve the rebels into submission," he continued. "However, a protracted siege only heightens the risk of foreign intervention." He looked up at Akane. "I'm not in a very happy position, am I?"

Akane decided it was time to chance another try at selling Jubei's plan. "*Chichive*, those farmers are not in revolt because they're Christian. They were driven to desperation by outrageous taxes which took them to the brink of starvation and beyond. I won't deny that men like Alcala and Sanjo took advantage of their suffering to advance their private dreams of power, but it was the misguided repression of the *bakufu* that handed them the weapon they're using against us."

"Are you suggesting that we let this rebellion go unpunished?"

"When a murderer uses a weapon to kill, it's the murderer who gets punished, not the weapon. Wouldn't it be wiser to save your vengeance for the schemers. End the persecution

of the farmers and the threat ends. Let them have their
religion, just deny them their padres. As you've said many
times, 'Kill the head and the body dies.'"

Tajima got up and paced the room. Once or twice he
seemed to reach a decision, only to start pacing again. Finally
he made up his mind. "I can't say that I'm convinced by your
arguments, but the alternatives are so distasteful that I'm
willing to let you take your case to the Shogun. I warn you,
though, Lord Iemitsu doesn't share your benign view of the
Christians. Furthermore the prospect of seppuku can't be
ignored. Think carefully. Are you prepared to lay down your
life for Christians?"

"I'm prepared to tell the Shogun the truth. If he listens,
thousands of lives, both Christian and samurai, can be saved.
If not, then I'll accept whatever comes."

"And Jubei—will he go with you?"

"No. He's decided to remain at Hara Castle."

Something resembling youth drained out of Tajima's face,
and suddenly he looked old. The Christian contagion had
spread to his own family. His son was allowing himself to be
used as a hostage, and his adopted daughter was in league
with him.

"So it's come to this." Tajima took a deep breath and let it
out slowly. "I suggest that you leave for Edo quickly, before I
change my mind and place you under arrest for treason."

The last person Tajima met with that morning was a messenger from Nagasaki. He reported that a boat had been
found drifting near Yushima Island. Everyone on board was
dead, including a foreigner whose throat had been slashed.
The Jesuit mission in Nagasaki identified the victim as a
priest named Alcala.

The news of Alcala's death soothed his spirit like a hearty
draught of hot sake on a cold winter's night. "Do we know
who is responsible?" he asked.

"All those on board had been stabbed except for a woman
who died of a gunshot wound. Apparently one of the crew
survived long enough to fire a single shot at her. When her
body was examined, they found the mark of the spider tat-
tooed on her thigh—the mark of the *Ichiko* women who
practice sorcery on Yushima Island. The dead woman was
their Rendai."

After the messenger had gone, Tajima leaned his elbow on

his writing desk and closed his eyes. The gods are with us, he said to himself. There will be no Portuguese interference and no concessions to the Christians.

Now he knew he had time to lay a proper siege. Mitsui's ship could be used to patrol the coast, cutting off access to Shimabara Bay. The Dutch, in exchange for certain trade advantages, had already indicated their willingness to put warships at the Shogun's disposal. Relentless bombardment from land and sea would reduce Hara Castle to rubble. Starvation would decimate their ranks and shatter their will to resist. When the time came to order the final assault, those still alive would be too feeble to put up much of a fight, thereby cutting samurai losses to acceptable proportions.

He took out his ink stone and writing brushes and began to formulate his report to the Shogun. It would be imperative that Iemitsu keep the news of Alcala's death a secret from Akane. He could keep her waiting in Edo for Alcala's message to arrive. Let her—no, let them all, he thought, believe that amnesty for the rebels was still a possibility. It would allow him time to get the siege under way before another attempt was made to reach Manila. If everything worked out according to plan, Christianity in Japan would be exterminated before word of the *konzetsu* reached the outside world.

Tajima picked up his brush, but the words did not flow easily. Lingering in the margins of his mind was the painful knowledge that he was setting in motion a course of action that could result in the death of his only son. He resolved to go to the temple that very night and beseech the gods to bring Jubei to his senses before it was too late.

Something about Iemitsu was wrong, Akane thought. It was more than the slightly exaggerated formality, more than the forced charm. Akane hadn't seen him since the Emperor had officially named him Shogun, and she had heard that the abduction had changed him. Still, sitting at Iemitsu's feet, she experienced a sensation not unlike going into a familiar room after some insignificant item had been removed.

After waiting over a week to see him, Akane was anxious to have done with the obligatory small talk and get to the business at hand. If the Shogun sensed her impatience, he seemed in no hurry to relieve it. The ritual chatting went on and on, and she knew it would have to continue in that vein until Iemitsu saw fit to rechannel the conversation.

A voice came from behind a decorative screen. "You may retire now, Shingo."

The Shogun rotated his position to face the screen, bowed deeply, then left by way of a side exit, leaving Akane utterly bewildered. Her confusion was compounded when Lord Iemitsu stepped out from behind the screen and smiled at her. "Do you like magic, Akane?" Iemitsu chuckled merrily.

"My lord." She put her palms on the floor and bowed.

"Are you sure *I'm* the Shogun?" Iemitsu said, taking his place on the dais.

"Your double is a remarkable copy, but a real coin has a familiar ring."

"But you admit that Shingo had you fooled, don't you?"

"I admit that I feel foolish."

"Akane, please understand that I wasn't playing a childish prank on you. It was a test. If someone who grew up with me can't tell us apart, then I feel secure in keeping Shingo on as the Shadow Shogun."

Iemitsu explained that the Shadow Shogun was used as a stand-in at any ceremonial functions where security might be a problem. "Once burned, twice cautious," he said. "But in fairness, the credit goes to your father. It was his idea."

Without further delay Iemitsu invited Akane to speak her piece. He listened attentively as she talked, punctuating the monologue with a few shrewd questions. Having anticipated every possible objection beforehand, Akane fielded the Shogun's questions deftly. At the conclusion of her remarks, Akane was satisfied that she had laid Jubei's case before Iemitsu as effectively as she could state it. Although neither one of them would ever refer to the debt Iemitsu owed them, Akane knew their role in his rescue added considerable weight to any request they made.

"It's a bold plan, and not without risks," Iemitsu said, carefully measuring out a tiny dose of hope. "However, it would mean passing up a golden opportunity to stamp out the Christian disease once and for all."

"My Lord, Christianity is not the disease, it's hunger and privation. The farmers aren't concerned with conquest, they're concerned with food!"

"Surely you're not suggesting that the padres never had any designs on Japan?"

"Not all the padres are schemers," she said, thinking of Jan Kriek. "But that's a moot point since all padres, good and bad, will have to stay away from Japan."

"If they agree to Jubei's conditions."

"They'll agree," she said confidently. "They have no choice. You have forty thousand Christian hostages."

Iemitsu let a few moments of silence pass, to give the impression that her arguments were having an effect. "I must say that the loss of all those farmers would deal a severe blow to the economy. But no final decision can be made until we receive a signed pledge from Manila."

Akane's spirits soared. "So you won't—"

Iemitsu cut her off with a wave of his hand. "All I can promise you is that I'll give Jubei's proposal serious consideration."

"That's all I ask."

"Just one more thing," Iemitsu said as Akane prepared to take her leave. "I'm curious to know why Jubei sent you to me with his proposal for amnesty. Can you tell me why he didn't come himself?"

Akane's heart sank. This was the very question she had feared he would ask. "He decided to remain in Hara Castle."

Iemitsu sat in stony silence, waiting, letting the pause hang in the air as an indictment of her inadequate response.

"I can only tell you what I believe is his reason," she continued. "Casting his fate with the farmers seemed to make the strongest statement about the depth of his commitment to see justice done." Judging from Iemitsu's expression, Akane realized that the Shogun had not found her explanation compelling.

"*Soka*," Iemitsu hissed. "I wonder if he's considered seppuku as an even stronger 'statement'?"

Akane stared straight at him, refusing to lower her eyes.

"No matter," he said, suddenly shifting to a lighter tone. "The problem should be resolved soon enough. But in the meantime why don't you remain here as my guest, until we see the shape of this . . . Alcala's proposal."

It was not a request, it was a command. In spite of her disappointment at not being able to return to Hara Castle immediately, she knew any attempt to get him to reconsider

would only antagonize him and needlessly prejudice Jubei's
peace plan. She bowed and left the room, believing that at
least the Shogun was considering a peaceful conclusion to the
problem.

After Akane had gone, Iemitsu shook his head sadly. It
grieved him to learn that his boyhood friend, the man who
saved his life, the son of his most trusted counselor, had
turned against him. The resentment he felt at the way the
Christian toxin had poisoned Jubei's mind only served to
harden his resolve to eradicate this foreign menace in one
decisive stroke.

He couldn't help wondering what Jubei's reaction would be
when Tajima unleashed the siege. Perhaps, he thought, it
will bring him to his senses.

19

Hara Castle
Year of the Boar—1635
Hour of the Rabbit

More than forty days had passed since the siege began. The
twin cannons on the great earthen mound Tajima had constructed pounded away at the castle day and night. On the
bay side Dutch ships patrolled the straits, bombarding the
seawall with devastating effect. The splintered hulls of fishing
boats littered the beach. At night women and children scav-
enged the shore for mussels and seaweed. The little bit they
gathered barely dented the collective hunger of the besieged
rebels.

By late February starvation, disease, and the constant bar-
rages had reduced their number to half of the original force.
Nearly every building in Hara Castle had been severely
damaged. Still, people huddled inside the ruins, using the

shattered timbers for firewood. Because of its great height and solid wooden contruction, the central donjon had come through the shelling relatively unscathed. The rooms and hallways were filled to overflowing with the sick and wounded. Each morning the dead were taken out to a mass grave that was never big enough to accommodate the vast number of corpses, and their places in the donjon were quickly occupied by more, always more, casualties. There was nothing anyone could do for them but try to make them comfortable, and pray for a miracle.

Jan Kriek had long since given up hope of Portuguese help, although whenever anyone asked, he always responded with unqualified optimism. He seriously doubted whether his litany of hope was believed, but since desperate people have little use for the truth, he continued to tell them what they wanted to hear.

As Kriek and Shiro left the central donjon for their morning tour of the castle grounds, the dying reached out their hands to touch the boy. Wherever he went, faces lit up and spirits soared.

"*Tendo!*" someone rasped in a feeble voice.

Shiro smiled and waved back.

It amazed Kriek to see the way Shiro had accepted his elevation to a demigod without allowing the adulation to turn his head. He had taken on the responsibilities that fell on his shoulders with an intuitive grace that filled Kriek with admiration and pride.

When they reached the burial ground, both of them were struck by the grim sight. As usual the burial teams had not been able to keep up with the terrible attrition rate. But this time the sight of so many bodies stacked shoulder high around the open pit, penetrated the numbness that comes to those who have seen too much death, and found a new place to hurt.

Shiro turned away. Kriek put his arm around the boy and led him back through the crowd of mourners who had gathered to wait for the moment when their loved ones were lowered into the pit.

As they approached the central donjon, it was Shiro who broke the silence. "Padre," he asked, "am I really a *Tendo*?"

Kriek gave the boy's neck a little squeeze. "You're a very special child," he said to Shiro.

"Do I have special powers?"

"Perhaps so," Kriek said. "God's using you to bring hope to the hopeless. That's a very special power."

"But I'm supposed to lead them to victory." Shiro stopped and looked up at Kriek. "I don't know how."

"Let me tell you a secret," Kriek said in a conspiratorial tone. "Nobody knows how to win. They say they do, but they always say it after they've won something. It doesn't matter that a million little things had to come together just at the right instant to cause success. No, they pick out one thing . . . and it's always something they did, and they'll tell you *that's* the secret to success."

"So it doesn't matter what I do?"

"Of course it matters. You have to put yourself in a position to win. It's like fishing. Remember, we always tried to get the fattest worms we could find, ones that looked so good that even a fish who just ate might be tempted to nibble. Then we'd go to good places where there was fast water and deep holes . . . and we'd go early in the morning, when the fish were the hungriest."

"And we'd put out our lines near old stumps or close to the reeds where fish like to hide," Shiro recalled.

"That's right. Then what did we do?"

"We waited."

"How?"

"Quietly."

"Did we always catch fish?"

"Not every time . . . but we caught a lot!"

"That's because we did all the right things. But sometimes fish do all the right things too, and that's when we go home hungry."

Shiro closed his hand around Kriek's little finger and they walked on. His face glowed with pride. "We were good, weren't we?"

"The best." Kriek squeezed his hand. "The best."

Later that night Kriek and Maria went to Jubei's room. They stopped outside the door and Maria scratched on the screen. A moment later Jubei slid the door open. Despite the evening chill, his kimono was open to the waist. Even in the dim candlelight Maria could see how thin he had become.

"I came here earlier," Kriek said, "but you were gone."

"I was out walking," Jubei replied without elaboration. He stepped aside and invited them in.

Except for a single candlestick and a tatami mat, the room was bare. He lives like a monk, Kriek thought as he sat down on one end of the tatami. Maria took a position behind him and to one side.

"Jubei, earlier this evening your father sent an emissary to the castle," Kriek said. "I just concluded my meeting with him, and there are some things I need to discuss with you."

Jubei nodded. "Of course. But first, was there any word from Akane?"

"I'm sorry, there wasn't," Kriek said. "I asked about her, and all he could tell me was that your father had sent her to Edo."

Jubei wondered if she even knew of the siege. If so, he was certain she was being held there against her will. Otherwise she would have returned long ago. His terrible longing for her, his emptiness, was mitigated somewhat by the knowledge that she was safe. "Has my father heard from Alcala?" Jubei asked.

"Father Alcala is dead." Kriek replied.

"Dead!"

"His boat was found drifting near Yushima. His throat had been cut."

"How did it happen?"

"We can't be sure, but Yushima is the island of the *Ichiko* women. Their leader, the Rendai, had reason to want him killed."

"So." Jubei's shoulders slumped. "Now there's no incentive to bargain with us."

"That's exactly what I thought," Kriek said. "Then your father's emissary surprised me by offering a peace proposal."

Jubei wrinkled his brow, and he bristled with suspicion. "What kind of peace proposal?"

"He promised to lift the siege in exchange for tribute."

"Tribute?" Jubei gazed at him incredulously. "What do you have of value to offer him?

"It's not money or gold he wants—it's birds."

"Birds!" Jubei laughed bitterly.

"I know it sounds crazy, but he promised to end the siege if I bring him a thousand live swallows."

"Is this some kind of twisted joke?"

"The emissary swore that Lord Tajima was absolutely serious."

"Ask yourself why!" Jubei slammed his fist down on the mat. "Our situation is hopeless. It's only a matter of time now. It doesn't make any sense."

Maria turned toward Jubei. "As you know, for samurai this is a battle without honor. The very notion of an army of perhaps a hundred thousand samurai being held at bay for nearly two months by a ragged collection of farmers is a thing beyond shame. The loss of thousands of samurai in an assault on the castle could only compound the ignominy. And if by some miracle the attack failed . . . your father's entire army would either desert or commit seppuku."

"Maria may be right," Kriek added. "Your father may be having second thoughts. Perhaps this is a face-saving gesture."

"But the birds . . . ?"

"They could be purely symbolic," Maria suggested. She turned back to Kriek. "When Japanese want a special favor from the gods, they often make an offering of a thousand paper cranes."

Jubei got to his feet and looked out the open window at the thousands of campfires burning on the hillsides. "It's too simple," he muttered to himself.

Kriek came up behind him and laid his hand on Jubei's shoulder. "Forgive me, but can we trust your father to keep his word?"

"I wish I could tell you that he is a man of honor, but I have too often seen his honor compromised in the name of peace and stability."

Maria came over to the window where they were standing. "If you doubt your father's word, there's an easy way to put it to the test. Give him the swallows. What does it matter why he wants them? If he takes his army and goes away, we've won . . . if he doesn't, the mistake will cost us a thousand birds."

"Everything you say is perfectly reasonable," Jubei replied. "but I can't help feeling uneasy about the birds."

Maria glanced up at Kriek. She said nothing, but her eyes were filled with hope.

Kriek took her drawn face in his hands, and in that instant he made his decision. By loving Maria he had separated himself from God's grace and condemned his immortal soul to an eternity of agony. Whatever risk was involved in complying with Tajima's demands paled into insignificance in the face of an opportunity to live out his natural life with the woman he loved.

"Tomorrow," he told her, "Lord Tajima will have his swallows."

It began at dawn.

Kriek gave the signal. The men on the roof of the central donjon dropped their fishnets over the eaves and began banging clubs on the roof tiles. There was a sudden rush of birds, some pitching and diving, others plunging headlong into a prison of nets where they stuck in the webbing like corks in jugs.

The commotion brought children out of warm sleep, women to windows, and men into the streets to watch. Half-starved cats, battle scarred and scruffy, paced the fences and alleyways with necks craned up, tails twitching.

One hundred bamboo cages hastily constructed during the night had been stacked shoulder high in the courtyard. Next to the cages a contingent of farmers waited for the nets, heavy with the catch of swallows, pigeons, and doves, to be lowered to the ground.

"Remember," Kriek reminded the men, "ten birds to a cage. Swallows only."

After Kriek finished verifying that the tally had reached a thousand, the excess birds were released. "What a waste!" he said to Maria as they watched the freed birds rise in the sky. "Letting all that food go while people are starving to death."

"This is Japan, Jan-san," she reminded him gently.

"Yes," he grumbled, "where the taboo against eating animal flesh is stronger than hunger."

"Don't be so quick to judge," Maria cautioned him. "I imagine there are a lot of Europeans who'd starve before they'd consider eating a sea slug or a raw squid."

"That's true," he conceded. "But the Buddhist prohibition against eating animal flesh does not apply to Christians, even Japanese Christians."

"Be patient with us, Jan-san," she chided him. "Life is not always governed by reason."

Jubei mounted a horse and led the procession of porters out of the courtyard. Fearing that the request for the birds might be a trick to lure Kriek out of the castle, he had convinced him to stay behind with his people. "Lord Tajima is my father," Jubei had insisted. "If there's going to be treachery, let it fall on me."

As Jubei approached the main gate, the all clear sign was given and the great door swung open. Maria and Kriek watched the march proceed down the road toward the enemy camp.

"God go with you," Kriek prayed.

By the time the procession neared the foothills, both sides of the road were lined with curious samurai who stared silently at the long file of porters with their peculiar cargo of caged birds. Jubei rode past them—back straight, head high— looking neither to the right or left, keeping his eye on the hillside where hanging sheets of white bunting identified Tajima's headquarters.

Outside the entrance to the enclosure a wall of samurai formed to block his progress. The captain of the guard stepped forward and demanded an explanation. "State your business," he said gruffly.

"The swallows . . ." Jubei said. "I've brought the thousand swallows."

"So I see," the captain replied, hoping his ignorance was not obvious. "We thank you for your . . . gift," he added, because he could think of nothing else to say.

"Tell Lord Tajima his son wishes to see him," Jubei responded curtly.

There was an awkward lull, during which the captain stared at Jubei. The only sound was the slapping of the war fan against his open hand. Finally the captain cleared his throat and spoke. "Stay here. I'll inform Lord Tajima of your arrival."

By the time the captain reached Tajima's residence, his face was flushed, more from humiliation that exertion. What was the meaning of this bird offering? If Lord Tajima knew, why had he kept it secret from his officers? He paused by the stone cistern to drink and clear his mind. When he thought he had regained his poise, he ordered an attendant to request an audience with Lord Tajima.

"*Soka?*" Tajima purred like a well-stroked cat. "Is that so?" he said to the captain.

"Of course I was at a shameful disadvantage, not knowing the meaning of this encounter," the officer complained.

Tajima chose to ignore his display of wounded feelings.

"When you return to the camp, ask my son if he would do me the honor of joining me for tea."

The audience was over. There was nothing for the captain to do except go away as ignorant as he had come.

Jubei was taken to the waiting bench outside the tearoom near the house Lord Tajima was occupying. He was told to rest until his father appeared. There were no deciduous trees in the outer *roji*, only evergreens, lending an air of elegant simplicity to the scene. Before him stood a wooden gate with a sloping bamboo roof. The stepping-stones that formed the "dewy path" had been immaculately cleaned. The stillness and pure air, the patterns of light and shadow, conspired to calm his spirit.

Tajima appeared, and they greeted each other with a single bow. Not a word was spoken as Jubei followed his father through the middle gate into the inner *roji*, carefully taking each stone of the "dewy path" one at a time, to avoid stepping on the moss. They stopped outside the tearoom, where Jubei crouched to rinse his mouth and wash his hands in the clear water of a stone basin. Then he removed his sandals and entered the tearoom through the "crawling entrance"—a tiny sliding door designed to prevent anyone from entering while wearing swords, thereby symbolizing the peaceful nature of the tea ceremony.

Tajima handled the tea utensils with the perfection of a master. Each unhurried gesture was done with supreme tranquility and care. In a small alcove to his right there was a hanging scroll inscribed with a one-line Zen poem that read; "Paired butterflies, yellow with spring." Below and to one side Tajima had set his flower arrangement—a sprig of winter-blooming camellia with a single crimson bud still damp with dew.

After Jubei had finished all the small tea cakes set out for him, he took the *shino* cup Tajima offered and rotated it in his hand so that the most attractive side faced his host. Then Jubei drank the frothy green tea in three equal swallows, letting the bitter taste remind him of the bitterness of life, and as prescribed by the ritual, complimented his father on the perfection of the tea.

"Foreigners have given us much over the years, but perhaps the Chinese gift of tea is the best," Tajima said as he cleaned the utensils. "In these troubled times it is good to have something to quiet restlessness and restore us to our centers."

"I didn't know you were a follower of the Rikyu School of Tea," Jubei commented.

Tajima nodded. "Rikyu's emphasis on simplicity helps me keep my perspective." He rotated the tea whisk in his fingers, inspecting it for cleanliness. "From time to time it's good to remember what the poet Ikkyu taught us:

"We eat, excrete, sleep and get up;
This is our world.
All we have to do after that
Is to die."

They laughed together, and Tajima began telling stories and anecdotes about people he had known and the military campaigns he had been involved in. Jubei responded with stories and observations of his own. The hours passed like seconds, and neither one of them violated the sanctity of the tea ceremony by discussing their differences.

At dusk the shoji screens on the western wall took on a crimson glow. Tajima leaned forward and said, "As you know, at the end of the tea ceremony it is customary for the host to grant his guest any favor it's in his power to bestow."

Jubei understood it to be an act of trust as simple and complex as the tea ceremony itself. Whatever was asked of a host must never place him in the awkward position of having to refuse. Yet it must not be such an insignificant request that the gesture was robbed of its dignity. Although he realized he might be stepping across the boundary of propriety, Jubei asked his father to explain the mystery of the swallows.

"Before I can honor your request, I'm afraid I must ask if you plan to return to Hara Castle."

"I do," Jubei said with unshakable conviction. "Why do you ask?"

"Because if you go back, I cannot reveal the secret of the birds," Tajima replied. "But this much I can tell you. Tomorrow at dawn Hara Castle will fall, and no one inside will survive."

Jubei's gaze hardened. "You gave your word—"

"I promised to lift the siege," Tajima said, interrupting.

"And I will," he added, "but not until after the Christian rebellion is crushed."

"Semantics!" Jubei snarled. "Don't insult my intelligence. A lie is a lie!"

"Jubei," Tajima said in a quiet, firm voice. "Why can't you understand? Do you think I'm the kind of man who breaks his word, tarnishes his honor for some trivial reason? Can't you see that purging this land of the Christian menace will ensure peace for generations to come and ultimately save untold lives?"

"Can't you understand that peace, true peace cannot exist without justice?" Jubei replied, and shook his head. "No, you don't want peace, you want obedience. You want docile subjects who suffer and starve in silence. That is only the illusion of peace."

"Be that as it may, at the moment I'm concerned about you. If you return, I cannot save you." Tajima's fists were clenched. "You are my son . . . my only heir. All I've worked for, all the power I've attained, can be passed on to you. Right now you despise me, but someday you might come to see what I'm doing in a different light. I beg you not to throw your life away so carelessly."

Jubei looked at his father a long time before he answered. "You're wrong," he said. "I don't despise you. I despise the world you live in . . . a world inhabited by old men clinging to old ways. You open the door and invite me into your musty world, and all you ask of me is to accept old men's lies. For what? A society corrupted by privilege and power . . . a decrepit old war-horse, gone in the teeth."

The light in the tearoom had failed. "It's late," Jubei said, bowing to his father. "I have to go back to the castle."

The idea of trying to restrain him by force flickered in Tajima's mind, but he realized it would serve no useful end. "I wish we had not allowed such distance to grow up between us," he said as Jubei bent down to crawl out the door.

A great sadness crept over Jubei's spirit. "For a time, during the tea ceremony, we were close," Jubei said to him. "I thank you for giving me that moment."

He disappeared out the door, and rode back to the castle without learning Tajima's secret.

*   *   *

Jubei climbed the last flight of stairs to Kriek's room at the top of the donjon, where he and Maria were waiting to hear the details of his meeting with Tajima. As he paused outside to catch his breath and compose his thoughts, the door slid open and Maria invited him in.

The first thing he noticed was the look of strain on her face. She exuded the pent-up tension of a tightly reined horse. A quick glance at Kriek told him that the waiting had been difficult for both of them. They listened to Jubei's account in stunned disbelief.

"Why?" Kriek asked. "What could your father hope to gain by making this strange peace offer, then breaking his word?"

"I wish I knew," Jubei said. "Although I can't explain it, I'm convinced the birds play some crucial role in the deception. Whatever else my father is, he is not a frivolous man."

Kriek and Maria sat quietly, wrapped in a private moment of despair. She stared down at the floor, twisting a long strand of hair between her fingers. Kriek gnawed on his lower lip, his eyes fixed on nothing.

"Jubei," Kriek said finally. "You've been a good friend. You've fought for us and suffered with us through the worst of the siege. Even if we can repel the attack tomorrow, there will be another, and another . . . until we are all dead. Those of us who are Christian are here because there is no place else for us to go. But Jubei, you're not a Christian. There's no need for you to die with us. Another useless death serves no purpose . . . so leave now, before it's too late."

"Jan-san is right," Maria pleaded. "Go to Akane. You have a long, full life ahead of you. Don't throw it away out of anger or misplaced shame over something your father did."

Maria had touched a vulnerable spot. She intuitively understood the unspoken longing he felt for Akane—the agony of knowing he could die without ever seeing her again.

"At first I stayed here to make it more difficult for my father to order an attack, knowing that his only son might be one of the victims of the slaughter. It seems I overvalued my importance to him. Now I'm staying here because I've seen too much to be able to turn my back and run away from this fight."

"Forgive me, Jubei." Kriek gripped his arm. "But I confess there's a selfish reason for wanting you to leave. You see, it's not just your life at stake . . . I want you to take Maria with you."

Jubei glanced over at Maria and saw her eyes flash. When she spoke to Kriek, her voice was charged with emotion.

"Jan-san, how can you be so blind! When I gave myself to you, I gave you my life—all of it!" Then, seeing the pain in his eyes, she touched his cheek and smiled. "Once, a long time ago, you told me that whatever happened to you, one moment was sunlit. I turned away from you that time because I was afraid. It wasn't until later that I knew the sunlit moments with you were the only light in my life. Nothing can make me turn away from you again."

"Maria, please listen—"

"No, Jan-san. There's so little time left to help you understand me. Let's not waste it arguing."

Each of the officers in charge of the castle's defense accepted the news of Tajima's treachery with stoic equanimity. There were a few grunts, some exchanges of looks, but no one uttered a word of condemnation or even disappointment during the meeting Kriek called to tell them to prepare for an attack at dawn. Their reaction left him feeling foolish for having allowed himself to imagine that peace could be bought at the price of a thousand swallows.

Earlier, plans for the defense of the castle had been revised several times to take into account the terrible attrition rate. But despite the losses, Hara Castle remained a formidable obstacle. The walls were steep and the main gate stout. The streets were narrow and winding, designed to confuse the enemy and slow down his advance. There was significant ammunition, and many of the farmers had proved to be superior marksmen. Those who breached the walls would find their mobility restricted by barricades set up in the streets, making them easy prey for well-concealed archers. The ones who got past the archers would be met with sword and spear. None of the officers were willing to predict victory, but they did assure Kriek that the outcome was by no means a foregone conclusion.

It was past midnight when he returned to his room. He found Maria standing at the window, watching the plain outside Hara Castle fill up with samurai. The battle formations, etched in torchlight, had blasted away the last remnants of hope from her mind.

Kriek came up behind her and enfolded her in his arms. At his touch Maria broke down and began sobbing. Kriek turned her to him and held her while she wept.

Maria fought to get control of herself. "Shouldn't you be with the men?" she asked, wiping her wet cheeks with the back of her hand.

"They sent me back." He smiled. "I think I was getting in the way."

Maria smiled through her tears. "Jan-san, it's been such a short time, but it feels like we've grown old together."

Kriek lifted her hair aside and kissed her ear. "We have, my love," he whispered, guiding her to the futon. "And there's almost an eternity left to us before dawn."

When first light broke over the plain, Tajima folded his battle maps, put on his helmet, and walked to his command post on the top of a low hill. There would be no speeches, no rousing cheers. It was going to be an ugly battle, leaving a bad taste in the mouth of every samurai who lived through it. It was small consolation that he had found a way to end it quickly.

At his signal the thousand samurai he had positioned in the rear began taking the swallows out of their cages. Each bird had a waxed string tied to its foot. On the end of the string was a wad of cotton, soaked with whale oil. One by one the cotton wads were set on fire and the swallows thrown into the air.

Tajima watched as the frenzied birds circled to get their bearings. Overhead the sky danced with flecks of fire. Suddenly the whirlwind flattened out into a stream and the swallows streaked back to their nests among the eaves of Hara Castle.

Shiro grabbed Kriek's arm. "Look, Padre," he said, pointing to the sky. Kriek stood on the battlements and watched as a stream of fiery swallows streaked overhead and descended onto the central donjon. An eerie hush fell over the castle grounds. Faces tilted upward, mesmerized by the uncommon beauty of the sight. No one spoke or moved as one after another the swallows plunged into their nests, trailing burning wicks behind them. In a matter of seconds tufts of flame could be seen licking at the eaves.

"Fire!" someone shouted, and the spell was broken.

Kriek snatched up Shiro's hand and ran for the courtyard, where a bucket brigade was forming. When he arrived there, the roof of the donjon was ablaze. By the time the first bucket of water was tossed, the entire top floor was already a raging inferno. Showers of sparks rained down on the roof below, and new fires began breaking out all over the castle town.

Maria passed Kriek a bucket of water and he passed it on. "Why don't Japanese have the sense to build their castles out of stone?" he shouted at Maria, as if she were to blame for the oversight.

"Earthquakes," she said simply, handing him another bucket.

Those close to the fire could only make a few tosses before the heat and smoke drove them back. Others rushed forward to take their turns, but it was clearly a losing battle. When the roof suddenly collapsed, killing many of the firefighters at the head of the chain, the effort to save the donjon was abandoned.

Arcing flames leaped from building to building so rapidly that the bucket brigade began to fall into disarray. The heat was becoming so intense in the courtyard that no one could get close enough to throw water on the flames.

Over the roar of the fires Kriek could hear the staccato percussion of musket fire. He knew the attack had begun, and nearly half of the castle's defenders were occupied fighting the fire. All around him people were keeling over from the effects of the heat and smoke.

"We've got to get away from here!" he yelled to Maria.

"Where's Shiro?" she shouted back.

They both began groping their way through the smoke, searching for the boy. They found him kneeling beside a fallen man, wiping the man's soot-blackened face with a wet cloth.

"Come on!" Kriek called to Shiro, who got up and started toward them. Maria reach out for his hand.

"*Tendo!*" the fallen man cried out to him.

Shiro stopped, then spun around and raced back toward the man.

Maria ran after him, when she suddenly heard the piercing

crack of splitting wood, looked up, and saw a massive beam tumbling down from the top of the donjon.

"Shiro!" she screamed.

The boy looked back, then vanished in an explosion of sparks.

Maria ran to him and dug her fingers into the charred wood, trying to pull the smoldering beam off his crumpled body. Kriek came up behind her and pulled her away. He bent down and brushed the hair away from Shiro's face.

"He's dead," Kriek said softly. Maria stifled a sob and gripped Kriek's shoulder as he leaned over and kissed the boy's cheek. "Good-bye, my son," he whispered. "May you live among angels."

Another flaming timber crashed down into the courtyard.

Kriek quickly made the sign of the cross over Shiro's body and led Maria away.

Getting out of the courtyard proved to be no easy matter. The streets were clogged with people trying to escape the fires. Each time they turned down a street, they were forced back by others fleeing from some fire farther down the same street. Finaly Maria found a narrow alleyway that took them to a larger street, which she said led toward the main gate, where the command post had been established.

Although the fires had not yet reached that section of the castle, a heavy pall of smoke made it difficult to see where they were going. Only Maria's intimate knowledge of the castle grounds kept them on course.

As they approached the main gate, a sudden gust of wind blasted away the blanket of smoke. When it cleared, Kriek saw something that stopped him dead in his tracks. A large band of defenders were forcing the main gate open.

"What are they doing!" Kriek gasped.

"I think they decided it was better to die fighting than to remain inside and burn to death."

The cool breeze that wafted through the gate felt good. Kriek put his arm around Maria. Behind them the fires roared out of control. In front of them men were pouring out of the gate with their swords raised high, their throats resonant with battle cries.

"So this is the way it ends," Maria said, nestling closer to him.

A ray of sun broke through the smoke and clouds, bathing them in a soft light.

Kriek pressed his lips to her hair. "But at least this last moment was sunlit."

The fires spread out from the central donjon, effectively cutting the castle town in two. Jubei found himself caught on the opposite side of the fireline from where the fighting was taking place. He tried to find a way through the flames, but the dense smoke and panic all around him defeated every attempt. Finally he gave up and retreated to the seawall, where others trapped on the sea side of the fireline were waiting for the fires to burn themselves out.

Since it was going to take a while, Jubei wandered up and down the beach looking for Maria and Kriek. The priest would be the easiest to spot if they were there, he thought, since Kriek stood a full head taller than most Japanese, and no one else had hair the color of raw silk.

After an hour of searching without finding them, the sea bombardment began again. Dutch ships tacked back and forth across the bay, laying down a devastating barrage of cannon fire. People ran for cover as huge chunks of seawall broke lose, spraying the beach with shards of splintered rock. Jubei picked a spot and leaned back against the seawall to marshal his strength for the coming battle.

Most of those crouched against the wall were women and children. Jubei realized there were not enough men to try to organize any kind of effective defense. When Tajima's troops broke through the fireline, it would be one against one, then two against one, until all resistance was crushed under the weight of superior numbers. Jubei looked around at the families huddled together and felt a twinge of sadness at the thought of dying alone.

As the flames at the epicenter of the fire began to die down, he saw the first contingent of samurai break through the wall of smoke. The farmers nearest the spot where they emerged rushed toward them, the clang of steel against steel and the sound of battle cries filling the air.

Jubei swallowed the last piece of dried squid he had been chewing and got to his feet. More troops charged onto the beach. He stood his ground and took each one as he came.

Within a short time he'd killed or wounded more than a dozen attackers.

Soon they began to come at him in groups of two and threes. One after another they dropped at his feet. During a brief pause in the fighting, Jubei glanced to each side and saw that he was the last defender standing. A large group of samurai had formed a semicircle around him to prevent his escape.

Jubei braced himself for another onslaught, but there seemed to be few left who were willing to test his sword, and some indecision among the officers about how to finish the fight. Using the lull to his advantage, Jubei eased his way down the seawall toward a spot where the barrage had blasted a gaping hole.

"Jubei!" an unfamiliar voice called out.

He saw a tall samurai come out of the crowd, carrying a long chain with a sicklelike blade attached to one end. Jubei did not recognize the man's face. The *hajimaki* tied around his head identified him as an infantryman, but Jubei had never seen a foot soldier carry such a weapon into battle.

The man stopped about five paces away. "I've been looking for you Jubei-san," he said. "I feel fortunate to have found you alive."

"Who are you?" Jubei asked.

"Today I am an infantryman in your father's army. In better times I was a prince in the Imperial Court. I believe you know me as Sanjo."

"*Soka!*" Jubei smiled, slapping the blade of his sword against his palm. "This could turn out to be a pleasant end to a very unpleasant day."

Sanjo let the chain slip through his hand until the sickle blade hung at knee level. "Out of respect for your skill with the sword, I've decided to test you against the *kusarigama*." Sanjo began twirling the chain at his side. "I think you'll find it a most challenging weapon."

As Sanjo moved toward him, he let out a little more chain and lifted his arm above his head, whirling the blade in a circle around his body.

Jubei, who had never faced a weapon like this, began retreating step by step toward the seawall. It was difficult to gauge how quickly to move away. Sanjo cleverly disguised how much chain he let out with each rotation of his arm.

At the last instant Sanjo released a long length of chain. Before Jubei could leap away, the sickle blade sliced into his left shoulder, sending the sword tumbling out of his hand.

A look of triumph came over Sanjo's face. Instead of going for the kill immediately, he decided to toy with Jubei. With each arc of the circle, he picked a spot and drew fresh blood.

Jubei coolly measured each rotation, calculating in his mind the length of the chain and the time it took Sanjo to complete a full circle. Mustering the last of his strength, Jubei lunged forward. The chain wrapped around Jubei's body, and the point of the sickle blade embedded itself in Sanjo's back.

Sanjo gasped, his eyes bulged, and he pitched forward, sending them both tumbling through the hole in the wall and into the sea below.

Day by day Akane grew more anxious. The isolation was maddening. Messages sent to Jubei through Tajima had not been answered. Her requests to see the Shogun were being politely, but routinely denied. More than forty days had passed since Alcala had sailed for Manila. Where was he? she wondered. What was he doing? Surely he had to understand there was a limit to the Shogun's patience. He had to know that the stores of food at Hara Castle were running out. A host of dire scenarios plagued Akane's mind, and time passed by as slowly as a funeral procession.

To relieve the tedium, Akane spent most of her days at the dojo practicing kendo. At first all the students had been glad to see her. But as her frustration mounted, her dueling took on a savage intensity that even the most reckless students found daunting. Fewer and fewer of them were coming forward to offer her a match, so she had to content herself with practicing her *kata* exercises alone.

Despite the bitter cold Akane had managed to break a sweat. She laid down her wooden practice sword and leaned back against the trunk of a large pin oak. Exhaustion drove out her worries and brought her some temporary peace. She watched the steam lift off the bare skin exposed to the chill.

"Akane."

The voice came from behind her. She turned and looked over her shoulder. "Musashi-sama!" she shouted, springing to her feet. "What brings you to Edo?"

"I came to collect my son's belongings," he replied. "I wanted to see you before I left for Kyoto."

"How long can you stay?"

"Not long. I'm looking for Prince Sanjo."

"*Umm*," Akane grunted. "I wish I could be there when you find him."

"Then why don't you join me?"

"I've been ordered to remain here in Edo until the situation at Hara Castle gets resolved."

"Then I have some good news for you. The siege is over."

"What!"

"Lord Tajima won a stunning victory. All of Kyushu is buzzing about the brilliant tactic he used to burn out the Christians. He got them to deliver a thousand swallows—"

"Where's Jubei?"

"He's not here?"

"No, he stayed behind in Hara Castle."

"I see," Musashi said gravely, assuming Jubei had been planted there to spy for his father. "I hope he got out in time. No one inside survived."

"It can't be true! The Shogun promised to wait until Alcala sent word from Manila!"

"Akane, Alcala is dead."

"Dead!"

"I came to Edo on Mitsui's ship. There was a Japanese padre on board who had been arrested at the Portuguese mission in Nagasaki. He told me Alcala had been murdered over a month ago. They found him drifting in a small boat near Yushima."

Akane's eyes were brimming with tears of rage. When she spoke, her voice was shaky. "Did anyone tell my father?"

"It was his samurai who had the body identified."

The enormity of the deception broke over her like a sudden storm. All she could think of was Jubei trapped inside Hara Castle. If he was alive, she had to find him. If he was dead, she had to know.

Without another word Akane broke for the stables on a dead run.

An ominous feeling enveloped Musashi as he watched her go.

* * *

Akane arrived at Shimabara in a drizzling rain. She learned that the number of Christian dead was reported to be fifty thousand, a figure inflated by nearly ten thousand in order to justify the heavy losses sustained by Tajima's samurai. Within days another ten thousand suspected Christians had been rounded up in Kyushu, and their heads were added to the stakes that bracketed the road leading to Hara Castle.

The pewter sky was thick with vultures and crows. She tied a bandana over her nose and mouth, then started the long walk to the place where Hara Castle once stood. The faces of the dead were damaged beyond recognition—the carrion and the fires had seen to that. Still Akane looked, compelled by the gut feeling that she would somehow know it if she came across Jubei's head.

The fine rain soaked her clothes and blurred her vision. Restless thoughts prowled through her mind, searching for reasons for the unreasonable, sense in the senseless. The grotesque legions of discorporate heads seemed to mock her as she passed by.

Where were you, Akane?

I was in Edo pleading your case.

For so long?

I didn't know Alcala had been murdered.

But you did know we were starving.

I knew that your supplies were running out, but I hoped—

You hoped . . . and what gave you hope?

Lord Tajima's only son was inside.

Jubei? One person weighed against the chance to extinguish Christianity in Japan?

They lied to me.

A lie is only effective if it's swallowed. You must have had quite an appetite, Akane.

I was a fool.

Oh, well, a live fool is better off than a dead genius, neh? Where's Jubei?

Silence.

Silence.

Silence.

Silence.

She stopped and peered up at a face streaked with wet strands of ash-light hair. Jan Kriek stared down at her through sightless violet eyes. A few stakes away Akane found the head of a woman whose hair was tied back with a familiar gold lamé *emotoyui*. Although her features were partially destroyed, Akane was sure it was Maria. She drew her long sword and hacked down both stakes. Then she carried their heads to the plum orchard where she and Jubei had parted, and buried their remains in a common grave.

She walked on, desperately afraid she would find Jubei's head among the last stakes. When she did not, her relief was spoiled by the thought that she might never find him alive *or* dead.

Inside the smoldering ruins of the castle Akane came across a huge plot of freshly turned earth, marking the site of the mass grave where so many of the sick and mortally wounded had been buried. She kneeled down and scooped up a handful of mud, remembering the last moments she and Jubei had together before they separated.

Her fingers tightened and the mud oozed through her clenched fist. "Jubei, if you can hear me, know that I didn't abandon you. Others, men we both trusted, were guilty of unspeakable treachery. But I let myself believe their lies, and my stupidity cost you your life. Although I can't undo what's been done, I can make them pay for what they did to us. Somehow I'll find a way to show them the meaning of suffering."

Akane stood up and wiped the mud off her hands. The only sounds were the hiss of rain and the quarreling of crows. She mounted her horse and headed back toward Edo, consumed with a passion for vengeance that bordered on ecstasy.

20

Edo
Year of the Boar—1635
Hour of the Monkey

In a small room near the Shogun's private quarters, Lord
Tajima was putting the finishing touches on a document for
Iemitsu's approval—a document designed to isolate Japan
from continued foreign contamination. Except for a handful of
Dutch traders permanently confined to Hirado, all other
Europeans were being formally expelled from the Sunrise
Land. The era of foreign intrigue was at an end. As the
architect of this edict of expulsion, Tajima was confident that
he was laying the foundation for generations of peace and
order under the banner of the Tokugawa.

Tajima heard the door to the Shogun's inner chambers
slide open and closed. He listened to Akane's footsteps coming
down the hall, but did not look up from his work when he
heard her pause by his door. If the Shogun felt it was necessary to grant Akane an audience, he thought, that was his
business. But he was still furious with her for meddling in
affairs that did not concern her. Let her fume! There would
be no explanations, no apologies. Unlike his son and adopted
daughter, he had not allowed himself to be blinded. He had
done what had to be done for the greater good of the country.

In no mood for confrontation or contrition, Tajima sat still
and waited until he heard her footsteps fade away. Then he
got up and went to the door. Akane was gone, but she'd left a
hempen basket outside his door. There was a note attached to
the lid.

Tajima set the basket down beside his writing desk, and

more from spite than lack of curiosity, went back to work
without bothering to read the note or look inside.

Shopkeepers were closing their shutters. The aroma of
miso flavored the air. A bird vendor called out to Akane,
"One more bird to free! Just one more." She stopped and
paid the man his price without dickering. A pawnbroker's
wife with a long-stemmed pipe clenched between her teeth
watched from the doorway of her husband's shop as Akane
released the sparrow into the air.

"Ah," the bird vendor said in keeping with tradition, "a
freed bird warms the heart of Buddha."

"Then why do you put them in cages?" Akane asked.

"So good people like you can set them free."

Tajima read over the finished document. Satisfied, he put
aside his writing brush and stretched out his arms, accidentally tipping over the basket. The lid popped open and a
severed head rolled onto the tatami. Tajima grimaced, certain
that Akane had brought a head back from Shimabara as some
kind of sick reprimand.

He reached out and picked up the head by the topknot,
turning the face toward him to see if it was someone he was
supposed to recognize. Tajima's mouth jerked open in a
soundless shriek of horror.

It was the Shogun!

Akane's pace was steady and unhurried, one foot in front of
the other like an old workhorse plodding along through a
lifetime of streets. There had been a brief flicker of triumph
at the climax of her vengeance, then the fuel had run out,
draining the heat from her eyes, quenching the fire in her
belly. All that remained was a profound sense of loss.

What had been accomplished? she wondered. One more
life had been snuffed out, another ruined. There would be a
spasm of shock inside the walls of Edo Castle, followed by a
mad scramble for power. But out on the streets the vendors
would continue to hawk their wares. Women would still
gather at the wells to gossip, children would still come home
with dirt on their clothes. The sun would still rise and set—
and Jubei would still be dead.

Like all who grieve, Akane was tormented by thoughts of

what might have been—opportunities lost, time recklessly squandered. She cursed herself for the years wasted while guilt postponed her physical union with Jubei. Now he was gone forever. But thoughts of him remained like ghost pain after an amputation, and revenge had been shoddy compensation for all that had been taken from them.

Outside what had once been Saru's tavern, a radish farmer laid down his sack of unsold *daikon* and went inside to warm himself. Akane followed him inside.

"*Irasshai!*" the manager greeted them cheerfully.

Akane returned his greeting with a reflex nod and climbed the stairs to Jubei's old room. She had decided to wait there until the *doshin* came to arrest her.

Something about the darkened room alerted her senses. "Who's there?" she called out to the darkness.

"Akane?" a voice answered.

The breath stopped in her throat.

"Akane, is that you?"

"Jubei," she whispered, not daring to believe.

Jubei stepped into the light and Akane rushed to him, flinging her full weight against him. The feel of his body, the familiar scent of his skin, the powerful arms that held her tight savaged her understanding. For a long time she clung to him, whispering his name over and over again like an incantation. She explored his back with her hands, gripped his hair and breathed his breath. Finally she stepped back, turning him full into the light. He looked so frail! Questions swirled in her mind. There was so much to ask him, so much she wanted to tell him, but everything was too jumbled to sort out. So she kissed his lips and let the warmth spread through her, filling her gutted spirit with fresh vitality.

"Oh, my love," she said in a voice vibrant with emotion. "I thought I lost you."

Akane gazed up at him out of almond eyes moist with tears. She dug her fingers into his back and pressed closer. "Never leave me, Jubei . . . never again."

"Never again," he responded from the depths of his being. "All our days have been spent living for others, doing what we were told, believing in old men's lies. No more! From now on our lives belong to us. No one will ever use us again!"

"I came to look for you as soon as I found out what had happened. I searched everywhere, afraid I'd find you . . .

afraid I wouldn't. When I saw Maria and Kriek's heads impaled on stakes, I was sure you were dead too."

Jubei's shoulders slumped. "I didn't know," he said softly. "We got separated by the fire. There were so many killed, but I hoped they might—"

"I made a grave for them in the plum orchard," she told him.

"And the boy . . . Shiro?" he asked.

Akane shook her head. "I didn't find any trace of him. They told me no one escaped . . . but you got away! How did you do it?"

Jubei told her about his encounter with Sanjo. "We fell into the sea, and I almost drowned before I managed to get free of the chain. I tried to swim, but I was weak from the blood I lost in the duel. I found a piece of piling floating in the water and hung on until I lost consciousness. The next thing I remember was waking up in a small hut. A fisherman's widow had found me washed up on the beach. She took me in, dressed my wounds, and hid me from the search parties until I recovered enough strength to leave for Edo."

Akane lifted his kimono aside and saw that his upper body was swathed in bloody bandages.

"Jubei, we have to leave here right away!" she exclaimed, suddenly remembering that precious time was slipping away before Tajima sent the *doshin* for her. "Are you strong enough to travel?"

"What happened?"

"I just killed the Shogun."

Tajima sat by the overturned basket with the Shogun's head cradled in his lap and Akane's note in his hands. His lips moved silently as the words she had written slid over his comprehension like quicksilver on glass.

At first I only wanted to kill you for your treachery, but then I realized that an instant of death could never compensate for all you had taken from me. So instead I took away the one thing you cherish above all else—the Shogun, the source of your power. Now live with that!

Akane

Tajima crushed Akane's note and slammed it to the floor.

His son a traitor! His adopted daughter an assassin! The Tajima name cursed for generations to come! The Tokugawa succession passing from Iemitsu to his brother Tadanaga, who viewed anyone connected with Iemitsu as a mortal enemy. All the sacrifices he had made, negated in one mad stroke of a sword!

Tajima rushed to Iemitsu's private chambers and found his crumpled body sprawled on the floor. A tray of untouched food was by his side. Apparently a servant had brought the tray, then left him alone with Akane. Moving quickly, he dragged Iemitsu's corpse behind the standing screen and flipped over the bloodstained tatami. Then he went outside and summoned the chambermaid.

"Have Shingo sent to me immediately," he ordered.

"Shingo, my lord?" she asked, not recognizing the name.

"The Shadow Shogun," he snapped.

Her face lit up with understanding. "Of course," she said, "the Shadow Shogun."

Akane and Jubei hurried out to rent two horses. When they stepped out into the street, they saw that the tavern had been completely surrounded by soldiers in brown uniforms with the hollyhock mark of the Tokugawa on their helmets. The captain recognized them instantly.

"I've been ordered to ask you to wait inside the tavern until Lord Tajima arrives," he said.

Akane looked up at Jubei. His face was drawn and pale.

"It's pointless to resist," she said to him. "Let's not spend the last few moments we have together in meaningless combat."

Jubei nodded, and they went inside to await Tajima's arrival. Jubei looped his arm over her shoulders and let her help him up the stairs. Seeing how weak he was, Akane realized that escape from Edo had only been an empty dream. In Jubei's condition a hard ride would have killed him.

She lit a candle and spread out a futon for him to lie on. "Where would we have gone?" she asked when Jubei was resting comfortably.

"North to Ezo to live among the hairy Ainu," he said. "It's cold there, but I heard the mountains are beautiful."

The manager of the inn scratched on the door, and when Akane opened it, she found a large bowl of steamed rice and a pot of tea.

"Are you afraid?" Jubei asked as she handed him the bowl of rice.

"No," she said simply. "I prefer death to living without you. When you are gone, my spirit withers like a flower brought to deep shade. It feels like a lingering death."

Akane poured the green tea over his rice and added a pinch of *shiso* for flavor. She kneeled close by his side while he ate. Before he could finish, they heard Tajima's voice, followed by the sound of his footsteps on the stairs. Jubei set down his bowl and forced himself into a sitting position.

Tajima pulled the door open and started in when he saw Jubei staring at him from across the room. He stopped, unable to believe his eyes. "Jubei . . ." he stammered. "You escaped!" Jubei continued to stare at him while Tajima came closer. "I suppose Akane's told you what she has done."

"She killed a man," Jubei said sardonically. "You killed forty thousand."

"She killed no one!" Tajima responded sharply. "As far as anyone outside this room is concerned, the Shogun is alive and well and in complete command."

"Are you telling me I didn't kill Iemitsu!"

Tajima moved closer and lowered his voice to a whisper. "The Shadow Shogun will stand in his place and I will continue to rule through him just as I did when Iemitsu was alive."

"Impossible." Akane shook her head. "Shingo was a good copy, but those closest to Iemitsu will see through your deception."

"Those closest to Iemitsu have as much to lose as I do if Tadanaga becomes the next shogun. If they suspect, they will keep silent."

"And what about his wives? Do you think they will be silent?" Jubei asked.

"Now that Iemitsu has his heir, he rarely visits his wives. His absence will stir no surprise in the women's quarters." Tajima brushed his hair back with the palms of his hands. "I have every expectation of keeping the secret until Iemitsu's heir comes of age. At that time Shingo will retire into a monastery and the Tokugawa line will continue without interruption."

Jubei couldn't help marveling at his father's ingenuity. It

was a bold gamble, but no one was more skilled at manipulating a game than Tajima. It just might succeed.

"What happens to Akane?" he asked.

"How can anyone be punished for a crime that has never been committed?" Tajima said. "Take her out of Edo. Go someplace far away, and never return. If you cannot agree to that, I promise that neither one of you will leave this tavern alive."

Jubei turned to Akane, and her face radiated joy. "We will leave Edo immediately." Jubei promised.

"My men will escort you as far as the Nihonbashi Bridge."

Tajima started out the door, then paused and turned to them. "All my life I have acted as a wind shadow for others, and now I am as alone as that great rock that stands in my garden."

The night was crisp and cool, and there was barely the trace of a wind as Jubei and Akane set out for Ezo.

AUTHOR'S NOTE

Someone once described the novelist as a liar who always tries to tell the truth. In that spirit I set out to create a fictional story that tells the truth about a fascinating period in Japanese history. It was a time when powerful forces from within and without came together in a life and death struggle for control of feudal Japan. The conflict between the Shogun and the nobles was for political power, but the clash between the Shogun and the Jesuits was for the soul of Japan.

However, since fictional and non-fictional characters mingle freely throughout this novel, I have compiled a list of the historical personages who appear in the story as a guide for the reader.

The first Tokugawa Shogun (Ieyasu/Hidetada)
Hideyori Toyotomi
Lady Sen
Takuan
Lord Arima
Lord Tajima
Jubei
Lord Iemitsu
Iori
Okubo
Lord Matsukura
Musashi
Shiro (Amakusa Shiro was actually in his teens when he was proclaimed "Tendo.")

Although I took great pains to represent these characters as they are depicted in both history and folklore, and to wrap the story around actual historical events, this work does not pretend to be history. But, inasmuch as it succeeds in conveying a sense of the true nature of those extraordinary times—to that degree truth has been served.